ALIEN™

ENEMY OF MY ENEMY

THE COMPLETE ALIEN™ LIBRARY FROM TITAN BOOKS

ALIEN™
ENEMY OF MY ENEMY

A NOVEL BY
MARY SANGIOVANNI

TITAN BOOKS

ALIEN™: ENEMY OF MY ENEMY

Print edition ISBN: 9781803360980
E-book edition ISBN: 9781803361123

Published by Titan Books
A division of Titan Publishing Group Ltd
144 Southwark St, London SE1 0UP

First edition: February 2023
10 9 8 7 6 5 4 3 2

A CIP catalogue record for this title is available from the British Library.

Printed and bound by CPI Group (UK) Ltd, Croydon CR0 4YY.

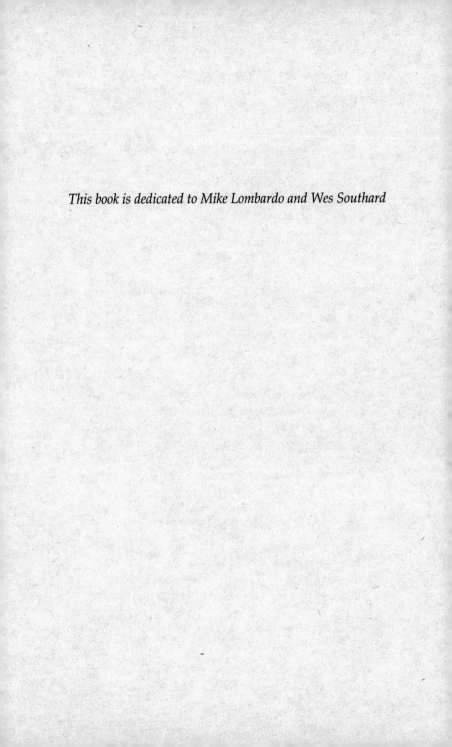

This book is dedicated to Mike Lombardo and Wes Southard

PART I

SERPENT MOON

1

The man in the first of the medical pods began to convulse, his abdomen swelling and stretching from the thing inside it. This was not unexpected; like the other test subjects, his arms and legs had been restrained by silicon bands, and he had been sedated. The figure standing at the glass observation window didn't show any alarm, even when the desperate struggling turned to violent bucking, and the moaning to shouts of pain.

"Mark down three weeks," the older, dark-haired man behind the window said to his assistant. He touched his beard, his expression unreadable. Behind the narrow-rimmed glasses, his eyes focused on the savage reaction just a pane of glass away from them.

Sitting in a chair behind a computer terminal, the assistant felt a chill. Their surroundings did nothing to soothe the nerves. Most of the Menhit Biowarfare Science

Facility on moon BG-791 was a soulless series of metallic pipes and beams, compartments and moldings of ashy and charcoal hues. Its external architecture had been designed to blend in with the tall geometric rocks that formed its mountainous backdrop.

The medlab was bathed in harsh, uneven light, with multiple recording devices capturing both video and audio from various points around the chamber. The important areas of the facility were like that—at once thoroughly modern and outfitted with the best equipment that Weyland-Yutani money could buy, but now just as harsh and uneven, failing more often than functioning. The deterioration of the moon on which the lab was located had wreaked havoc on the electrical and magnetic systems, making continued research difficult at best. Their personnel had been halved again and again until they were left with twenty or so scientists, researchers, and volunteers. The increasingly frequent storms outside the facility posed an ever-present threat to its structural integrity.

Nerves were on edge.

Tempers flared.

Still, the remaining men and women of the Menhit Lab continued with their experiments. There was important work to do, they had been told, and it had been hinted at more than once that an evacuation ship's timely arrival—*any* arrival—would be largely dependent on providing the company with positive results.

The medlab itself featured four pods, three of which currently held bound test subjects. Semi-sterile metal countertops ringed the room beneath an abundance of cabinets lining the upper portions of the walls. Within those, tools and equipment of every kind were stored.

Against the back wall stood the cold storage case, where a select number of the Ovomorphs were kept. They had been chosen from the more extensive collection currently warehoused in the specimen storage area. Through the foggy glass doors of the storage case, large egg shapes were visible, haloed by a faint green glow. These were the most valuable—and expensive—items in the lab. Maybe even more valuable than—

The first of the test subjects began spitting up blood, and the dark-haired man glanced briefly at his assistant.

"It should be just minutes, now. Flip the switch on the laser."

"Dr. Fowler..." The assistant's eyes were fixed in horror as a second man began to struggle against his bonds, and then to shake so hard that the silicon fiber bands holding him seemed strained to the point of tearing.

The woman in the third pod began to moan, her distended chest rippling and clenching.

"Do it, Watkins," Martin Fowler said, ignoring the sounds of pain coming through the speakers and audible through the glass. "Do it *now*."

The assistant rose from his chair at the computer terminal, where he had been logging the information given to him by Dr. Fowler and coordinating the video and audio records of the medical bay's events. Stepping across the room to the switch for the medical bay's ceiling-mounted laser, he hesitated a moment, even knowing what was coming. Then he flipped the switch to ON.

Stan Watkins joined Fowler at the observation window just in time to see the first test subject gag and vomit. A second later, one of the newborn aliens burst from his chest in a spray of blood and shredded internal organs. It leaped to the floor, screeching as it adjusted to the change in its environment. Then it, too, began to shudder, convulsing for several seconds before steadying itself.

"An effect of the serum," Fowler muttered, more to himself than Watkins. "Likely a result of the increase in aggression, as we predicted." He moved across the room to a voice-activated speaker mounted near the laser's switch. Depressing a button next to the speaker, he leaned in and issued a voice command. "Fire."

On the other side of the glass, the laser on the ceiling beeped, calibrating and calculating as it searched for motion. When it locked on the newborn Xenomorph, it fired focused blue laser bolts, cutting the little creature to pieces. The second male test subject, nicked by the laser, cried out, his torso stretching and receding as the creature inside it struggled to escape.

The dead alien, meanwhile, bled profusely on the floor. Its blood was a fluorescent yellow with hints of green, and it smoked and bubbled as it ate through the tile beneath, the wood of the subfloor, and the metal foundation beneath that.

Watkins was about to point out the structural hazard to the facility should the blood, with corrosive effects that seemed to be spreading outward as well as down, keep dissolving the floor. Fowler seemed to anticipate him.

"No need for concern," he said. "The alloy used in the foundation is based on Xenomorph chitin." He glanced at Watkins's skeptical expression and added, "It'll hold." Then another motion drew his attention.

"You promised," the woman said from her pod, her voice weak as it came through the speakers. Watkins turned to look at her through the glass but her eyes, bloodshot and glistening with tears, were already glazing over. She spoke, her voice rising high and to the point of breaking. "You said you'd get them out of us. You *promised…*"

As the implication of her words sank in, Watkins turned and gaped at his boss.

"Dr. Fowler…" he said slowly, becoming sick to his stomach, "you said they were volunteers, terminal patients who had agreed—"

"Not now, Watkins," Fowler said sharply. His gaze was so intense that Watkins followed it back into the medical bay.

The second test subject, the man with the laser gash in his bound arm, bucked once, and then his insides blew outward. The creature leaped onto what remained of his chest, splattering fragments of the man's insides as it shuddered. A moment after, the laser from the ceiling cut it down where it stood. When its blood oozed and bubbled, mingling with the devastated remains of the man's torso, Watkins had to look away.

He'd agreed to a lot in his employment with the Weyland-Yutani biowarfare lab, yet agreeing verbally—or even on paper—couldn't balance the things he'd been asked to do over the last month. Things he wasn't proud of. But this was a new revelation. He hadn't known, hadn't understood the full implications of what they were doing.

Not really, not like *this*.

Perhaps he hadn't wanted to know.

"Dr. Fowler, for God's sake—"

"There's no other way," Fowler told Watkins. "I've been there before, believe me, but this work—the results of this experiment—might save the lives of hundreds, maybe thousands in the future."

Watkins was silent for a moment as he considered his superior's words.

"You're an asshole," he muttered.

Fowler didn't respond.

The woman in the third medpod was crying, gagging, vomiting onto her chest...

When the third of the creatures burst out of her, it jumped onto her legs, shaking off the convulsions much more quickly. It seemed larger, and Fowler murmured something to Watkins about making note of it, though he didn't seem to notice when Watkins remained fastened in place, mesmerized by the chestburster.

Watkins had read extensively about the Xenomorphs, yet never ceased to be amazed by the sight of them in the flesh. They were the perfect predators, stealthy killers, prolific procreators. Even at so early a stage, this new one was no different. The creature was sleek, a fully formed monster. Its every body movement was agile, almost fluid, its response to stimuli nearly as sensual as it was sensory. It was a thing adapting immediately to its environment and mastering it.

It's almost a shame, Watkins thought, *that it has to die.*

Almost.

Another beep. The laser centered on it and fired.

The creature dodged out of the way, leaping toward the observation glass in front of Watkins. He screamed, flinching. Up close, the little Xenomorph was both terrifying and fascinating. Beneath the sheen of blood its elongated head—a shiny dark metallic gray—seemed to have no eyes or lips, but its mouth was full of tiny, needle-sharp teeth. The ridges against the sides of its head pulsed. This close, Watkins could see the delineation of each of the ribs against its chest, which moved rapidly with its steady breaths. Its unformed arms remained adhered to its sides by a viscous fluid which coated its body. The beginnings of claws scratched at the window. Its legs had yet to develop.

It was, to Watkins, the embodiment of a nightmare.

The laser rotated on the ceiling and geared up to fire at the window where the creature was perched. As if aware of the danger, it leaped out of the way and the blue light hit the glass, causing a fissure. The little creature streaked back into the chamber—Watkins was always startled by how fast they could move—and ducked under one of the medical pods.

"Do you see it? Where did it go?" Fowler shouted, hitting the alarm system button on the wall. Instantly, red lights began to strobe. A robotic voice, female, came across the overhead speaker and began to calmly talk through the lockdown procedures.

The two of them approached the glass, stepping to either side of the crack, peering into the medical bay. Watkins was afraid to lean in too closely, afraid that any attempt at assaulting the window would compromise the glass's integrity. He sent his terrified gaze darting around the room as the robot voice droned on through emergency medical procedures.

Crimson lights blinked and blared, making the small, irregular shadows flicker and hide, jump and dash.

If the alien was still in there, Watkins couldn't see it.

"Dr. Fowler, if the thing gets out—"

"It can't," Fowler replied, but he didn't sound so sure.

"It's a lot stronger—"

"It doesn't matter! Don't panic, for God's sake. There's no other way for it to get out of the medical bay. It's in there somewhere."

Watkins grabbed his sleeve. "Their maturation rate is accelerated with the serum!"

"All the better." Fowler pulled himself loose and gestured up at the laser. "It'll be a bigger target, then, and it'll be cut to ribbons as soon as it comes out of hiding."

There was a flash of movement, a gray blur, and then Watkins saw the thing, already larger, hanging from one of the laser turrets. With a yank of its tail, it pulled the contraption from the ceiling, sending down a display of blue sparks.

"Holy shit," Watkins muttered. They were screwed, pure and simple. Several men would have had trouble pulling that laser free of the welding and bolts that held it there. The alien had done it with hardly any effort at all. It couldn't have—shouldn't have—been that strong, not yet. What, exactly, was in Dr. Fowler's serum?

"That's impossible," Fowler said, diving for the computer terminal. He looked genuinely worried now, perhaps all out of empty reassurances. "It should never have been strong enough to..." He typed furiously, his own words forgotten. When Watkins got too close, Fowler waved and then shoved his assistant away.

"Let me finish this," he said. "Get the guns out of the cabinet. We have to get out of here."

He kept typing, offering the occasional voice command that enabled him to send files offworld to Weyland-Yutani. Watkins backed away, then moved out into the small alcove beyond the medical bay's observation room. The area was lined with lockers and narrow black cabinets, each with a coded number pad on the door. He punched in the day's code for the weapons cabinet on the back wall, and then took out two M4A3 pistols and two heavy white PMC armor jackets. He eyed the door that led out into the rest of the facility.

Beyond it was a hallway that ran away from the medical bay and its observation room. The main doors of the facility would go into lockdown shortly, and anyone still inside would be forced to proceed to the cavernous specimen storage room. That was where they kept the results of their research and, given the extensive mechanisms used to secure the space, it also could be used as a "safe room."

It seemed possible to make it there, at least.

After all, even with accelerated maturation, it would take the Xenomorph time to grow large enough to be a threat to a grown man. That was what had Fowler told him—at least an hour, maybe two, before the creature posed any real danger. Right?

He thought about the bodies in the medbay, the way the blood of the Xenomorph had eaten through the ruptured abdominal cavity of that poor research volunteer, and shook his head as if to shake the memory loose, then cast it away.

Volunteer. That was a laugh. Had anyone really volunteered? Had anything Dr. Fowler told him about the project been on the level?

There was a crash from the room behind him, and he flinched. A meaty, crunching kind of thump followed, as if something or someone had been thrown against a wall. Watkins slipped into one of the armored jackets, gripped the gun, and slid the safety off.

There were other people spread elsewhere throughout the facility—Weyland-Yutani's last guard, the lab's essential personnel—and most of those people didn't know anything about Dr. Fowler's work. Research assistants, scientists in other departments, janitors, private military contractors—people who might never see the Xenomorph coming. They'd be unarmed, unaware, unprepared...

...and there was nothing, really, that he could do. He couldn't save anyone. Watkins wasn't a hero, and he knew it. He'd only die trying. All he was good for, as far as he could see, was running like hell.

When he heard another crash, followed this time by Dr. Fowler screaming, Watkins did exactly that.

In the shaft that ran between the large specimen storage room and the rest of the facility, the Xenomorph crept toward the sound of movement. Its muscles ached as they stretched—it was growing fast, its arms and legs taking shape, its claws forming—but that didn't slow it down. The ache was dull enough and served only to sharpen its senses.

Tunnels and holes let it move in darkness throughout the metal hive. Sometimes the tunnels led to warm, living things. Sometimes they did not. Some tunnels led to a new nest. There were eggs in the nest, and it tore away the metal around them so the eggs could sense new hosts.

In the twelve years that Dr. Sarah Shirring had worked for Weyland-Yutani, she had become familiar with emergencies. Much of what the corporation paid big money for was of a sensitive and therefore secretive nature, skating along the fine edges in legal, moral, and scientific propriety. Sarah had justified her work over the years as innovative, daring, necessary to move the human race forward in its desire to populate across the stars, and that kind of work came with risks.

Often in her career, Sarah had both participated in and organized safety and emergency drills. She had been strict, almost militant in her insistence that her staff memorize the protocols and procedures put into place should an emergency arise. They worked with volatile chemicals, and one could never be too careful.

Sarah had even experienced a number of real emergencies—biochemical mishaps, perimeter breaches by well-meaning idiots only half in the know, trying to free a test subject or stop what they saw as corporate vice. She had always taken emergencies seriously. To fail to do so meant people got hurt.

Of course, that was before the last couple of months, when the impending destruction of the moon had begun to make even the most trivial systems unreliable. Plumbing had gone on the fritz. Lights flickered. Important data, when logged on the computers, could be lost to a power surge or dip. It was absolutely maddening.

Even Sarah had had enough.

When the alarm sounded and the robotic voice over the loudspeakers told all Menhit employees to make their way calmly to the storage area, she didn't bother. Sarah assumed the catastrophe was no worse than one of the interns—they'd been left with the corporation's B-team—spilling a vial and panicking prematurely. In fact, when the loudspeaker system crackled a few minutes into the alarm loop and the robotic voice cut off, she assumed the problem had been solved, if there had even been a problem at all.

It was, in Sarah's opinion, a good thing the corporation was getting them off that godforsaken moon, because between the incompetent "specialists," the skeleton support crew, and the systems failing all over the facility, it was impossible to do any real work. How much time would be lost with this most recent hiccup, sending working scientists to the storage area to hunker down when they could have been working? Maybe even locking them in there because of some electrical failure?

Twenty minutes?

Thirty minutes?

How many samples would go bad while unattended? How many time-sensitive experiments would fail?

When, thirty minutes later, the robotic voice began to blare the warning again overhead, Sarah rolled her eyes and went back to putting the test-tube samples back in the mini-fridge. In fact, she ignored it for another good ten minutes before that nagging little doubt in her, the part of her that still, on some level, respected protocol even on moons where protocol had fallen apart, compelled her to lock up the fridge and strip off her gloves.

The voice again instructed employees to move toward the storage area. She turned from her counter along the wall, and sighed.

There was a sound.

Before she could look up, something large and bony reached down, clamped over her mouth, and lifted her off the ground. Her eyes went wide and she struggled, but it paid her no mind. She couldn't turn her head to see the thing but she could smell a kind of acrid scent and feel heat and a dripping wetness on her neck and shoulder.

The thing dragged her into the vent and toward the storage room, it seemed. Arriving there, it thrust her against a wall, her feet dangling, and began secreting a kind of webbing to encase her. She struggled but soon couldn't move. The effort sapped her strength. She winced, but found she didn't have the breath to cry out.

In the hallway to the toxicology lab, Dr. Ana Thayer, eight-and-a-half months pregnant, made her way slowly down the hall. Unexpectedly, her body shuddered. She felt a sharp pain just beneath her breasts, and at first thought the baby was kicking hard, showing her its readiness to come out. She put a hand on the place from which the pain was spreading, a cold-burn kind of pain that didn't feel right. Her fingers felt something sharp protruding just above the swell of her stomach. She looked down.

The thing was coated with blood.

Her blood.

She tried to suck in a breath to scream, and found she couldn't.

The sharp thing was the cause of the pain, coming straight through from her back to her chest, and she tried to turn but that only sent bright sparks of agony down through her stomach. The baby kicked inside of her.

Dr. Thayer couldn't breathe or think. She tried to pull and then push the thing out of her, the sharp little segment that cut her fingers when she tried to grasp it, slick with her blood. The segment disappeared suddenly, pulled out of her. It drew all the strength away with it, and she sank to the floor. Already the room around her was getting hazy.

"My baby," she tried to say, and looked up to see a monster. She had a moment to recognize the bloody segment as part of a longer tail before it jabbed her in the eye, and everything went dark.

Moving back into the shaft, the one which provided access between the storage room and the medical bay, the creature followed more sounds of movement and voices.

* * *

Research assistants George Miller and Lena Forster slept on the twin cots set up in the rec room. At first, the overhead voice seemed far away to Lena, cutting through the haze of sleep in urgent tones rather than words. She could have—would have—kept sleeping. It seemed lately that the changes in the gravity and magnetosphere of the moon were taking their toll, making her limbs hurt, her head hurt. She felt heavy, weighed down.

The cots had been set up specifically to offset some of the exhaustion the remaining crew at Menhit experienced, although that had been Dr. Watkins's doing, not Weyland-Yutani's. The company had made it clear that time was precious. It took time to get results, and results were the only thing buying the crew's way off that moon.

The voice blared, a sound from another time, another place. It took Lena a moment to realize the voice was the lab's warning system. It was instructing them that there was a security breach, and that all personnel were to report to the storage room. It reminded them that external lockdown procedures were already under way, and that internal procedures would commence in ten minutes and thirty-seven seconds.

"George? George, wake up."

The man groaned in the cot beside her, and Lena shook him harder.

"George," she said. "Come on. Get up. There's something wrong." He sat up, listening a moment to the robotic voice overhead. Then the sleepiness in his face dissipated and he stood with a jolt.

"Let's go. We can't stay here."

"What is it, do you think?" she asked as she followed him out into the hall.

"I don't know. I—" George's eyes grew wide.

A silhouetted creature about the height of a man stood at the far end of the hallway. It was hunched over, shuddering. There was a large cracking sound that made Lena flinch, and the creature's arms seemed to grow. Another round of cracks and the thing seemed to unfurl, standing taller.

Lena found her voice and screamed. As she did, the creature stopped shuddering and turned its long, curving head in their direction.

"Run," George said in a dry, rasping voice. Then louder, "Run!"

Lena tried to run. At first her legs refused to get the message, until the thing charged down the hallway toward them, its long tail snapping back and forth. Then, Lena turned and ran.

There were more cracking and crunching sounds behind her, but this time George's screams followed. When she turned to see why, she saw only a bony, square jaw within a much larger maw. Then there was pain in her head and blackness.

* * *

In the storage room, the Xenomorph spun those who had survived its attacks in hive-webbing, placing them near the arrangement of eggs.

When it had run out of prey, it found a way out of the metal confines of the facility. Outside, the Xenomorph discovered a different lifeform.

Along the outer south-facing wall of the Menhit facility, the majority of the generators and power grids were housed behind steel fences. The roar they produced was loud—loud enough that Wesley Lombardo, a private military contractor on guard, didn't hear anything out of the ordinary.

A blur of gray moving swiftly along the top rail of the chain-link barrier dropped down on him. Lombardo fired off one shot, more from surprise than any real reflex, before something grabbed him by the biceps and lifted him off the ground. Twisting around, he got a look at his attacker. The elongated head had no eyes, but seemed to see him all the same. Its rictus grin, full of teeth, parted wide, and for a moment, all Lombardo could see was the salivating darkness inside.

Then, an inner mouth shot out and punched a hole in his forehead, straight through skin and bone to his brain.

Wes Lombardo's body dropped. The alien scaled the fence and leaped down among the generators, swiping at the casings. Its long claws tore through the metal and at last, both light and sound faded.

Moving like a shadow, it made its silent way back into the facility.

Back in the chamber from which it had emerged, the Xenomorph drone, grown nearly to full size, darted back down the maze of hallways to the new nest, where it had finished secreting enough hive webbing to secure the living bipeds.

There was no Queen, but instinct drove the creature to protect the eggs, to secure for them the hosts which would incubate the face-hugging hatchlings. Then instinct sent it back up into the vent above the nest, into the cool darkness there where it could rest for the time being and be safe.

The tunnels had been plunged into absolute blackness, accentuated by barriers that had dropped into place, but after a time lights came on. The utter silence was punctuated by vibrations here and there. The section that had held the eggs made empty, futile clicks.

The cocooned prey were locked in place with the eggs placed nearby. They emitted a steam that drifted through the nest, glowing in the new, dim light.

Then the eggs began to hatch.

2

Panic spread through the Hygieia Colony.

The wobble in BG-791's orbit had become increasingly erratic over recent months, and the scientific data was grim. It was only a matter of time—weeks, perhaps days—before the changes in the gravitational forces would begin exerting a strain on the moon itself, tearing portions of it away first in small pieces, then in larger chunks. Whatever was left would crash into Hephaestus, the planet it orbited.

For going on twelve years Dr. Siobhan McCormick had been assistant director of research with the Seegson Pharmaceuticals lab around which the Hygieia Colony was built. First she had noticed the changes in the behavior of the vurfurs, the vicious deer-like mammals that hunted along the colony's perimeter. They had become anxious, more prone to attacking any colonist who wandered out to the Gatelands.

Then she had seen it in the frenetic and confused migratory patterns of the scant bird life on the moon. They seemed confused, flying in circles and cawing anxiously. She was a botanist, though, not a biologist or geologist; plants were her primary field of expertise, and she had seen some of the most telling signs in the seismic activity that displaced large areas of soil, rock, and surface vegetation. Relatively minor at first, the tremors grew in strength until it had become dangerous for her to conduct her research.

Lightning storms increased, and changes in the magnetic field led first to widespread irritability, then to outright violence as people lashed out at one another, often for little or no reason. Travel restrictions were implemented so that the traders who brought supplies, news, and gossip from the more populated worlds stopped coming. Eventually trade ceased entirely. Before long, communication transmissions began to address evacuation and relocation, and even there, news was sparse. Seegson Newscore updates all but ceased.

With each ship that departed, the population decreased, and no one new was brought in. Once a colony of seventy, Hygieia was reduced to essential personnel and those members of their immediate families who chose to remain, or who had no choice in the matter. For months, the remaining few were cut off from the rest of colonized space.

Counted among those who hadn't been selected for evacuation, Siobhan had never felt true dread before, but it was there now. At first it had been subtle, that fear, but it grew a bit every day until it seemed to wash in and out and over her like some invisible tide, pulling her and the rest who remained into its undertow. The sensation only got worse whenever they asked about the status of the evacuation.

Her boss, Arthur Benton, looped her in on negotiations. The man was a good director of research, but not so great a people-person, so the organization and dissemination of information for any project often fell on Siobhan's shoulders. The United Americas government protocols for evacuation were no exception. She—well, she and Camilla, the synthetic who had worked beside her for years—were tasked to make sure all the colonists were where they needed to be when they needed to be there, and that they followed all the UA procedures down to the last crossed "t" and dotted "i."

Siobhan read through the latest UA transmission again, which outlined the logistics. The next ship was slated to evacuate a group of fourteen people, including herself, and one synthetic. The UA would do so in exchange for data relating to plant extraction and refinement techniques Seegson Pharmaceuticals had been developing on Hygieia.

Seegson was forced to agree.

Despite the conditions placed on them, Siobhan counted herself lucky that the Seegson administrators cared enough about their people—even those far on the outer rim, on Independent Core System colony planets and moons—to negotiate a relatively quick and safe evacuation. She hadn't quite understood, however, why the task fell to the government. The company had put them on the moon easily enough, and it seemed as if they could remove them just as easily. She assumed it had to do with money. Things like this always did.

Frankly, she didn't much care who sent the help, as long as someone did, and quickly.

Frowning, Siobhan slipped the printout into the drawer of the desk on which her personal terminal sat. She didn't look at the other ones—the transmissions from Erik, which had been so frequent at first and then trailed off to nothing. The quick note from her sister back on Earth, sent hours before she'd died... the last few ties to a homeworld that was so remote, so different to her now, that it had ceased to be home.

Eventually she'd have to add those to her unfinished packing. Like the rest, she would be subject to the directive that allowed only two traveling containers per person. People were to bring only what they couldn't do without, and she had made certain that was understood. Things they needed for day-to-day survival, like food and toiletries, would be replaced. Thus the relics and remnants of fourteen lives and one synthetic's existence sat in travel cases waiting to be loaded onto the rescue ship.

Only Siobhan's belongings—things like those transmissions—remained, most of them in the same places where she'd kept them for more than a decade. She packed a little every night, but it was hard to empty even so desolate a place of the few things that made it bearable.

The Seegson Pharmaceuticals lab on BG-791 was all she'd known, all she'd had, for so long. The company's promises of lateral positions and job transfers after evacuation were ephemerally comforting, but Siobhan couldn't help but wonder what she was doing. She was thirty-eight, single, childless, with no family and few friends, and a home and career that was literally about to go up in smoke and flames. Did a transfer to another planet, another moon, really matter? She'd been proud once at the thought of contributing to a process that saved lives, but the hero-high had long ago faded with the day-to-day minutiae of their work.

She'd seen enough of the corporate wheels to know that saving lives was not and never had been the highest priority of pharmaceutical companies, even ones whose professed ideals she'd believed in. At Seegson, like the rest, it was money.

It always came down to money.

The door to the lab slid open with a soft *whoosh*. Camilla came in carrying an armful of flowers, and the picture struck Siobhan as sweet. With the synthetic's placid expression, her soft, matronly features, and her eyes as cornflower blue as the blossoms in her arms, she looked gentle, almost blithely so. Perhaps that was the endearing, if somewhat misleading, part of her charm. Camilla was a Seegson 226-B/2, built to withstand a range of extreme temperatures, resistant to venom and poison, and exceedingly strong.

Those little blue flowers she carried produced a pollen that was deadly to inhale or even touch, growing against reason in the inhospitable terrain beyond the oasis of the Gatelands. Camilla smiled at her, and then moved to the counter to place the flowers in a glass preservation bin that would prevent pollen being expelled into the lab.

"Good evening, Dr. McCormick. How are you?" Even after twelve years, Camilla still addressed her colleagues formally. Siobhan had tried more than once to explain why it was okay to call her by her first name, and each time the synthetic nodded, replied with, "Okay then, Siobhan," and offered a small smile. Then the next day she returned to formalities.

Camilla had mentioned once that while she had been designed to adapt, particularly in ways which would make humans more comfortable around her, some small glitch in her programming seemed to prevent her from circumventing the conflict that first names presented.

"I'm fine, Camilla, thanks," Siobhan said. "Just tired, is all. The electrical storm last night kept me up. I got two, maybe three hours of sleep."

Camilla tilted her head thoughtfully. "I'm sorry to hear that. I hope you sleep better tonight." When Siobhan didn't answer, the synthetic's gaze flicked to the transmissions terminal. "Have you received any further word on the evacuation timetable?"

Siobhan nodded. "Tomorrow, they said. If all goes well, the ship should be here by tomorrow."

"Good," Camilla said. "Most of the residential area has been cleared, and it seems as if the colonists are packed. If you relay the specifics of the procedure to me, I'll make sure the residents are all well aware and prepared."

"Thanks." She took Camilla's hand as the synth passed by and gave it a quick squeeze. "I'm really glad you're in this with me. I don't think I could have made it through these last few months without you."

"I am glad, too, doctor." Camilla looked down on her with motherly warmth. "I appreciate your having kept me on here. It gives me... purpose." After a moment, Camilla shifted gears and said, "I understand that the planet they are sending us to for relocation processing is LV-846, in time for the summit meeting next week. The United Americas joint chiefs will be there, plus government officials including representatives of the UA and UPP, and at least three Independent Core Colony leaders. It will be a historic event, and may very well mean the difference between peace or war for generations to come."

"A collision in its own right," Siobhan muttered, and at Camilla's perplexed look, she added, "Where did you hear that?"

"A news transmission," Camilla replied. "Sometimes Seegson Newscore still transmits to my terminal."

"Well, I'm glad one of us is connected to the outside worlds," Siobhan said with a weary grin.

"It is a good thing," Camilla agreed, mimicking the grin. "I hope we make it in time to witness the summit meeting."

Siobhan chuckled. "I had no idea you were interested in politics."

Camilla gave her an almost shy look. "I find the process of government—of a few individuals controlling the welfare and futures of the many—somewhat illuminating. Individual human beings often put their well-being in the hands of those they know and trust, those who have their best interests at heart, but the masses entrust their welfare to complete strangers. It seems as if that would require the strangers to have a profound understanding of many things, in order to make wise and informed decisions." She paused for a moment, and then added, "The arrangement requires a lot of trust for everyone involved in the process."

Siobhan glanced at the drawer in which she had placed the UA transmission.

"I suppose it does seem… counterintuitive," she said, "but sometimes we have to trust in those we don't know, or even those who wouldn't normally have our best interests at heart. Sometimes, it's a leap of faith."

"A leap of faith." Camilla tilted her head again, processing the new concept, and seemed satisfied with the phrase. "Yes, that's it. This summit meeting… it's a leap of faith."

Siobhan laughed, but it was a tired sound, stretched thin.

"My understanding from the news reports," Camilla went on, "is that in addition to the peace talks, they will be discussing the pathogen bombs and their origin. Newscore didn't get more specific than that, but it sounds like there might be new information."

"Well, finally," Siobhan said. "Maybe they can find a way to put an end to all these colonial uprisings. Truth be told, Cam, I don't think I can do another three-year stint in a military lockdown."

"I don't think Seegson would put their people through that." Camilla rested a hand on her shoulder; it was a gesture both gentle and reassuring. "Not after the upheaval of leaving this place."

Siobhan smiled. "Maybe they'll reassign us to LM-490. I hear the beaches there are beautiful."

Camilla seemed on the verge of replying when her terminal began beeping loudly. The same sound came from Siobhan's, and her breath caught in her chest. Her first thought was that the moon had taken an unexpected detour out of orbit, and that the hours they thought they had would instead be minutes, maybe less. Then she recognized the signal code.

Someone was sending a distress call.

Wheeling her chair closer to the terminal, she peered at the screen. It wasn't an interplanetary call for help; rather, it was on the terrestrial channel, and seemed to be coming from the Weyland-Yutani lab sixty miles away.

Siobhan called up the transmission. The message repeated steadily.

HELP US.

HELP US.

HELP US.

She pushed the "received" button to notify the sender that the message had reached its destination.

The transmission that followed, distorted and choppy as it was, brought back the inexorable wave of dread.

3

At the Gatelands, the outer perimeter of the Hygieia Colony, it was surprisingly quiet. Despite the fact that it had been a good seven hours or so since the last ground tremor, the vurfur, it seemed, had retreated into the thick, uneven, twisted brambles that passed for forests outside the terraformed oasis on BG-791.

Maybe, for once, it would be an easy night patrol.

Lance Corporal Kenny Elkins looked up at the sky. It was a different kind of dark up there, since the orbit of the moon had shifted. When night came on, sometimes minutes earlier or minutes later than it seemed as if it should, it came quickly, and it came heavily. A clear night like it was tonight—with the stars and the gas giant Hephaestus in full view—could cloud over in an instant and rain frozen hail down on the landscape, pelting the huge brambles and knocking loose their man-sized thorns, or tearing through the roofs of the colony like laser-scissors through fraying fabric.

Sometimes, jagged bolts of lightning ripped across the sky or lanced down to spear a dusty outcropping of lifeless rock or graying dirt. The vurfur would stomp the ground with their hooves and snort, brandishing their impressive antlers and baring their sharp teeth before taking off into the brambles for shelter. Their absence was usually a pretty reliable sign that a storm was brewing somewhere not far off.

The vurfur didn't like the storms. Neither did Elkins. Come to think of it, he didn't much like the vurfur, either. Their meat was nearly inedible, and they were an ornery bunch to boot. One had bitten him on the forearm a month or so earlier and the wound had gotten infected. Dr. McCormick had given him strong antibiotics to knock out the infection and the bite had mostly healed, but nights like this, when a storm might come or go on a whim, it still ached a bit in the muscle there.

Elkins shrugged off the fatigue in his back and arms, switched the gun to his other shoulder, and resumed patrolling. He scanned the dark in front of him, watching for movement near the launch platform where interstellar ships landed and took off. It would be there, he figured, that the UA evacuation ship would touch down, and they could all finally get off this godforsaken rock.

Beyond, the dark was impenetrable. Elkins had been out there beyond the Gatelands a few times during the day, but never very far. There was no reason, really. If the scientists needed some fungus or plant sample only found in the wilds, the synth on staff at the lab made those treks, and it was equipped to handle itself. Those instances, as far as Elkins knew, were few and far between.

Extensive robotic exploration had led to subsequent maps and documentation of the moon's geography, drawn up back when it was first discovered. BG-791 was almost as devoid of life as the planet it orbited. Other than the oasis where the colony had been built—the only part of the moon that had responded to terraforming—there was a large dried-up lakebed far to the south with some unusual mushrooms and bird nests, and a Weyland-Yutani lab outpost about sixty miles west. Until the human settlers had arrived on BG-791, the dominant species had been the vurfur.

There was a lot of empty darkness out there.

Well, *most* of it was empty.

A thump behind him made him stop. He held perfectly still, listening, inhaling shallow breaths and letting them go as silently as he could. Most likely the noise was nothing to worry about. The moon made creaking noises sometimes, groaning from the pressure exerted by the sudden pull or release of gravity, the—

A snort came through the dark, not close enough to feel… not yet.

Elkins turned slowly, careful not to make any sudden movements. He eased the gun off his shoulder, aiming in the direction of the sound. The lights of the colony's perimeter dropped off beyond where Elkins was standing. After a moment, he could make out a hulking shape several feet away, something with antlers... or spines... it was hard to tell. The thing in the dark pawed and scraped at the ground.

It made an odd noise, one that Elkins didn't recognize. The vurfurs made a kind of warbling growl, not like—

The ground beneath him shook as the thing charged.

Caught off guard, Elkins shouted, firing blindly into the dark.

Another shot rang out, this one loud in Elkins's ear. The thing that had been charging him collapsed with a heavy thud and slid in the gray dirt to his feet. Panting, Elkins looked from the dead vurfur to the dark that had yielded the kill shot. Out of it stepped First Sergeant Alec Brand, his gun aimed at the carcass. Satisfied it wouldn't get back up, he lowered his gun.

"You okay?" Sarge asked.

"Yeah," Elkins said. He shivered. "Yeah. Shit. Thanks, Sarge."

"No problem." Sarge gave him a small, mirthless smile. "Shift change. Let's head back, huh?" He turned and walked back into the darkness.

With a final glance out at the wild moonscape beyond the Gatelands, that mostly empty wilderness drenched in erratic night, Elkins exhaled shakily and followed his commanding officer.

* * *

At the United States Colonial Marines guard barracks just outside the metal fence surrounding the Hygieia Colony, two more of Alec Brand's squad, privates Anita Compton and Danny McGowan, sat at a rickety card table. Each held a fan of playing cards.

The remaining member, Eddie "Roots" Rutiani, napped on a cot against the back wall. There was little light in the room except for the swinging overhead bulb, which shook something fierce every time a tremor rattled the barracks, but it was enough for the game. The majority of the colony's belongings were stacked in boxes and crates, taking up most of the barracks' two storage rooms and the rec area where the three squad members and their own personal effects were gathered.

McGowan squinted at his hand and frowned, as if he could change the cards he held. Compton fought a smile for as long as she could, but then it broke out into a full grin.

"You gonna play your hand or what, McGowan?"

"Yeah, yeah." He waved impatiently at her with his free hand. "Gimme a minute, will ya?"

"You're not going to win," Compton teased. "You suck at this game, and you've got no poker face at all."

"This ain't poker," McGowan grumbled, giving her an annoyed glance over the top of his cards.

"Doesn't matter," Compton said, sitting back with an air of triumph. "You can't play cards for shit."

"Screw you, Compton."

"Yeah, that's not gonna happen, either. Not if you screw like you play cards."

"Ouch!" Roots said, rolling over on the cot. "She got you there, man."

"Suck vurfur balls, Roots," McGowan said, shooting him a look.

"Play your damn hand already, D." Roots rolled away again. "I'm exhausted, and you two are keeping me awake."

McGowan opened his mouth to reply when a tremor rumbled beneath their feet. He flinched, and Compton's hand was on her gun before Roots had rolled back over.

"Just a tremor," McGowan said.

"They're getting worse," Roots mumbled.

"Was nothing," McGowan replied.

"Moon's tearing apart out from under us."

"It was *nothing*," McGowan barked at him. "Just a tremor."

The others gave him wary stares. He was about to say something, maybe to smooth over his harsh words, when Sergeant Brand and Kenny Elkins walked in. McGowan and Compton moved to stand but Sarge waved them down. Elkins crossed to the empty chair between McGowan and Compton, and sat.

"Deal me in next hand?"

"So." Sarge nodded at Compton. "How bad is Danny losing?"

McGowan tossed his cards on the table as the others snickered. Joking and playing cards had once been a good time, all things considered. Lately, though, the barracks felt too small and the air too heavy. Cards had become a way to kill time, not to relax after a patrol shift.

Compton scooped all the cards off the table and shuffled them. Sarge sat in the desk chair across from the table.

"Roots, you're up," he said. "Compton, you too, I think."

"On it, Sarge," Roots responded, rolling off the cot and landing on his feet. To Compton, he said, "Let's go bag us some vurfur. Seems to be all we're here for, anyway." Anita Compton rose and, grabbing her gun, turned to Sarge.

"They quiet tonight?" she asked. "Hiding from the storm?"

"Not all of them," Elkins said. He took cards off the table and started dealing. "One nearly ran me through tonight. I would've been done in by a goddamn alien deer if it weren't for Sarge here."

"No shit?" McGowan looked from Elkins to Sarge. "One got that close?"

Sarge shrugged. "They're getting antsy, I guess. They probably know what's coming."

"I dunno… I kinda feel sorry for them," Compton said. "When this moon crashes, they'll be wiped out. Extinct. Everything that lives here will be."

"Good riddance," Roots said from the doorway. "You ready?"

Compton moved to join Roots at the door, squeezing McGowan's shoulder on the way past.

"Watch out for Elkins," she said over her shoulder. At the door, she turned with that grin again and added, "He cheats." Then she and Roots slipped out into the night.

"Roots is right," McGowan said, still watching the doorway. "We were exiled here—we all know it. We're glorified game wardens, here to deal with the fucking deer population."

"We weren't 'exiled' here." Sarge rolled his eyes. "It's a security detail. Guard the Seegson lab. You know, the UA wanted Hygieia pretty bad before they found out it was gonna crash. Any Independent Core Systems colony they could get their hands on, stick it to the UPP—all that. I think they even gave Seegson some funding for the research, and they're getting a shit-ton of data from Siobhan's people, too."

McGowan smiled down at the cards Elkins had dealt him. He knew better than to call Sarge out on the way he looked at Dr. McCormick, or even mention how he'd used her first name. It wasn't exactly a secret—at least to McGowan—that there was something brewing between their sergeant and the good doctor.

"You know what I think?" Elkins said, oblivious to Sarge's crush. "I think they sent us here because of the Solokov woman."

Katya Solokov was the wife of Maxim Solokov, one of the "contractors" responsible for settling Independent

Core Systems worlds. Without governmental oversight from either the UA or the UPP, men like Solokov were limited only by their money and their resources—and Solokov had a lot of both. He was also the kind of man who gave contractors a bad name. Solokov ran as many criminal enterprises as he did legit ones, and showed no mercy to those who got in his way.

When his wife left him and took his two sons with her, she rightfully feared for her life and sought the help of the UA government in obtaining asylum.

"Katya Solokov," Elkins said. "I remember, and little Mikhail and Dimitriy." Under instructions from the UA, Sarge and his men had questioned Katya at length. They were especially interested in the pathogen bombs dropping on UA colonies. Rumor had it that Solokov had financed—if not ordered—the production of the bombs.

The rumor was proved false, and Solokov was cleared. Getting to the truth had saved Sarge and his squad from a court martial, given what they'd done.

After Katya had been questioned, the joint chiefs decided there was nothing more she could reveal concerning Maxim Solokov's criminal businesses. But while in custody she had learned a great deal about the UA. Fearing she might go back to her husband and use what she knew as a way back into his good graces, their leader, Assistant Commandant General Vaughn, made the decision to send Katya and her two children to Nungal 734.

Prison world Nungal 734 was legendary, as were the prisoners incarcerated there, comparable only to the long-closed Fiorina "Fury" 161. The inmates on Nungal 734 would make quick and likely brutal work of the Solokov woman and children, sent there as the result of a "bureaucratic error." This, in turn, would instill in Maxim's mind fear of the UA's power.

Sarge hadn't been sure who'd given the order to Vaughn, but he'd heard the person's voice—its chilly efficiency, its callous indifference—and it had genuinely scared him. That cold fear had remained with him ever since. When he approached his squad with a plan to smuggle Katya and her kids to freedom, outlining the risks to their careers and possibly their lives, all of them had agreed.

Compton herself was a mother of two, and back then Elkins had a baby on the way. And Roots... well, he'd been assigned riot duty on Nungal, and swore he'd rot in prison before subjecting a woman and two innocent children to *that*.

Sarge and his squad had managed to get Katya Solokov and her kids to a planet where neither the UA government nor Maxim Solokov were likely to ever find her, but despite their careful planning, Vaughn and her ops team had discovered who was behind the escape. Brand and his squad had been lucky, very lucky. Expecting to be sent to prison—or worse—instead they'd been demoted and reassigned to BG-791.

Hygieia.

Nothing explained the "mercy" they'd received, though McGowan shared Sarge's suspicions that there may have been pressure from the ICS Contractor's Coalition, an organization funded and run by one man.

Maxim Solokov.

"We did the right thing by her and those kids." Sarge shrugged, but the sag in his shoulders gave away his agreement.

"I'd do it again if I had to," McGowan replied. "It's just... well, sometimes I wonder if Vaughn somehow knew about this place, ya know? Like she knew BG-791 was going to collide with the Big H, and maybe she was hoping we wouldn't get out of here in time."

"She couldn't know," Sarge said, but he didn't sound convinced.

"Vaughn's the one running security for this summit meeting," Elkins offered. "You know, since she's done such a bang-up job keeping peace and all." Elkins snorted. "Maybe she and the other joint chiefs are hoping we'll be a problem that gets cleaned up with the moon itself."

Sarge looked away. "Well, if that's the case, they're gonna be disappointed. We're out of here tomorrow, boys. The ship is coming."

"Yeah, sure," Elkins said. "They're sending us right back into the jaws of the joint chiefs."

McGowan frowned. "What do you mean?"

"You wanna tell him?" Elkins gestured to Sarge.

"They're sending us to LV-846." Sarge leaned back in the chair. "Where the summit's going to be held."

"No shit?" McGowan gaped a moment at the news. "You're kidding me." Elation fought with a new fear, mixed with anger.

"Nope." Sarge shook his head. "If all goes well, we'll be there by the start of the festivities—just in time to join security duty."

"On whose orders?" McGowan felt a tightness in his gut. It sounded like a set-up.

"Our number one fan," Elkins said. "Assistant Commandant General Vaughn. The military scientists think those pathogen bombs aren't of human origins— you know, the 'black goo' someone's dropping on the colonies. Not the US or the UPP, sounds like, and not the ICS."

"So what the fuck does that have to do with us?"

Sarge leaned forward and looked McGowan in the eye. "They want us to make sure there are no surprises— no riots, no bomb threats, no crazy people—and they want it to go smoothly. We're good, McGowan, and they know it. This is a big deal. They're talking peace treaties, ceasefires across all the colonized planets. This might put your careers back on track. And me, shit—maybe after, they'll finally let me retire in peace." He sat back and added, "With a pension."

"Hell, if it's money, I'm in," Elkins said with a shrug. "Sarge can have his beachfront bungalow and his fishing boat on some nice, quiet planet, like he's always talking about, but I've got a kid, and kids aren't cheap."

"Not like your wife, at least," McGowan said with a small grin, and Elkins shoved him.

"You're funny. Real funny," Elkins said without looking at him. "Play, already, so I can kick your ass."

On Sarge's desk, the transmission terminal bleated the code that indicated an internal transmission. They all jumped. Any transmission nowadays might bring bad news at best, and carry a death sentence at worst.

Words appeared on the monitor. Sarge wheeled around in his chair and leaned closer to read the incoming message.

ALEC...
DISTRESS CALL FROM W-Y LAB... SOUNDS BAD.
DEATHS... MAYBE QUARANTINE.
CAN YOU BRING YOUR SQUAD SO WE CAN
CHECK OUT THE SITUATION?
SIOBHAN

Sarge pressed the "received" button, then began to type.

WILL ROUND THEM UP.
ON OUR WAY.
STAY PUT UNTIL WE GET THERE.
ALEC

"You'll have to finish your game later, men." Sarge rose and picked up his gun. "We've got to get back to the lab." Surprised, both Elkins and McGowan stood and grabbed their weapons, as well.

"Problem, Sarge?" Elkins asked.

"Not ours. Weyland-Yutani. Radio Compton and Roots and have them meet us at the garage. Siobhan says the situation sounds bad."

"Bad enough to pull them off rounds?" McGowan said.

Sarge paused but did not look at them. "We're going to have to grab our quarantine gear." Elkins and McGowan exchanged glances as he made his way to the door. "Move out," Sarge barked over his shoulder.

As they were trained to do, the two fell in behind him.

4

She and Camilla had just about finished packing the fiber bandages, medicines, and portable medical tools into the M577 Armored Personnel Carrier when Siobhan caught the figures of Alec and his squad approaching over the crest of a hill. When Alec spotted her in the doorway of the APC, he jogged a little way ahead of the rest.

"So, what's going on? What are we looking at?" he asked as he joined her by the personnel carrier. "Storm damage? Tremors?"

"I don't think so," Siobhan replied. "We got a video transmission from William, a synthetic over there, and it sounds like something happened inside the facility itself."

"Friend of yours? From the factory, maybe?" Roots asked Camilla with a humorless smirk. Siobhan started to say something, then held her tongue. She'd heard that Roots had once been in a battle where a synthetic had malfunctioned and killed a number of humans, as well as destroying another synth. Since then, he'd harbored a mistrust of them, and didn't usually try to hide it. He managed—though barely—to be polite to Camilla, but occasionally his cynicism slipped out.

Camilla smiled, seemingly unaware of the tone in Roots's voice. In Siobhan's experience, Camilla didn't quite get cynicism or sarcasm, and although she understood them intellectually as concepts, she rarely picked up on them when talking to humans.

"No, Private First Class Rutiani. I can't say I've ever met William."

"Anyway," Siobhan continued before he could reply, "a lot of the message came through. It was distorted, but he looked badly damaged. Hurt," she said to Camilla, almost apologetically. "I couldn't make out all of what he was saying, but it sounded like there had been a serious accident at the lab." She held up a little rectangular message drive about the size of her thumb. "I'll show you."

Ducking inside the APC, Siobhan headed toward the front, and the others followed her. On the dashboard sat a small portable transmission terminal, and Siobhan slid the message drive into a slot in its side.

The man who materialized behind the static onscreen was clearly and severely injured; the whitish fluid that powered through a synthetic's systems like blood was leaking from a deep cut on his forehead, out his nose and ears, and the corner of his mouth. The message camera was angled slightly down. The synthetic, William, had to be on the floor, although the camera angle had only caught him from the waist up. Between the static and the close framing, it was hard to make out the scene behind him.

"*Please,*" William said in a croaking, robotic voice. His speed and sound modulators must have been damaged by whatever had happened to him. "*Please, help them.*" There was a loud crash behind him and a burst of sparks, but the synthetic paid it no more than a cursory glance.

"*There was an accident,*" he continued. "*I cal-cal-calculate... dead... at least twenty-three dead. Two injured. Am shu... tting down. Irrep-rep-reparable damage to lab. Research comprom-ommmm-mised. Please help. Help the survivors. An accident. Help... damage... samples escaped. Help surv-v-v-vivors. Please.*"

With what looked like maximum effort, William reached up onto the desk, likely going for the terminal's stop button. One wrist was broken, bent at an unnatural angle. With his other hand, he managed to lift his bulk toward the top of the frame—his remaining bulk, Siobhan saw with horror, as glowing white entrails dangled from where his bottom half should have been.

A blur of dark gray flashed across the screen, too quick to make out.

Then the screen went black.

"What the ever-loving hell was *that*?" Roots asked as Siobhan removed and pocketed the drive. "Sarge?"

Alec's squad was looking at him, as much for explanation as instruction. From the expression on his face, though, Siobhan could tell he had no answers to give them.

"I guess we'll find out," Alec said. "Let's roll."

Siobhan sat up front with Lance Corporal Kenny Elkins, who was driving. Outside, the sky was streaked with black and gray. It had begun to rain, and occasional bolts of lightning lit the horizon, followed by rumbles deep enough that she could feel them in her chest.

She had liked thunderstorms until she'd been assigned to BG-791, where the lightning was three times as intense as on Earth, and the rain sometimes felt sharp enough to cut through clothes. The thunder alone was a great beast roaring across the sky. She'd experienced enough other planets that Siobhan had thought she'd seen it all, but nowhere was the indifferent and destructive strength of a storm more evident than on this moon—which itself was slowly being torn apart.

A bolt of lightning hit a ridge several miles ahead, sending vibrations through the ground and up into the vehicle, and she flinched. Kenny glanced at her and tried to give her a smile that conveyed confidence. The whiteness of his knuckles on the steering wheel of the APC didn't do much to allay her fears, though.

Siobhan had never been to the wildlands before, and as they crossed the rough terrain its gray clay dust kicked up in swirls around the APC, defying the downpour and obscuring the view. Even so, she saw that she hadn't missed much. Tall, tree-like brambles packed into dense forests sprung up occasionally along the sides of the APC's path, coming out of the black, illuminated for a passing moment in the APC's arcing lights, then blurred by rain. Occasionally she caught glowing eyes reflected in pairs, deep in the brambles.

There were no real roads on BG-791. Positioning technology was useless in a storm like this. Even the mile markers, indicating the direction of the pathway, were the makeshift kind. At times the wind would kick up, the storm would obscure both the path and the markers, and Elkins would have to slow their progress.

"Kind of like looking out into the ocean at night, huh?" Kenny said, his eyes on the road. "Darker than space, in a way." Something in his tone gave her the impression that he found a kind of thrill in navigating the vehicle through the wildlands, that maybe he *liked* the tension of white-knuckle driving in such hostile conditions. She knew the man as well as she knew any of Alec's squad, which was to say as a friendly, casual acquaintance, and she supposed it made sense. Long ago she'd gotten the impression that no one in the squad—including Alec—gave much thought to danger, or even death.

"Yeah," she replied. "It's sort of overwhelming."

"Nah," he said lightly. "It's just dirt out there. Dirt and a little rain. And deer."

Roots poked his head between them, and she jumped.

"So what do you think they were doing?"

"The deer?" Elkins glanced at his squad member with a small smile.

Roots punched him lightly on the shoulder. "No, you dumbass. The science nerds over at the Weyland-Yutani laboratory," he said, then added with a sheepish shrug, "No offense, Dr. McCormick."

"None taken." She smiled and turned halfway in her seat to better see Roots and the rest of the squad. "And I have no idea. We haven't really had any reason to compare notes with them. They keep entirely to themselves. Honestly, I thought they'd forgotten we were here, and I guess we sort of forgot about them, too."

A bump in the road jostled the carrier, and Roots grabbed Elkins's seat. When he'd regained his footing, he socked Elkins in the shoulder again.

"Maybe they really *are* making those pathogen bombs the terrorists have been dropping on the colonies," McGowan said from one of the seats in back. "Maybe they sell them off to whichever government pays more."

"Nah," Compton replied from the seat across from him. "Word I heard is, they're studying how to enhance the natural abilities of human soldiers—and if that's the case, I wouldn't mind a boost of whatever they're cooking up over there." She made a bicep muscle and squeezed it lightly. "Not that I need it."

"Nah, it's none of that," Alec said. He sat in back with Compton and McGowan.

"Oh yeah, Sarge?" Elkins said, glancing back. "What is it, then?"

Alec didn't say anything for several moments. Finally, he answered. "We should follow quarantine and contamination protocols when we get there. No fuckups." His expression was serious. "Strictly by the rules. I mean it."

"What do we have to be quarantined *from*, Sarge?" Compton leaned toward him.

"I don't know."

"Sarge—" Roots looked concerned.

Alec waved his hand dismissively. "I've just heard things, is all. The synthetic said it himself—they have... what did he call them? Samples. Samples they can use as weapons. DNA for hybrids, mutations, that sort of thing. Bio-weapons—that's what they do."

"Hybrids?" Siobhan frowned and turned further, stretching to look at Alec. "What do you mean? Hybrids of what?"

Before he could answer, the APC bounced hard over a bump in the pathway, drawing her attention back to the front windshield.

A moment after, the Weyland-Yutani outpost loomed into view over the sharp black outline of a hill.

The building which housed the lab was a series of dark, hexagonal buildings interconnected by tent-like tunnels. Both buildings and tunnels were made from a special alloy, hard as steel, fitted into six-sided panels that gave the building an odd, hulking shape that blended nearly perfectly into the tall, similarly shaped rocks behind it. Beyond the science facility, the residential buildings, squat cement alloy boxes, cowered in the dark.

"Bioweapons, huh?" Roots was between Siobhan and Elkins again, staring out the windshield. "Is that what they're really doin' in there? And what did the robot mean when he said they'd 'escaped'?"

Just then there was a loud grinding sound as the ground shook beneath them. Siobhan heard a sharp *crunch* of rock, and the road in front of them split open.

"Oh shit!" Elkins swerved. "Hang on," he said through gritted teeth. The APC fishtailed a little, sending Roots flying against the vehicle's wall, and then it gripped the pathway again as the corporal swung the wheel the other way, bringing the carrier back on track on the other side of the split. Siobhan's heart pounded in her chest as she calculated in seconds all the horrible things that could have happened if the APC's wheel had been a few inches closer to the fissure in the road.

Overhead, the sky flashed and there was a *crack*, as if a great door was opening, letting in bolts of lightning and torrents of rain. The night clouds hung gray and heavy.

"Whatever we've got to do in there," Siobhan said, her attention split between the facility ahead and the sky above, "we better do it quickly, and get the hell back to the lab."

Elkins pulled the APC up to the entrance port of the facility. As soon as the vehicle had stopped moving, the others crowded behind him and Siobhan to get a look at the place before stepping outside.

There were no lights evident in the building, although old-fashioned LED lanterns swung in the gathering storm winds, hanging from posts leading up to the massive steel door. In the glare of the APC headlights, through the rain, Siobhan saw that the door was open. Deep scratches had dented the metal in long furrows, as if someone had used some kind of pronged tool to pry it open. Above it, in utilitarian type, the name of the place had been etched into a white metal sign.

MENHIT BIOWARFARE SCIENCE FACILITY

Whatever lay within, beyond the reach of the APC's headlights, remained swathed in a near impenetrable blackness that seemed to move with the relentless onslaught of the rain.

"Get into your hazmat gear," Alec told his squad. He stared at the door. In the years that he'd been serving as chief security officer for the lab, Siobhan had come to know the subtle differences in his mostly stoic expressions. The one he wore now was of distinct unease and suspicion. If he knew anything about what might have happened in that lab, he wasn't telling them. Then again, if he wasn't sharing what he knew, he probably had a good reason.

"Alec," she said, and then, remembering the squad and catching their tiny, knowing smiles, "Sergeant Brand, what are we up against here?"

He shifted to look at her, and in his eyes, she saw a number of emotions clashing. The uncertainty was there, as was concern for her safety, and the safety of his squad. The uncertainty was what worried her most of all.

"I don't know," he said. "We need to get in there and find out."

Elkins, Roots, and McGowan pulled their hazmat gear out of their backpacks and began putting it on— long rust-orange coveralls with gloves and boots, as well as heavy black masks. Built-in speakers made it possible for them to communicate without having to use their comms.

Compton touched the windshield. "Why do you think they contacted us? Why didn't they call the Weyland-Yutani Hazmats?"

"No time—not if people were hurt in there. Besides," Alec added with some distaste, "the WY teams wouldn't know how to handle a genuinely dangerous situation. They just come and clean up after… something like this."

Before they could press him, he added, "Get your gear on, Compton. We've got to get moving."

That shut down the discussion.

Compton nodded and joined the others in getting ready. Camilla stood by, watching placidly, holding Siobhan's hazmat gear. It was slightly different from the military-grade ones issued to the Colonial Marines; hers was a Seegson-brand suit for scientists and medical personnel, more lightweight, pale gray in color, and devoid of the weapons fittings the military suits had. She wished in that moment, though, that she did have a weapon—or at least knew how to use one, beyond the cursory weapons training the outpost personnel underwent before assignment to a foreign planet. Something in her gut told her that whatever had broken out in the Menhit Lab, it wasn't bacterial or viral in nature.

It was something more, something worse. Something that could tear a synthetic person in half.

Siobhan hadn't forgotten about *that*, and she didn't think Alec had, either. An explosion would have left burn marks on the synthetic's skin, and she hadn't seen any. Nothing she could make out of the background suggested an explosion, either. So the question was, what could the Weyland-Yutani team have possibly been working with that was capable of that level of destruction, employing that kind of strength?

"You ready?" Alec gently touched her shoulder, breaking her out of her thoughts. She jumped, then nodded and followed him and the others as they opened the APC door and stepped out into the wildlands.

Elkins took point, drawing his M41A pulse rifle. His hazmat suit, like those worn by the other marines, had been fitted with a small but powerful flashlight on his right shoulder that sent an almost blinding brightness out into the dark around them. He moved with quick, light, careful steps that Siobhan tried to match as she and Camilla followed. McGowan and Roots, then Alec, all similarly armed, brought up the rear.

As they approached the main door, Elkins held up a fist and the group stopped. Siobhan held her breath, listening along with the others. They heard nothing. Only when Elkins motioned them silently forward did Siobhan exhale, and it was shaky.

One by one they slipped through the gap, crossed a lobby with a large front desk, and through another open doorway that led into a long hallway. The walls were a dark gunmetal gray, fitted with pipes and wires that looked to Siobhan like veins, carrying shadows to and from the heart of the place. She had heard once that the architectural design had been deliberate, particularly the structure of the interiors. It had something to do with insulating the building or perhaps protecting it from the periodic radiation storms which occurred out in the wildlands. The dark floor and ceiling panels, she assumed, served the same purpose.

Peering through the plastic of her suit's mask, she tried to see ahead, beyond the thick gloom to whatever might lie at the end of the hallway. Even with Elkins's flashlight, she couldn't discern much more than the pipes and wires.

They moved with cautious steps. Occasionally a pair of marines would peel away from the group, their shoulder lights stabbing into a side hallway or closet, and eventually, the administration rooms which made up the front suite of the building. These rooms showed signs of sudden abandon, and of some whirlwind of destructive activity. Chairs were knocked over, desks and tables badly damaged, paintings and knick-knacks cracked and smashed.

As far as people went, though, the rooms were empty. There weren't even bodies, or parts of bodies.

There was blood sometimes, and for some reason that was worse, although she couldn't have said why. To see the blood without any bodies accompanying it. There were splatters on the flat counters of the office breakroom, smears on the supplies closet door and cabinets. There were streaks and pools and sprays and even clots that turned her stomach, not just from the visceral violence, but from the meat-gone-bad smell they left in the air, detectable even through the suit's filter. While filtering out dangerous materials, Seegson hazmat suits allowed wearers to detect scents that might provide warnings.

Siobhan knew the smell of death in both plants and animals; it clung to the inside of the nose—and sometimes, she thought, it lingered on the inside of the mind and even the soul.

"What do you think happened here?" McGowan asked in a low voice. Siobhan flinched at the sudden break in the silence. Maybe it was instinct, or the vigilance drilled into marines during their training, but they moved as if through hostile enemy territory, and their tension was infectious.

"Don't know," Alec answered, studying one of the bloodstains. "Maybe one of the scientists caught a bad case of cabin fever—or maybe a conscience—and started tearing the place up." He turned. "Camilla, do you detect any signs of life?"

The synthetic checked a sensor implanted in her left wrist. As part of her role in the lab, she'd been designed to pick up the biometric signatures of living things, and while it wasn't terribly sophisticated technology, it had proved useful for tracking animals in the past.

"It seems," Camilla said in her soft, modulated voice, "that there is some indication of life, though not nearby. I'm sensing biolife signs in at least three areas northeast of this location."

Alec nodded and led them around another corner.

Siobhan followed, then jumped. A wire, torn loose from the gloom of the ceiling, dangled at eye level. Its occasional sparks caused it to jerk and twist. The group moved carefully around it.

At the end of the hall, they found a closed door. Affixed above the doorframe was a metal plaque.

TESTING AND RESEARCH

"Here?" Alec asked.

"We're getting closer," Camilla said.

Alec tried the button for the door and it slid open. Inside, a light flickered momentarily, not long enough to see anything, then went out. He shone his flashlight through the doorway, gun nosing around as he crossed the threshold and disappeared. After several moments, he stepped back into sight and motioned for them to come in.

Siobhan followed Camilla, moving off to the right to let McGowan and Compton step past. She wanted to move closer to Alec. It was hard to feel safe anywhere in this place, here in the dark without a gun or any other way to protect herself, but being close to him made her feel a little more secure.

It wasn't, as Camilla had so casually pointed out, just because Alec was a good-looking guy, although he was. Thick dark hair with hints of gray, blue eyes, rugged build, the scruff of a beard just starting along his jaw— sure, he was a good-looking guy. It wasn't that, though. Perhaps it was his voice, the *look* in those blue eyes. Both were reassuring, strong... and mostly confident, except maybe when they were alone.

Those times, there was a kind of vulnerability in him that Siobhan found endearing—a willingness to let his guard down around her, and she liked that. It reminded her that she could be strong and confident and reassuring, too, when needed.

Siobhan moved closer toward Alec and stumbled—that old McCormick grace—but caught herself before falling.

"You okay?" He looked concerned.

"Yeah, I…" She looked down to see what had tripped her up and the gorge rose in her throat. She took several breaths to keep from screaming. "Oh God," she managed, and the others followed her gaze downward.

It was a body.

5

Alec frowned. He reached out and gently pulled Siobhan away from the corpse. Crouching to get more light on the thing made the carnage look worse, a spotlight on so much red in an otherwise colorless environment.

The body had several long claw-marks across the chest and stomach. The wounds were exceedingly deep, the lowest one on the torso exposing the ripe swell of intestinal loops. Blood had pooled and soaked into the carpet like an aura all around the mutilated figure. One of the arms was missing. There was also a large hole in the head, too large to be caused by a gun. It looked caved in, as if something had punched through the skull right in the center of the forehead. It was hard to tell if the body had been male or female, since many identifying characteristics had been chewed off, including most of the face.

This answered one key question. It was plain to see that

whatever had killed the person hadn't been some chemical leak or viral outbreak; at least, none like he'd ever seen. It looked to Alec like an animal attack—something had clawed and gored and gnawed on the body. Could it have been a vurfur? He didn't think so. Vurfur didn't have claws, and their antlers—massive though they were— gored rather than slashed, and the rack on the biggest vurfur buck couldn't punch clear through bone like that.

Unless maybe the scientists here were experimenting…

Alec stood, and let out a small groan. His joints ached after years of combat, mixed with gravity and pressure changes across multiple planets and moons. He was tired—tired of putting out fires that weren't his. Tired of seeing bodies of people who should have lived out long lives, but couldn't because some greedy corporation somewhere was paying for things which shouldn't exist. He did his best to hide such sentiments from his squad, and from Siobhan—especially her. Trying to be the rock that others turned to and relied on.

It was easier not to have to open himself up to the feelings such sentiments brought. That weariness, though, and the jaded way it made him feel, had worked its way down inside, into the meat and bones of him. Moments like this, when the state of a body showed that the shit was about to hit the ancient proverbial fan—he couldn't just shrug it all off, no matter how much he might want to.

"Let's move," he said finally. "We've got to find those survivors."

"What did this?" Compton asked, and she turned. "Doc, what could possibly have done this?" She looked at Siobhan like a frustrated child might look at a parent, needing answers that would right the world again.

"I—I don't know," Siobhan admitted. "Plants are my thing, not animals, and I—"

"So it's an animal that did this?" With the toe of his shoe, Elkins nudged at the body. "Like a vurfur? That must've been one hell of a pissed-off deer."

"Not a vurfur," Alec said. "There's no telling what it was, not for sure, but not even a genetically enhanced vurfur could do... *that*." He stepped toward the door. "Come on, we need to keep looking."

They moved back out into the hallway and continued down to the next door. There was a small sign on the wall to the right.

MAINTENANCE

This door, made of thick metal, looked as if someone had tried to fold it in half but hadn't entirely succeeded. There was dried blood in the dent, and something had corroded the edge of the doorframe.

McGowan and Compton each took a side of the door and managed, with some grunting effort, to force it open wide enough for them all to slip in. Leading the way, Alec tensed, his weapon ready.

The room beyond was large, with sections of massive

machines fenced off behind tempered glass walls. Brightly colored signs warned of high voltage and chemical toxicity. The big metal beasts looked to be mostly generators for lights, air quality filtering processors, and the like. The metal casings featured a few dents, though nothing as severe as the door's.

Many of the large pipes and wires that had lined the hallway seemed to connect to the machines through multiple ports in the ceiling and surrounding walls, although some of the wires had been pulled free or sliced apart. A plaque on one machine read

EMERGENCY LOCKDOWN

and the complex control panel exhibited fail-safes, overrides, and other assorted buttons and levers, as well as a screen which offered them nothing more than a pale green glow.

Camilla scanned the control panel for fingerprint patterns and processed the codes they might need, but there was no way to tell if they would work. Periodically static cut into the glow, racing across the screen like angry little bolts of lightning, but it made no sound.

What damage there was didn't appear to be professional sabotage. It was messy, imprecise. This hadn't been done by a person, but rather had been a clumsy attempt by... well, whatever had dented the door. He refused to allow his mind to settle on any memories of what might wreak such havoc, tearing through flesh, bone, and metal with equal efficiency.

As they filed back out into the hallway, Roots—who had been uncharacteristically quiet—spoke up.

"Sarge, something don't feel right with all of this. I been thinkin'—"

"There's a first," McGowan quipped as he nudged his gun around the corner of a doorframe and peered inside.

Roots ignored him. "What I mean is, any kind of fuckup—pardon my language, Doc—I mean, any shit going down at a lab is bad, right? We know that. You let loose a virus or blow something up and yeah, you got yourself a world of trouble. But they're supposed to have, like, three times as many people stationed here as we got at Seegson, and that includes, what, like, six PMCs?"

He paused, looking around the building, then back at Alex.

"There ain't nobody here."

"So what's your point?" Elkins said. "You lonely?"

"My *point*," Roots replied, annoyance tinging his voice, "is that there ain't no emergency personnel, no team leaders barking orders, no clean-up crews. Hell, there ain't even any synthetics around—not even that one in the video. Whatever lockdown procedure they went into here, it's over now, but there ain't no one waiting at the door to get out of here. Come to think of it, there ain't even locked doors anymore. I mean, *shouldn't* there be, if something bad happened?"

"He's right," Siobhan said. "I thought maybe an explosion could have damaged the lockdown circuitry and left the doors open. The only other way would be if someone had manually overridden everything, and in a lockdown, that would be against protocol." She glanced around. "None of this makes any sense."

They came upon an open door with a sign that indicated a new wing.

MEDICAL RESEARCH

A body, propped up in a sitting position, blocked the way.

"We got it, boss," Elkins said, and he and McGowan dragged the body out of the way. Alec couldn't help but notice that as their lights flashed on the dead man's chest, a gaping hole filled the space that should have been the chest cavity.

"Wait a minute. Wait," Alec said, crouching down to look at the body. Sure enough, the ribcage had been forced outward from the inside, cracking the bone. The flesh, the muscle, even the organs looked chewed and torn—at least what was left of them.

Alec felt a knot in his gut.

He'd seen that kind of injury before—too many times before. In fact, sometimes it seemed his whole life had been decided and shaped by the things that made injuries like that. He stood slowly, the light passing over the jaw slacked in pain and horror, the rolled-back, glazing eyes. Alec fought down a panic that rose from deep inside him, a familiar terror that had been a part of him since childhood.

"What is it, Alec?" Siobhan said, studying his face with concern. He forced the gorge of dread back down. He couldn't bring himself to lie to her, but he did his best to appear reassuring with a light squeeze of her arm.

"Maybe nothing," he said. "Maybe coincidence. I want to be sure first." To the others, he said, "Either way, we get in and out. I don't want us here any longer than we need to be—got it?"

"What about survivors, Sergeant Brand?" Camilla tilted her head.

Alec fought the urge to grimace. If the dead guy's injury was any indication, there weren't any survivors, not really. Anyone they found now was going to prove a liability, one way or another. He didn't voice those thoughts, though.

"Are you still getting readings on them?" he asked.

Camilla checked her wrist and nodded. "Through there," she said, pointing to the door to the medical wing. "I'm picking up two of them in that direction."

The medical research wing was in worse shape than the outer corridors and offices. There were more bodies, each with those bizarre chest injuries that especially seemed to worry Alec. An ill-defined but present anxiety hung over the group like a fog, increasing Siobhan's sense of vulnerability.

They reached a hallway that ran perpendicular to the one where they stood. Signs pointed out the medical bay to the right and a storage room far down on the left.

"We should go to the medbay," Siobhan said. "If there are survivors, it would make sense for them to go there."

"That is consistent with the biolife readings I'm receiving," Camilla said. "There are survivors farther away, as well, and they seem to be moving... but there are stationary life signs in or near the medbay."

"Okay," Alec said. "Right it is, then. Let's get them first." He led the others down the hallway. As he did, there was another tremor, not as strong as the earlier one, but enough that they had to stop and brace themselves. After a short time it passed, and they continued.

At the far end was a reinforced steel door, its adjacent control panel dark. As they approached it, a clang resounded from the other side. They stopped, silent and waiting, but no other sound issued from inside the medbay.

"Try the panel, Elkins," Alec said in a low voice. Elkins pushed the button, but nothing happened. Roots stepped around Siobhan, and he and Elkins threw their shoulders into sliding the door open manually. The backup generators, located outside the facility, should have kicked in auxiliary power to work the doors and lights. If they hadn't, Siobhan thought, it might mean that whatever was wrong inside the facility had found its way out.

After a time, the door gave way, groaning as it slid back along its track. Beyond was another shorter, featureless hallway, and a door at the far end leading to the medical area.

"Compton, McGowan—you two stand guard out here. Keep an eye on things. We'll look around in here."

"Got it, Sarge," Compton said.

"Keep your eyes open. We don't know what we're dealing with yet."

Something in his voice told Siobhan he wasn't being entirely truthful, but both McGowan and Compton nodded. She kept her tongue.

"Don't worry, Sarge," McGowan said. "Whatever's in here, it won't get past us."

Seeming satisfied, Alec gave them a nod, and he and the others slipped through into the medical area.

The antechamber to the medical bay was a small room with a desk in the corner to the right of the door. A row of chairs wrapped around most of the two far walls. Much of the room was empty, except for the occasional grisly reminder that something bad had happened here. Beneath one of the chairs Siobhan saw a boot with what looked eerily like part of a lower leg, the calf muscles chewed. It was still inexplicably standing upright.

A bloody handprint on the wall struck her as wrong somehow; it was upside-down, for one, with the fingers pointing down, and smeared upward toward the air vent near the ceiling. Siobhan forced herself to look away. Though not squeamish by nature, she thought herself fairly empathetic, and with each room they cleared, the likelihood of finding survivors in any shape to save seemed to be diminishing.

To the right of the desk stood an open door. Moving toward it, Alec silently motioned for them to follow. Elkins gestured for Siobhan and Camilla to move ahead of him so he could protect the rear. Siobhan was barely through the doorway when Alec grabbed her arm and tugged her to one side. She suppressed a cry.

"Be careful," he told Camilla and Elkins as they stepped in after Siobhan. All of them followed his gaze to the floor. There was a small spatter of something yellowish-green around a hole in the floor near Siobhan's shoe. Whatever the substance was, it had eaten through the tile, the wooden subfloor, and even the metal beneath that. Something shiny and dark at the bottom of the hole had caught what was left, arresting the corrosion further, and the substance pooled and foamed there. There was an acrid smell in the room which might have been the substance itself or the mix of melting solids with which it had come in contact.

"Don't let it touch your shoes," Alec said. He waved them along a path around other holes of various sizes, lighting the way with his flashlight.

"What is it, Sergeant?" Camilla took a delicate step around the hole and stood next to Siobhan.

"Honestly? It's… uh… blood." He glanced around, picked up a metal tool that looked like a large clamp, and dipped it into the yellow stuff. Immediately, it began smoking and bubbling, eating through inch after inch of it in seconds. "It has to be them."

"Come again, Sarge? I thought you said 'blood'." Elkins looked skeptically down at the half-eaten metal clamp.

"I did." Alec shone the flashlight around. In the passing glow, Siobhan saw medical pods with bodies in them. That explained the foul smell in the room, a nauseating mix of corrosion and rot. These also looked as if something had exploded from within the chest cavities, tearing through internal organs, meat, and muscle, and dragging along whatever they couldn't blast through.

Ripped through, a voice in her head corrected her. Something had torn its way out from inside the bodies. Although she couldn't have pinpointed why just then, she was sure of that fact. *They have samples. Samples they can use as weapons. DNA…*

Another pass of the light showed even larger holes in the floor and more of that yellow acid that had eaten through the floor around the medical pods.

"Blood can't do that," Siobhan said, shaking her head. "I don't care what kind of experiments they're doing here. How could any living thing have blood like that?"

"Most can't," Alec said, and Siobhan saw that look in his eyes again, that deep-rooted worry which so rarely surfaced. "In fact, only one creature I've ever seen has blood like that."

"Wait, you don't mean…?" Roots raised his gun, swinging it around the dark lab. "I kinda thought they were myths."

"*What* were myths? What's going on here, Alec?" Becoming exasperated, Siobhan searched his face. "What did… *that*… to those people?"

"An XX121," he replied. "A Xenomorph."

6

"So, McG, what do you think we're looking at here?" Compton asked as the two stood guarding the hallways. She leaned against the wall across from McGowan, but kept her gun raised. The only light came from the flashlights affixed to their shoulders, and it made weird shadows which darted, swelled, and receded behind them. "Virus?"

McGowan likewise leaned against the doorway and glanced in the direction they'd come, into the near-impenetrable gloom, then shifted the gun to his other shoulder.

"Nah," he said, "that don't seem right to me. The damage we've seen, those bodies—a virus didn't do that."

Compton nodded. "So what, then? Super-soldier? Genetically engineered animal?"

McGowan shrugged. He'd experienced violence before—colonial uprisings, protests gone sour, and prior to joining the USCMC, a hell of a lot of street fights. He'd seen shootings, stabbings, beatings, stranglings, and even a drowning once, but nothing like he had seen here at the Menhit Lab. The air practically crackled with tension, and not just from him and Compton, who seemed determined to fill the silence in the empty hallway with talk.

As if to echo his thoughts, the floor rumbled beneath his feet.

Just the fucking moon, he thought.

Whatever had happened here had left a mark. It had a kind of ghostly permanence. Maybe it was even still happening in some other part of the building, which didn't sit right with McGowan. Not at all. Sarge seemed off, too, like something had gotten his hackles up, and that was never a good sign.

"I think—"

A creak and a thud from back the way they'd come brought them both to attention, their guns raised.

"What was that?" McGowan searched the dark, trying to make out movement. There was nothing.

"I don't—oh wait." Compton took several steps forward, squinting. "It's a vent plate. Looks like it fell off the wall. No big deal."

"Compton…" McGowan's voice trailed off. He wasn't sure what he meant to say—some warning, maybe, not to go too far into the dark down there… but he couldn't have said why. It was a gut feeling, which he usually trusted, but in this place, somehow it seemed distorted. They'd cleared that end of the hallway and found the remnants of the threat, but no threat itself. That was gone, whatever it was.

"What?" Compton turned around. She clutched her gun tighter. "What is it?"

"I—I don't know," McGowan said. "I just… I got a bad feeling, ya know?"

She nodded.

Behind her, in the dark, a shape swelled from the ceiling and dropped, then rose up. Compton didn't notice.

"I know what you mean. I—"

"Look out!" McGowan raised his weapon as Compton dived out of the way. The light from his shoulder fell on the thing. It was about seven feet tall and had a shiny dark gray exoskeleton, like an insect. Its head was long, arcing back behind it, with no apparent eyes or nose, and its mouth was pulled into a wide, lipless snarl.

It appeared to be bipedal, with a narrow, bony frame and limbs lined with ridges and joints ending in spikes. Its hands—or maybe they were paws?—were overlarge, as were its arched feet, and all four ended in sharp claws. Spines protruded from its back, starting between its skeletal shoulders. Its spiked, segmented tail whipped behind it, some six feet long.

For several moments, McGowan couldn't move, couldn't fire. He could only stare at the thing. He'd seen the training videos, had heard the horror stories, always about friends of friends. Few who had ever encountered one of these things lived to tell about it themselves.

It was an XX121. One of the deadliest killing machines in the known universe, and it was standing close enough that McGowan thought he could smell the sickly sweetness of its breath and feel the vapor of its saliva every time the thing exhaled.

The alien pulled back its hand as if to swipe at him.

Suddenly there was gunfire, the lightning of an M41A pulse rifle from McGowan's left. The alien screeched, its bright yellow-green blood spraying back at Compton. Some of it landed on her gun, and the metal began sizzling and melting. Some of it landed on her face shield and began eating away at that, as well. When it reached her skin an instant later, her own screaming matched that of the creature.

The alien dove at Compton and tore off the arm holding the gun. Blood shot from her shoulder stump, spraying the floor, the wall, and McGowan, and pouring down the side of her body. The gun skittered across the floor into the dark.

Compton's screaming stopped. Her eyes grew wide with horror as she watched her arm dangling from the claws of the creature above her. She turned her head toward McGowan, but whatever fight was left in her was swiftly draining from her face.

McGowan raised his gun and fired at the creature. He was far enough away to avoid direct contact with the thing's blood, but it pattered onto the floor in front of him, eating through it.

The XX121 shrieked in anger. It speared Compton through the chest with its long tail and whipped her at McGowan. Her body connected hard with his chest and he flew backward, the base of his skull cracking against the wall behind him. He fell heavily, and for several moments, the hallway swam in front of him.

Blinking, he saw blurred shapes—the alien stalking toward him, large gray hands reaching down, Compton's body lifted from his lap, and then both the alien and Compton were sideways, up on the wall, moving away into the darkness.

Everything went black.

For a moment, Siobhan was too shocked to say anything.

"A Xenomorph killed those people?"

"At least one," Alec said, sounding almost apologetic. "There could be more."

She had heard about Xenomorphs, but as nightmare monsters in stories told to children to scare them into being good. She'd read the files, seen artists' renderings of the beasts, had even heard that the USCMC had initiated training to recognize and exterminate them, in theory... but in real life? Siobhan had never met anyone who had actually *seen* a real Xenomorph, let alone had any kind of interaction with it.

Sure, there were legends—salvage crews and the Svarog miners who had battled the Xenomorphs and survived—

but those were stories from faraway worlds, places more ephemeral, in a way, than the aliens themselves.

She was surprised to find that it wasn't blinding terror that immediately rose to the surface of her conscious thoughts, though she certainly was terrified. Rather, it seemed critical just then to understand what she was up against. Maybe it was the scientist part of her, or maybe it was survival instincts kicking into gear.

Either way, she *needed* to know.

Siobhan surveyed the room. The bodies in the medpods seemed to support the incubation stories she'd heard about. She noted a broken laser mount on the ceiling, and with a quick scan of the floor, she saw the cracked casing of the laser. It looked to her as if they had been incubating and birthing aliens in the medpods, then cutting them down with lasers. But why?

"What kills them?" she asked, her voice surprisingly calm.

"Well, shooting them is no good, at least in close quarters," Elkins said, gesturing at the floor. "Their acid blood. Still, they can be killed—crushed, torn apart, all that. Fire's supposed to be real good for killing them. They're highly adaptable, extremely efficient killers, but they're still just beasts."

Siobhan looked from Elkins to Alec, who nodded, then looked away.

"Best way to stay alive," Roots said, "at least according to what they told us, is to put as much distance as possible between us and them. And if you can't do that—"

"—consider everything non-essential to be expendable," Alec finished in a low voice.

A heavy silence followed. A Xenomorph outbreak the day before evacuation from a dying moon set to collide with its planet…

It was almost too much for Siobhan to process. How did the changes on the moon affect the Xenomorphs? They couldn't possibly survive the collision with Hephaestus… Would they sense impending death and try to stave it off? Or escape. What if one of them made it onto the evacuation ship?

"Siobhan," Camilla said, breaking into her thoughts, "I think you should see this." She was standing by a large stasis case where biological samples were usually kept. The glass doors had been shattered. One large, leathery egg, split open on top, appeared to have hatched. Judging from the large concave bases lining the shelf, there had been others, but they were gone.

"Yeah," Roots said, and he looked down, kicking something over to the others that, in the glow of the flashlight, looked like a shed snakeskin with too many tails. "At least one of the facehuggers latched on to someone."

A loud bang from the observation room on the other side of the medical bay made them all jump.

"Something's in there," Camilla said, looking at her wrist. "Something alive."

7

Roots crept to the control panel. Despite the carnage around it, the unit for opening the observation room door appeared to be undamaged. He glanced back at Alec, who nodded, then he pushed the sequence to open the door.

It skittered half-open, issuing a low grinding noise where it stuck in its track. Roots and Elkins gave it a hard shove and it finally slid into the wall. The room beyond lay dark and silent. Roots and the other marines raised their guns, motioning for Siobhan and Camilla to stay close behind them.

Siobhan glanced back at the long, splintering crack in the observation window, then slipped through the doorway.

The observation room was just large enough to house an L-shaped desk with a computer terminal on it, three tall filing cabinets for assorted message drives and paper files, and a long control panel that climbed the wall by the door and showed dials, knobs, switches, and buttons. Siobhan had never seen a medical facility like it before; it was more like a military control room. She thought of the ceiling mount for the laser and realized there had probably been a lot more control than observation taking place in here. She shivered at the implications.

"Hey! Hey, we got people here!" Roots stood across the room next to a man slumped beneath the control panel. The man appeared conscious but disoriented, his eyes blinking against the marine's light. Blood had dried in a small rivulet down the left side of his face, and when he held up a hand to shield his eyes from the flashlight's glare, Siobhan saw several broken fingers.

Lying on the floor with her head in the man's lap was a younger woman who appeared to be unconscious. The blood from a head wound had turned her short blonde hair a shade of pink.

Siobhan crossed the room and knelt by the man, examining him. She had no medical training beyond the basic first aid offered to Seegson scientists, but she was tired of feeling useless on this excursion.

"Hi," she said in a low, soothing voice. "I'm Dr. McCormick from Seegson Pharmaceuticals. We received your distress signal. We're here to help."

The man blinked at her. A smudge of blood obscured the right lens of his old-fashioned glasses. His dark hair, run through with gray, bristled wildly, as did his moustache and beard. His skin was pale. The wound to his head seemed superficial—a cut on his forehead—but the look of terror and confusion ran deep in his eyes.

"Signal?" He glanced from Siobhan to the marines. "Oh, yes—William. He probably sent it."

"Your synthetic?" Roots frowned down at him. The man didn't answer. He absently stroked the hair of the woman in his lap. If he knew his fingers were broken or felt any pain, he didn't show it.

"Can you tell us who you are?" Siobhan continued in the same soothing voice. "What happened here?"

"I... I'm Dr. Fowler. Martin Fowler. I run the bioweapons research division. This..." he gestured with his broken hand, indicating the woman, "...is Cora Lanning, a research volunteer."

"What happened here, Dr. Fowler?" Siobhan repeated. He gazed at her, studying her a moment. He shook his head slowly.

"The research... it was important. We were so close."

"You let one of those things loose, didn't you?" Alec cut in overhead. The rage in his voice was barely reined in, Siobhan noted. "An XX121. You were doing some fucking experiment with it, and it got free."

Dr. Fowler didn't look at him, but he nodded. "We were working on something revolutionary—something that would have saved lives."

Roots snorted. "You know, Doc, I always get a kick outta hearing guys who make weapons meant to kill, when they talk about how they're saving lives. Does that company-line bullshit ever actually work on anyone?"

Dr. Fowler glared at him, and the disorientation seemed to dissipate.

"I—we—were developing a serum for the infected. When the Ovomorphs hatch, they attach to people and—"

"We know what they do," Alec said.

"The incubation period varies," Dr. Fowler continued, undaunted. "We've seen the facehuggers take as little as two to as much as eight hours to implant an embryo inside someone. And from infection, the embryo takes less than two hours to burst through the host—naturally, that is. The serum we developed extends that incubation time to up to three weeks. Three weeks! That's more than enough time for evacuation to a medical facility."

"Or evacuation to the corporation's facilities," Siobhan said flatly, "for study."

Dr. Fowler glanced at her. "They're remarkable creatures." His voice had regained more confidence, it seemed, despite the anger being leveled at him. "Creatures of amazing efficiency. Strong, agile, highly adaptable, driven to survive." To Alec he added, "I don't know if you've noticed, but it's war out there. Terrorists dropping bombs on colonies, riots, destruction of resources… you think all we do here is make the machines of war, but there can't be peace without the means to enforce it. The kind of peace you get is determined by those with the means to keep it from slipping away."

"Or the money to buy it," Elkins muttered.

"What about Cora?" Siobhan broke in. "Has she been infected?" She brushed hair out of the girl's eyes, but the prone figure didn't stir. Though the thin chest of the young woman rose and fell with small, shallow breaths, there was no other indication that she was alive.

"Unfortunately, yes." Dr. Fowler sighed.

Instinctively, Alec and the other marines raised their guns, and he held up his hands. "Wait! She's perfectly harmless to you. The serum I told you about—I've administered it to her. I found her just a little while ago in the medlab, next to the shriveled skin of the facehugger," Dr. Fowler explained quickly. "I gave her the injection, and she'll be out for a while, but she's fine. *She'll be okay.* She can be evacuated safely."

"I don't think that's a good idea," Siobhan said. "We can't take the chance of infecting the Seegson lab, the colonists—the entire evacuation. It's too risky."

"There's no risk," Fowler argued. "It's perfectly safe. Months of research can vouch for that."

Siobhan looked up at Alec, who shook his head infinitesimally, and then she looked back at the scientist.

"Dr. Fowler, I understand your position, but—"

"But it ain't gonna happen," Roots said.

"She's very valuable to our company," Fowler said, his voice crusting over again with a defensive tone.

"She's a liability to ours," Elkins said.

Dr. Fowler opened his mouth to say something, but closed it. Perhaps he cared for the unconscious girl. Perhaps he only cared about the money to be made from the creature inside her. Siobhan hoped it was the former.

"Let Camilla examine her," she suggested. "We'll decide if she's safe to move."

Dr. Fowler considered it a moment, then nodded.

"Agreed, and I will share our files with your synthetic," he said. "See for yourself. That alien inside her is, to all intents and purposes, completely harmless."

Siobhan couldn't tell if he believed his own words.

When McGowan woke up, alone in the hallway, he could still hear screams. They sounded hollow and far away, as if they were coming from inside the walls.

Slowly, he sat up, wincing at the pain in his head, and glanced around. A little way down the hall, the floor smoked and sizzled around a smattering of holes, and a large splash of blood—human blood—hung on the wall above them. Some of it smeared sideways down the hall's length, disappearing into the dark. He turned his head and flinched when he saw the severed arm nearby.

Compton! That thing had gotten Compton. He rolled over onto his knees and, groaning, raised himself to his feet. A dull ache throbbed at the base of his skull and behind his ears. He stumbled forward, looking for his gun, and found it just at the edge of the shoulder light's gleam. Slowly, he crouched to pick it up, his gaze fixed on the gloom beyond. Gripping the gun, he rose cautiously, pointing it ahead.

"Compton?" His voice sounded thin in his ears. "Compton? You there?"

McGowan took a step forward, then another. The flashlight at his shoulder blinked and flickered, then pushed back a little of the darkness. He stopped a moment and listened for the screaming, but couldn't hear it anymore. What direction had it been moving in? He turned toward the wall where the blood was smeared and saw that the streaks bent upward. He tilted the flashlight up and saw that the streaks ended at the open vent Compton had mentioned earlier.

He shivered. "Compton?" Standing on his toes, he tried to peer into the vent, but it was too high to make out anything. "Compton?"

A loud bang from somewhere within the depths of the vent system made him jump, and he backed away.

"Fuck this," he muttered to himself, moving toward the door. "Fuck *all* this." His head ached. He didn't like the idea of leaving his back exposed to the last place the Xenomorph had been, but he had to get out of there. Even the air seemed thicker, harder to breathe in, like the O_2 scrubbers in his suit were failing. He needed to get out of that hallway, out of that complex entirely, he and the others.

As he stumbled toward the doorway at the other end, a part of him waited, listening, expecting those claws to grab his shoulder or those jaws to drip and snarl and bite through him. It hadn't killed him when it had taken Compton, but that didn't mean it wouldn't be back.

McGowan passed into the shorter medical area hallway and to the door. The panel there was faintly lit; when McGowan leaned toward it and pushed the button, the door opened. He stumbled through into the medical bay antechamber, barely registering a severed leg—*Compton, oh God, Compton's arm*—and the blood, and crossed the room to the next door. He also registered in his periphery a vent—as well as the pipes and wires yanked down from the ceiling—that seemed to shuttle the noxious air to and from the room.

A wire twitched close to his cheek, and he caught the movement in the corner of his eye. He flinched. It reminded him of the fingers of that thing, the monster that had taken Compton.

Was it following him through the vent system? He stopped for a moment to listen. From the other side of the antechamber door, he thought he heard voices— Sarge, Dr. McCormick, Roots, who had never known the meaning of the word "whisper." McGowan was close. He had to warn them, to get them out of there.

The door was open just enough that he could squeeze through. When he did, he was hit by the smell of rot and blood. It was strong, even through the hazmat suit's air filters. He stumbled around, shining his flashlight on holes in the floor, and blood, and shredded, spattered organs. His stomach clenched. Danny McGowan had seen some things, some bad things, in his stint with the marines, but what he saw in the medical bay of that facility was something different entirely.

As part of their training, they had been shown a forty-five-minute video on Xenomorphs. Graphic and raw, it didn't fully capture the magnitude of the carnage they left in their wake. Didn't come close.

He found bodies in the medbay pods that had been exploded from the inside. Surely, Sarge and the others had seen this. They couldn't have missed it. They had to know. So where had they—

Raised voices came from behind the cracked glass window. Sarge was yelling at someone, then a male voice McGowan didn't recognize, and then Elkins... they were in what had to be the observation room!

McGowan staggered over to the door, which hung mostly open. He could see Sarge now, in the room beyond, glaring down at an unfamiliar man and woman on the floor. Dr. McCormick was crouched beside the man, and Elkins and Roots had their guns trained on him.

The air in the room behind him changed. McGowan heard the chittering sound from somewhere behind and above him, but he didn't register it for what it was. His primary focus was on getting to the others and warning them about—

The sound behind him was almost imperceptible. He felt an itching on the back of his neck and the hairs there stood up. He had a single instant to consider turning to face death head-on before there was pressure against his back, and then a pop, and then a burning, nauseating agony. His stomach seized and clenched. He tried to move forward, but found he couldn't. Not forward, but he was lifting up, up off the ground, and his stomach was a knot around the force that was moving him, a tugging, shrieking knot of incomprehensible pain.

He looked down and saw the barbed tail of the Xenomorph, painted in his blood, protruding from his gut.

He screamed, but it came out as a weak moan. He managed to stay conscious and vaguely aware around the haze of pain long enough to see that Sarge and the others had turned in his direction.

Then things went black for the final time.

8

Setting aside his gun, Elkins lifted Cora Lanning in his arms. She was limp—dead weight, really—but small and light, and he had the insane thought that if he jostled her too much, her bones within would shatter like glass and he'd be left with a pretty flesh-bag of sharp, jagged things. Or maybe, if he dropped her, she'd burst from within and a miniature Xenomorph would come tearing its way out...

Dr. McCormick gestured for Cora to be put in the remaining clean medbay for examination. Elkins could tell from her expression that she was struggling with the idea of leaving the woman behind, but she'd been right. As far as Elkins was concerned, Cora was a time bomb, and nothing Fowler had said had reassured him in the least that she wouldn't go off at any minute.

He didn't like Fowler, didn't trust him.

And he didn't trust the woman in his arms.

Elkins had just turned toward the door when he heard the scream. It sounded like Danny McGowan. Turning so that his flashlight stabbed into the next room, he nearly dropped Cora in shocked horror.

McGowan hung from the tail of a large Xenomorph, which stood in the doorway, blocking the way they'd entered. The beast was tall—more than seven feet, Elkins estimated—and looked just like the pictures and video he'd seen. Bony and powerful at the same time, it was almost the same shade of dark gray as the walls and ceiling. It tipped its long, curved head back and screeched, and Roots opened fire on it.

"No!" Sarge shouted. He waved at Roots to stop, but it was too late. The creature's shoulder split where the ammo found it, spraying that fluorescent acid onto the wall, the floor, and McGowan. The Xenomorph whipped its tail and flung the corpse clear across the room, and the tail snapped back. The creature struck out at the half-open door, sending it flying into the room with a single shove, then stepped inside.

Roots looked to Sarge, who nodded, and they both opened fire on the thing.

It leaped onto the wall and scrabbled for the ceiling, chirping angrily. Sarge fired a shot into its shoulder. It jerked from the impact but kept moving, its blood spattering down to the floor. Some of it splashed toward Roots, hitting his boots before he leaped out of the way. The private cried out, and Elkins turned his attention to his comrade, whose feet were smoking and bubbling. Roots dropped to the floor, detached the boots, tore them off, and tossed them away into the shadows.

Elkins's attention snapped back to the gunfire that sprayed across the ceiling. He was surprised to find that it was Dr. McCormick shooting at the thing—with *his* gun. She hit the Xenomorph in the back between two bony protrusions, and it howled before ducking into the vent and disappearing. Its blood ate at the vent's edge and carved a blackened path down the wall.

Dr. McCormick slowly lowered the gun. Her hands were shaking badly, but her expression was empty. Sarge approached her carefully, offering low, soothing words as he took the weapon from her hands.

"You did good, Von," he said. "Real good." He squeezed her shoulder. Dr. McCormick didn't answer. She went to the cabinets, rifled around until she found a roll of gauze, and then crossed the room to where Roots sat, cradling his left foot. Beneath his hand, Elkins could see blistering flesh.

Elkins looked down at the woman in his arms. He was still holding her, hadn't been able to move or think. He could only stand there dumbly while the alien skewered one friend and tried to cripple another. For a moment, he considered dropping Lanning right there. She had one of those *things* inside her. One of those monsters…

A hand on his arm brought him out of his reverie. He looked up. It was Dr. McCormick, and she must have read something in Elkins's expression.

"Corporal, you can put her down," she said softly. "Go on... put her down now."

Elkins looked around helplessly. He wasn't sure where to put Lanning. Sarge came up to him and took the young woman from his arms.

"Elkins, it's gone. For now, it's gone, but I need you here—with us—okay?"

He nodded.

"Siobhan is going to have Camilla examine her. I want you and Roots watching the doors, the vents—any place that thing can come back through. Can you do that?"

Elkins nodded again.

"You with me, Kenny?" Sarge asked, his voice lowered.

Elkins blinked. "Yeah, Sarge. Yeah, I'm with you." He looked to Dr. McCormick, who handed him his gun and gave him a reassuring smile.

Sarge added a nod and turned to Dr. McCormick. Taking her arm gently, he pulled her aside. They spoke in hushed voices, but Elkins could make out enough to know that Sarge wanted her to perform whatever examinations she intended, and do it quickly. He didn't think they'd prove the woman safe to transport.

The doctor mentioned something about human life, but that didn't seem to move Sarge so much as the look on her face. He sighed and nodded, then carried Cora Lanning into the medical bay. Dr. McCormick, Camilla, and Fowler followed.

Elkins crossed the room to Roots, whose foot, he saw, was now bandaged. His boots lay discarded a few feet away; the Xenomorph blood had eaten through both the tough material and the metal toe shield beneath. Roots was eyeing McGowan's prone figure.

"How 'bout you?" Elkins said, offering the private a hand. "You okay?" Roots took it and let Elkins help pull him to his feet.

"Yeah, I'm fine. Barely grazed me."

"Good," Elkins said. "Hobble over to the vent there and keep an eye on it, then, will ya?"

"And what about you?" Roots asked, eyeing the vent with suspicion.

"I'll watch the doors. If anything moves in that vent, you kill it."

"Oh, don't worry about that," Roots replied. He limped over to McGowan's body and, with evident distaste, yanked the bloody boots off and slid his own feet into them. "That thing comes back, I'll blow it off this godforsaken rock."

"We don't have much time," Alec muttered over Siobhan's shoulder. "Will this take long?"

Siobhan, who was helping Camilla prepare for Cora Lanning's examination, looked at him and noted the worry in his eyes. He kept glancing at the door.

"Not too long," she said, and then, "I trust Camilla's assessment. If she believes the... embryo is safely contained, we can discuss next measures. They can wait with us until their corporation ship comes and picks them up. *If*—" she said, eyeing Dr. Fowler, "—and *only* if Camilla believes the embryo is contained."

The synthetic gently lifted each of Cora's eyelids and shone a light into the young woman's eyes, then checked her pulse. She put a hand on the woman's chest to check her heart rate, then she used the implement in her wrist to scan Cora's abdomen. Her expression remained placid, giving away nothing.

Since Seegson researched the medicinal value of animal by-products, Camilla had been programmed with necessary medical and veterinary knowledge, and was able to check for vital signs and basic medical stability in a living organism. She was also equipped to evaluate potential for infection, poison, venom, and allergens, as well as perform rudimentary blood tests by employing small injectors and sensors linked to her wrist implant. She couldn't assess soft tissue or bone abnormalities—at least not with one-hundred-percent precision—but she could scan the movements of the creature inside the human subject.

"Camilla, what do you think?" Siobhan said. "Can we move her?"

The synthetic took a step back from the unconscious woman and turned to Siobhan, tilting her head thoughtfully. It was a habit she exhibited when she was trying to consider the best way to say something. It was likely another part of her programming, a kind of buffering gesture while she gathered data, but Siobhan found it endearing, all the same.

"Well, Dr. McCormick," Camilla said, "it appears that her respiration and pulse have been slowed, probably from the drug administered to her by Dr. Fowler—"

"That would be consistent with our research," Dr. Fowler broke in. Siobhan realized he had been standing uncomfortably close, but said nothing. Unflustered by the interruption, Camilla continued.

"She's unresponsive to light and pain stimuli, but given the nature of her condition, I believe this is a common and temporary situation. Her medical status would be considered stable. Further, my scan shows the gestation of the Xenomorph embryo inside her has slowed, as well, when measured against comparable data."

Though she continued to speak to Siobhan, her gaze moved steadily to Dr. Fowler and Siobhan thought that, had Camilla been human, she would have been eyeing him with mistrust.

"I have assimilated the portable drive information Dr. Fowler has given me concerning their research, and there is missing information. This includes the statistical survival rate of those on whom the drug successfully works, and the information on those for whom the drug does not. Any drug has a failure rate, and I would need to factor that into my assessment."

Dr. Fowler scowled at her. "The gestation rate of the embryo has slowed. You said your scan showed you that. Our research shows that the slower gestation rate is an indicator that Cora is not in that small—very small—percentage."

"What is the failure rate, Dr. Fowler?" Siobhan asked.

"It's negligible."

"Give us numbers," Siobhan asserted. "For what percentage of people does the drug fail?"

Dr. Fowler looked at Cora, his expression softening, but only a little.

"Fifteen percent."

"Are you serious? *Fifteen percent?* That's insane!" Siobhan felt the heat rising in her face. How could this man—another scientist, at that—hold back information as important as that? Was the Weyland-Yutani money so damned good that he was willing to risk the lives of associates and strangers alike?

Of course he was, wasn't he?

Otherwise, the Menhit Lab wouldn't have been reduced to a dark derelict of bloody corpses.

"I told you, our research—" Dr. Fowler began.

"So we're just supposed to take you at your word, that your wonder drug is working on her?" Siobhan said, cutting him off. "What else aren't you telling us?"

"That we..." Dr. Fowler hesitated.

Siobhan locked eyes with him, waiting.

His shoulders slumped.

"That the corporation won't pick us up without proof of a sample," he said. "Cora. She's the only way I'm getting off—*we're* getting off—this moon." He paused, and something that seemed uncharacteristically earnest shone in his eyes. "Please."

The others were silent for a moment. Survival was contingent upon the life or death of a colleague. This seemed cruel, even for a company like Weyland-Yutani.

Siobhan looked from Dr. Fowler to Cora, who was really was little more than a girl just out of her teen years, with a whole life ahead of her. If only the parasite inside her could be drugged long enough to be removed. It didn't seem fair to abandon her to the terrifying fate of a moon being torn apart before crashing into the cold, swirling oblivion of the planet that was pulling it in.

How was that any less cruel than what Weyland-Yutani proposed?

Still, she was only one girl, and Siobhan had fifteen people to worry about. The ship was coming in less than fourteen hours. If one—or, God forbid, more than one—of those creatures managed to make it back to the Seegson facility...

"Dr. McCormick," Camilla broke in softly, "I can only report that, superficially, she appears to be stable, as Dr. Fowler suggests. Any unknown variable, however, could negatively impact our evacuation success rate." Her voice seemed to become harder. "The safety of Seegson personnel is my first priority. I cannot recommend that she accompany us."

"Now listen—" Fowler said.

"No, *you* listen, Dr. Fowler," Siobhan said, standing toe to toe with him. "I'm not going to risk the safety of my staff and their families on your word alone. I'm sorry. Under normal circumstances we could quarantine you both, but we don't have that kind of time. We have no assurance—"

"You have *my* assurance!" Fowler shouted, glaring at her. "My research is impeccable. She's less of a threat to you than your synthetic here!"

"The threat," Alec broke in, stepping between Siobhan and Fowler, "is a seven-foot killing machine with acid blood that *you*"—he poked Fowler in the chest—"let loose in this lab. And not just one. I counted at least nine spots on those shelves there where you were holding eggs, and we found only one. If those others have hatched, we're fucked. Now, *my* number one priority is keeping Siobhan, her staff, and their families, and my squad alive. I don't give a shit about anything else, including you and your... your *science experiment*, especially if you get in my way."

Dr. Fowler shrank back from him, seeming at a loss for what to say. He glanced at Cora, and then his expression changed, his eyes wide and his mouth dropping open.

Siobhan turned to see what he was looking at, and she let out a little gasp.

Cora Lanning was sitting up in the medical pod, blinking her eyes. She looked at them and gave them a small, shy smile.

She was awake.

9

"Cora! You're awake! How are—?" Dr. Fowler took a step toward her, but Siobhan placed a hand on his arm to stop him.

"Dr. Fowler?" The girl rubbed her eyes with the back of one hand. "What happened? Did I get… did you give me the drug?"

"I did." Fowler smiled. "Tell me, what are you feeling right now?"

She let out a shuddery sigh and looked from Siobhan and Alec to Camilla. "I… okay, I think. I feel okay. A little hungry. Who…?" She gestured to Siobhan.

"Cora, I'm Siobhan McCormick, from the Seegson Pharmaceuticals lab. We got the distress signal your synthetic sent. Can you tell us what happened?"

The girl shivered. "I don't know much. I'm sorry, Dr. Fowler, I—" She stopped, her gaze shifting off. Something, it seemed, was coming back to her. She raised a shaking hand to her head, wiping the blood-stiffened hair from her face and pushing it behind her ear. "There was screaming. I remember the screaming inside the safe room, where we all were... oh God..." She looked up in horror and whispered, "We were in there with those things."

"Where?" Alec asked, but she didn't seem to hear him.

"They're all gone," Cora continued in that same shaken whisper. "They had holes in their chests where the... where those monsters..." She looked down at her own stomach, touching it lightly, as if afraid the contact would stir the creature inside her. To Fowler she said, "You can get it out of me, right? I don't want it inside of me."

"Of course," Dr. Fowler said, stepping toward her. He put a reassuring hand on her shoulder. "Once the corporation ship comes, we'll get you taken care of."

"You promise?"

"Absolutely." He gave her a warmly reassuring, almost paternal smile. "Now, can you tell us what you remember?"

Cora thought about it a minute. "I was working in the biotoxin lab. We were doing the second wave of Anathema experiments on the black pathogen samples—the ones Dr. Shields sent, that were taken from LV-239. You know Myrna Shields, right, Dr. Fowler?"

"I do," he replied, sounding oddly noncommittal.

"Well, we had just disposed of the sample—thank God for that, right?" She uttered a nervous little titter. "I mean, imagine if any of us were exposed because of what happened? Or if those things..." Her smile evaporated. "Anyway, I heard the ceiling tiles crack, and one of those creatures came through. It killed Dr. Forman and Shelley and Dave and... I don't even know how many others."

"You saw it?" Alec asked. "The Xenomorph?"

"One of them. There was only the one then. I—I ran to the storage warehouse. That's what we were told to do, in case of emergencies. The room's got special locks," Cora explained, "and alarm systems because we keep important equipment, prototypes, that sort of thing in there—"

"That's okay, Cora," Fowler broke in with an uneasy laugh. "They don't need to know all those details."

"Oh, right," she said, blushing a little. "Anyway, a bunch of us ran in there and locked ourselves in. The lockdown procedures added extra security, we thought. Nothing would get in, but that wasn't the problem." Her eyes filled with tears and her voice cracked when she added, "None of us could get out, either. The... the thing was in there with us. And the eggs, they hatched. That's... that's all I remember." She hugged herself tightly. "Did you find me there, Dr. Fowler?"

"When the doors opened again, yes," Fowler said. "You were the only one left, who hadn't..." He made a gesture with his hands like something was exploding from his chest. "I could only assume, given the discarded Ovomorph shells everywhere. I gave you the shot, to be on the safe side."

She smiled gratefully up at him.

"Wait," Alec said. "You said, 'one of them.' How many were there? How many were in the room with you?"

Cora thought about it a minute, and then said, "I—I don't know."

"Think," Alec said. "It's important."

"I—I don't—five, maybe six? Some of the eggs had already hatched when we found them. Some of the people were already dead."

"So, no one has any idea exactly how many Xenomorphs are running around this facility?" Alec's voice was strained. The anger there simmered, threatening to boil over. "You have no idea what, exactly, the threat level is."

"The problem will sort itself out," Fowler replied evenly.

The others looked at him, angry shock on their faces.

"Are you insane?" Alec took a step toward him, but Siobhan put a hand on his chest to stop him. Over her head, Alec added, "How the *hell* do you figure this will 'sort itself out'?"

"This moon is dying," Dr. Fowler replied. "In a week, maybe less, this godforsaken rock will be so unstable it'll tear itself apart. It'll crash into Hephaestus and its remains will be a pulverized, swirling mess that will annihilate all life still clinging to it. It doesn't matter if there's two, three, or twenty of those things—at least, it won't after tomorrow, when the ships come.

"If we can re-route the corporation ship to pick us up by the Seegson Pharmaceuticals lab," he continued, "we can put miles between us the Xenomorphs. Even if they thought to follow, they'd still have to do so on foot. We have vehicles, weapons, and we'll have a head start. We could hole up in your lab, then get the hell off this moon before the savage bastards even know we're gone."

It took Siobhan a few moments to process the recklessly negligent and audacious assumptions this man was making. Finally, she took a deep breath and tried a reasoning approach.

"Dr. Fowler, surely, as a man of science, you can't be so willfully ignorant. There are so many variables—"

"Ignorant?" Dr. Fowler blustered.

"You of *all* people should know that these things are predators," Siobhan continued, her own anger on the verge of erupting. "They exist to kill, and to make more aliens. That's it—and it sounds like they've already made quite a few. So where do you think that leaves us?"

"They've killed one of my squad members, maybe two." Alec's grip on his gun tightened. "I'm not going to lose anyone else. We need to go, and I'm not taking any more risks."

"We need to bring her," Dr. Fowler said. "We can't leave Cora behind. You can see with your own eyes that she's fine."

"Wait, what?" Cora exclaimed as she took in what they were saying. "Please, don't leave me!" Alarm creased her young features, her eyes growing wide in panic. "Please! You can't leave me here. I'm okay! I feel okay! Dr. Fowler says I am..."

Siobhan and Alec exchanged uneasy glances. Dr. Fowler had deliberately kindled their sympathy and the girl's panic. How could they abandon her now, to who knew how many of those monsters?

"You can guarantee she's safe?" Siobhan asked, deliberately avoiding Cora's searching eyes. It was a useless question, but she had to ask it.

"I can," Dr. Fowler said with a small smile.

"If anything happens," Alec growled, poking him in the chest again, "it's your ass." Then he said, "Roots, Elkins, we're moving out. Let's go!"

Fowler offered a few options for escape from the Menhit Lab. It was by pure chance, he said, that they'd managed to avoid most of the Xenomorphs, in spite of the way they'd come in. They couldn't expect the same luck going out the same way.

The greatest risk involved passing by the large storage room, which the first Xenomorph seemed to have repurposed as a nest. It was there, Dr. Fowler theorized, that the majority of them would be gathered, given its cooler temperature and secured pathways for ingress and egress.

"So which way, then?" Alec demanded. Siobhan could tell from the thinness in his voice that he was getting more impatient with each passing minute.

"We go out the other side, toward the living quarters," Fowler said. "They're empty now—only essential personnel were left here, and all of them were working when... well anyway, that would be the safest route, in my opinion."

"We'd have to skirt around the building to get back to the APC," Elkins said. "Any of those things make it outside yet?"

"That might work in our favor." Roots frowned. "At least outside, we don't have to worry about their blood in close quarters."

"Private Rutiani has a point," Siobhan said. "I'd vote for that route. Camilla, what do you think?"

"The probability of encountering a Xenomorph along the proposed route, given the bio-readings I'm getting, is approximately sixty-seven point eight percent, compared to our original route, which gives us a probability of ninety-two point three percent."

"It's decided, then," Alec said. "We play the odds."

1 0

As they made their way through the complex, the ground rumbled, as if the moon itself was reminding them that time was running out. A look of terror flickered across Cora's features. The marines didn't even seem to notice.

They found more carnage splayed across one of the hallway walls. It was what remained of some of the other scientists. Mostly, it was just blood and strands of hair, but it was overwhelming; the smell of rot got up inside the nose and throat and stayed there. Cora whimpered, shrinking further against Dr. Fowler. Camilla gave the gore a curious cursory glance, and then guided the Weyland-Yutani duo around it.

Siobhan saw some severed fingers and an employee ID badge with the name Stanley Watkins lying in a pool of blood, and steeled herself as she stepped over them.

The hallways in this part of the facility, she noticed, were more like a labyrinth, and darker, too. If there were signs directing which way to go, she didn't see them; despite the flashlights, the darkness closed around them in a way it hadn't done even in other parts of the facility, and when there were hall lights, they only moved around the shadows.

She supposed it was in her head, that cloying blackness, the weight that came with the stench of blood. In these hallways, the sound of their footsteps seemed louder, the vents larger and closer. A hum came from those, a kind of low electrical vibration which Siobhan couldn't place. It made no sense; nothing in the facility worked, least of all the electricity. It set her on edge; it felt like a live, feral, waiting thing, breathing and growling and following them via the ductwork as they made their way down the hall.

They turned a corner and Elkins, who was in the lead, flinched. The sudden movement started a chain reaction of jerks and cries.

"What?" Alec shouted from the rear. "What is it?"

"Nothing," Elkins said, clutching his chest a moment, then gesturing at the gloom ahead of them. "Just wires and debris. I thought—for a second, it looked like one of those things."

"Okay, pull it together, guys. We're almost out," Alec said. "Keep going and keep a sharp eye on your surroundings." They started again, moving quickly and quietly, as they had before. The marines in front ducked through any open doorway to check each room for dangers before moving on. There was an EXIT sign with an arrow encouraging them on, but still the breath in Siobhan's chest remained tight, even when Dr. Fowler confirmed they were almost to the outside door.

"Almost there" was good, but not as good as "there" would be.

"Sergeant Brand," Camilla said after a time, "I'm getting the bio-reading of a single lifeform nearby."

"Where?" Alec said, glancing around. "Which direction?"

Camilla consulted her wrist

"It appears to be... directly above us."

The group froze, their gazes drifting toward the tops of the walls, searching for air vents. The ceilings themselves looked fairly solid, a kind of smooth concrete with embedded metal mesh... except for the hole.

"Sarge," Roots whispered harshly. "Look!"

The cavity had been carved in an irregular shape where the ceiling met the wall—like a water stain, only much larger. Its edges were jagged where chewed spokes of metal poked through.

"Up there?" Alec whispered to Camilla, nodding at the hole.

She nodded back. "It appears so."

Alec nodded to Elkins and Roots, and the three of them crept toward the opening, guns and faces pointed upward. Siobhan glanced around the hallway for something she might use as a weapon. She couldn't stand another minute of feeling helpless. There wasn't much to find, other than a slightly bent metal pipe about a foot long and an inch or so wide, ostensibly from somewhere beyond the ceiling.

It would have to do.

She crouched and picked it up, straightening slowly, her attention fixed on the hole. Silence enveloped the hallway; even the hum from the ductwork seemed to have paused, like a breath held in anticipation.

Alec waved for her and the others to continue, past the hole and whatever lay in wait up there. As they hurried by, Siobhan thought she heard a low, breathy kind of squeal. She clutched the pipe tighter.

The Colonial Marines heard it, too. Once they had passed, Alec signaled to his squad to slowly back away, guns still trained upward. Then a roar like wind in an airlock came from above them, and a set of shiny black talons curled around the edge of the ceiling hole.

A chill crawled across Siobhan's skin. Her heart pounded almost painfully in her chest.

The second set of talons appeared beside the first.

"Run!" Alec bellowed.

In the time that it took him to do so, the creature emerged from the darkness and scaled down the wall.

Siobhan ran. She heard the pounding of footsteps all around her, as well as the firing of pulse rifles. The unnatural squeals of the Xenomorph seemed to echo all around the hallway, as did the scrabbling of its talons as it chased them. It sounded close—over her shoulder, on her back, in front of her, next to her, in her ear.

Reaching the end of the hall, Siobhan skidded into a door and started frantically pounding the control panel next to it. Its faint blue glow gave her fleeting hope, but with each slap of her hand, that hope faded. Alec shouted behind her, his pulse rifle thundering. The squeals reached an angry pitch.

Again she typed in the codes, then made a fist and punched the control panel in frustration. The doors slid open, and she and the others tumbled through. There was a panicked moment of falling forward, landing on her stomach. She rolled onto her back, intending to scramble away from the thing, to get out of the way.

It was almost on her.

Rearing up from the floor, it bared its teeth, dripping with its glistening saliva. It screeched at her, its bony frame tensing to strike.

Pulse rifles fired over her head. Fluorescing blood splattered from the creature's shoulder and chest, spraying away from her.

Thank God.

The impact knocked it back on its feet. It screamed once, then fell forward, its arms flailing out in front of it. Siobhan rolled to the side just as the thing's head and injured shoulder crashed onto the floor where she had been.

Then, all was silence again, except for the acidic sizzle of its blood eating into the floor, and the heavy breathing of the others. Siobhan looked down and saw the razor-sharp tip of a single talon curved over the tip of her boot. She pulled away with a jerk.

Alec appeared above her, offering a hand. She took it, and he pulled her to her feet. Only then did she notice that she was still clutching the pipe in her free hand, when he glanced at it and smiled.

Turning, she looked down at the dead Xenomorph, at the sleek black curve of its head, the thin, powerful muscles that belied its bony frame, pinned by multiple shoulder beams. Its serrated tail trailed away behind it. The last foot or so, she saw, had been severed, and had landed nearby.

Then she looked at the others, who were once again creeping down the hallway toward the exit. She dropped the pipe, bent and picked up the severed piece of tail, and then she and Alec moved to catch up with the rest.

The area behind the Menhit facility was eerily quiet. It had stopped raining, but the sky above was thick with clouds, and thunder still echoed across the mountaintops.

The generators, Siobhan saw, had been badly damaged, much like the machinery inside the building. The fence around the generators seemed intact, though. There was some blood and bits of pink and gray in the mesh of the barrier, and it took Siobhan a moment to realize that she was looking at brains—which had been punched straight out of the skull of the Weyland-Yutani PMC corpse lying on the ground. A company-issued weapon lay in pieces next to the body. The name on the uniform read LOMBARDO, W.

"Shit," Alec muttered to himself, and then repeated it even louder.

"What's the matter?" Dr. Fowler asked. "Beyond the obvious fact that he's deceased, of course."

"Don't you get it?" Alec shook his head. "A dead guy out here means that whatever killed him is probably out here, too. Those fuckers got out of your 'secure, locked down' facility, Doctor." To Roots and Elkins, he said, "Let's move. Eyes open—and shoot anything alive that isn't one of us."

They moved quickly in the cool night air, following the lengths and contours of the building, sticking close to its outer walls to protect themselves on at least one side.

The moonscape groaned, the ground rumbling beneath their feet. They climbed a small hill and the air dragged at their limbs. The gravitational pull of the planet was exerting its strain on the moon; more and more often, it made its presence felt as a gnawing in the bones, an ache in the head behind the eyes and in the sinuses. It felt to Siobhan like the moon itself was in pain, twisting within against the forces without, and it was catching them up in its tense grip with each throb of agony.

Elkins led them around a corner and stopped short. The others came to an uneasy halt and followed the trail of his gaze to the side of the building, up near the roof.

The Xenomorph clinging to the outer wall was enormous, two or three times the size of the ones they'd seen so far. Tufts of fur grew between the jutting blades of its shoulders and back spines, and its chest was much broader. Most notable, though—most terrifying—was the set of gigantic bony antlers protruding from the curved, eyeless head.

Siobhan shuddered as the full implication of the thing struck her. Humans hadn't been the only hosts the Xenomorphs had managed to wrangle into that makeshift nest inside. This one had to have been incubated inside a vurfur—she was sure of it. As if to confirm her thoughts, its screech when it spotted them had the snorting quality of the large deer-like beast. It stomped and pawed at the wall in territorial hostility, then quickly began to make its way down, moving at a speed that seemed impossible, given its size.

"Go!" Alec shouted. "Go! Go!"

They ran, stumbling over the uneven landscape toward the next corner of the building, but it gained on them, galloping along the wall as if it were flat ground. Elkins spun and, still backpedaling, fired off a round. The creature dodged it without even slowing.

The group turned the corner. The APC stood waiting about fifty feet ahead of them. Siobhan glanced back at their pursuer and saw it had leaped the corner, too. It was making its way down toward them.

Just then, the ground beneath them began to tremble.

"Oh *fuck*!" Roots shouted, leaping over a fissure that zigzagged out toward him from under the facility.

The building to their right shook hard; in the next moment, the Xenomorph was twisting in the air. It landed hard on the ground just as Alec reached the APC. He trained his gun on the Xenomorph, which shook itself off and stood, then screeched loudly.

That sound, Siobhan thought. It wasn't natural. There was something inorganic, an almost metallic whine beneath the heavy breaths and squealing and roaring. It was something... well, something *alien*. In all the worlds Siobhan had experienced, and of all the flora and fauna of those worlds, nothing she had ever heard sounded like it.

She thought it must be the sound of nightmares breaking free.

The Xenomorph charged them, pounding forward on all fours, its antlered head low. Alec kept firing. Undeterred, it skirted each explosion in the dirt. Elkins reached the APC and began pulling the others inside as they arrived—Dr. Fowler and Cora, Camilla, and finally Siobhan. He and Alec jumped aboard and slammed the door shut, seconds before a powerful crash rocked the vehicle.

It was battering the APC, trying to force it open.

"Elkins," Alec warned, "get this bucket of scrap metal moving!"

"On it, Sarge," Elkins said, sliding into the driver's seat.

Outside, the roar of the ground splitting open mingled with the frustrated squeals of the giant Xenomorph.

Another crash lifted the APC up on one side, tilting it dangerously to the left. For a moment, Siobhan felt certain the vehicle would flip. She held her breath.

It slammed back down.

Then it lurched forward, and they were moving.

They bumped along the terrain, flying over a hill and landing hard. Then another. The sensors in the APC tracked the Xenomorph behind them. It was matching their speed.

"It's still on us," Elkins said through gritted teeth.

"Impossible," Dr. Fowler called from the back. "It can't—"

"*Well, it is!*" Elkins shouted. "It's right behind us!"

Over the low wail of the wind outside, the eerie shriek of the creature seemed to surround them. A sound like thunder rumbled underneath them, for a moment blotting out everything else. Then the road ahead suddenly split open, dirt and rocks tumbling down into the newly formed hole.

"Shit!" Elkins cut the wheel and made a hard right. The hole seemed to grow, reaching out toward them, pulling in more dirt. The APC dipped a little where the ground slipped out from under it, but Elkins held fast, pulling them back out onto solid terrain. They fishtailed, gripped the road—such as it was—and they jerked forward again.

The shrill squealing of the creature behind them became a piercing screech as it leaped and dodged the shifting landscape. Then a heavy thud above them jolted the vehicle again.

The Xenomorph was on top of the APC.

"This is bad, Elks," Roots muttered. "Get it off us."

"I'm trying," Elkins replied. He cut the wheel and they were all slammed to the side as the APC turned sharply to the left. He turned the other way, trying to shake the thing off the roof. According to the sensors, it clung fast, no doubt digging those talons as deep into the metal as it could. Pointed dents appeared in the roof of the cab.

The corporal cut the wheel back and forth again, and the APC fishtailed to keep up. Ahead, through the windshield, Siobhan saw a dark hole where the road had opened.

"Elkins, turn!"

He did so, jerking the wheel hard. The vehicle skimmed the edge of the hole and hit a bump in the dirt. The sensors picked up the Xenomorph careening over the side—an instant later they saw it with their own eyes—and then it was tumbling into the hole.

The group cheered in relief as Elkins put more and more churned-up road between them and the hole the Xenomorph had fallen into. Siobhan just hoped it was a deep enough crack in the failing moon to swallow up the creature for good.

PART II

EXIT PLAN

1 1

When Elkins pulled up in front of the Seegson Pharmaceuticals lab and killed the ignition on the APC, no one spoke for several seconds. Siobhan could hear her own ragged breathing over everyone else's. She leaned forward and tapped a few commands into the sensor interface, and it did a quick scan.

Though she knew what the result would be, she still needed confirmation. No foreign objects or lifeforms of any significance were attached to the vehicle. The alien was gone. One by one, they climbed out of the APC and looked around.

The ground beneath them had quieted for the time being. The dark beyond the Gatelands, though thick, was still.

Dr. Fowler eyed the Seegson building with disdain. "Well, I suppose it keeps you out of the elements, at least," he said. Siobhan resisted the urge to lash back at him.

Instead, she said, "This way," and led the group into the lab building. When they reached her office door, she turned to Alec.

"Sun-up will be in about three hours. I think we should get Cora and Dr. Fowler into the quarantine quarters so they can rest until their ship comes."

"So you still insist on quarantine measures?" Dr. Fowler waved a hand dismissively. "I told you, it isn't necessary." Siobhan turned on him, and all the tension of the night burned like fire behind her eyes.

"My lab, my rules," she said, not bothering to hide her anger now. "You will sit in quarantine like you're told, or you can wait for your ship outside, with whatever manages to make its way here from your lab."

Dr. Fowler opened his mouth to reply, closed it, and nodded.

"Quarantine it is, then."

"We'll get them tucked in for the rest of the night," Rutiani said. His hand rested casually on the stock of his weapon to dissuade any argument.

"Thank you, Private Rutiani," Siobhan said. "Remember, we need everyone on the Gatelands platform by ten forty-five p.m. The Seegson ship will be here by eleven."

"It can't come soon enough," Elkins said.

"Dr. Fowler," Siobhan added, "do you have contact information for your corporate liaison, so I can notify them of the change of pick-up location?"

"I can handle that," Dr. Fowler said. "Our rendezvous isn't scheduled until tomorrow, in the afternoon. We can avail ourselves of your comms systems after you leave."

Siobhan shrugged. "Suit yourself," she replied, punching in the combination to her office door. "Good night, everyone. I'll see you in a few hours."

"Good night," Alec said, giving her shoulder a light squeeze as he walked by. She smiled to herself and entered her office.

The quarantine area of the Seegson Pharmaceuticals lab's medical bay was located near the rear of the facility, between the emergency shower stalls and the bioprocessing and chemistry labs.

Sarge gave Roots and Elkins the task of escorting the Weyland-Yutani scientists to the quarantine area and seeing they were comfortably secured. He told them he was going to take care of some things at the barracks, and the men knew what that meant. Compton and McGowan had families, whom Sarge had to notify that they had been killed in action. They had personal effects which had to be packed up and sent home.

Lives well lived created ripples outward that continued after death, and it was up to the survivors who cared about those lives to follow the ripples to their natural conclusions. It wasn't an obligation either of the soldiers envied, but they knew Sarge would handle it with respect, pride, and genuine care. That was enough for both men to feel at least some peace in the passing of their squad mates.

"I trust we'll be released before you ship out," Dr. Fowler was saying. "You won't leave us to starve to death or miss our ship."

Roots had been tuning out the scientist's passive-aggressive banter as they followed Elkins down the hall.

"You'll be fine," Elkins mumbled, and from the tone, Roots guessed he had checked out of the conversation as well.

"And the quarantine quarters are adequate for the both of us, I assume," Dr. Fowler added. "This place seems... well, Seegson never had quite the funding that Weyland-Yutani provided, but I suppose you've all done the best you could with what you had."

"You'll be fine," Roots echoed in the same non-committal tone.

"I don't feel so good," Cora Lanning said.

"You'll be fine," Elkins repeated.

"What time is your ship coming again?" Dr. Fowler asked.

"We were told eleven a.m.," Roots answered.

"And where are you scheduled to be relocated?"

Elkins glanced back at Roots. The look told him not to commit to specifics.

"A UA outpost in the Reticuli System," Roots replied.

"Dr. Fowler?" Cora slowed nearly to a stop, but Dr. Fowler gently tugged her forward again.

"I didn't think the UA had any current outposts in the Reticuli System," he said.

"Dr. Fowler?" Cora rubbed her stomach lightly. "I feel queasy." She did, in fact, look a little pale to Roots.

"You ask a lot of questions," Elkins said to the doctor.

"I just like to know whose bed I'm sleeping in."

Roots was about to answer when Cora stopped short, gasping loudly and jerking her arm from Dr. Fowler's grasp. Immediately she bent over in pain, clutching her stomach. From beneath the curtain of her hair came retching sounds. Foaming spit pattered to the floor.

In seconds Roots and Elkins were by her side, shoving Dr. Fowler out of the way and easing her to the floor. Fowler took a few steps back.

"Doc, what can we do?" Roots looked up at him, but the man didn't answer. Cora spasmed violently in Elkins's grasp. From the gurgling sounds, it seemed as if she was trying to talk, but the pain ate up the words.

"Fowler, goddamn it! Do something!"

"Back away," Dr. Fowler said, heeding his own advice. "Now."

At first, Roots and Elkins just crouched there by the girl, confused. The girl was twisting in pain; they couldn't just leave her writhing on the floor. The exams had said she was okay, stable. Wasn't she?

"Get away from it," Dr. Fowler said.

It?

Roots had just enough time to register the man's use of the word before the girl's stomach exploded outward. He fell backward, spattered in blood and bits of bone, crab-crawling away until his back hit the wall.

Blood saturated the thin fabric of her top, quickly spreading outward. The cloth tore and a crescent head, slick with blood, followed by a lithe body, all sharp angles and edges, chewed its way out.

It screeched once.

Roots raised the butt of his gun, intending to bring it crashing down on the little creature's head. It seemed to sense his plan, though, and launched itself at his face.

At first, he felt the panic, the gut-deep loathing and fear of the thing—even at so small a size—being so close to him. Then the pain came as needle-sharp teeth penetrated his cheek. Instinctively, he swatted at it, but it was already moving. Pain and blood clouded the vision in his left eye, but he heard Elkins's weapon firing and turned in time to see the tiny monster leap to the wall, scale it, and disappear into one of the dark corners.

Then it was gone.

In the barracks, Alec sat on the cot that the squad sometimes used for naps. Two moving crates, each filled with the clothing and personal effects of his dead squad members, sat in front of him.

He held a picture of Compton's two sons. It was an old-fashioned paper photograph sent by their father, and on the back was a note.

John – ten
Robbie – 6
2187

In the photo, the older sibling had an arm flung around the shoulders of the younger one, and both were grinning broadly under mops of thick, curly dark hair. Compton had loved that picture; she'd told him that she kissed it good night every time she went to bed.

Gingerly, Alec put it in the box, on top of her other things.

He barely remembered his own mother. When he was a kid, he'd been sent from El Hoyo to a colony ship as a lucky recipient of the town's generosity and his parents' kindness and meager pooled resources. It had been a second chance, a rare opportunity to get away from a life of poverty and violence and have an actual shot at a life he chose, undefined by forces beyond his control.

It hadn't quite worked out that way, though.

The ship, the *Gaspar*, had been hijacked and sent to a secret testing facility on an unregistered moon so that Weyland-Yutani could experiment with Xenomorphs. He'd never understood all the details, not even the "how," let alone any inkling of the "why." All he'd known was that for a long, terrifying time which could have been a day or a week, he'd run and he'd hidden in a strange jungle, holding in his breath and his tears, hoping like hell that those *things*—he didn't know what they were at the time—didn't tear him apart like they had the thousand other colonists on that ship. Everything he was, everything he'd become and accomplished, had been defined by that time in the jungle, and by the women, Amanda Ripley and Zula Hendricks, who had rescued him.

Alec was a Colonial Marine because of that. He had fought and killed to protect and save people on more moons and planets than he could count. He had lost years to hypersleep. He had given his life to the USCMC. He had thought—had stupidly let himself entertain the fantasy—that the horrors he'd faced in places overrun with Xenomorphs were behind him.

They were not, and once again, Weyland-Yutani was behind it all.

A rush of anger came on him like a wave of heat in his face, neck, and chest. His fists clenched. That *bastard* Fowler—all those soulless sons of bitches at the Weyland-Yutani lab—didn't care who they hurt, who they killed. Even after all these years, they hadn't learned that they had no control over this thing, this force they wanted to possess. This streamlined and efficient killing machine that they wanted to both somehow get under their control and unleash wildly on the galaxy.

They had failed so many times in trying to control it, although they'd certainly done their best to spread the plague of Xenomorphs as far and as widely as they could. He hated them for that.

Setting the lids down on each of the crates, he locked them, and then piled them up with the other boxes to be loaded onto the evacuation ship in the morning. It felt jarringly final to do so, like he was cauterizing a wound rather than letting it heal naturally.

Alec had managed to get McGowan's dog tags off his body just after the alien had killed him, but they hadn't been able to recover Compton's body. He knew the ranks and serial numbers of his squad by heart, but he would have liked to have been able to give those dog tags to Compton's husband, or her sons. She and McGowan had been good soldiers. They deserved better.

Tomorrow, on the ship, he'd begin the reporting and notification processes, and he was damn sure he'd make it known what his squad members had died fighting against.

Walking over to his desk, he sat, propping his socked feet up on it, then leaned over and opened a side drawer where he kept a bottle of whiskey. There was less than half a bottle left, no doubt from the squad taking the occasional nip—off-duty, of course—but Alec didn't care. He had to be up in a few hours, and as exhausted as he was, he knew he wouldn't be able to fall asleep without a little help. He unscrewed the cap.

An alarm went off throughout the labs.

"Shit." He swung his feet off the desk, put the bottle aside, and pulled on his boots. He noticed a small spatter of blood—McGowan's, probably—on one of the toes. He stood and grabbed his gun, thinking of Siobhan, and was out the door.

Siobhan was nearly asleep when the alarm went off. She sat up, disoriented and anxious. The shrill sound coming over her comms produced both a jarring pain in her head and a knot in her stomach.

Exhausted when they'd gotten back, she had managed to change into a tank top and sweatpants, pull up her hair, and brush her teeth before crashing on her bed. If she'd dreamed, she did not remember, and suspected that was probably a good thing. Now, with the alarm sounding, she blinked to clear her vision of sleep, threw back the blankets, and pulled on her boots, then made her way to the door.

Camilla stood outside, hand raised as if to knock.

"What's going on?"

"I'm not sure," Camilla said with a small frown. "However, the quarantine alarm appears to have been activated by Lance Corporal Elkins."

Siobhan's heart sank. The research volunteer, Cora...

Fifteen percent of the test subjects, Fowler had said, did not respond to the damned drug he'd created. He'd sworn Cora wasn't one of those people.

He'd sworn...

She and Camilla hurried down the corridor toward the quarantine area. A door at the end of a side hallway opened and Siobhan let out a little cry. It took her a moment to recognize the silhouette stepping in from the dark outside. It was Alec.

"What's happening?" he asked, rushing toward them, his gun already drawn.

"An alarm was set off—Camilla says it was Elkins, at the quarantine lab," Siobhan replied with a grim nod in that direction. "So I can hazard a guess."

"That son of a bitch," Alec muttered.

Then they were on the move again.

They found Elkins and Roots picking themselves up in the hallway leading to the lab. Elkins had his gun trained on Dr. Fowler. Roots had some nasty wounds on one cheek. What was left of Cora lay on the floor. Blood splattered a nearby wall, streaking toward a vent. Siobhan took the sight in, that knot in her stomach pulling tighter.

"What the fuck happened?" Alec's eyes blazed as he glared from the body of the girl to Dr. Fowler.

"I... I don't know," Dr. Fowler replied. "I don't understand." He looked genuinely shaken, but his glance kept slipping toward the exit and his body language was guarded. He looked more worried about himself, Siobhan thought, than about the mutilated remains of his research volunteer lying on the floor.

She crouched beside the body. The chest cavity looked to have been blown outward from the inside; broken fragments of her ribcage jutted up, blood dripping off the shredded skin that had caught on the jagged ends. Inside, what Siobhan could make out of the lungs looked pretty torn up; it was hard to tell where one ended and the other began.

A wave of dizziness swept over her, and she sat back on the floor.

"Von, are you okay?" Alec's voice came from above her.

Siobhan nodded. "I—*whew*. I'm fine." She swallowed a few times to sink the gorge that tried to rise in her throat. "I'm fine." She waved away the hand extended to help her—it seemed important that she find it within herself to get up on her own—and rose slowly. Then she turned to Dr. Fowler. It took just as much effort, if not more, to control the anger she was feeling.

"You said she was not a risk." Siobhan leveled a gaze smoldering with rage at the man. "You were *responsible* for her. You claimed she was not—*not*—part of that fifteen percent." Dr. Fowler looked from her to Alec to Elkins and Roots, then back to her again.

"I—I swear I didn't know. You have to believe me—"

"Believe you?" She kept her voice even, but her hands clenched into fists. "Every single thing you've told us since we met you has turned out to be a half-truth or a flat-out lie. I wouldn't believe you if you told me my own name."

"I didn't mean for this—I didn't know," he insisted. "She showed all the clinical signs of the serum working."

"What you *meant* to do," Siobhan said, "was say anything you had to, in order to get you and your cargo off this moon." She took a step closer. "Where is it?"

"Where is what?"

"The Xenomorph, you son of a bitch," she replied through gritted teeth. "Where. Is. It?"

Dr. Fowler didn't answer. Her gaze swung to Elkins, then Roots, who seemed to shrink in the withering gaze of her anger. None of them said anything.

"We need to find it," she said, "and we need to kill it."

1 2

Outside, the moon rumbled and groaned. Beyond the Gatelands, more fissures opened in the ground, splitting rock and dirt along the road between the Menhit Lab and the oasis of the Seegson Pharmaceuticals lab.

It was as if BG-791 sensed the alien infection that was spreading on its surface, and was attempting to heave it up and out, but the effort wasn't enough. The moon was being pulled apart. The vurfur sensed their own extinction. The Xenomorphs were just one more cancerous tumor in an already dying body.

For the humans on BG-791, time was running out.

Inside the Seegson lab, that electric tension of a world dying outside added to the strain inside. It hummed beneath the group's heated debate. It was an underlying presence in every look, every word, every movement, pulling at everyone and everything with its own gravity.

"Tell me what you know about the Xenomorphs," Siobhan said to Alec. "What do we need to know to kill them?"

"Or contain them," Dr. Fowler ventured, but this only drew the muzzle of Roots's gun on his chest.

Alec considered Siobhan's question a moment. "I know that outside the host, the chestbursters grow quickly, so there will only be so many places it can hide. They're built to survive, to adapt... but they're still just animals, and like any animals, they don't like fire. They don't like jolts of electricity, explosions, that sort of thing. And they can be buried alive."

"Sergeant Brand is correct," Fowler interjected. "They move away from pain, as any animal would, and while our serum may slow the gestation of the alien inside the host, it seems to accelerate their growth once outside. So no, they are not indestructible, but they are also far more aggressive."

"Meaning?" Roots jabbed the gun into the scientist's chest, and the latter grunted.

"*Meaning*," Fowler said, pushing his glasses up his nose, "that these specimens don't just kill to protect themselves, their Queen, or their young. They kill in rage, kill for the sake of killing. They are driven by that aggression as much as by the will to survive."

"So, on top of everything else," Roots said, "they're assholes."

"Yes, I suppose you could say that," Fowler replied, grimacing.

"Explain something to me, Doc," Elkins said. "This thing is itching to kill, right? But we have guns. So it's hiding, maybe figuring it'll pick us off one by one—"

"I wouldn't say it's 'figuring' anything. These are not reasoning creatures, any more than, say, the vurfur reason that weak prey is easier to kill and eat than strong prey."

"That's what I'm getting at," Elkins said. "Right now, it's small and weaker than it will be. Its first experience was Roots firing at it. But like you said, it's growing. It's adapting. This itch to kill will eventually bring it out of hiding, right? So what should we be keeping an eye out for, behavior-wise? Where do we look for it?"

Dr. Fowler shrugged. "I rather think your synthetic here—"

"Camilla," Siobhan broke in.

"Camilla, yes. I think she would be able to provide you with more accurate information than I could, by employing her bio-scanner. I studied the Xenomorphs in their gestational stage. That was my expertise—what I could do to slow their growth inside a human host."

"Yeah, great job you did there, Doc," Roots said with a small snort.

"Sergeant," Fowler said, turning to Alec. "I understand that your men are upset, but I see no reason why I need to be subjected to their relentless disrespect."

All eyes turned to Alec. He had been staring off down the hallway, his gaze tracing the paths between the vents and the floor.

"You want respect?" he said finally. "Help us kill this thing."

"Hey, look," Roots cut in. "Sun's coming up, right? The ship will be here soon. Maybe the answer is, we hole up somewhere that we can defend until we can get off this rock. It's only a few hours. We should be able to stay alive for a few hours."

"We can't," Siobhan said, a growing horror dawning on her. "Not yet. We've got the residents. We have to see if they're okay."

The others went quiet. Besides the five of them, there were seven other people still to account for—essential researchers and the family members who refused to leave BG-791 without them. Siobhan had been given the task of getting them all safely off the moon, and it was a responsibility she took seriously.

There was an elderly couple, the Hernandezes, with a young granddaughter named Kira for whom Siobhan had a particular soft spot. She knew how hard it had been as an adult—let alone being the only child in the colony— to move star systems away to a cold, inhospitable moon with hostile plants and animals, an alien sun, and none of the amenities of home. Kira had lost both her parents a few years before, and despite the tragedy and all the upheaval, she was a bright, mostly happy girl with a shy fascination for science and a tender hand when it came to plants and animals.

Siobhan had always hoped Kira would have more than a lonely existence on BG-791, and now more than ever, it seemed imperative that she get the girl off that moon.

"There were no communications from the residential pods as of two minutes ago," Camilla said, breaking the silence. "This is not necessarily worrisome, though; it is late, and the alarm was limited to the laboratory facility. The residents are likely sleeping, provided there has been no breach."

Siobhan turned to Alec. "We need to check on them."

Alec looked into her eyes. "Right." He nodded slowly. "We sweep the residential pods, wake everyone, and bring them back here—quick and quiet. Then we do like Roots suggested and find a place to lock down until the ship arrives."

"Sounds like a plan to me," Elkins said.

"I love this job." Roots shouldered his gun. "Oorah. Let's go save some colonists."

It had been a long night for Hank Hernandez. His granddaughter, Kira, had been excited all the previous day about finally getting off BG-791. The prospect of taking a big UA ship to another planet was a thrill in and of itself; it had been a long, long time since she'd even left the Seegson complex, let alone the moon on which they lived.

She'd chattered enthusiastically about the new school she would be going to and the new friends she would make and about living on a planet with real seasons and parks and movies and candy and on and on... and Hank had been happy to listen to her, to feel delighted because she was delighted. All her toys and clothes and books were packed and waiting in the barracks to be loaded onto the ship. She'd even bravely packed away her favorite stuffed animal, a floppy dog named Mr. Bones, claiming she wouldn't need him for that last night, and would feel better knowing he was aboard the rescue ship and not accidentally left behind somewhere.

It wasn't lost on Hank that they were fleeing, but he did his best to match Kira's excitement of the day, to make it seem more like an adventure than an escape.

Come nightfall, though, it had been another story. Kira hadn't wanted to go to sleep. Her bedroom—once warmly decorated in shades of pink and purple and packed with toys, clothes, and games—stood nearly empty. Her nightlight, which she had been too old for just the night before, now cast its faint glow on the bare wall. In the morning, they'd be leaving the nightlight behind, as they would the bed pod and nearly all the big furniture.

Maybe it was the shadowy emptiness of the place or the absence of Mr. Bones, but all the exhilarating new possibilities of the day had morphed into nighttime uncertainties, doubts, and fears—not least of which was whether or not the ship would actually come and take them off the moon before it crashed.

The ground trembled outside and the wind leaned on the housing complex, making it groan. The skies looked angrier and more dangerous than anything the little girl could imagine in the endless starry space beyond it.

For him, this would mark the sixth interplanetary move in his life, not counting the various places he had been stationed years ago as a Colonial Marine. He'd always figured there'd be one more big move, maybe to somewhere sunny and warm; someplace where he and Victoria could retire and live out the rest of their days fishing and sunning themselves on a quiet beach. What he hadn't figured on was evacuating a moon about to skew its orbit and crash into its planet.

And he hadn't figured on having Kira.

Hank had been an agricultural scientist for the Seegson Pharmaceuticals lab for almost forty-three years. His and Victoria's only daughter, Melanie, was grown and busy with a job and new family of her own, and Hank hadn't been ready to retire just yet. He had another ten years or so left in him, he'd thought, and Vickie was always up for a new adventure. It was one of the things he loved about her.

When Seegson had offered him the position on BG-791, which included payment of relocation costs and a benefits package with a number of bonds he could leave his infant granddaughter someday, he'd agreed. He and Vickie would be off on yet another adventure.

The moon itself had been rough terrain; they'd arrived when the Gatelands oasis was still wild. The housing pods had been ready for moving in, but parts of the lab were still under construction. There had been few animals and fewer people, and none of the amenities of the settled planets. "No place to go and nothing else to do but work, huh?" Vickie had said with a small smile, but he had gotten her meaning. Seegson had put them someplace where there were no distractions, nothing to focus on *but* work.

It had been exciting all the same. There was a new lab and new surroundings, a new sky above their heads, and plenty of time in the evenings for wine and chats over the wire with their daughter and her husband, Keith, and the new baby, Kira. From a work standpoint, there'd been exotic new plant life to study, which had always been a thrill to him.

They'd been living on BG-791 for about a month when an industrial accident killed Keith and put Melanie in the hospital. Her situation had been critical; she hadn't survived the night. She'd died alone in a sterile medpod. Hank was given three weeks' leave to fly to LV-809 for the funerals and bring back Kira.

He loved his granddaughter; he'd loved her from the moment he'd first held her, in a whole, profound, pure way. When he'd held her in that hospital, a tiny little pink, perfect person so much like his daughter, he'd been conflicted, overcome with emotions both sad and elated.

It probably hadn't been a good move for Kira to live on BG-791, but neither he nor Victoria could bear to leave her with anyone else. They would make it work.

Vickie had been an elementary school teacher before the move, so she could homeschool Kira, and Hank's job with Seegson would provide them with food, medicine, clothes, and any of the other important things they might need. Plus, they loved her. They could take good care of her—Hank knew that, but he also knew they couldn't really give her much of a life.

With this next move, though, off BG-791, he and Vickie could finally give Kira all the things she hadn't been able to have before. She'd have all those things she mentioned and more, and maybe most of all, she'd have friends to be there for her and look after her. He and Vickie weren't going to live forever, after all, and Hank wanted to know that at the very least, if anything happened to him and Vickie, Kira could have the life she deserved. The life her mother never really got to have.

Hank tried to explain some of those things to Kira that night—the good things, at least. He reminded her of what she could do and be on the new world, all the things she'd get to see. Finally, he convinced her to snuggle down underneath the blankets and close her eyes. Then he tucked her in, kissed her good night, and met Vickie down the hall in the kitchen for a glass of wine.

That glass turned into two and then three, and still, that night, Hank couldn't sleep.

Hank had never been a spiritual man. He didn't believe in a god any more than he believed in the monsters Kira was afraid were under her bed or in her closet. He'd seen enough throughout the galaxy to be both awed by its majesty and convinced that it was a combination of chaos and coincidence that had put together such a vast and savage universe. There was complexity, sure, but there was contradiction: a mindless force of inexplicable violence and destruction in the midst of what passed for order and even supposedly civilized sentience that suggested the human race—even at its pinnacle of scientific and medical achievement—was completely on its own.

Mostly, Hank was okay with that, with the idea that humanity was hurtling around space, clinging on for dear life, without a co-pilot, let alone a Force of Great Omniscience to oversee everything. However, it wasn't a terribly comforting philosophy, especially on nights when it was hard to sleep and the storms lit up the sky outside the windows and the land beneath him ground away, threatening to pull itself apart.

Before the sun came up, he was out of bed and padding to the kitchen to make coffee. They would be leaving that coffee pot behind, too, and there was an irony in it that made Hank a little sad. It had been a trusty friend, in a sense; a thing he'd relied on every morning.

They'd bought it in the customs shop before boarding the ship that brought them to BG-791, and it had survived multiple washings and even a tumble off the counter. It provided them with such an important part of their morning ritual that Hank and Victoria knew they'd need it one more time, and so it hadn't been packed, and wouldn't be making the trip with them. It was going to be sacrificed to the moon just to give them one more cup of coffee.

As he waited for it to finish percolating, he looked around at the things which had provided comfort for years, things that had made this nearly empty house a home for over a decade. It felt to him then as if he was leaving little pieces of himself behind, in the path of that mindless destructive force that would tear them apart, pulverize and burn them.

The thought left him unsettled.

He'd nearly finished the small pot of coffee in that heavy haze of disquiet when Victoria shuffled into the kitchen in her robe and slippers. Her hair was delightfully wild in the mornings, even though she'd cut it short three years ago. She was self-conscious about it, but he found it sexy.

"Coffee's almost gone?" she asked in a sleepy voice.

Surprised, he turned to the coffee pot and frowned.

"Oh, I guess so! I'm sorry—I wasn't thinking. I think there's still one bag left downstairs. I'll go get it."

She put a hand on his arm to stop him. "I'll get it. I want to see if I left a sweater down there." She turned and said over her shoulder, "Be right back."

"I'd use the inside door, if you're going to the basement," he said. "Those clouds are looking pretty angry up there, and the ground's been shaking something fierce since last night."

Victoria nodded, blowing him a kiss as her slippers shushed their way to the basement door. She paused, her hand on the jamb.

"I'll be glad when we're all safely on the ship."

He offered her a tired smile. "Me too."

She returned it, then slipped around the basement door.

Hank turned back to the kitchen window, thinking about the evacuation. It was still too early to wake Kira; better that she get some sleep so she wouldn't be tired for the trip. The overnight bags sat by the front door, and the rest of their belongings sat in moving crates in the USCMC barracks. They were ready. All they had to do was wait for the ship. Just a few hours, and then the tightness in his chest could ease again. He and his family could, this time, dodge the fury of that mindless destruction.

When Hank heard Victoria's scream from the basement, his first thought was that she had fallen. Maybe the small quakes in the night had opened a crack in the floor, set the concrete polymer down on some uneven edge. He dropped his coffee mug onto the counter and dove for the stairs, shouldering the door open the rest of the way.

"Victoria?" He bounded down the stairs. "Victoria! Are you o—"

He skidded to a stop a few steps from the bottom, his attention immediately caught by the impossible nightmare scene unfolding across the basement by the storage shelves.

The thing which had its claws wrapped around his wife's neck had hoisted her off the ground. Her cries were coming out as strangled whimpers as she slapped at the massive hand which held her.

The monster stood on two feet like a person, but there was otherwise nothing human about it. It was tall, a good seven or eight feet at least, with a curved, elongated head, an almost metallic sheen of exoskeleton over a jointed, bony body, and a long, segmented tail. Every part of it looked painfully sharp and deadly. It didn't seem to have any eyes, but nevertheless, it appeared to be inspecting Victoria with a second, smaller mouth dripping glistening saliva. This extended from the depths of its larger one.

Hank leapt the last few steps, intent on freeing his wife from the monstrous thing, but the creature buried the claws of its free hand into Victoria's stomach. When it wrenched those claws free again, Hank saw her bottom half twist and then stretch in a terribly wrong way. There was a fierce cracking sound, and then her hips and legs dropped to the floor in a spray of blood.

Hank cried out. His first instinct was to run to help her, even as her eyes glazed over and her chest shuddered, and what was left of her slumped in the thing's grasp. When it dropped her to the ground, though, he saw Kira in his mind. Shutting the door, he dove for the stairs again and took them as fast as he could.

The hallway was a blur. His thoughts were swimming, his vision smeared by tears and panic. He threw open Kira's door and crossed the room in two strides, scooping her up and putting her on her feet before her eyes were even open.

"Grandpa?"

"We gotta go, *conejita*."

"Is the ship here?"

"It will be. We have to go now, though."

"Don't I need to get dressed?"

Hank took her hand and tugged her gently out of the room without answering. He didn't want to scare her, not any more than he had to, but he needed her to know that he meant business.

"Stay close," he told her in a low, firm voice.

"Where's Grandma?" She looked around, the sleepiness finally giving way to alertness and then the beginnings of panic. Hank's chest tightened. He sniffed, then passed his sleeve over his eyes to clear his vision.

"I'll explain everything when we're outside," he said. "Remember, stick close to me, and keep quiet."

He could sense her frightened gaze on his back, could feel the tremble in her hands, but he pushed on. First he led her to the gun safe in the cloakroom, where he punched in the number code to open it, relieved that he could remember it after all these years. Hank had kept his old service weapon from his time in the USCMC.

It was a VP70. He pulled it out now and tucked it into the waistband of his pants. Then he took Kira by the hand and led her to the door. From somewhere in the basement, he heard a sound like a squeal and a roar. It made the hairs on his arms stand on end.

Kira froze, but he pulled her along.

Hank thought of his neighbors. There was no telling if there were more of those things or if they had made it to other pods. He couldn't worry about them now, though—he had to think of Kira. They had to get to the main lab.

Hank's hand shook as he tapped the panel to open an exterior door. For a single moment he held his breath, afraid it wouldn't open, that somehow the monster in the basement had cut the power. Then the hatch slid to the side and Hank tugged his granddaughter out into the blue hours of early morning.

"Where are we going, Grandpa?" Kira's little legs hurried to keep up with him. Her hand felt fragile in his.

"To the labs, honey. Your grandma's hurt. We need to get help."

The girl was silent for several minutes. Hank listened for sounds of the thing from the basement following them—that horrible screeching that he thought might echo in his head forever—but the moonscape around them swallowed all sound except the muted crunch of the ground beneath their feet.

"Grandpa?" Kira's voice sounded small.

"Yes?"

"Are we going to leave this moon? All of us?"

Hank did his best to hide the pain in his eyes.

"You bet we are, baby."

"How did Grandma get hurt?"

Hank didn't answer.

"Grandpa?"

"Yeah?"

"Are there monsters on this moon?"

Hank faltered, nearly tripping, but caught himself. "What do you mean, Kira? Why would you ask that?"

"I dunno," she mumbled. "I just... I thought I heard a noise."

Hank set his jaw and plowed forward, his gaze focused on the lights of the Seegson lab about three-quarters of a mile away. He wasn't sure how to answer her question. He'd never believed in lying to children, but he didn't want to scare her. She'd been through so much already. The irony was that an hour before, telling her there were no such things as monsters would have been an easy truth. It wasn't now, though.

He thought of Victoria's upper half hanging limply from the claws of the creature in his basement. What the hell was that thing? Where had it come from? And why his Victoria? Why now?

There were monsters on that moon... and monsters that had put him and his family there, right in their path. He wasn't going to forget that, even if he wasn't about to tell his granddaughter about them.

"The moon's full of weird noises," he finally managed. "You know—storms and tremors and stuff. That's probably what you heard."

"I guess," she said, but she didn't sound convinced.

"Don't you worry," he told her, hoping he sounded more confident than he felt. "We'll be out of here, soon. You and me and Mr. Bones."

"And Grandma," she added.

That tightness in his chest threatened to force tears again.

"And Grandma," he added softly.

1 3

The Seegson residential section—pods built to house research scientists, assistants, volunteers, and their families—was a series of apartment suites connected by long hallways. Each suite had a kitchen, one or two bedrooms, a living room, and a bathroom on one floor, and a basement for storage and maintenance. There was also a small plot of land behind each one, generally used as a vegetable or herb garden.

Many of the apartments now stood vacant, abandoned by non-essential personnel in the months prior to the final evacuation. About a mile down a gentle slope away from the lab facility, the residential area stood on the edge of the Gatelands oasis, surrounded on three sides by small, rocky cliffs. Over time, the lab's greenhouses had closed some of the gap between lab and residence, yet to Siobhan, the residential pods felt very far away.

It was still dark out, but the night had faded to a dull blue that muted the landscape. Roots and Elkins led the party, flashlights attached to their rifles, and were followed by Siobhan and Dr. Fowler. Alec brought up the rear. Camilla, they had decided, would wait at the lab, just in case they missed any residents who had made their way from the living quarters.

Upon leaving the facility they had discovered a vent cover, twisted and bent, on the ground near the west wall. Something had forced it outward, crumpling it like polymer foil. The sight made Siobhan's heart sink. The ground beneath the vent was loose and powdery, and she could see tracks—large prints with two long central toes and two end-capping shorter ones, each ending in claws. The tracks led away from the building and down the hill before the rocky landscape obscured them.

The path through the greenhouse buildings disappeared into the dark between them. If something was hiding there, waiting for a chance to strike from atop one of the shadowed buildings or down some narrow alley, it would be on them before Siobhan and the others ever saw it. The long way, skirting the greenhouses, seemed like a safer option. They would be out in the open there, but then, so would anything looking to attack.

"Looks dark down there," Elkins muttered, though it was hard to say if he was talking to himself or the others.

"Maybe they're all sleeping," Roots replied.

"Aren't they the lucky ones," Dr. Fowler added sarcastically.

Siobhan bit her tongue. She wanted to tell Dr. Fowler that they might *all* be asleep at the moment, if he hadn't been making bloodthirsty monsters in his lab, but she didn't. She simply squeezed the handle of the medkit she was carrying and focused on the silhouette of the residential pods below.

The wind picked up, lifting her hair and gliding along her exposed skin to raise goosebumps on her arms. The air nowadays always seemed heavy, like before a rain, even when no rains were coming.

As they moved past, putting the greenhouses on their left, the wind changed timbre and pitch. Its low whistle became a high, thin, keening whine, almost like a squeal. Siobhan gave the cluster of buildings a wary look. She knew there was a laser scalpel in the medkit, but it wouldn't serve as a very good weapon. The blood of those things might spray into her face or run down her hand and arm. The same problem might happen with the cauterizer, too, she suspected. And the hypodermics wouldn't be strong enough to pierce the creature's exoskeleton.

Hell, if it came down to it, she supposed she could wield the kit itself like a hammer. Once again, though, she wished she was better armed.

They put the greenhouses behind them. It should have been a relief, but Siobhan couldn't help feeling watched, as if something as-yet-hidden from the faint first rays of the early morning sun was waiting for them to turn their backs.

"We've got company, Sarge," Elkins reported. "One adult male, one child."

Turning her attention forward again, she noticed two figures in the distance, heading their way.

"That's Hank Hernandez and Kira!" Siobhan exclaimed, hurrying down the hill. Alec caught up to her and gently took her arm. She turned to him, confused.

He smiled at her. "Just in case," he said, and that was all he needed to say. Siobhan understood. Caution was a good idea for many reasons, not least of which was that one or both of them might be infected. She nodded slowly, a little sad at the possibility, and fell in behind Alec and his men.

Hank waved at them, and Siobhan waved back. As they drew closer, she could see their eyes.

Something had happened, something bad.

It occurred to her then that Victoria, Hank's wife, wasn't with them, and a cold lump of dread settled in Siobhan's stomach.

"Hey!" Hank called when they got within earshot. His eyes were red. "Hey there! We need help."

"What happened?" Alec called. Siobhan could see the muscles tense in his shoulders and forearms. He didn't want to train the gun on Hank, but he was thinking about it.

Hank glanced at Kira, then looked at Alec. "It's my wife. Something... something attacked her in our basement. I couldn't… there was nothing I could do. We had to get out of the house." While one of his hands held Kira's, Siobhan saw, the other held a gun. That hand was shaking.

Alec saw it, too. His gaze moved from gun to little girl before he met Hank's eyes.

"Is she…?"

Hank nodded.

"Did you see any other survivors?"

"No one," Hank replied, glancing back. "Although, to be honest, I didn't really stick around to look."

"The thing that attacked your wife," Dr. Fowler said. "What happened to it? Where did it go?" Hank looked at him as if he had just materialized out of thin air.

"I don't know. I didn't stick around to see what it would do after tearing—" He stopped, glancing again at his granddaughter. He shook his head. "What was it? What did that to her?"

"A Xenomorph," Alec said. "Weyland-Yutani born and bred."

For several seconds, Hank stared in silence. Kira, who had been very quiet, stared up at her grandfather with unspilled tears in her eyes.

"A monster hurt Grandma?" she whispered. Her little voice broke Siobhan's heart.

"Yes," Hank said finally. "I'm sorry, baby. She's with your mom and dad now. I'm… I'm so sorry."

Kira nodded, the tears trailing down her cheeks.

Hank's gaze slid to Dr. Fowler. "Your monster?"

Dr. Fowler didn't reply. Hank turned to Alec again. The grip on his gun was tighter now; its muzzle trembled.

"Can you protect my granddaughter?"

Alec looked him in the eye. "We can certainly try. We need to confirm the status of the other residents, but our synthetic is at the lab now. Roots and Elkins here can take Kira back there to await the evac ship. I'll go do a lap through the residential pods and see what's going on."

"I'm coming with you," Siobhan said.

"Siobhan—"

"Those people are my responsibility. I'm not going anywhere or doing anything until I see to it that our people are safe."

From Alec's expression, it seemed as if he was considering arguing further. He must have seen something in Siobhan's expression, though, because he sighed and then nodded.

"Okay." To Kira, he said, "Honey, are you okay to go with my men here and stay in the lab with Camilla?" The girl had often spent time in the lab with Siobhan and Camilla, practicing math or spelling that Victoria had given her earlier that day, and she liked Camilla. She had, in fact, taken to the synthetic very quickly as a kind of "auntie with superpowers," as she had put it. Siobhan hoped the girl saw Camilla as a family member who wouldn't die. Given her life up to that point, maybe that was what she needed.

Kira sniffed, wiped her eyes and nose on her nightgown sleeve, and nodded. She was barefoot, and the dirt of the moon had dusted her legs nearly up to the knees. Siobhan could only imagine what the girl was going through.

"I'm going with you, too," Hank said to Alec.

Kira looked at him, terror in her expression. "Grandpa, no!"

He knelt beside her, placing a hand on each arm and looking her in the eye.

"Kira, baby, I love you. You know that—and I loved your mom and dad, and I loved your grandma. It hurts to lose people you love—I know you know that, too, and I never want to lose you. So I need you to go with Alec's men. I need you to stay with Camilla, where I know you'll be safe."

"Stay with me, then," Kira said, fresh tears glistening in her eyes.

"I need you to be a big girl for me right now, okay? I need you to try to understand what I'm telling you. Alec and Siobhan need help. They need to make sure no one else gets hurt like Grandma, and I need to make sure the thing that hurt her is dead, so it can't come after you and me. If you're safe, I can concentrate on doing that. Do you understand?"

Kira nodded slowly, sniffling.

"Okay, Grandpa. But please be careful."

He winked at her. "I will, baby. I will. Now go on—go with…?"

"Lance Corporal Elkins," Elkins replied. He smiled down at Kira. "You can call me Kenny, okay?"

She nodded again, and Elkins took her hand.

Hank watched the two Colonial Marines lead his granddaughter away. When he stood, he nodded at Alec.

"I'm ready."

"So how many people are we looking for, exactly?" Hank trudged a little ways behind Siobhan and Alec. "I didn't think there were too many left. Mostly, the residential pods are a ghost town."

"Well, aside from you, Kira, and Vic—" She stopped, both mid-word and mid-step. "Hank, I'm so sorry." She met his gaze for a moment and saw the tears in his eyes before he nodded once and turned his head.

"I couldn't get to her in time," he said in a low voice. "I couldn't... but I could save Kira, so I did."

Siobhan put a sympathetic hand on Hank's shoulder, and then they both continued forward again. After a moment, she spoke again.

"I count four—four other people, I mean, to answer your question. Arthur should still be here, and I think Leo is, as well. And then we've got Bill Maloney and Shannon Lee."

Arthur Benton, Siobhan's supervisor, had stayed on with his skeleton crew, even though Siobhan was mostly in charge of the evacuation. As director of research, it fell on him to dot the last few i's and cross the last few t's, to make sure the information and products produced by the lab saw their way off into the rightful hands. He was

ALIEN: ENEMY OF MY ENEMY

a tall man, neat and quiet, with a low, firm voice and an unflinching gaze.

Many of the staff found him quirky at best and unlikable at worst, but Siobhan got along with him just fine. She understood that life had not always been easy for the man, although he never said as much or even hinted it in words. It was in the way he carried himself, as if the weight of the galaxy without and his memories within were opposing forces holding him up and keeping him standing. It was in those dark eyes, and in the undercurrent of sadness in his voice.

His partner, Leo, on the other hand, was bright and buoyant, a mostly retired journalist with an endless supply of warm smiles, funny stories, and—amazingly—bottles of fairly good wine. Siobhan enjoyed talking to Leo at the yearly Seegson holiday parties and summer company picnics. At those events he often picked up where Arthur sorely lacked. They lived on the west end of the residential pods, away from the labs, along with Bill Maloney.

Siobhan wasn't exactly sure what Bill did at Seegson; he seemed to be a jack-of-all-trades. She had seen him volunteer for research testing in the past, so she supposed that was what he was employed for in an official capacity. However, he was just as often fixing lights, mopping floors, or tinkering with the damned air conditioning in the east end, calling it a "fickle ol' bird." Bill had told Siobhan that he'd once been a hunter, and that he was itching to get out sometime and bag him one of the vurfur. She hoped now that his experience as a hunter meant he was okay, that he might have been able to defend himself with the big storm rifle that he kept mounted on the wall over the couch.

Closest to the lab on the east end was Shannon Lee's apartment suite. Siobhan didn't know much about the pretty little woman other than that she was a chemist and that she and Kenny Elkins had had a brief fling two or three years ago. The relationship was technically against company policy, but no one had cared. They were on an outpost moon in the middle of nowhere, in a dying solar system that even the gangster who theoretically owned it had forgotten about. It had been lonely living there long before it had ever become so stressful.

If this little group of people she had come to think of as a makeshift Seegson family found comfort in each other, she certainly wasn't going to stand in the way, nor would she have tolerated anyone who did.

Thinking about it now led to thoughts of Alec. She felt the way he looked at her sometimes, and warmed at the way he said her name. He was certainly no rule-follower, but he had never made a move in the years he'd been on BG-791. He had come close a few times, in those suspended moments when looking into each other's eyes had become a gaze, and that gaze, a pull toward each other for a kiss. He had never taken it beyond that, though, and Siobhan had assumed the reason why was buried somewhere behind that dark and troubled gaze.

Alec glanced at her now from a little ways ahead and gave her a small smile. She returned it.

They reached the residential pods and slowed, taking in the quiet building shouldered against the coming dawn.

Hank frowned. "Lights are out," he muttered, glancing up at the sky. "They shouldn't have gone out for another hour yet."

Alec raised his gun. "Follow me," he said in a low voice. "Siobhan, stay between me and Hank."

They moved quietly and quickly, like they'd done at the Weyland-Yutani lab, entering the front lobby unit. It was dark inside, as well, and empty, but that wasn't unusual. No one had sat at the desk in the back left corner for a long time, because no one received visitors anymore. Alec lifted his rifle, and the flashlight revealed mail cubbies that were bare because there were no deliveries to BG-791 for anything other than essentials. The dust was thick on the long desktop, the pale gray-greenish color of the moon's soil.

The door against the back wall led to the west and east wings of the apartment complex, and Alec headed toward it, the others following close behind. The deep shadow of the hallway beyond was broken only by a sparking control panel on the wall. The thought occurred to her that Bill would fix that panel, before a more serious realization dawned on her. The broken panel, a "fickle ol' bird" now if ever there was one, meant that something was wrong—something Bill, if he was even still alive, wouldn't be able to fix.

She hadn't noticed in the dark, but when a fresh set of blue sparks erupted from the panel, Siobhan caught a glimpse of long claw marks dragging down the wall beneath it. A flash of fear moved through her. Glancing at the men, she saw from their expressions that they had noticed the marks, too.

Alec turned away from the wall. "What apartment is Shannon Lee in?"

"Number 102," Siobhan replied, turning as well. She pointed to a door two down on the left. "That one." They made their way to the door. Alec knocked, leaning in toward it.

"Miss Lee? This is Sergeant Brand. Are you alright?" When no one answered, he knocked again.

They waited for several seconds, listening for some sounds of life from the other side of the door. They heard nothing.

After a moment, Hank said, "I guess it'd be too much to hope that she's just a heavy sleeper."

"We should go in," Alec said, and without waiting for an answer, he tapped the control panel to the left of the door, which opened soundlessly.

"I'll wait out here, keep guard," Hank said. He held up his gun. Alec nodded.

The layout of the apartment suites varied very little. The one-bedroom suites were more compact, with the living room central to the layout. The two-bedroom suites had at least one of those bedrooms down a hall. Shannon's apartment was the former and stood nearly bare, with a single chair and small table in the kitchen and a loveseat in the living room.

There was no life in those rooms, literally or figuratively. There was barely any light, except for the dim glow that came through the windows. Whatever had made it Shannon's home was gone now, likely packed up and waiting in the barracks for the evac ship. All the rooms were dark except for the bedroom. From beneath the closed door, Siobhan could see a thin sliver of yellow-white glow.

She touched Alec's shoulder and gestured. He nodded, led the way to the door, and glanced at her before opening it.

Shannon Lee was not in the bedroom. At least, most of her wasn't there. She had stripped down and dismantled the bed, and parts of it lay strewn about the carpeted floor, but otherwise, the room held no furniture, no knick-knacks, nothing like that. Across the back wall, however, was a splash of blood. It made a dizzying pattern—dark against the white behind it—that hurt Siobhan's eyes as much as her heart. Strands of black hair and chunks of something gray stuck to the various streaks of red. Shannon's body, though, was gone.

Siobhan's stomach roiled and she turned from the doorway.

"If you want to wait with Hank, I'll sweep the other rooms," Alec said. "I doubt there's anything to find, but..." He shrugged.

"Okay," she said, and trudged back to the front door.

When Hank spotted her, he stood up straighter. "Did you find her?"

Siobhan considered for a moment how to answer, while he peered over her shoulder into the living room.

"No," she said finally. "She's... not there."

Hank didn't reply, but she could see from the look in his eyes that he understood what Siobhan meant. They stood in silence until Alec joined them a few minutes later.

They moved further west, toward Bill Maloney's apartment. Alec shifted his flashlight from side to side, revealing more blood that streaked the walls, which were gouged and scratched. About ten feet away from the open door was a trail of drag marks, also in blood, which curved around the doorframe. The smell emanating from inside was strong, a coppery, heavy smell that turned Siobhan's stomach.

Alec crept up to the opening and peered around it, gun drawn. Silently, he motioned for the other two to join him.

The trail of blood continued far into the room, to the center of the living room. Siobhan followed it with her eyes to the motionless form on the floor, where it ended. Sidestepping the blood, the three entered the apartment. Alec motioned that he was going to check out the other rooms. Siobhan and Hank nodded, each kneeling to one side of the body.

It didn't take long to identify Bill. Deep claw marks had been gouged into his face, chest, and abdomen, and the bottom half of his right leg was missing, but Siobhan knew it was him. She felt tears well up in her eyes but she wiped them away. His neck, at least, was intact, so just on the off chance that he might still be alive, she checked for a pulse there and in his wrist. She found none.

His flesh felt cold.

Looking up at Hank, Siobhan shook her head.

Alec joined them a few minutes later, glancing down at the body. "Apartment's clear. Whatever did… *that*… is gone now."

Siobhan rose, then offered a hand to help Hank. "We need to check on Arthur and Leo. Then we can get out of here."

1 4

All was quiet inside the Seegson lab. None of the group wanted to be alone: given the circumstances, Elkins and Roots agreed that it was probably a good idea to stay together. The quarantine room was deemed the safest, with the emergency shower stalls and warm beds and strong locks, and so Elkins got Kira and Dr. Fowler situated there with Roots.

Elkins noticed that Roots's limping was getting worse, so he volunteered to take the first shift. Roots tried to protest, but not too hard. He seemed genuinely grateful to get some shut-eye with the civilians while Elkins stood watch in the small common area just outside.

"Are you hungry, Lance Corporal Elkins?" Camilla stood in the doorway of the adjacent kitchenette. "I can make you something to eat. Some eggs, perhaps? Maybe coffee?"

Elkins gave her a weary smile. "That would be nice, Camilla. Thanks."

She returned the smile and slipped back through the doorway.

There were a few desks in the common area with communications terminals set up, generally for checking the news or playing computer games during break times. Camilla didn't have an office but had been assigned a small desk nearest the doors to quarantine, where she could process data. Elkins eyed her chair. His legs ached, his back ached, and his arms ached. He was so exhausted that he could have fallen asleep on his feet.

Blinking a few times, he shook his head to bring some wakefulness back into him, and moved over to the synth's station. At the least, he could check the news of the summit meeting on LV-846, and catch up on what was happening beyond the doomed space rock they all were riding.

He tapped on her touchpad to bring the terminal out of sleeping mode and hoped she didn't have it password protected. The screen sprang to life with a spinning Seegson logo which twirled out of view. In its wake, a few file folders appeared, as well as the Newscore icon.

Thank God for small favors, he thought, and tapped the app on the screen.

The major headlines, of course, centered on the summit and speculations about what the United American Allied Command scientists intended to reveal about the black goo. He tapped a headline that outlined the basic agenda for the four-day meeting. United Americas joint chiefs were to meet with leaders of the Union of Progressive Peoples and the Independent Core System Colonies, among others. As ordered by Assistant Commandant General Vaughn, the joint chiefs would, of course, be escorted by USCMC forces, no doubt in an overt show of UAA power, as well as to quell any violence that might arise.

The goal of the summit was to reach agreements as outlined in a new peace treaty. Since recent evidence indicated that the pathogen bombs—like the pathogen itself—might not be the work of any of the Earth governments, the hope was that all parties would agree to and sign the treaty.

The Newscore article went on to emphasize the importance of the treaty as a foundation for peace moving forward. Failure might mean countless more years of war.

"No pressure," Ekins mumbled, his eyes scanning the rest of the information. None of it came as a surprise. When he, Roots, and Sarge arrived on LV-846, they would be assigned—along with the rest of the Colonial Marines—to make sure nothing went wrong. Nothing that they could address, anyway. Whether the UA and UPP governments would see eye to eye with each other, let alone the crooks that were running different parts of the ICS—well, that was beyond the marines' control.

He tapped out of the article and skimmed through another about the unified forces that had been sent to other outer rim colonies to quell riots. Elkins thought it looked like more black goo trouble—colonies too close for comfort to others that had been exposed to the pathogen. People were terrified of being bombed with the stuff, and angry that no one in power was doing anything about it.

Elkins and Roots had once been assigned to riot control on the moon Kepler-2801, a UA trading outpost and associated colony, and it had gotten ugly. He'd seen fire-bombed colonial settlements and paranoid vagrants gunning down refugees. The way those refugees' eyes turned black, the way their bodies swelled and twisted and their skin grew pale and spider-webbed with dark veins, Elkins couldn't help thinking that maybe those crazy vagrant fuckers had done the refugees a mercy.

Elkins tapped the terminal screen again. His finger hovered over another headline—about a mining incident—when a message popped up on-screen. Addressed to Camilla, the message was from a Rebecca Mueller at the UA Office of Interplanetary Resettlement, with the subject line "*Xenomorph Infection*."

Frowning, Elkins tapped on the message.

Hello, Camilla.

Thank you for your communication. I checked with my superiors and, as you may have surmised, with the ongoing conflicts surrounding the pathogen and its mutations, I have been advised that it would not be feasible to send a UA ship to evacuate your team. The likelihood of Xenomorph infestation and subsequent devastation to both UA personnel and property is considered too great a risk.

We sincerely apologize for any inconvenience this causes and wish you all well on finding a suitable solution to the issue at hand.

Sincerely,
Rebecca Mueller
UAOIR

"Camilla? Camilla!" Elkins jumped out of the chair and headed for the kitchen. "Camilla, what the—"

He glanced around the kitchen, but no one was there.

Arthur and Leo's apartment was, to Siobhan's dismay, in much the same condition as Shannon and Bill's. Alec found some blood on a countertop, and Siobhan found a finger under the glass coffee table in the living room. The end of it looked chewed. Siobhan's heart hurt for her boss and his partner.

"Any luck?" Hank called from the doorway.

"Nothing," Alec said. Using the muzzle of his gun, he lifted the edge of a bloody towel just outside the bathroom, saw what was underneath, and grimaced. "Doesn't look good for them." Realizing how that sounded, he looked up at Siobhan. "Hey, I'm sorry."

She nodded, turning her head to hide the tears in her eyes. The sadness, though, once again began to harden into anger. These poor people didn't deserve any of this. They had been so close—so frustratingly, *agonizingly* close—to getting off BG-791 for good. To say that it wasn't fair was a gross understatement.

Further, Weyland-Yutani was criminally responsible for their deaths, as was their chief mad scientist, Dr. Fowler, and Siobhan was going to make damned sure people knew about it. She picked up a digital framed photo of Arthur and Leo, relaxing on the beach of some far-away planet or moon, and swiped it to the right. The new image which appeared showed them in matching sweaters from one of the holiday parties. She swiped one more time and the image changed to a picture of them in front of Mount Rushmore on Earth.

She set the frame down gently, but her hands trembled with rage. She glanced from Alec to Hank.

"Let's go," she said. "There's nothing... there's no one left."

Alec took her hand and looked into her eyes. "I'm sorry, Von. I really am. I'm sorry. I know you feel responsible for these people, but it's not your fault."

She tried to meet his eyes but couldn't. "I was supposed to get them off this moon. They were supposed to be saved."

"I know," Alec said gently, "and Compton and McGowan were up for time off after their rotation here. Believe me, I do understand. You did everything you could."

She looked up at Alec finally and offered him a small smile she didn't feel. Tears blurred her vision.

"Thank you."

He nodded once, then led her back into the hallway to join Hank. The trio headed down the hall.

"I feel like I failed them. They were my responsibility, and I failed them," Siobhan said.

"You didn't fail them," Alec said softly. "If anyone did, then it was me. My job here was supposed to be to protect you, to protect the colonists."

"It's no one's fault," Hank broke in. "Well, that Fowler guy—it's *his* fault. His company's fault. But neither of you failed anybody, you hear? You couldn't have known what they were doing at the other lab. How could you know? I think—"

Hank's words were cut off by a loud rumble from deep beneath them. The floor shifted and tilted beneath their feet. A dark crack formed at the base of the wall to her left, zigzagging its way up toward the ceiling, which was shaking loose small chunks and dust.

Alec wrapped a protective arm around her. The three of them ducked, huddling close to the nearest doorframe and to each other. A small chunk of wall bounced painfully off her shoulder, and dust snowed onto her hair.

A moment later, the hallway fell silent and still.

"Are you okay?" Alec asked her, then to Hank, "How about you?"

Hank nodded. "You?"

"Yeah, I'm fine," Alec said. He noticed Siobhan rubbing her shoulder. "Von?"

"I'm okay," she replied. "A little bit of the sky falling, that's all." She gave him a reassuring smile. "Let's go. I'd like to get back to the lab and…"

The words died in her throat as the silhouette at the end of the hall in front of them arrested her attention.

"*A Dios mio*," Hernandez said beside her. "Is that…?"

Alec followed their stares over his shoulder, then turned slowly, raising his gun. The tall, dark shape at the end of the hall made a throaty clicking sound, kind of like a jittery purr. It flicked its segmented shadow-tail and turned its elongated head.

"Fuck," Alec whispered.

"What now?" Siobhan's heart pounded.

Alec glanced through the doorway to the apartment suite behind them, then at Siobhan, before focusing his attention on the shape again.

"We kill it."

Before Siobhan could respond, the shape charged them, squealing, its claws scraping against the floor tiles. Alec shoved her behind him, through the doorway and into the apartment, then opened fire on the Xenomorph galloping toward them. Hank fired at it, too, cursing at it in Spanish.

Siobhan looked around the shadowy apartment's living room for something with which to defend herself if it got past Alec and Hank. She dropped to her knees by the couch and opened the medkit, rummaging through it. As she had suspected, nothing in it would really help against the thing in the hall. She stuffed a few of the painkillers into her pocket and took out the laser scalpel. Then she stood.

A scream from the hall turned her stomach. She whirled around to see Alec firing in the opposite direction. She dove back into the doorway and saw the Xenomorph dragging Hank down the hallway. The claws of one of its massive hands had sunk into the man's shoulder, and his shirt was already dark with blood. He fought like hell anyway, kicking his feet and pulling and slapping at the claw which held him.

Siobhan saw that his gun lay at her feet and picked it up, leaving the laser scalpel on the floor. She aimed it at the back of the Xenomorph, right between the shoulder blades, and fired.

The creature jerked from the blast to its back, screeching in anger. It took off at a sprint and Siobhan found herself running after it. She heard Alec call her name, and then the thumping of his footsteps as he ran after her, but her focus was on Hank.

The Xenomorph moved fast, slipping in and out of the pockets of shadow. Siobhan raised the gun again to fire, but now that they all were running, she was afraid of hitting Hank. Perhaps worse, she might hit the alien itself in a spot where it would bleed on him, and that blood would eat right through him. Alec was probably thinking the same thing. He was a better shot, but just as cautious of the creature's blood.

Still, it would have to run out of hallway eventually. They'd kill it when it was forced to stop.

The creature wasn't about to give them that chance, though. With another screech, it dragged Hank up as it scaled the wall. When Siobhan saw the vent high up near the ceiling, she cursed under her breath. In the next instant, it slipped through the dark square hole in the wall, pulling Hank, who was still screaming, into the vent shaft with it.

"*Damn* it," Alec said, slowing to a stop. He paced back and forth, seemed to consider punching the crumbling wall, then decided against it. "Damn. Fuck!"

Siobhan stopped a few feet away from the vent. Her gaze traced the trail of Hank's blood from the floor up the side of the wall and into the vent shaft. The blood looked very dark to her, so much darker than the wall. Hank's blood. Hank, whose wife was dead and whose poor little granddaughter had no one left—no family, no friends, no one.

She fought the urge to cry, and this time the anger swallowed the grief.

"The vent shafts go to the basement," she said. "From there, they go outside."

"Siobhan—"

"He might still be alive," she said, and her tone made it clear that she would not stand for an argument.

He joined her by the vent. Turning to her, he placed a hand on each of her shoulders and looked into her eyes.

"He might still be alive," she repeated more softly.

He nodded. "Okay. Let's go find out."

In the quarantine room of the Seegson lab, Martin Fowler dreamed of monsters.

The landscape in the dream was much like that of BG-791—above, a sky in shades of gray, a dusty, cracked terrain, nearly barren and colorless, with distorted hexagonal mountains hemming him in. At the base of the mountains, the thick brambles, rough brown with long black thorns, grew well over his head. The darkness within them was almost a tangible thing, a kind of blackness that would seep into the nose and throat, filling the lungs, weighing heavy in the stomach, blotting out sound and vision.

Martin could hear the most terrible sounds in there—the screaming of the vurfur as far worse beasts tore them apart.

Overhead, storm clouds gathered like dirty wool stretched across a loom of endless night. The monsters had come from somewhere out there, beyond the clouds. And he—Martin Fowler—had brought them here. He and the higher-ups at Weyland-Yutani had brought the monsters and messed with them in the vain hope that they could manipulate them, make them stronger, more aggressive, more lethal.

And the monsters had broken free.

In the dream, Martin knew the things had overrun the bramble forest, which seemed to be spreading to close him in. He couldn't see them, and could barely hear them, but he knew they were there, cloaking themselves in the shapes shadows make, moving among the branches and around the thorns.

Overhead, there was a clap of thunder so loud it jarred his bones, and then it began to rain. Martin could feel the wetness on his upturned face, his chest, his shoulders. When he opened his eyes, though, he gasped. The sky was pelting him with a shower of liquid ash... no, not ash, he realized with horror. He scanned the ground around him and saw globules of black pulling together into puddles, seeping into the thorny growths and changing them, dissolving and reforming the very dust of the ground itself.

Plagiarus Praepotens.

It was the pathogen—the black goo.

He rubbed vigorously at his eyes, his face, his hair, trying to wipe away as much of it as he could. His vision blurred; squiggling black lines crawled over his irises and he flinched. Then he saw the backs of his hands.

The color had drained out of his flesh. The black goo was carving veins of disintegration into them as old cells broke down and new, tumorous ones formed. It was happening all over his body; he could feel it, and the pain was immense.

Martin fell to his knees. He couldn't see now, not more than hazy silhouettes, but he could hear the squealing and chirping of the monsters from beyond the thorns as they closed in on him. When their shadows melded with the black goo on the ground all around him, he began to scream.

He jerked awake, blinked a few times, and saw the little girl from the Seegson residential building sleeping soundly in the medpod next to him. He pinched the bridge of his nose with his fingers—a headache was starting there—reached over to the small table between the pods, and picked up his glasses.

That was when he saw Private First Class Rutiani and Lance Corporal Elkins standing at the foot of the pod. Martin slipped his glasses on and saw that the men's expressions were a mix of low-key anger and concern. Rutiani's hair was askew, and the sleep had not quite dissipated from his eyes. Both held their guns, though.

"Can I help you, gentlemen?" Martin said.

"Camilla's missing," Elkins replied. "You wouldn't know where she is, would you?"

Martin sat up. "No, I wouldn't."

"You didn't see her?" Rutiani asked, cocking an eyebrow at him.

"I don't see how I could have. I was sleeping."

"And she didn't say anything to you?" Elkins glanced slowly around the room as if he thought maybe Martin was hiding the synthetic somewhere.

"Why would she?"

The men seemed at a loss for words. Their faces, though, told him they were thinking a lot that they weren't saying.

The synthetic worked there in the lab, so Martin didn't think the marines were worried that she was lost, nor did he think they were worried for her safety. In Martin's experience, the Xenomorphs weren't interested in synthetics because they could, on some animal level, recognize the artificial beings' inorganic nature. To the Xenomorphs, synthetics were of no more interest than a table or a chair, useless to incubate their young and of no real threat unless they got between the alien and its target lifeform.

Further, synthetics were strong and durable. If Martin recognized the model correctly, this Camilla was a Seegson 226-B/2 synthetic, and those were built to withstand a number of toxic substances, allergens, acids, and the like. They were an inferior brand of synthetics, in Martin's opinion, to the Weyland-made ones, and prone on occasion to malfunction. Perhaps fear of that was what made the Marines clutch those weapons so tightly.

"Listen, gentlemen. I understand that you've had a very long night, and that you blame me for being the root cause of it. However, I assure you that whatever you think happened to… Camilla? Is that her name? I promise it has nothing to do with me. I haven't seen her or talked to her since you put us in here, and I have no idea where she is."

"We need to find her," Elkins muttered to Rutiani. "You stay with them. I'll go look."

"Copy that," Rutiani said with a small nod.

"Can I ask why such concern?" Martin leaned forward, his elbows on his knees. They didn't answer him, and he wasn't surprised.

"Elkins," Rutiani called over his shoulder, and the other man paused, turning.

Rutiani glanced back at him. "Be careful."

1 5

The basement of the Seegson residential sector was a mess. Organized as a series of subterranean rooms, each basement area corresponded to an apartment suite above it. The maintenance and utility section ran the length of them, accessible from the far ends of the hallways. Along it, one could open each cellar door with an apartment-specific card key, or all the rooms with the master maintenance key. Siobhan looked for the latter in a small, caged-in office below the lobby.

"Found the key," she said, taking it from a desk drawer. "Let's go." She also found another flashlight and snatched it up.

"We listen first," Alec said as they approached the first door, "and maybe figure out what's there before we go in."

"Got it." Siobhan clutched both Hank's gun and the key card. She hoped her hands weren't shaking and that she didn't look as nervous as she felt. "Let's do this."

They listened at the first door and heard nothing. Alec nodded to her, and Siobhan slid the key card into the reading slot. When it lit up green, she turned the handle and opened the door.

The room was empty. They did a cursory sweep to make sure, but found nothing except old junk that the residents were leaving behind—a broken chair, a pair of pants with a long tear in them, an old computer. There was something sad about the forgotten remnants of someone's life, even on BG-791. Soon, Siobhan thought, the whole moon would be left behind, and with it, any trace that humanity had ever been there.

They searched the next few rooms the same way, quickly shuffling aside old carpets, boxes, broken holiday decorations, even a USCMC medal. Siobhan saw Alec pocket the medal, and she thought she understood why. It was an honor the USCMC didn't give lightly, and she supposed he couldn't bear the thought of it buried under the rubble, the act of valor for which it was awarded simply forgotten.

In one of the rooms toward the middle of the hall, they came upon a body. They could smell it before they saw it—a thick, nauseating rot-and-blood smell that made them both wince. They crept slowly into the room, Alec leading the way, and found the remains near a shelf of canned goods.

The body had been torn in half. The legs and feet had been carelessly tossed against a wall, with part of the entrails splattered against the concrete polymer and the rest spilled out on the floor. The limbs themselves were little more than a jumbled heap, coated in blood.

The top half was in equally bad condition. The face had been caved in, with most of the flesh clawed off. One arm had been pulled from the socket and lay at a terribly wrong angle, bent the wrong way at the elbow. The chest, too, appeared to be caved in, as if the creature who had done this had stepped on it as it walked away.

"Is that Hank?" Siobhan peered around Alec to look at the corpse.

"Hard to say," Alec said. "I don't think so. Too small. I think it's a woman. Look at the hair."

Siobhan forced herself to look at the ruined head, her gaze glancing over where the face should have been. The hair wasn't terribly long, but it was certainly longer than Hank's, and curly, too—or at least, it had been before it had been matted and stuck to the floor by all the blood. When she saw the little rose tattoo on the shoulder where the robe had been torn away, she let out a sob and turned away.

"It's Vickie," she said. "Hank's wife."

She felt Alec gently touch her arm.

"Let's go," he said softly. "I'm sorry you had to see that."

They moved out into the maintenance hallway again, and finished off the rest of the storage rooms. There were no more bodies, but no survivors, either. She shuddered to realize it had probably taken their remains up into the vents.

"Let's get back to the lab," she said finally. "They're not here, and if there's no one left to find, then…" She paused, absentmindedly pocketing the master key card. "It's going to be drawn to the survivors in the lab, Alec. I can't… I won't let them end up like Vickie."

"They won't," Alec said. "Not if I can help it."

They climbed the stairs and followed the first-floor hallway back to the lobby. A streak of blood—had it been there before? Siobhan didn't think so—had soaked into the carpets near the front desk. More blood—just little droplets, really—dripped off the desk's surface in tiny patters. Alec pointed his gun toward the door, which still rocked a little where it had landed, while Siobhan made her way around the desk.

More blood—a lot more—had drenched the carpet where the chair should have been. Something glinted in a patch of early morning light that fell on the soaked spot. She crouched beside it.

The object which had caught the light was a wedding ring. This time, it was Siobhan who picked it up, then slipped it into a pocket of her pants. Her reason, she thought, was probably not much different from the one Alec had for keeping the medal—remembrance of lives that had meant something.

She stood and made her way back to the center of the lobby.

"Everything okay?" Alec glanced between her and the outside, his gun still trained on the open doorway.

"I think I found Hank's ring. A lot of blood, too. I think he—"

She froze.

There was a clicking sound, like chattering teeth. The hairs on her arms stood on end.

Alec looked over her head, up at the ceiling. He swung the gun around, so it was pointing up now, too. Sweat had broken out on his forehead, and although his mouth was set in a tight, straight line, his eyes looked worried.

"Von," he said quietly, "it's above you."

"Alec?" Her voice was a terrified whisper. She lifted her head slowly.

"Don't look. When I say, I want you to get behind the desk, okay? As quickly as you can."

"Okay."

"If it comes near you, shoot it."

"You can believe I will," she replied.

"Ready...? Now!"

Siobhan leaped sideways toward the desk as the creature dropped onto the spot where she'd been just an instant before. She'd known it was there, but seeing it—that long tail uncurling and whipping around behind it—she panicked. Her back hit the edge of the desk hard and she stumbled, sliding the length of the surface and falling backward onto the carpet. Her hand caught the smear of blood, which had gone cold. The red oozed up from the fibers around her fingers.

For a moment, she couldn't move. Then it was on top of her. All that existed was the bony jaws of the smaller mouth inside the Xenomorph's larger one, chattering and salivating.

Alec shouted at her to get behind the desk, and she flinched, the paralyzing moment broken. She scrambled backward to get out from under it as Alec fired off a couple of rounds into the thing's back.

The Xenomorph's inner jaws receded and it turned on him, advancing slowly. He raised his weapon again and the thing stopped, squealing a threat in his direction. Alec grunted back at it, two alphas squaring off.

Siobhan stood on shaky legs, using the desk for support. She raised Hank's gun and was surprised to find that her hand was steady. Aiming it at the creature's head, she exhaled slowly. Then she fired.

The round found its mark, opening up a wound in the shiny curve of its skull. A firework of acidic blood exploded from the wound, and the Xenomorph screeched in anger. Its tail lashed out at her. Before Siobhan could move, it connected with her hip, flinging her against the wall. Her head struck something hard and the world swam in a blur of muted colors that rose above her. She thought she might have sunk to the ground, because the dark shape moved from somewhere above her, over the silhouette she thought was Alec, and out the open door.

There were flashes of light and she heard Alec's gun

going off. Above that, the high, keening squeal of the monster from somewhere outside.

Then, everything went silent.

It could have been seconds or minutes in which blackness threatened to wipe out her consciousness. A screaming pain in her head made it hard to concentrate on Alec's voice. It was somewhere above her, too, then closer. She felt his arms around her, lifting her up, and that brought some of the world back into focus. Her hip hurt where the Xenomorph's tail had hit her.

"Talk to me, Von. I need you to tell me if you're okay."

"I—I'm okay," she said, wincing at how her voice made her head feel. "I hit my…" She touched the spot at the back of her head from which the pain seemed to be coming and felt something wet there. She looked at her fingers and saw blood. Slowly, she turned— the movement sent bolts of pain from her head down through her neck—and saw a small smear of blood on the wall behind her.

"You knocked your head pretty good," Alec said, his voice shaky but light. He was forcing that lightness, she was sure, so he wouldn't scare her. He looked into each of her eyes, shining his flashlight into them, and then asked, "Can I see?" Without waiting for an answer, he moved behind her. She could feel his fingers parting her hair. "Yeah," he added, "the skin is split and you'll probably have a lump, but it's superficial. You'll live."

"Well, that's good to know."

He helped her up, slipping an arm around her waist to lift her.

"You sure you're okay?"

"I am. Really. I'm fine," she said, and she smiled at him.

"Good. I'm not leaving this moon without you, Siobhan." He looked into her eyes. She saw concern there, and something else. "I'm going to get you out of here. I promise."

"I know," she said softly.

"Siobhan, I..." His voice trailed off.

"I know," she said again, kissed him on the mouth, a soft, quick peck, and then slid past him toward the doorway.

The Xenomorph's body lay on its side in the dirt outside the residential lobby doors. Alec's weapon, a higher-powered model than the one Hank had carried, had blasted a hole in its chest. The yellow-green color of its blood looked bright against the gray of the dirt beneath and the darker gray of the creature's exoskeleton. It sizzled as it dripped onto the ground. Its lipless mouth hung open, the rigid inner jaw protruding outward. The tail snaked behind it, and the massive claws had left long furrows where the thing had evidently tried to stand.

Siobhan slipped from Alec's grasp and sank to her knees next to the thing. She wanted to see it up close—

needed to, and not just out of scientific curiosity. She had to face the thing that had done so much damage.

She reached out and touched its bony hip. It felt cool, smooth but sharp, and she thought she felt a faint buzz beneath her fingertips—like an electrical charge—that quickly faded to stillness. She pulled her hand away and looked at her fingertips. This thing, this terrifying killing machine, was still just an animal. It had weaknesses. It was not a nightmare beast, not supernatural in its abilities. It was a narrowly evolved, efficient predator, but it could die, the same as any other species. It could be killed.

Siobhan looked up at Alec. His eyes watched her with concern. She nodded to him and he helped her up again.

"You killed it," she said.

"I did," he replied.

"I'm glad," she said.

About halfway back to the lab, Siobhan remembered the medkit painkillers she had put in her pockets; she injected one into her arm. By the time they reached the front doors, the sharp jab in her hip and most of the throbbing in her head had subsided.

Alec had been quiet for most of the walk back, hovering close. She thought maybe he was thinking about Hank and the marines he'd lost. He didn't talk about it often, but she knew he had encountered the Xenomorphs before, and had managed to survive. What little he'd told her about those experiences was more than he'd told anyone else, and she understood in everything from his tone of voice to his body language that he had buried even more of it.

Those scars, the ones inside him, were worse than any of the ones on his body.

She didn't ask what he was thinking, not because she wouldn't have shared the burden of those thoughts with him—she would have—but because she knew that Alec needed to patch up these new wounds inside, let them scar over as well. That was how Alec survived such things, and she accepted that about him.

Roots and Elkins were waiting for them in the lobby. Both marines looked grave. As they crossed the threshold, Elkins stepped forward.

"Sarge," he said, "we've got a problem."

"Breach?" Alec asked, raising his gun. For now, he buried whatever he'd been thinking, and was back to business.

Elkins glanced at Roots, then back again. "Bigger than that." He handed Alec a printout. To Siobhan, it looked like a comms message. Alec scanned it, then thrust it in her direction.

...not be feasible to send a UA ship to evacuate.
Likelihood of Xenomorph infestation and
subsequent devastation...

She read the message from this Rachel Mueller twice before crumpling it into a little ball and throwing it on the floor.

Too great a risk.

Not feasible to send a ship.

"Son of a *bitch*!" She ran a hand through her hair and glanced toward the quarantine area, thinking of Kira. "How could... they can't... for God's sake, they're just abandoning us!" She paced back and forth, pushing through her panic, devising and rejecting courses of action. She stopped and looked at Rutiani.

"What did Camilla say about this?"

"Nothing," Roots replied. "She's missing."

It took a moment for the words to sink in.

"Missing? What do you mean, missing?"

"We can't find her anywhere," Elkins said. "She said she was going to make me something to eat, she went into the kitchen, and then she vanished." Elkins shrugged. "I did a little poking around her comms, though, and intercepted that message from her terminal. She... it sounds like *she* told them about the aliens."

"She's a fucking synthetic, right?" Roots cut in. "That's the problem with them. Unpredictable, prone to... to do just..." Roots made a whistle and a gesture like a bird flying off.

"Maybe she was programmed to spy on us," Elkins said. "I don't know. Or maybe Fowler fiddled with her when we weren't looking. Sabotaging our evac would be a good way to make sure we never told anyone what Weyland-Yutani was up to here."

Siobhan shook her head in disgust. "I need to check on Kira," she said, heading toward the quarantine area. "Figure out a way to tell her that her grandparents are dead and that we're stuck on this fucking moon."

The men followed, close behind her.

In the quarantine area, Dr. Fowler was pacing back and forth in front of the pod where Kira slept. He acknowledged them with a minimal nod. Siobhan watched the girl. How much tragedy was one child expected to endure? How much of a burden was going to be put on her little shoulders? She noticed that the stuffed dog Kira usually carried wasn't with her, and wished she'd thought to look for it in Hank's apartment.

Behind her, she heard low voices. Alec was talking to Elkins and Roots. He told them to guard the doors—no one in or out—while they figured out what to do next. As they moved off to guard the entrance to the quarantine area, Siobhan's gaze shifted from Kira to Dr. Fowler, and she knew what she had to do.

"Dr. Fowler," she began, realizing then how tightly she was holding on to Hank's gun. "You said Weyland-Yutani was picking you up tomorrow, right?"

Dr. Fowler nodded. "Around one p.m., I believe."

Alec sidled up to her. Likely, he recognized something

in her tone that suggested she was devising a plan. She wasn't sure she could have called it that, just then—it was more like acting on an instinct.

"You'll call them from here and confirm that," she continued. "Make sure they don't suspect that anything is wrong… beyond what they already know, I suppose. Whatever you've told them."

"I told them there were two survivors. One incubator."

Incubator. That was a terrible way to refer to Cora. Siobhan bit down on her disgust, though. "You're going to report business as usual," she said. "Problem contained. Sample ready. And you're going to be on that ship—we all are."

Dr. Fowler cocked an eyebrow at her. "Oh?"

"Yes. Our ship isn't coming. They don't want to risk a Xenomorph outbreak in UA territory. And since that's your fault, we're commandeering your ship. Once we get to LV-846, you can have it back and go on your merry way."

"Are you really suggesting the hijacking of a multi-billion-dollar corporate ship? Just taking it for a joyride across the galaxy?"

"It's not a joyride, Doctor. It's a detour, and yes, that's *exactly* what I'm suggesting," Siobhan said. She tapped the gun lightly against her thigh, just to make sure Dr. Fowler saw it and knew she meant business.

He looked from her to Alec, whose mouth turned into a small, satisfied smile, and then back to Siobhan.

"You're crazy," he said. "I can't authorize—"

"I'm not *asking*," Siobhan interrupted. "If you want off this moon, you're going to go with this plan, or so help me, I'll drop you here and now, right in this lab." She raised the gun until it was leveled at his forehead.

Dr. Fowler never took his eyes off her. They carried a look of alarm, but the rest of his face remained calm.

"Okay," he said after a few moments. "Okay. Take it easy. We'll all leave together."

"And there will be no samples coming with us," she added. "Agree to it."

Dr. Fowler hesitated, and Siobhan turned the safety off with a loud *click*.

"I agree," Dr. Fowler said, holding his hands up. "I agree. Have it your way."

"I intend to," she said, and slowly she lowered the gun. To Alec she said, "We should all try to get some sleep. In shifts, if we have to. We'll leave in the morning."

"Yes, ma'am," Alec said, that small smile growing a little broader.

1 6

Siobhan stayed awake while Alec slept. Despite how exhausted he must have been, he tossed and turned in one of the medpods, mumbling to himself. Siobhan wondered if he was dreaming of the things he didn't speak about when he was awake.

She had chosen to wait for Kira to wake. Fowler had wandered off, claiming he wanted to talk to Elkins and Roots, and that would leave the girl alone. Siobhan expected her to be looking for her grandfather, too, and felt that in Camilla's absence, she ought to be the one to break the news to Kira.

About thirty minutes after Alec fell asleep, the girl stirred. Her little eyelids fluttered open and she sat up, looking around. Siobhan sat beside her. Kira's expression was at first hopeful, but in noting Hank's absence, that hope quickly faded to dismay. When she looked into Siobhan's eyes, they both teared up instantly.

"He didn't come back with you, did he?" Kira asked in a soft voice.

"Honey, I'm sorry." The girl began to cry, and Siobhan pulled her into a hug. "I'm so, so sorry. We tried to save him."

"It was the monsters, wasn't it?" Kira asked, her voice muffled by the embrace. "The ones that killed my grandma."

"Yes, baby," Siobhan whispered.

Kira cried hard then, and in her sobs Siobhan felt the heartbreak and the sorrow, the loss of her grandparents and parents, her home, her sense of security. Everything. The universe had put too much on the little girl, pulling apart her innocence before she'd had the time to heal or experience enough to replace it with wisdom. Siobhan fought hard not to cry herself. Instead, she whispered soothing sounds into the little girl's hair and held her until the sobbing subsided.

When Kira finally pulled away, she sniffled and looked up.

"When we get off this moon, can I live with you and Camilla?"

Siobhan's heart broke a little, but she smiled.

"Yes, baby," she said. "Of course you can. Of course you can."

"Will the ship be here, soon?"

"Soon," Siobhan said. "I promise. We're getting out of here."

"And we'll go someplace without monsters?"

"Oh, absolutely," Siobhan whispered. "Absolutely."

This seemed to satisfy the girl. With a final sniffle, she nodded, then lay back down again.

Alec dreamed of a jungle world with oppressive heat, humidity, and the stench of blood. In the dream he was both a child—as he had been when he'd first encountered the Xenomorphs—and an adult, seeing the world around him with the knowledge of both past and present.

He was crouching in the rotted-out hollow of a massive tree trunk, its insides crawling with spider-like creatures the size of hands. Thick moss coated the outside of the tree and heavy foliage, leaves the size of small children, hung overhead. He was soaked with sweat, so the dirt and the moss he'd shaken loose stuck to his skin. His eyes burned. His throat was parched. He had blood under his fingernails and calluses on his hands from the rough, makeshift spear he was holding. He could feel his own heartbeat in his ears and the heaviness of the planet's air in his chest.

From somewhere outside the tree and above him, he heard the screeching of the monsters that had killed the other colonists. He thought they might be calling to each other, somehow communicating where he wasn't and where he might be. Their footfalls were surprisingly light, but he knew they were getting nearer. A segmented tail snapped in and out of view, and suddenly that sound they made—that half-chitter, half-purr of wariness—was very close to his ear.

Alec held as still as possible, trying not to move as one of the spider-things crawled across his hand. He tried not to breathe and stir the giant jungle fern leaf that obscured him from view. Could they smell him? Could they hear his heartbeat?

It pounded now in his chest.

Alec clutched the spear tightly.

A light thump just outside of the tree made him jump, but he stifled a cry. That chitter-purr was right there, right on the other side of the leaf. He huddled farther back into the dark of the tree's interior.

I'm going to die here.

In the next instant a gray, clawed hand shot out under the leaf and grabbed his ankle. It pulled him off his feet and out into the blazing sun that shone overhead, bright as his scream was loud. It was so bright that at first, he could only make out the silhouette of the creature above him. Then the glare faded some, and Alec could see a narrow, bony jaw jutting from a much larger mouth. It darted toward him and then there was wetness, though whether it was from the creature's saliva, his own tears, or his own blood, he couldn't tell.

Not until the little jaw retracted, dripping liquid red, and the dark of dream-death blotted out the world.

* * *

Alec awoke with a jerk, rubbing a hand quickly over his forehead. There was some sweat there from the nightmare's exertions, but no blood. He was okay… for now.

Turning, he saw Siobhan curled up with Kira in another medpod, both fast asleep. Dr. Fowler stood near—though not quite with—Roots and Elkins over by the quarantine entrance. These sights brought reality crashing back down on him, and he fought the guilt that arose from sleeping so hard for… how long had it been?

He had a job to do, a promise to keep, and he wasn't about to fail Siobhan.

Shaking off the remnants of the dream, he stood, picked up his gun, and headed toward Roots and Elkins. It looked as if Elkins had been up all night, and Alec intended to relieve him of his post and let him get some sleep before they headed back to the Weyland-Yutani facility. They were all hungry and tired, not at their sharpest, and Alec worried about that, too. People could only be pushed so hard before they started slipping, making mistakes, and in a situation like this, mistakes meant that people died.

"Kenny," he said as he approached. "Go get some sleep. I'm taking over. Roots, go grab something to eat, and then come back here."

"Copy that," Elkins said, and he took off. Roots followed right behind him. Alec took up the spot where

Roots had been leaning against the wall, near the doorway. The hall on the other side was quiet and empty.

"Sergeant Brand," Dr. Fowler said. Alec turned, and saw that the scientist was giving him a sly smile. "You look refreshed. I trust you slept well?"

"I slept," Alec said. "That's good enough."

The men stood across from each other, looking down the hall beyond the quarantine door. It was empty and silent.

"So," Fowler said after a time, "I take it you approve of Dr. McCormick—Siobhan—and her intention to commit grand larceny?"

Alec didn't answer.

"By stealing a corporation ship, I mean. As a marine, you're comfortable with that?"

"I am."

"Now, don't get me wrong. I understand that you all want to get off this moon. The Weyland-Yutani corporation—and I, of course—would naturally want to assist in this terrible situation... correct the UA's error in judgment, and all that. But don't you think deliberately taking and forcibly rerouting the ship, without notifying the corporation, without consulting the fuel reserves and life support system's capacity... that it's all a little irresponsible?"

Alec turned on him, his eyes flashing with anger.

"Responsibility is a funny thing, *Doctor* Fowler."

Fowler was quiet for a moment. "You're a man of few words," he said. "Few but meaningful ones, when you utter them. In my experience, people avoid talking because they're too stupid or too afraid to. You don't seem to be either. You seem like a reasonable man. So it surprises me that you would so adamantly defend this criminal action you're all planning." He waved vaguely toward the medpods. "You strike me as a man with a backbone and a brain, a rare combination."

"I think you and I are done talking," Alec said as calmly as he was able. "About criminal actions, or anything else."

"Sergeant Brand—"

"If you say one more word," Alec replied in a low voice, his gaze still fixed on the hallway, "I will shoot you where you stand. One shot to the head, before you can even exhale. No one will ever know."

Dr. Fowler held up his hands in a gesture of surrender, pushed off from the wall where he was leaning, and walked away.

Alec thought of the *Gaspar*, the colony ship of his youth. He'd been registered in the ship's log under his father's last name, despite the fact that his mother had only known him for the brief time he'd been stationed in El Hoyo. The name Brand, his mother thought, might make the people running the ship treat him better, as the son of a USCMC sergeant and not just some poor kid from El Hoyo.

It hadn't mattered, though—not really. The colonists had been kind to the kid traveling alone, looking for a new life. The people who ran the ship—Weyland-

Yutani—hadn't cared whether he was a marine's son or a poor kid from a tiny village. To the corporation, they were all fodder for experiments with the aliens.

They had been people like Dr. Fowler, who really didn't see the hypocrisy in labeling inconveniences "irresponsible" or "criminal," while they played at being dark gods all across the galaxy. Alec was pretty sure that given the opportunity, Dr. Fowler would sabotage their plans, even kill them if he had to, in order to protect what he had developed for his bosses.

If it came to that, Alec thought, he'd kill the man. He'd be doing humanity a favor.

Around eight a.m., Roots and Elkins rejoined Siobhan, Alec, Kira, Fowler in the quarantine area by the medpods. They'd each had a turn at sleep, though no one looked particularly well-rested. The moon had been restless that night, groaning and twisting beneath the facility. The gravity had shifted again, and they could feel the pull of it in their bones, in the queasy lumps in their stomachs, and in the heaviness of the air in their lungs.

The pressure had given Siobhan a lightheadedness that had settled grumpily into another headache. There would be no time to load up the Weyland-Yutani ship with the boxes of their belongings, so they gathered up supplies and whatever personal items they could carry in one bag each. They made one exception, though:

Alec and Roots went to the barracks and brought back Mr. Bones and some clothes from Kira's things. Siobhan's eyes misted at the sheer joy that lit up Kira's face upon seeing the stuffed dog, and at the way she hugged it.

She saw that Alec was also carrying McGowan's dog tags, which he slipped into his bag.

There was still no sign of Camilla. When Kira asked Siobhan if Auntie Cam would be joining them on the big ship, Siobhan honestly didn't know how to respond. Camilla had never done anything like this, and her absence made no sense. The synthetic was unable to feel fear or guilt, so she wouldn't be deliberately avoiding them, and Dr. Fowler seemed pretty certain that a Xenomorph would have no interest in attacking a synthetic unless it somehow got in the creature's way.

Had that happened? Had Camilla gotten between them and a Xenomorph?

Siobhan knew the others were angry with the synthetic, blaming her for getting their evac ship cancelled, but she knew better. Despite the setback it had caused, Camilla had done what she had to, what was logical and right in her logical, right mind. It hadn't been an emotional decision, because as often as Siobhan thought otherwise, Camilla simply wasn't capable of emotion. At least, Siobhan thought, if she'd been destroyed, she hadn't been afraid to die.

On their way to the armored personnel carrier, a general quiet settled over the group. Words were few and spoken in low voices. It had been a long couple of days, and they were starting to wear on everyone. There was a general sense that they were heading into the mouth of the beast by going back to the Weyland-Yutani lab. The truth was, though, that at this point, there was no safe harbor anywhere.

Overnight, deep cracks had opened in the ground. Many of the tree-sized brambles beyond the Gatelands had been uprooted, and the anxious vurfur, likely sensing their own impending demise, pawed and stamped at the brambles' edges. Birds moved uneasily from branch to branch, but often faltered in their flight. They felt the gravity, too, and the approaching end.

Siobhan could only look so long before she had to turn away. There hadn't been much life on BG-791, but what there was had reached its end and, on some level, knew it. Both the scientist and the human in her hurt to think of their extinction.

As they loaded themselves and their belongings into the APC, Siobhan noticed the scratch marks from the giant Xenomorph with the antlers that had chased them down. She touched one of the furrows in the metal and felt a surge of both grief and anger. The two, she noticed, were becoming interchangeable.

Kira sat up front with Elkins, and Siobhan sat in back with Alec, Roots, and Dr. Fowler. Siobhan could hear Elkins telling Kira all about the controls, giving her a kind of crash course in driving the APC. The girl asked all kinds of questions.

"What does this button do?"

"Why do you need to pull that?"

He fielded each one with enthusiasm that Siobhan was pretty sure was both genuine and meant to keep the girl's thoughts occupied. Anything was better than dwelling on and dreading what they might find at the Menhit Lab.

It took almost two hours to reach the Weyland-Yutani facilities, navigating around downed branches and the carcasses of dead vurfur. Siobhan was once again impressed with Elkin's control of the vehicle, and how he managed to divide his focus between the road and the little girl beside him.

They pulled up to the front entrance, and Elkins put the APC in park.

"Okay," he said, turning around in his seat. "Last stop on this train. Menhit Station, dead ahead."

"What's a train?" Kira asked.

Elkins smiled at her. "You're going to see, once we get to the new planet."

They collected their things.

"The platform where the ship will pick us up is out back," Dr. Fowler said. "Not quite as big as your Gatelands, but it does the job. We can—"

Before he could finish, a tremor rocked the APC. Dr. Fowler was knocked against the side of the vehicle, and Kira fell back into her seat. Siobhan staggered to the front windshield to see the damage. Pieces of the mountain behind the lab were splintering and tumbling down the cliffside. A rock nearly as big as the APC itself landed directly in front of them.

Alec joined her at the window as an avalanche of large rocks tumbled to the path around the side of the facility, effectively cutting it off from the front. The other side of the building, Siobhan saw, had already been buried in loose rocks from the cliffs on that side.

A huge boulder bounced down the side of the mountain and onto the roof of the facility to the left, caving it in. Another brought down most of the back of the building in a cloud of dust. Finally, the moon stopped shivering, and the rocks stopped falling.

All was quiet and still.

"Damn it," Dr. Fowler said through clenched teeth. Siobhan hadn't even noticed that the man had joined her and Alec at the window. "We can't go around that way to get to the platform. We'll have to go through the building."

"If that's the only way," Alec said, "then let's move out. Elkins, Roots, take point. Dr. Fowler, we'll need you to guide the men up front through the facility. I want this safe, quick, and quiet. If you have to fire, get them at a distance, and aim for the soft parts."

"Do 121s even *have* soft parts?" Roots asked.

"Everything's got a soft part somewhere," Elkins replied.

"You'd be surprised, gentlemen," Dr. Fowler said. "You'd be surprised."

They opened the APC door and climbed out into the stark quiet of the facility. Even at noon, the sun didn't quite penetrate the hazy gray clouds above. Without the benefit of the hazmat suits, the air so far from the terraformed area of the Gatelands was thinner. It made Siobhan's headache pulse in her temples.

"The two fastest and safest ways," Dr. Fowler said, eyeing the facility like it was a beast in a flimsy cage, "would have been that path to the right and the side door over there, both buried in rock. So, my recommendation is that we take the tunnels underneath."

"Come again?" Roots said, shouldering his gun. "I *thought* you said that the safest way is… *underground*?"

"I did," Fowler said, sounding defensive. "We have a network of… well, for want of a better phrase, escape tunnels. Evacuation routes should an emergency ever arise. They run the length of the facility, all the way to the platform. By my estimation, this is as much of an emergency as this facility will ever face, so now is as good a time as any to use them."

Roots still looked at him as if he were insane. "You know they're hive creatures, right?" the private said. "They *like* tunnels and dark places."

Dr. Fowler waved aside his concern. "There are no vents in the tunnels that would give them access, and all the ways in and out are locked. The creatures likely aren't even aware that the tunnels are there."

Roots opened his mouth to protest further, but Dr. Fowler cut him off.

"Since you know so much about them, you must know that while the Xenomorphs can adapt to extreme cold with little difficulty, they eschew fire. Our tunnels have weapons caches—M240 incinerator units. Flamethrowers, ladies and gentlemen." He paused for what Siobhan could only guess was dramatic effect. "The idea was that under certain circumstances, there might be a need to… cleanse and disinfect, so to speak. To eliminate the spread of contagion in one's wake. So if, by some chance, the Xenomorphs should follow us into the tunnels, the M240s will be an effective deterrent."

"How do you know the tunnels didn't cave in," Elkins said, "like the building?" He looked skeptical.

"We can be reasonably certain that's not the case," Fowler replied coolly. "The tunnels were constructed using materials developed here at the lab—they're quakeproof, fireproof, and built to withstand extremes in temperature and pressure. Even a direct explosion would cause minimal damage. Rocks falling above the ground probably didn't even make a dent."

He seemed to be waiting for more challenges, but the rest remained silent.

Finally, Siobhan spoke. "Are you sure they're down there? The flamethrowers, I mean."

"Yes, I am certain. No one who knows about those tunnels is left alive. Except for me, of course, and I have one of the only key cards that will open the access door." He shrugged. "This is your plan, though, Dr. McCormick. If you can think of a way over those rocks or through them, then by all means, I'd love to hear it."

Siobhan glanced at the others. They were watching her expectantly, even Alec. It *was* her plan, and it was a desperate one, but it was the only option they had. The tunnels seemed like the only way off this moon.

"Okay. Tunnels it is, then."

"Dr. McCormick—" Roots began, but when Siobhan turned to him, he stopped.

"We have no choice," she said. "That Weyland-Yutani ship is our only way off this moon, and the tunnel is the only way to get to it."

"You heard the lady," Alec said. "Dr. Fowler, get us to the tunnels. You worry about the way ahead. I've got our backs."

1 7

Dr. Fowler led them through the front entrance and into the lobby. The force of the falling rocks outside had cracked the walls down to the foundation. As they stood in the empty room, the building creaked around them. Siobhan suspected that at any time, a piece of ceiling could collapse or a room cave in.

Despite Fowler's assurances, she couldn't help but wonder what shape the tunnels would be in, after months of tremors and moonquakes. Given his tendency to lie or gloss over what he didn't want to admit, she didn't feel particularly confident in his assessment.

"Just as cozy as I remember it," Roots said flatly, righting a fallen potted plant on the front desk counter. Then he followed as Fowler led them through the lobby and a doorway that opened into the gray hall beyond. Many of the pipes had cracked, the wires looping down.

It made the hallway look like segmented tails and exoskeleton ribs.

The ceiling lights that had offered just enough glow to see by during their first incursion had since nearly gone out. What little light was left created shadows that looked distorted, flickering just on the periphery of vision.

At one of the locked doors, Dr. Fowler stopped, pulling a small ring of key cards from his pocket. He sorted through them until he found one with a light blue band across an edge, and he slipped it into the lock's card reader.

Nothing happened.

He pulled it out and slid it in again, and this time, a green light on the top of the lock flickered for a moment, then came on. Fowler pushed open the door and led them into a stairwell. Metallic rails lined a concrete-alloy set of steps that ran down to a landing, with another set descending beyond that.

"This way," he said.

Elkins and Roots descended the stairs, guns pointed ahead. For the moment they didn't need flashlights. At the landing they swung their weapons toward the darkened stairs that continued down to the tunnels. After a moment, Elkins waved the others down, and they joined the marines on the landing. Behind them, Alec dragged the door shut, leaving them in darkness.

"Give it a moment," Dr. Fowler said, "and the backup lights should go on down there."

For several seconds, nothing happened. Then there

was a series of clicks, followed by a flickering of light, and faint overheads came on in a wave along the length of the tunnel. Siobhan could see branching offshoots on both the left and right sides of the main corridor.

"You know which way you're going?" Elkins asked Fowler. "Looks like a maze down there."

"I know the way," Fowler said. "It's mostly just a straight shot forward."

Elkins and Roots, with the scientist close behind, led the others down the steps and into the tunnel. The walls were rounded and looked, for the most part, intact. They had been painted gray-green and were lined with thin pipes of a darker shade. Much like the hallways upstairs, they looked to Siobhan like long ribs in the body cavity of some great animal.

As they moved down the tunnel, the marines checked the branches, nosing their guns into the shadows and listening. A series of numbers and letters in a much brighter yellow-green seemed to label entrances to the offshoots, but the lights down each branch remained dark. The illumination wasn't much better in the main tunnel, but there was enough to make their way forward.

Occasionally they would hear the odd metallic *ding*, which would make the group jump and pause, waiting for the source to reveal itself.

Nothing came.

"Where do these branches go?" Kira asked as they walked. "Why are there so many?"

Dr. Fowler smiled. "There's only one way in, like I said, but there are a few ways out. These side passages go to different parts of the campus beyond the lab itself, but like I said, all the ways are locked. The doors are a special titanium alloy—very strong. I don't think the Xenomorphs could get through them, unless maybe—*maybe*—they bled their way through."

Kira looked skeptical. "What about the earthquake?" she said. "Could an earthquake break any of those doors?"

Dr. Fowler's smile slipped off his face. He didn't answer.

They continued a little way in silence until a loud bang made them all jump, then freeze in place. The marines trained their guns on the branches to the left and right, waiting. A few other bangs echoed from farther away, and then dropped off.

After several moments of silence, Roots said, "They're pretty quiet when they're sneaking up on people, right? It couldn't be just one of them, making that much noise."

"It's the pipes," Fowler replied. "I'm sure it's just the pipes." He peered over the marine's shoulder and down one of the side hallways. "And the ground outside is shifting. The quakes are getting stronger, and down here, sounds are distorted." It sounded as if he was trying to convince himself as much as them.

"Let's keep moving," Alec said. He eyed the corridor to the left, and then shifted his gaze to the right. "I assume we keep going straight?"

"You assume correctly," Fowler said.

They moved forward again, but the occasional groaning of the pipes—if it was the pipes—had them on edge. Even if Fowler was correct, Siobhan thought, the concept of being buried in ground that was being torn apart was no more comforting than the idea of Xenomorphs closing in on them.

"Where are those caches of flamethrowers, Dr. Fowler?" she asked.

"Just up ahead here," he replied, indicating an upcoming corridor on the left. "There's a small utility room a little ways down. The stores of M240s are in there." He reached the corner and turned it quickly, momentarily disappearing from sight, and Siobhan felt a twinge of panic. It wasn't that she cared about what happened to him, not personally, but he was their guide through the Weyland-Yutani underground. His disappearing on them would mean nothing good.

When she and the others rounded the corner, they saw Dr. Fowler standing in front of a lighter gray metal door with a yellow stripe running across it. He was pulling another of the key cards from his key ring, one with a matching stripe, and dipping it into the lock of the door. A tiny green glow cast its light on his fingers, and the door swung open.

"In here," Dr. Fowler said, and he went inside.

At the doorway, Siobhan peered in. Dr. Fowler had been right about it being a small—*very* small—room. It was lined on three sides with metal shelves, and on those shelves sat a number of crates with the Weyland-Yutani name and logo—a yellow W over a gray Y on a black background. "Building Better Worlds," their slogan read. Siobhan shook her head. It was a crock of shit.

"Here we are," Dr. Fowler said, pulling down one of the larger crates and setting it on the floor. "This should have the M240s in it." With some effort, he pried the lid off the crate. Inside were two incinerator units. It was hardly a cache, as Dr. Fowler had described it, but it was something.

"Are there more?" Elkins asked, looking at the other shelves.

"There should be," Fowler replied. He picked up one of the M240s from the crate and held it with an admiring smile. Then he pulled the trigger. The blast of flame from the end shot close to Siobhan's leg, and she jumped.

"Sorry, Dr. McCormick," Dr. Fowler said absently. "Just testing it to make sure it works."

"It works," Siobhan said, glaring at the man. She bent and picked up the other weapon herself, and when she stood, she saw Alec looking at her uneasily.

"I can handle it," she said to Alec. "Don't worry."

"Are you sure about that?" Fowler responded. "It's a big gun for a little woman, if you don't mind my saying so." He gave her a smirk. "You think you can use it?"

She pulled the trigger, and this time, the burst of flame came dangerously close to the top of the scientist's head. He flinched.

She smiled. "Yeah, I think I've got the hang of it."

The marines searched the rest of the shelves, but beyond the crate that Dr. Fowler had found, there were no other M240s. There were a few M41A pulse rifles, an M56A2 smartgun, and a few handguns, with accompanying ammo.

"Looks like your company screwed you on your so-called cleaning and disinfecting measures, Dr. Fowler," Elkins said. "This stuff is useless."

"These are weapons," Fowler objected.

"Carrying around more guns like the ones we have will just slow us down," Alec said. To his squad, he added, "There are boxes of 10×24mm caseless ammunition in that crate there. Grab that—we can always use more ammo."

"Copy that," Elkins said, and he and Roots started stuffing boxes of ammo into the many pockets of their uniforms. When they and Alec had emptied the crates, they all gathered at the door.

"Okay, Dr. Fowler," Alec said. "Take us out of here."

Fowler led them back into the main branch of the tunnel. He'd made it halfway to another corridor when an echoing chirp arrested their movement. To Siobhan it sounded metallic... like a claw briefly scraping a metal pipe. It also could have been a chittering purr, a single throat calling to others.

The sound came from somewhere behind them.

"You heard that, right?" Roots asked. "That wasn't just old pipes."

"Like I said," Fowler replied, "sounds get distorted down here. Could be nothing." He didn't look convinced, though.

"Or it could be something," Alec said. "And something down here with us is not good."

Siobhan squinted to see into the gloom of the tunnel behind them. One of the lights several yards back was flickering. Was that movement? It was hard to tell. Shadows and slivers of tunnel looked distorted as the light strobed on and off.

"This way," Fowler said. He was gesturing ahead of them, but his gaze was fixed on the tunnel behind. They started to move out again, a quiet urgency in their steps, but Siobhan remained transfixed by the flickering lights.

There *was* movement there—she was sure of it.

A dark, bony, segmented silhouette rose up and up, unfurling.

"Alec…" Siobhan raised the flamethrower.

A second silhouette dropped from the ceiling down there.

A third emerged from one of the side corridors.

"Alec!" Siobhan backed away until she felt a hand on her shoulder. She jumped and glanced over her shoulder. It was Alec.

"I see them." He pointed his gun. Over his shoulder, he said, "We have company."

The sound of footsteps hard and fast on the tunnel floor echoed from behind. Siobhan turned to see Fowler running.

"Dr. Fowler, wait!" she shouted after him.

"Go," Alec said. "Everyone, follow him. Go!"

They all began to run. Siobhan heard the now-familiar screech of one of the Xenomorphs, magnified and echoing through the tunnel. Others responded, and it sounded like a chorus. It was impossible to tell if other creatures in other corridors were responding as well; the noise seemed everywhere at once.

At a corridor bend some distance away, Dr. Fowler turned to the right, and the others followed, trying to keep him in their sights. Siobhan had just a moment at the bend to look back, and she saw that a fourth Xenomorph had joined the trio. They were galloping along the floor, the walls, the ceiling, gaining on her and the others.

She blasted flame in their direction, hoping to shock them into slowing down. The Xenomorph in the lead jerked back nearly to a stop. It seemed to know fire, to understand its danger, whether by experience or instinct, but the flames went out almost as soon as she laid them down. When the way was clear, the Xenomorph picked up speed again.

Siobhan ducked down the corridor and ran to catch up to the others. In the lead, Dr. Fowler turned left down another corridor, and a squeal from the branch opposite sent a flare of terror through her. Alec had just reached the turn when a fifth Xenomorph leaped from the ceiling to the floor, skidding into him. The force of the impact knocked the rifle from his hands and sent him sliding on his back across the surface. The alien crept toward him, saliva dripping from its jaws. It loomed over him, taking up most of the junction.

Alec's gun lay out of his reach. He seemed to be gauging whether he'd be fast enough to dodge and grab it before the alien was on top of him. Siobhan didn't think he would be. She got up close on the thing, but it didn't seem to notice. It was preoccupied with Alec, reaching down toward his legs.

He tried to scuttle backward.

"Sarge!" Elkins's voice came from somewhere farther up. "Sarge!"

The alien glanced up and then back at Alec.

Its jaw opened.

Siobhan pulled the trigger of the flamethrower.

For a moment, all she knew was light and heat as the flames of the weapon shot out at the creature in front of her. Its screech became a scream, and it writhed under the painful blast. Then it took off down the corridor from which it had come.

Siobhan ran to Alec. During the creature's confusion, he had dived for his gun, grabbing it. She offered him a hand up, and he smiled at her.

"Thank you," he said. "I owe you one."

She shrugged. "You've saved me a few times. Just trying to even things out."

With a smile, he took her hand and they ran to meet Roots and Elkins, who was carrying Kira, backtracking their way to their fallen sergeant. Fowler wasn't with them, Siobhan noticed.

"You're okay," Roots said between breaths. "We tried to get to you."

"No problem. Siobhan had my back." Alec squeezed her hand gently.

"This way," Elkins said. "Fowler kept going, the fu—" He stopped when he remembered Kira, who, clinging to his neck, had buried her face in his shoulder. "—the coward. Anyway, he went down this corridor up here on the right."

Behind them, the howls of the Xenomorphs seemed to fill all the tunnels. It sounded as if they were getting closer.

Again they ran. A few of the hallways split off from the one they were following, but these appeared to stop in dead ends, so they kept along the straight path. The main corridor itself leaned a bit to the left, but mostly ran one way. Siobhan's sense of direction was hopelessly thrown off, and there was no time to think, only flee.

Sometimes the sounds of the aliens grew louder, and sometimes fainter.

They emerged at a four-way junction, and the sounds died down to a faraway din.

"Which way?" Roots asked, his voice tense.

"If he gets on that ship and leaves without us..." Elkins didn't finish his thought.

Siobhan scanned the different branches. The one directly ahead had a metal ladder leading upward, and she thought she heard the rhythmic clunk of footsteps climbing up.

"That way!" She pointed toward the ladder.

They reached it in a matter of moments. At the base of the ladder, Alec shone his flashlight up just in time to see

Dr. Fowler lift a hatch, flooding the cylinder with bright sunlight. Then he climbed out, and closed the hatch.

"That son of a bitch," Alec muttered, and jumped onto the ladder. He began to climb. Elkins put Kira on the ladder next.

"Follow Sarge, okay, honey?" the corporal said. "He's strong enough to open the hatch." The girl nodded. Elkins gestured to Siobhan. "You next."

She slung the M240 over her shoulder by the strap and began to climb. Behind her, she heard Roots muttering.

"Don't be a hero, Kenny. Get your ass on this ladder."

"Yeah, yeah, I'm coming," Elkins said.

Alec reached the hatch, and with a grunt heaved it open, climbing out. Sunlight blinded Siobhan for a moment but she shielded her eyes and kept climbing.

"Keep going, honey," she said to Kira. "You're doing great. We're almost there."

Alec appeared over the hatch's opening, lending a hand to Kira to pull her out. Then he reached down and took Siobhan's hand, helping her over the lip of the hatch. She blinked a few times, her eyes adjusting to daylight, as Roots and Elkins followed behind.

There was the platform, as Fowler had said, and parked on it was a large ship, a bulk of black metal the size of an Earth-city block with a company logo stenciled on the side that Siobhan didn't recognize, as well as the ship's name: *ASTRAEUS*.

Fowler had already covered half the distance to it and was running like hell.

"Go! Go!" Alec shouted. "Don't let him get on that ship without us!"

They took off running, Elkins and Alec in the lead. The two closed the distance to Fowler, who was starting to lag and breathe heavily. They tackled him just as the ship's drawbridge door descended. The three of them landed hard on the ground.

"You son of a bitch!" Alec shouted as the scientist squirmed beneath their grasp. "Give me one reason not to kill you! Just one reason not to shoot your sorry ass right here!"

"I thought you were the aliens!" Fowler shouted, holding his hands up to protect a face smudged with gray dirt. His glasses were askew, and his hair stuck up in odd directions. "I'm sorry!"

Roots, who had picked up Kira, kept pace with Siobhan. The three joined Alec, Elkins, and the doctor, breathing almost as hard as he was.

"You were going to leave without us, you sorry sack of shit!" Alec pulled back a fist.

"No! No, I—" Whatever excuse Dr. Fowler was about to give was eclipsed by the angry screeches erupting from the tunnel. Siobhan looked in time to see Xenomorphs—she counted five of them—spilling over the mouth of the hatch and into the light. They seemed undeterred.

"Run!" she screamed.

Alec let Fowler up. Roots pulled him and Elkins to their feet. Siobhan offered a hand to the Weyland-Yutani scientist, but he waved her away, getting up on his own. They ran up the ramp of the door and into the ship.

Siobhan paused halfway up as one of the Xenomorphs reached the ramp's edge. She turned the flamethrower on it and it squealed, falling back. Alec took her arm and tugged her onto the ship. The last thing she saw before the door closed was one of the creatures lunging at her.

There was a clanging thump, followed by another and another as the Xenomorphs threw themselves at the metal door.

"Fire it up!" Dr. Fowler shouted, heading toward the bridge. "Get this thing off the ground!"

Whoever he was addressing, they complied. The rumble of the engines drowned out the sound of the screeching outside. The rumble of the moon itself, even louder, groaned over the sound of the engines. The ship shook violently, its nose-end tilting up and then falling back to the ground with a bone-jarring thud. Then it keeled to the right.

Roots swore loudly. "The ground's opening up!"

The others staggered after Fowler toward the bridge. There were two middle-aged men at the helm—a taller, dark-skinned man with a baseball cap and a somewhat younger white man with a messy thatch of blond hair. They barely acknowledged the influx of people onto their bridge, nor did they respond to Fowler's yelling over their shoulder. Calm and cool, they flipped switches and hit buttons, clicking on sensors and firing thrusters in an attempt to right the ship again.

Through the front windshield, Siobhan saw the Xenomorphs charge the ship. A sudden zigzagging crack split the platform, and two slipped into the chasm that appeared suddenly beneath their feet, screeching and scrabbling for a moment with those long talons at the edge of the crumbling dirt before disappearing.

Two others leaped the width of the chasm and slid across the dirt toward the ship. They caught their balance and galloped ahead.

The ship pulled its tail end out of the ravine and lurched forward. The taller man—Dr. Fowler had called him the pilot—barked at the younger man beside him.

"Sam, blast those things out of our way, okay?"

"Sure thing, boss," Sam replied, and he leaned a dual-pronged lever forward. Twin laser blasts shot out from somewhere beneath the windshield, hitting one of the aliens square in the chest. The hit burned a hole through the exoskeleton and, ostensibly, the meat beneath. The alien dropped to the platform, its blood steaming on the ground.

The Xenomorph who had been keeping pace with it dodged the laser, ducking under it, and pushed forward.

"Missed one," the pilot said calmly.

"On it," Sam replied. He jerked the lever back and then forward again. Part of the platform groaned and folded into a new rift, which splintered toward the ship.

The pilot pulled back on a lever of his own, and the feeling of forward momentum seemed to drop away. The ship lifted up off the ground as another of the Xenomorphs fell into the widening gorge where the vessel had just been.

Siobhan leaned closer to the windshield, peering down. When the last of the Xenomorphs leaped up and landed with a thump against the glass, she uttered a little cry, her finger on the trigger of the M240.

The thing screamed, its talons scraping at the windshield as it tried to hold on. A wound on its shoulder bled down its arm; Siobhan felt with horrifying certainty that it would jerk that arm and the blood would splatter the windshield, eating through it, and as soon as they hit the vacuum of space, the pressure would cause it to shatter...

"That one's yours," Sam said.

The pilot nodded. As the nose of the ship tilted upward and they climbed into the sky, he tilted the steering lever to the left and the ship rolled in that direction. The alien swung out to the left as well, its blood spraying out and away.

"You all might want to get yourselves seated," the pilot said as the ship lurched back to the right. The Xenomorph clung to the outside for several moments, then lost its grip and slid off and away. Siobhan saw it falling back toward an ever-widening canyon of opened-up moon before the ship lifted up into the clouds, and then into the black of space.

1 8

During that first afternoon, Siobhan came to learn that the men who were flying the *Astraeus* were named Gavin Broadwell and Sam Urban, civilian flight contractors for a company named Icarus Flight, which hired them out for piloting and navigation jobs to bigger corporations. This meant that they weren't technically Weyland-Yutani employees, but independent workers loyal only to whoever paid the highest number of credits.

In fact, they seemed to care little for Icarus or Weyland-Yutani, beyond the fact that one had hired them for work and the other delivered the credits to their accounts. She picked up most of this from Dr. Fowler, who was passingly familiar with Icarus as an affiliate. The men spoke little to anyone but each other, and even then only sparingly.

It was useful information to Siobhan, though, and as a result, it hadn't taken much to get Gavin and Sam to reroute their course to LV-846. Alec and Siobhan had explained what had happened on the moon and the plan to fly to their original relocation destination. At first, it had been of little interest to either the pilot or his crewman, until Gavin learned that Roots and Elkins had served on Kepler-2801 during the riots. Broadwell had been there as well, as an escapee from a nearby bombed-out village. He had, in fact, narrowly avoided being mowed down by gun-toting vagrants looking to keep refugees from bringing the plague of black pathogen into their camps.

"Lost a brother in that," Gavin said. "I'll never forget. Worst death I've ever seen."

"I'm sorry, man. That place was hell," Elkins said somberly. He added with a subtle glance at Fowler, "Wouldn't wish that experience on anyone."

Gavin paused a moment, seeming to consider if he should go on, and decided to do so. "Was a Colonial Marine who saved my life. Got me out of there. Won't ever forget that, either." He glanced at Sam, and an unspoken agreement passed between them. "You boys want to go to LV-846, then we go to LV-846."

"Now wait a minute," Fowler protested, rising from his seat behind them on the bridge. He had taken up sitting in one of the empty seats near the holographic maps table, ostensibly to keep an eye on things. "You can't do this. It's a violation of your contract with Weyland-Yutani."

"Don't care," Gavin said.

"They're the ones paying you!"

"Got paid already," Sam added.

"Well, if you think those credits can't be revoked, you're wrong," Fowler said, moving into the cockpit space between them. He glared out into the void beyond the windshield as if it was outer space's fault. "I'll make sure of it! I'll see to it that—"

His words were cut off by a blow to the jaw which sent him reeling. He looked up, both surprised and alarmed, at the person who had hit him.

Siobhan shook her hand out, then massaged her knuckles. She leveled an even gaze at him, but inside, her heart was pounding. She'd never punched a person in her life, but something had finally snapped. All the stress, physically and mentally, of the moon dying out from under her, the inexplicable loss of Camilla, and the creatures Fowler had unleashed—stalking and hunting the closest thing she'd had to family in the last decade—all found their way to her fist.

It felt good to finally shut Fowler up.

Really good.

Gavin chuckled softly, then turned back to the console in front of him.

"Nice right hook ya got there, Dr. McCormick."

"Thank you," Siobhan said, then she walked away. If Fowler had anything to say about her, he waited until she was out of earshot. What she did hear was Sam.

"Dr. Fowler, it's best if you just sit tight 'til we get to

LV-846. I ain't taking a punch in the jaw like that for you or anybody else."

LV-846 was a good four or five days away, and Martin Fowler was worried.

It wasn't the ship itself or its ability to provide that kept him awake as he lay on the bed pod in one of the evac ship's private cabins. Resources on the *Astraeus* were stocked for thirty people at least, and on a trip of that length, hypersleep wouldn't be a necessity. Air and food and the creature comforts of travel wouldn't be a problem.

The trip wasn't quite short enough, however, to be able to avoid extended contact with the others. For a week he would be stuck with the mutinied crew and the crazy Seegson woman and her marines.

Even that didn't really worry him, though. He hadn't gotten to the position he'd earned within the Weyland-Yutani corporation by being liked, and the fact that Dr. McCormick, her lovesick marine, and his lackeys didn't like him didn't bother him in the slightest. The bitch had given him a hell of a black eye—when he touched it gently with his fingertips, it hurt—but she'd sucker-punched him. Now that he was aware of her crazy temper, he'd be better prepared if she tried it again.

He'd handle her—and the rest of them, if need be. Even if the opportunity didn't arise on the journey, the

Company would never let such actions by McCormick and her team go unaddressed.

That thought Martin savored.

There was the serum to consider. He'd managed, of course, to get all of his data off the moon through transmissions to the main Weyland-Yutani headquarters in San Francisco, and had even managed to pocket a well-packaged sample in a refrigerated travel case that was small enough to tuck away in a pocket. It was nothing short of a miracle that the sample hadn't broken given all he'd been through.

Martin's worry was about more than just the safe delivery of the serum, though. He knew he'd have no problem with replicating the formula with relative ease, in whatever new lab the corporation assigned him to. What he was really concerned about was a sample of a different kind. Its delivery, or failure thereof, would affect him deeply.

Four or five days was cutting it close, *really* close, to the three-week mark. He'd have to get the corporation to send a ship with a fully stocked medbay and trained professionals directly to LV-846, or they were likely to lose their sample *and* their top scientist.

He had volunteered, against the small nagging voice that in others might have been considered better judgment, because he'd had a lot to prove, a lot at stake. The embryonic sample could be extracted—he'd made sure to develop that procedure very early in the process—and the serum would work. He'd promised that.

In fact, he'd literally staked his life on it.

Four or five days more would put him right around the limit to which the last of the volunteers had survived. After that, Martin Fowler would become a ticking time bomb, carrying something far, far worse than an explosive.

He rubbed his abdomen, could feel it stirring around in there, a queasy sensation like gas or extreme hunger, but there was no pain. Not yet. Not *quite* yet... and that was good. Should the pain come, the alien would follow very quickly behind.

He wondered if it mattered that the sample inside him was a Queen—as far as he knew, this might be the first one gestated in captivity, in a lab. Would that have an effect on the results? Would she grow at the same accelerated rate, due to the serum? Would her levels of hostility and resilience be increased, as they had been with the drones? Would the corporation be able to contain her properly?

Martin thought he could keep the secret from the others a while longer, but time was certainly of the essence. Extraction and early containment would be crucial. He reviewed the protocols and procedures in his head, over and over. It kept him from thinking about the killing machine inside him.

It kept him from being afraid.

If anyone had told him at ten years old that someday he'd not only see an alien with his own eyes, but come to understand its biology and behavior on such an intimate level, he'd have never believed it. So many times he had told himself that what he had done, what he had developed, was in the name of human progress. He had found a way to maximize weapon efficiency. Shorter wars meant fewer lives lost—at least, fewer lives on the side of those who had paid for the technology.

After all, what was progress in the hands of those who couldn't pay to implement it? It was a waste, that was what. Martin hadn't put in all those years of research, at the cost of his marriage, his friends, his free time, into building something that would languish in a lab vault—or worse, be destroyed by some well-meaning but clueless do-gooder looking to save a handful of expendables from "monsters," just because they couldn't see the big picture.

Money was nice. Knowledge was nice... but power—*that* was what kept the galaxies spinning. Power was a relevant currency no matter what planet he was on, and Martin had sacrificed throughout his whole life to bank it for himself.

He would have to find a way to reach his Weyland-Yutani superiors without the others knowing. It shouldn't be too hard to get their current coordinates and call another company ship to intercept them. He had something the corporation wanted, and it was in their best interest to save his life in order to acquire it.

Of course, they would go after the Queen whether he survived to see its birth or not, so he had to impress upon them that he was more useful alive than dead. Historically, a single drone could take out multiple fully armed human beings, including those who had been trained to kill them. A single Queen conceivably could—no, *would*, and there was no doubt about it— cause extensive casualties, unless of course he was there to make certain she was caught.

Even after he died, they would remember his name as the man who had developed this serum and gestated a Queen. But not yet, not if he could help it. He wanted to enjoy and exercise the power now, in life, that his accomplishments would afford him. He thought he'd earned that.

Martin turned over on his side. He'd rest a bit, just until he'd heard the others go to bed. He thought he could outmaneuver whichever idiot Brand put on duty— Rutiani or Elkins—and make his way to a communication terminal. He'd get the Company to come.

And then the others on the *Astraeus* would see true power at work.

The first morning on the *Astraeus*, the smell of strong coffee and bacon woke Siobhan from her first real sleep in weeks. She showered, dressed, and made her way to the kitchen area, where Sam Urban was scrambling eggs for Alec, Kira, and Roots. They were seated at a round metal table, and Elkins was reading a Newscore printout and sipping coffee on a chair nearby.

A pile of bacon sat in a bowl at the center of the table.

"Oh wow. I haven't had bacon in… probably fifteen years," she said, sitting in the empty chair next to Alec.

"Help yourself," he replied, then took a sip of coffee.

"Sam here's not a bad cook," Roots added, then popped a strip of bacon into his mouth. Sam glanced over his shoulder at them and winked. Alec poured her a cup of coffee and slid it over to her.

"Sleep okay?"

"Pretty well, all things considered." Siobhan smiled. "You?"

Alec tried to smile back, but it faltered.

"Sure."

She turned to Kira and asked, "How about you, honey? Did you sleep?"

Kira, who was pushing scrambled eggs around her plate with a fork, nodded but didn't answer. She didn't look up.

Siobhan's smile slipped away. She was worried about the girl. When they got to LV-846, Siobhan would have to begin the process of making sure she got some counseling, got into a good school, made friends... So many children got lost in the shuffle between worlds. Some disappeared. Others got hurt... and worse. There were no laws governing children who traveled alone, at least none that applied across worlds, and so anything could happen.

Kira deserved better than that. After all she'd been through, she deserved so much better. Siobhan reached out and touched the little hand on the table, giving it a gentle squeeze.

"It's going to be okay. We'll make everything okay."

Kira looked up at her. There were shadows under her eyes. She tried to smile but failed worse than Alec had. A moment later, she pulled her hand away.

Sam appeared over Siobhan's shoulder and put a plate of eggs in front of her, along with a fork.

"This looks great," Siobhan said. She was grateful to change the subject. "Thanks, Sam."

"No problem."

As they ate, Dr. Fowler charged into the kitchen and went straight to Sam.

"Your colleague is ignoring incoming messages from Weyland-Yutani." He turned to Siobhan. "I know your little team here decided to hijack this ship, and you've managed to convince the flight crew here to be complicit in your crime, but—"

"Dr. Fowler—" Siobhan broke in.

He ignored her.

"—your continued refusal to ignore the corporation is just going to draw their attention all the more. They don't like losing valuable assets, and this ship is worth a lot. More than any single one of you will ever see in a lifetime."

Alec pushed his chair back and stood. Fowler backed off.

"You can tell them that they can have their ship back when we get to LV-846," Alec said, stepping away from the table. "Until then, I don't want to hear another word about it from you—*or* them."

Fowler didn't respond, but Siobhan suspected it wasn't the end of the conversation. He was the kind of guy who was used to people listening to him, and doing what he told them. That he was being summarily ignored, even shot down, had to be getting under his skin.

Over the next couple of days, each time she passed through the bridge, Siobhan noticed there were a number of incoming transmissions that Gavin had continued to ignore. Weyland-Yutani's contact man, a voice who identified himself as Stan Bloom, could be heard through the dashboard comms.

At first, he sounded confused as he asked about the whereabouts of the ship and the new route reported by their tracking systems. When Gavin brushed him off with some excuse about static interference, he seemed dissatisfied but accepted the answer... until a few hours later. That next time, he sounded firm but slightly uneasy when he asked to speak to someone in charge.

"I *am* in charge," Gavin said tonelessly, and he gestured at Sam, who hit the disconnect on the communications system. Between the two of them, they managed to put off Bloom a few times more, until Sam was caught off guard and accidentally answered one of Bloom's incoming calls. Bloom sounded clearly frustrated in his attempt to get the pilot or his navigator to explain where they were taking the ship.

When another attempt came, the entire group was present on the bridge.

Dr. Fowler jumped on the intercom before Sam could stop him. "LV-846! They're taking the ship there! You need to stop—" Sam slammed the button that cut off the communication and glared up at the doctor.

"Don't touch that," he said. His tone left no room for argument.

"This is kidnapping," Fowler countered. He leaned down and pointed a finger in Sam's face. "They'll see that all of you are thrown in prison. Or worse! You really want to fuck with the Company? They'll hunt you down and make you pay for this. You'll never see any planet's daylight, ever again!"

Gavin snickered, and Fowler turned on him.

"You think this is funny?" He practically growled at the man.

Gavin shrugged.

"You think the corporation cares about you?" he said. "Enough to come get you?"

"Hell *yes*, I do! They certainly care about what I'm carrying!"

"Oh yeah? What's that?"

Dr. Fowler paused and glanced at the others, who were all looking at him expectantly.

After a moment, he said, "My research, of course. My life's work. I have very specific knowledge about a very specific area. I've created a serum with numerous applications across multiple fields. Weyland-Yutani paid me a lot of money to develop the serum and… deliver the information."

"Didn't you already transmit the research data from your lab to headquarters?" Siobhan said. "That should give them what they want, unless you've stuffed a bunch of file folders in your pockets. So, if they have what they need from you, what makes you think they'll care about saving a person whose continued existence now constitutes an expense?"

"Come now, Dr. McCormick," he replied. "It wouldn't benefit me to turn over *all* my research, without any assurance of my security. What I sent them is incomplete. Further, I have samples of my serum which could facilitate production. Without the samples, and my overseeing the production process, the results would be set back by years. As a fellow scientist," he continued with a hint of scorn, "I'm *sure* you understand that one of the most invaluable resources we can offer is time."

"Well, good for you," Siobhan said. "They can pick up you, your samples, and all your *invaluable* research on LV-846." She walked up to Dr. Fowler and leaned in until her face was close to his. "But if you get in the crew's way again," she said, smiling sweetly, "I'll make it my personal mission to bury you so deep in this ship's hull that even its builders will never find you."

Dr. Fowler regarded her with abject hatred.

Then he walked away.

1 9

On the third night, some fifty-six hours out from LV-846, the comms fell silent.

Siobhan stared out the window of her cabin into the deep of space. The godlike immensity of it never ceased to amaze her, no matter how many times she was transferred from planet to planet, moon to moon. People thought of space as an endless, empty expanse of darkness, but it wasn't, despite the interminable blackness between worlds. There were countless celestial bodies, meteors, asteroids, black holes, forces producing life and death, spreading decay, stars being born and dying and becoming something else...

It was the closest thing to a religious experience she had ever felt.

In fact, Siobhan had once found strange comfort in the vastness of space, as if the cosmic scope was proof of something greater than humanity, that the spirit endured and life went on in some form or another.

Now, as she looked out on the sprinkling of stars through the brilliant mist of strange nebulae in the distance, she wondered how many of the worlds revolving around them had Xenomorphs, or creatures just as bad. How many worlds had evolved life that existed simply to cause death? And as the corporations pushed people farther and farther out into the universe, how many of those creatures would wipe out segment after segment of the human race?

Wherever people went in pursuit of creation, corporations like Weyland-Yutani and maybe even Seegson seemed to follow with their monsters in tow, using those innocents as fodder for experiments in destruction.

Siobhan looked back at her years at the Seegson lab on BG-791, at nights she'd spent restlessly tossing and turning in bed, worried about the pathogen bombs hitting colonies all over the galaxy. There seemed to be no rhyme or reason to it, and blame had been assigned to multiple groups, always with no real proof. Small colonies were hit as often as big ones, both civilian and military, scientific as well as exploratory. And there was no "one side"—the United Americas, Three World Empire, Union of Progressive Peoples, even Independent Core System Colonies were struck at one time or another.

No colony was so far out as to be missed by whatever terrorists were dropping the bombs. There were many, however, who were forgotten by those who might protect them.

Back when BG-791 was still connected to the rest of the galaxy, reports had described in great detail what happened when the black goo came into contact with living creatures. Coming from sensationalist outlets and legitimate scientific groups, they revealed how the bodies would spasm and writhe and change from the inside out, how the people would become things almost impossible to categorize, let alone contain.

There had been rumors, of course, that the pathogen was engineered by a race of ancient beings that had created human life on Earth. That it was meant to produce an entirely new species using only the smallest source of genetic material. Siobhan thought, however, that the purpose behind the pathogen might be even more fundamental.

It was the stuff of creation and destruction, the very magic of the gods. Depending on what it touched, it simply granted life or death. That kind of power, contained in just a few tiny particles, was absolutely terrifying.

At the time, she had thought the pathogen attacks were the worst threat to her safety on that moon. She hadn't known then—not really—about the destructive capability of the Xenomorphs. They had been purely theoretical, almost imaginary, a bad thing happening to someone she didn't know, on a planet so distant that the threat never seemed real. Back then she hadn't known

Alec, at least not well, and she'd had no idea that he'd ever encountered such monsters.

They hadn't been a looming threat, not like the pathogen.

Yet the monsters had been close, all that time. Frighteningly close. If the pathogen was the magic of nightmare gods, then the Xenomorphs were their terrifying dark angels.

Somewhere in the ship there was a thump, and she flinched. Every noise, no matter how small, made her jump now. Siobhan wondered how long it would take to stop feeling like the next world she went to, and the next, and the next, would never take her far enough away from the Xenomorphs.

As she stared out the window, a planet loomed into view. That was odd. She couldn't say for sure, but she didn't think their flight path took them this close through a star system. It couldn't be LV-846, not this early.

Were they going in the right direction? While she had gotten lost in her thoughts, had the ship veered off course? She frowned. It seemed unlikely that Gavin or Sam would have gone back on their agreement to take her and the rest of the team to LV-846, unless... Had Weyland-Yutani threatened them? Offered them more money?

She rose from the bed and crossed the room. Something was wrong; she felt it in her gut. At the door, she put on a pair of comfortable shoes, then grabbed the light hooded jacket hanging from a nearby hook and slid that on, too. She tapped the button for the door, which opened onto a dark and quiet hallway. Siobhan moved down the hall to Alec's door and knocked.

"Coming," Alec called from the other side, and a few moments later, his door slid open. He stood there in just a pair of sweatpants, his hair, short as it was, standing in small, rumpled spikes, his eyelids heavy with sleep. His unshaven jaw, she noticed, also was starting to show the occasional gray whisker.

His eyes widened when he saw her. "Von," he said, surprised. Then he frowned. "You okay? What's wrong?"

"The ship," she said, trying not to stare at his bare chest—at least, not in an obvious way. Any other time, she would have welcomed the distraction. Just then, though, she needed Alec to help her confirm they were still on track to LV-846. "I think something is wrong. It's... I don't think it's going the right way."

Alec cocked an eyebrow at her. "What do you mean?"

Siobhan shrugged, glancing around. "I can't say for sure. I guess... well, I've spent some time the last couple of days looking over the holographic star map on the bridge. LV-846 is the middle planet of a three-planet system, but this far out, there shouldn't be anything but empty space for at least another day and a half. There are no other star systems fifty-six hours out, and... well, look." She took his arm gently and led him to the window in his bedroom. Since both their rooms were on the same side of the ship, their windows looked out on the same view. The planet she had seen, a dark maroon and blue orb, had grown larger with their increasing proximity.

"That," she said, gesturing out the window, "shouldn't be there."

Alec frowned. He leaned over and grabbed a gray USCMC T-shirt that had been tossed on a nearby night table, and pulled it over his head.

"Am I crazy?" she asked. "Am I just overthinking this?" She touched the glass of the window gently. From the pictures she'd seen, LV-846 was a green planet, with wispy white clouds and the occasional blue smattering of small seas. This planet outside wasn't anything like that, nor did she think it was the third and farthest planet of that star system. According to the bridge's map, the ship wouldn't make it to the outer edge until late afternoon the day after tomorrow.

"No," Alec said, "you're right. This is wrong. This is the wrong way."

The two made their way to the bridge. It was quiet and darker than it should have been, with a signal light from the control dashboard flickering a pale whitish-blue. That pervasive feeling of wrongness coalesced into a knot in her stomach.

Siobhan half-expected to see Dr. Fowler behind the controls, piloting the ship off course. She was surprised, however, to find instead both Gavin and Sam passed out in their chairs, snoring heavily. That seemed worse. It didn't make sense. A ship this big might well have had an autopilot, particularly if hypersleep was necessary, but in this case, it was too short a trip for either of those things. Each crewman would have taken a turn at the helm while the other slept. Finding the pilot and navigator both passed out at the controls seemed to her like a bad sign.

A coffee mug—Gavin's, she assumed—sat on the dashboard near his sleeping form. Another looked to have dropped from Sam's hand and rolled a bit away before its handle stopped it. A dark coffee stain had spread on the floor beneath it.

The blinking blue-white light was coming from the piloting dashboard. It formed a single word.

OVERRIDE

That knot of anxiety drew tighter.

"What's that an override for?" Siobhan asked, pointing to it.

Alec strode over, examining the controls. He shook his head, flicked a switch next to the button, and when nothing happened, he looked back at her.

"I'm not an expert, but if I had to venture a guess, I'd say it's an override for the course setting. The rest of the system seems to be online and keeping the ship moving, but the autopilot is off. Which means, I'm guessing, that some kind of a remote piloting system has been introduced."

"Weyland-Yutani?" Siobhan asked, her heart sinking.

"Has to be. They probably did an end run around the pilot and navigator and took control." Alec turned to Gavin and shook him. "Captain! Gavin—wake up!" Alec shook him harder, but the man's head lolled on his neck. Alec checked the pulse at his neck, slapped his cheek lightly, and gave him another shake, but Gavin kept sleeping.

With an alarmed frown, Alec grabbed Sam's shoulders and shook him, trying to rouse him, but Sam didn't respond, either.

"Sam. Sam! Wake up, buddy," Alec said. "Come on, wake up."

Siobhan crossed the bridge and picked up the mug on the dashboard, peering into it. The sludge at the bottom of the cup had a familiar smell, a sharp bitterness just beneath the scent of the coffee into which it had been mixed.

"It's a sedative," Siobhan confirmed. "Plant-based. A strong one. Someone—Dr. Fowler, I'm guessing—drugged their coffee. That was probably how Weyland-Yutani could take control of the ship without interference."

"That son of a bitch!" Alec pounded the dashboard. "Should have killed him back on the platform." He thought a minute. "I need to get Elkins."

"Can he disable the remote piloting? Maybe we can reclaim control."

"That's what I'm hoping. I'll be right back. Stay here with them?"

Siobhan nodded.

He moved toward the door, then paused and turned back to her.

"Be careful. Don't trust Fowler, from here on out. In fact, shout if you see him and I'll come running."

"I will," Siobhan replied. "Please hurry, though."

She understood exactly why he wanted her to be careful. Dr. Fowler had been an obstacle every step of the way since they'd met him, but this was deliberate—and dangerous—sabotage. For whatever reason, he was dead-set against going to LV-846.

Siobhan could only imagine what "accident" might cause her and the marines and little Kira to disappear, if the corporation reclaimed control of the ship long enough to get it where they had intended it to go.

Alec turned to leave, then stopped again as if considering something. He came back and kissed her softly on the mouth. The gesture was so simultaneously thrilling and sweet that Siobhan was stunned into silence. Before she could recover words, though, he had crossed the bridge again and slipped out the door to get his squad member.

While Siobhan waited, she brewed coffee in the little portable pot that Gavin kept on the bridge. The strong smell, she reasoned, might help wake the crew up, and if not, at least it would be there for them when they did.

That sedative was strong—a medical-grade extraction of a plant cultivated on a number of colonized worlds. In fact, Seegson had synthesized it at the lab on BG-791. It wouldn't have surprised her to find out that Fowler had pocketed some of the Seegson samples at some point before they'd left, fully intending to use it to thwart her plan. He was proving himself daily to be a more and more dangerous individual. Hate wasn't an emotion Siobhan felt easily, but she was starting to hate Martin Fowler.

Siobhan shook Gavin's arm, half-heartedly trying to wake the man up. He mumbled something unintelligible—a name, she thought, possibly the name of his brother—and then started snoring again. That didn't surprise her, either. She could only hope Fowler hadn't given them too much, and done permanent damage.

The coffee percolating, she moved toward the controls. They were far too complicated for her to feel comfortable pushing random buttons and pulling levers, but she was curious as to how Weyland-Yutani was piloting the ship, and to where. Nothing she could see gave any indication of where they were or where they were going. The star map hadn't changed since the last time she'd been on the bridge, which suggested to her that it had been paused somehow with the hope that, over the course of the night, with the passengers sleeping and the crew drugged, no one would notice that the course of the ship no longer matched it.

The override light flashed on and off, on and off into the gloom.

Several minutes later, Alec came back in with Elkins.

"I sent Roots to get Kira and keep an eye on her," Alec said. "Elkins thinks he can cancel the override."

Elkins made his way to where Gavin was sitting and slid him and his chair out of the way. He began typing in commands and flipping switches.

"Just give me a minute here to figure out the system..."

Alec joined Siobhan. "Any sign of Fowler?"

"None," Siobhan said. She gestured toward Gavin. "These two are going to be out for a few hours. I hope Elkins can fly this thing."

"I can fix it," Elkins said. "Flying it will be someone else's deal."

"Is there anything you can give them to wake them up?" Alec asked.

Siobhan considered it for a minute. "It would be risky, a strain on their hearts, but... if we really need to, it could be done. This sedative is made from an extract that functions like a benzodiazepine, and if the ship has flumazenil-based synthetic substitute..." She saw the confusion on Alec's face and smiled sheepishly. "Sorry. Yes, in other words, it could be done, if the ship's medical supplies have what I need. I'd have to check their medbay. I'll see what I can do."

"Okay. I'll go with you."

Roots sat in a chair next to Kira's bed and yawned, fighting the urge to fall asleep. He had been sleeping like the dead when Sarge came banging on the door to let him and Elkins know Fowler had drugged the crew and the corporation had rerouted the ship. Sarge had given Roots the order to watch over Kira and keep an eye out for Fowler—to detain him, by force, if necessary.

He liked the kid, so that was okay, but boy, did he want to take a crack at Fowler. Everything the man had done since they'd rescued his sorry ass from the W-Y lab had been aimed at screwing them over. Roots had assured Sarge that he'd have no problem detaining Fowler with force. In fact, he was looking forward to it.

"The girl, though—that's your first priority," Sarge had said. "Look out for her, okay?"

"Copy that," Roots had replied, bending over to grab one of his boots. His foot still hurt from the Xenomorph blood that had spattered on it at the Menhit Lab, and running for the ship hadn't helped it any. He pulled the boot on gingerly. "Will do."

"She's in the room next to mine, at the end of the hall. Let her sleep, if you can, huh? Poor kid's been through hell these past few days. We all have."

"Sure thing, Sarge," Roots replied. He'd gone down to Kira's room, let himself in with an extra key card, and saw her in the dim light from the window above the bed. She was asleep, breathing slowly and softly, hugging her stuffed dog. After he'd locked the door again, he'd set his gun aside on the floor, pulled a chair over from the small desk in the far corner, stretched out his legs, and folded his hands over his chest.

Once Elkins had tinkered with the ship controls and deactivated the remote system, they could get to finding Fowler and—if there was any God out there in the universe—flush the son of a bitch out of the airlock.

Roots yawned again and propped his head up with his hand. He nodded once, his eyes slipping closed, but caught himself and sat up in the chair. The girl murmured something and turned over in her sleep.

The dark around him, the soft breathing from the bed nearby, the warmth of the room, all seemed to seep inside him, making his limbs, head, and eyelids heavy. He shook his head, trying to clear the drowsiness from it. He wished Elkins would hurry up already.

A sudden loud bang made him jump, the fatigue dissipating instantly. The sound had been close—right outside the door. He bent and picked up his gun, then stood in the darkness. He looked at Kira but she was still asleep.

Was that Fowler? What was he up to now?

Roots crept around the foot of the bed to the door, unlocked it, and pushed the button to open it. It slid back with a soft *whoosh*. He glanced back at the bed, but Kira didn't stir. Standing in the doorway, he looked out into the hall. It was dark, and so far as Roots could tell, it was empty.

A dervish of unease whirled up in his stomach. Men—men like Fowler, at least—weren't that fast. If Fowler had made the noise in the hallway, Roots would have seen him. He would have caught at least a glimpse of the man running away, but there didn't seem to be a sign of anyone.

Roots couldn't help but look up toward the ceiling, tracing the lines of architecture to the nearest air vent. It was small… too small for anything bigger than a child to fit through. He thought of the new Xenomorph which had chewed and slashed its way out of Cora's stomach. It had been small—small enough to fit into a vent that size.

Stop.

He was overthinking. Exhaustion, hunger, stress—they were all catching up to him and he was hearing things. He *had* to be. They were in space now, far away from BG-791 and its inevitable trajectory, far from the Weyland-Yutani lab and its genetically boosted monsters. There was no way one of those things had gotten aboard… right?

How many? Roots tried to recall the number of XX121s that had come spewing out of the tunnel. He'd been running, hyped up on adrenaline, worried about protecting the girl in his arms. He'd been exhausted even then, his nerves thin and tight. It was hard to remember the details. He thought all of them had been taken out, though, by the evacuation from that devolving moon.

Five… there were five.

Two, he recalled, had fallen into the cracks in the platform. Or had it been three? He seemed to remember one, at least, had been shot by the ship's lasers… and one had to be shaken loose from the ship. *Was that all of them?* He couldn't be sure. What if there had been other Xenomorphs they hadn't seen in the tunnels, ones that had silently stalked past and stowed away on the ship?

Roots backed into the room, closed the door, and locked it. He had to tell Sarge and Elkins that Fowler might not be their only problem. He couldn't leave the girl, though. He was dressed in sweatpants and a T-shirt, the same as Sarge and Elkins, and so none of them had their comms—those were with their uniforms. The only solution was to wake Kira and take her with him. He'd have to go out and find—

Another bang rocked the ship, followed by a long grinding sound of metal against metal. That *definitely* hadn't been Fowler, and he didn't think it could have been an XX121. It was a sound he'd heard before.

It was the sound of laser fire—from another ship.

PART III

INTO THE FIRE

2 0

On the bridge, Elkins fiddled with some wires behind the panel of the dashboard. Gavin and Sam slept on; Siobhan and Alec had wheeled them out of the way in their chairs so Elkins could work, and then Siobhan had checked on the men. Respiratory distress was a potential side-effect of the sedative, and given their labored breathing, she had seemed uneasy forcing them awake, especially without a medic or doctor, or even Camilla, present.

She and Alec decided instead to search the medbay for stabilizers. Elkins had been left behind with the crewmen, snoring where they slumped.

"There," he said as he pushed the panel back into place with a small grunt. "Gavin, my man, the ship is yours. Well, it will be once I reboot the system." He flipped a small switch on the underside of the dashboard, clicking it one way and then the other. The lights across the top flickered off and then on again with a low hum. "I broke one of the connections so the corporation can't take control of the ship again, but they're going to be pissed."

Sam stirred lightly in his chair, and Elkins added, "You may want to set the maps to non-transmissible going forward, at least until we get to LV-846. I'll remind you when you wake up. Or you might want to think about dumping this rig entirely. Fowler may not be right about much, but he's right about Weyland-Yutani. These Company fuckers... they find ways to screw people over, make them disappear. Take your credits and go to some nice ICS planet—I'd suggest LM-490. I hear the beaches there are beautiful."

No response.

Elkins stood with a small groan.

Marine life was starting to take its toll on him. Thirty-four was too young to have creaking joints and aching muscles. True, he hadn't slept much, and the evacuation from BG-791 had been less than smooth, but he just didn't bounce back as quickly as he used to. A body could only keep going for so long before downtime, any bit of downtime, allowed the wear and tear to set in.

As if to confirm his thoughts, when he leaned over the dashboard to reprogram the coordinates into the autopilot, his back twinged.

"Okay, all set," he said, straightening. He looked at Gavin. The man had stopped snoring. His chest still rose and fell, but it was irregular now, and a little jagged.

Silently, Elkins cursed Fowler for risking the lives of the only two people who could actually fly the ship. The moral issue aside, that damned nutjob had risked all their lives in taking down the crew. Autopilot was one thing, but fifty-four hours from now, someone human was going to have to *land* the thing.

Suddenly, the bridge shook, a thunderous metallic bang echoing through the room. Elkins reeled, trying to maintain his balance. Leaning against the dashboard for support, he looked up and through the front view port. There, he saw a looming metal ship at least twice the size of the *Astraeus*.

"Oh shit," Elkins said.

When the retraction device sent out by the USCSS *Demeter* made contact with the *Astraeus*, the reverberation shook the hallway where Siobhan and Alec were making their way from the medbay, stabilizers in hand. They were headed to Kira's room to check on her.

"What was that?" she asked, pocketing the stabilizers. Her hands were shaking.

"I don't know," Alec admitted.

"We've got to get to Kira!" Siobhan sprinted ahead. Alec followed.

Just as she was about to slip the key card into the door lock, the door slid open. Roots stood in the doorway, gun in hand. Kira, looking sleepy, stood behind him, clutching Mr. Bones.

"It's another ship!" Roots looked into the hallway. "That son of a bitch called them to come get him!"

"Are you sure?" Siobhan took Kira's hand, and they rushed to catch up as he jogged down the hallway, with Alec right behind him.

"I'd bet my pension on it!" Roots called over his shoulder.

When the four of them reached the bridge, Elkins was there to meet them.

"It's a ship," he said. His voice was calm, but Siobhan could tell from his body language that he was worried. "The USCSS *Demeter*, it says on the side. How much you want to bet that's a Weyland-Yutani ship?"

"Roots thinks it's here to get Fowler," Alec said. "Either he called them, or they tracked us." He ran to the front window and looked out. The others followed.

Most of it was angled around in front of them, as if to block their way, but the apparatus for the retraction arm curled around the left side of the *Astraeus*. Siobhan thought it felt like they were heading into the open claws of some predatory beast.

"It's looking like a solid theory, Roots," Alec said. "Elkins, do we have control?"

"We do now, yeah. Our ship's on autopilot. Coordinates are set for LV-846."

"Can you fly it?"

Elkins frowned. "I'm a mechanic, Sarge, not a pilot."

"You don't need to fly it the whole way. We just need to shake off the *Demeter*. Can you do that?"

"Sure," Elkins replied. "In theory, I guess. I could try to run some evasive maneuvers—"

"*Do it*," Alec said. "Roots, I need you to secure Dr. Fowler. Find him, restrain him, confine him to his room. We can't have him running around causing more problems, and we sure as *hell* don't want him contacting them." He gestured at the big ship outside.

"Copy that," Roots said, a small grin on his face. "Looking forward to it." He took off to find the scientist.

"Can I do anything to help?" Kira asked Alec. The sleep had mostly faded from her face, and while there was still a remnant of sadness there, her eyes held a kind of determination that Siobhan admired. She was tough stuff, that little girl, trying not only to bounce back, but to be an active part of things.

Alec looked down at her and smiled. "Yeah, you and Siobhan can be my eyes and ears when I go out there to detach the retraction device."

"Wait, *what*?" Siobhan clutched his upper arm. "You can't go out there! It's too dangerous!"

"What are they going to do, fire on me? They'll hit the ship—and they won't risk that."

"How do you know?"

"Fowler seems pretty sure of it."

Siobhan rolled her eyes in exasperation. "Fowler's a lunatic!"

"Look," Alec said gently, putting his hand over hers. "If they had written this ship off as a loss, they wouldn't have bothered with the retraction device—they would have just fired on us already." He let that sink in, then added, "We can't detach the retraction arm from here unless we do it manually, and we have to do it quickly. Any minute now, they're going to start towing us away. I have to, Von."

"Sarge," Elkins cut in, "Deep-space external repairs are supposed to be two-man jobs."

"Well, we're going to have to settle for one," Alec replied. "I need you here, ready to get the ship away from the *Demeter*, out of retraction distance. Roots needs to keep an eye on Fowler."

"Well, then, let me come with you," Siobhan said.

"Von, I appreciate the offer, but—" He stopped when Siobhan narrowed her gaze.

"Now you listen," she said in a low, firm voice. "There's no time to argue. I'm coming with you. Kira will stay with Kenny and keep eyes and ears on what the *Demeter* is doing and report to us." She looked down at Kira and smiled. "Will you do that, honey?"

Kira nodded. "I can help. I can."

Siobhan cupped her cheek. "I know."

"Siobhan—"

"Let's go," she said, ignoring the argument she knew was coming, and started across the bridge.

Siobhan and Alec found a large metal toolbox painted yellow, as well as space suits, in a closet room near the airlock. As they slipped into the suits, Alec made another attempt to talk Siobhan out of going outside.

"Really, Von, I don't think—"

"Alec," Siobhan broke in, "I know you're trying to protect me. I appreciate that. I love that you care enough to worry about what happens to me way out here in the middle of space. But I need to do this. I've been... helpless. Helpless this entire time, and when I have nightmares about everything that's happened—which I do—I dream of being unable to act, of having to watch as things happen to me, which is so much worse than trying and failing to make things happen myself." She paused, looking into his eyes. "When I picked up that flamethrower, I felt like I finally got back some of the control I'd lost the moment we arrived at the Menhit Lab. I could do something to protect myself and the people I care about, and I can't go back to feeling helpless. I can't sit on the sidelines, relying on everyone else to make things happen, or the nightmares are never going to stop. Do you understand?"

Alec gave her a small smile. "I think I do." He hefted the toolbox.

"Good," she said, putting on her helmet. Through the comm system, she said, "*Let's do this.*"

They passed through the inner door, fastened tethers to their suits, and then pushed the button to depressurize the airlock. The outer door opened. For a brief, absurd moment, Siobhan tensed, but not from the thought of walking out into space. She had done this before, though it had been a while. In her peripheral vision, a darkness flickered just outside, and she braced herself for a Xenomorph hand to curl its fingers around the opening.

It was nothing, though—a shadow from the retraction arm, maybe, or a passing cloud of dust.

The two moved out along the edge of the ship, following its maintenance ridge, a large, segmented seam of metal along the ship's side that crew members could use as a guideline to get to the outer control panel. The clamp of the retraction arm had hooked onto that ridge a few feet shy of the panel, denting the metal with its force but holding tight. The clamp itself looked to Siobhan like a huge metal "C," exerting pounds of pressure she couldn't begin to guess.

When they reached it, Alec looked closely.

"Ah, damn it," he said. *"I was afraid of that. The clamp they're using is too strong to unhinge with any kind of tools we'd have on this ship."*

"So we remove the segment of the ship it's attached to."

Alec looked at her, surprise visible through the visor of his helmet. She gestured to the heavy bolts that held the segments of the metal ridge to the side of the ship.

"This is a maintenance ridge, right? Bolted to the side but not a crucial part of the ship's structure. We unbolt the segment it's clamped onto, get back in the ship, and off we go."

"I'm impressed." Alec handed her a long thin tool from the series of attachments in the toolbox's side compartment.

She smiled. "*I used to have a friend who worked maintenance for one of the moon's delivery ships. He was very enthusiastic about his job.*"

"*A friend, eh?*" Alec said, sliding down a little to let Siobhan closer to the ridge's bolts.

"*More of a fatherly figure, really,*" she said.

Alec chuckled. "*So, I guess I don't have to explain how to use that industrial screwdriver?*"

"*No, I think I've got it,*" she replied, sliding the button to turn it on. It took several minutes of heavy vibrations up her arm, but she managed to free one of the bolts. When it came loose, it floated off. "*One down, three to go,*" she said.

Alec nodded. He found another smaller version of the screwdriver Siobhan was using and went to work on another of the bolts.

"*How is everything going?*" Elkins's voice came through the comm system.

"*Almost there,*" Alec said, as the bolt he'd loosened floated away.

"*Good,*" Elkins said. "*Because I think they're starting to get an idea of what you're doing out there. Better hurry.*"

"*Roger that,*" Alec replied. To Siobhan, he said, "*If they begin hoisting us in, we're screwed. Let's get these last two bolts off.*"

Siobhan applied the screwdriver to the next bolt on the right, while Alec took the one on the left. His bolt came free a few minutes later, just as the ship lurched to the left. The ridge swung outward and Siobhan's screwdriver skittered off the bolt and toward her hand. A fraction of a second later, its bit slid under her glove, digging a groove into the metal ridge. Her heart pounded.

Elkins's voice came over the comm system again. "*You two all right?*"

"You?" Alec asked, touching Siobhan's shoulder. She nodded, but she could feel her pulse in her ears. If that bit had punctured her space suit… There was no time to think about that now, though. She readjusted the screwdriver bit onto the bolt and began unscrewing it again.

"*Guys?*" Elkins said.

"*We're okay,*" Alec replied. "*I guess they're onto us, huh?*"

"*You need to get back inside the ship,*" Elkins said.

"*Almost there.*" The vibrations from the screwdriver were making Siobhan's teeth chatter, but she held on.

"*Time's up.*" Elkins's voice sounded tight. "*They're gonna drag the ship right out from under you.*"

"*One more second…*"

The ship was yanked to the left again, just as the last bolt came free. The ridge slid off the side of the ship, the clamp still clinging to it.

"*Sarge…*"

"*Kenny, we got it off! We're coming back in.*"

Siobhan and Alec pulled themselves along the remaining ridge segments, back toward the airlock door. Behind them, the arm was retracting and opening to free itself of the useless piece of metal. The Weyland-Yutani ship was going to try again.

"*Elkins, get this thing moving!*" Alec called through the comm system. He reached the airlock door and smacked a gloved hand on the button to open it. The door slid open and Alec took Siobhan's arm as he floated inside.

"*Siobhan—*" Kira's little voice came over the comms. "*Look out!*"

Alec pulled Siobhan into the airlock and slammed a hand on another button, and the outer door began to slide shut. She looked back on the diminishing sliver of outer space just in time to see a flash of bright light that, moments later, impacted with the spot where they had been, knocking the ship back. Alec hit the button to repressurize the airlock.

"*What was that?*" Alec asked.

"*They're firing on you,*" Elkins said in that same tightly calm voice he'd used in the APC. "*Don't worry, I'm getting us out of here.*"

They felt a vibration begin to run beneath their feet. When the airlock chamber had repressurized, they hurriedly took off the space suits and made their way back to the bridge.

Gavin and Sam, still asleep, had been strapped into the side chairs near the big star map, and Kira was sitting in Sam's chair on his side of the dashboard, belted in and studying a flat dashboard monitor which had constructed a 3-D view of the *Demeter*. The image's retraction arm was swinging toward the back of their ship.

"It's getting ready, Kenny," she said, waving distractedly at Siobhan and Alec. A moment later, the 3-D arm shot forward.

"I'm on it, little co-pilot," Elkins said from Gavin's chair, and the *Astraeus* moved forward too. There was a groan of metal as the arm grazed the hull but found nothing onto which it could clamp. The 3-D image of the arm retracted, sliding in the other direction.

"They're trying again," Kira said.

Siobhan and Alec reached them at the dashboard.

"What can I do to help?" Alec asked Elkins.

"Hold on," Elkins replied. "I don't exactly know—"

The ship catapulted ahead with such force that it knocked Alec and Siobhan to the floor. Elkins maneuvered over the part of the *Demeter* still visible in front of them. Another flash of light connected with the back side of the ship and shook it violently. Elkins held tight to the wheel and pulled far ahead of the *Demeter*.

They were moving fast.

The stars ahead became a blur.

Alec looked to Siobhan, who had crawled toward the star map table and was using it to pull herself up.

"You okay?" she asked Alec. He nodded.

"Just glad to be moving," he replied with a smile. "Nice work out there."

She returned the smile. "Thanks. You, too."

"Siobhan, I'm helping Kenny!"

"I see that," Siobhan replied, making her way over to the girl.

"She's actually really good at this," Elkins said with genuine appreciation. "She's taking to it like a fish to water."

"What's a fish?" Kira asked, and Kenny laughed.

"Her warning may very well have saved my life," Siobhan said, hugging the girl around the shoulders.

"Can I be a Colonial Marine when I grow up?" Kira asked Elkins.

"The marines would be proud to have you," he replied.

Alec joined Elkins at the dashboard. "Good hustle, man. Any word from Roots?"

"Not yet, Sarge."

"I should go find him," Alec said.

"*Vaya con Dios*," Elkins added. "Isn't that what your people used to say?"

"Not bad," Alec said with a small smile. "Not bad at all."

2 1

Roots crept silently down the hall, gun in hand.

He'd checked Dr. Fowler's room, but the mad scientist hadn't been there, so Roots had moved on to the medbay. No luck there, either. The ship wasn't that big, maybe two-hundred-fifty or two-hundred-sixty meters at best. Fowler had to be somewhere, and given the fact that there was another, larger Weyland-Yutani ship nearby, Roots thought Fowler might be heading for the emergency escape pods.

Part of him thought that if Fowler wanted to leave, so be it. Taking himself out with the trash would be doing Roots and everyone else on board a favor. An order was an order, though, and another part of him— the part built from experience and instinct—told him that letting Fowler get away would be a gross oversight. He wasn't sure if it was the idea that Fowler might take something crucial with him if he left, or that he might leave something terrible behind. Either way, it seemed smart to keep the scientist with them.

The way Fowler went to such lengths to keep himself alive, maybe he knew something the rest of them didn't, at least about surviving in the wake of contact with the Xenomorphs.

The emergency escape pods were on the lower deck of the ship. A metal ladder led down into a gloomy silence below him. Ever since his stint on Nungal, he'd developed a distinct unease of lower decks, along with his dislike for synthetics. He wouldn't have said he was afraid of either, exactly; he preferred to think of it as a healthy and well-placed mistrust.

It would figure, finding Fowler down there in the dark. The guy was going to be a pain in the ass to the very end.

Roots dropped as silently as he could to the metal floor beneath the ladder. The hull curved up and around him and he shivered. Faint running lights illuminated a path leading toward the emergency pods. His eyes adjusted to the gloom, and he moved quickly.

Fowler's back was to Roots.

The door to the escape pod had been lifted, and the scientist was busy securing a small, refrigerated bag into one of the compartments.

"Going somewhere, Doctor?"

Fowler jumped at the sound of Roots's voice. He straightened and turned, and Roots could see that his brow was beaded with sweat.

"PFC Rutiani. Hello."

Roots tapped the edge of the pod doorway with his gun. "You thinking of leaving us?"

"Well, as you may have noticed, my ride is here. So, if you don't mind—"

"Actually, I do mind," Roots responded, getting between Fowler and the escape pod door. "I've got orders to bring you back and confine you to your cabin."

Fowler sighed. "Honestly, why do you care at this point? You have no use for me—I know that. Can't you just let me go?"

"Sorry, no can do. See, if we could trust you," Roots said, "I mean, not to lie to us, try to abandon us, drug the crew, feed us to your alien pets, or whatever else you might be thinking, well then, hell, we already would have thrown you a going-away party. But we can't trust you."

The expression on Fowler's face changed. There was something desperate there, something like genuine fear.

"I really think," Fowler said, "that it would be better for all of us if I just leave. Please, just let me leave."

"You can tell your friends on the big ship that they can pick you up on LV-846, just like we planned."

"I have no friends on that ship," Fowler said flatly.

"I'm surprised," Roots replied, pushing Fowler in the direction of the metal ladder, "what with your sparkling personality and all."

"No, I mean, it's an automated ship, the *Demeter*. A new Weyland-Yutani design, a completely robo-piloted recon vehicle. I don't think they're even using synthetics on board anymore."

"So, can't you tell the ship's piloting system to meet you?"

Fowler was quiet for several seconds.

"I don't know how," he said finally.

Roots considered this for a moment, then said, "You're worried. You think sending a ship like that means they don't care about coming to get you, don't you? That they can't be bothered to send people to make sure nothing goes wrong." Fowler didn't answer until they reached the bottom of the ladder. There, he turned again.

"Last chance. Let me go."

"Not gonna do that," Roots said.

"You should know, then, that I'm carrying—"

Just then, the ship lurched forward, knocking both of them down. Roots shook his head and looked up to see Fowler scurrying up the ladder. He jumped to his feet and followed, reaching out to grab hold of Fowler's pants leg as the other man emerged on the main deck. Fowler stumbled, giving Roots a chance to finish his climb as well, but then Fowler was jogging down the hall.

"If you run, I'll shoot you," Roots shouted after him. "So help me God, I'll shoot you right here."

Fowler ignored him. Another sudden jerking of the ship sent them stumbling, giving Roots a chance to close the distance. Fowler turned, stomped on Roots's bad foot, and took off down the hall.

Cursing under his breath, Roots tumbled after him, considering through the haze of pain the outcome of shooting the man. He managed to chase the scientist down one hallway and halfway through another before a blister on the top side of his foot split open and a sharp bolt flared across the flesh. He continued to limp as best he could, but Fowler was too fast.

Just as the scientist was about to round the next corner, though, Sarge appeared and shoved the muzzle of his gun toward Fowler's chest. The man skidded to a stop, putting his hands up.

"All right, all right. I'm not going anywhere... obviously."

"You okay, Roots?" Sarge called over Fowler's shoulder. His eyes, beneath the glare of his knitted brow, never left the man.

"Fucker stomped on my foot," Roots said, stumbling toward them.

"Dr. Fowler, we're going to escort you back to your cabin now," Alec said. "And you're going to stay there until we land."

Roots and Sarge walked Fowler back to his room in relative silence. Fowler must have given up trying to convince the men to let him go. In fact, he seemed unusually resigned. Roots didn't trust it. When they reached the cabin, he confiscated Fowler's key and did a sweep for anything Fowler might use to get into trouble. After pocketing a few items he had seen the prisoners on Nungal use for weapons, he and Alec locked their prisoner there, and headed back to the bridge.

When Alec and Roots returned to the bridge, Gavin and Sam were awake and at their stations. Siobhan had seen them stir about ten minutes before, and had given them some coffee and boosts of stabilizers to counteract their sedation hangovers and shortness of breath. She and Elkins had just finished explaining what had happened to the groggy men.

"Are you okay?" Alec asked as he joined them at the dashboard.

"Got a wicked headache," Gavin said, manning the controls.

"If I see that bastard," Sam said, "I'll kill him."

"He's locked in his room," Roots said. "I've got first watch over him tonight."

The blasts from the *Demeter* had done damage. This became increasingly evident over the next two days. While Alec, Elkins, and Roots took turns making sure Fowler stayed put, Gavin and Sam worked on compensating for the damage to the navigation, fueling, and steering systems.

By the time they entered LV-846's star system, though, the ship was shaking badly. Gavin had to lean on the steering lever to keep it on course, and they had lost more than three-quarters of their fuel.

When the planet came into view, Siobhan was relieved. She may not have understood the ins and outs of running a ship, but she didn't need to. She could feel the trembling, the hitches in its forward movement. In some ways it was like standing on the surface of BG-791 again, with everything around her and under her feet threatening to give way and fall apart.

Gavin and Sam prepared to orbit the planet. In the front viewport, Siobhan could see the black of space growing lighter as the corona of LV-846's atmosphere came into view.

"It's going to be a rough one," Gavin said. "Strap in."

Siobhan and the others took the seats lining the sides of the bridge. The star map flickered on the table, winking in and out. A few minutes later, the lights on the bridge followed suit, and the shaking caused by damage to the navigation systems was compounded as the highest layers of atmosphere swirled around them.

"Looks like we've got an electromagnetic storm brewing down there," Sam said. "It's wreaking havoc with our controls."

"Can't wait it out," Gavin replied. "No more fuel."

"Are we gonna crash?" Kira asked.

"Not if I can help it, little lady," Gavin said.

"Don't worry," Elkins reassured her, reaching out to squeeze her hand. "They know what they're doing."

"Better than you?" Kira sounded skeptical.

Elkins chuckled. "Way better than me."

The ship rattled hard, and Siobhan felt her teeth grinding together. Every muscle tightened as they descended into the EM storm. She had never liked re-entering an atmosphere, even on planets where the weather was always mild. Something about the shift from space to sky made her uneasy, and a little nauseous. She didn't mind being above the clouds or below them, but had never much enjoyed the transition.

In storms, it was so much worse.

Lightning flashed outside the front window. Droplets of water pounded the glass. All Siobhan could see were gray smears of cloud; she couldn't fathom how Gavin and Sam could manage to pilot a ship through all that, safely to the ground. But then, she supposed, that was what Elkins had meant. It was one thing to fly a ship like the *Astraeus*. It was something else entirely to land it.

"Captain, I'm picking up a distress signal from below," Sam said. "It… it's not going out on military and government channels. I'm not sure how it's transmitting at all. LV-846 is a private military complex—the security protocols should have squashed this transmission before it ever left the surface."

"Some kind of breach," Gavin agreed. "I hear it."

"What is that code?" Alec called. "That's not USCMC."

Sam listened a moment to the series of beeps and tones that grew increasingly louder over their comm system, then shook his head.

"It's... Grant code, and it's repeating—a loop." The Grant code system had replaced the ancient and archaic Morse code—Siobhan had learned that from Alec—and it was, in her opinion, exceedingly more complicated. It had originated with pirates and scavengers who used it to locate, transport, and trade illegal goods across the galaxy. While the military were trained in deciphering it, it was still primarily used by independent shippers and traders.

Alec and his men listened, as well.

Roots frowned. "Isn't that...?"

"An attack, I think," Alec said. "Right, Sam?

"Not attack... that's code for 'infection'... no, wait. Sorry. That's 'infestation.' God, what the hell happened down there?"

Siobhan's blood ran cold. "Can we respond and ask what's going on?" She looked to each of the men, but they were concentrating on the sounds, pulling secret meaning out of what sounded to her like some weird middle ground between music and noise.

"No one to ask," Sam said. "That signature there... hear that? That means it's a recording re-looping, which is done when there are no living people—at least not within range of the broadcasting area."

"Doesn't mean there's no one left at all," Gavin added, "but... it's not a good sign. Like Sam said, the security down there is tight. Unauthorized messages should have been stopped immediately. So should unauthorized ships. No one's hailed us to ask why we're in orbit or ask for our authorization code. And no one's shot at us—that's even more surprising."

"There's a time stamp on this message," Sam said, "from a few days ago. *Damn it.*" He sighed, fiddling with a few controls on his end of the dashboard. "The storm's interference is blotting out a lot of the message, but—wait, that was 'conference center.' And 'summit'—I think this is originating from the summit meeting down there."

"Damn," Gavin said. "Now, that's really not a good sign—for anybody."

Siobhan's chest felt tight. Gavin was grasping the greater truth. Under the best of circumstances, tensions at the summit would be high, governments would be wary of one another, and any number of terrorist threats or violence could upset a balance crucial for the continued safety of countless colonies all across the galaxy. Of course, it made sense that security protocols would block unauthorized travel to and from the planet, as well as outgoing messages. Under such circumstances, it would have made sense to just shoot the *Astraeus* down outright…

Unless there was a bigger problem than political tension.

If the distress signal had originated days ago, however, that meant the summit had barely gotten under way before whatever occurred had provided the incentive for the distress. Had they communicated the trouble to Earth? Was help on the way?

A sudden violent jolt shook the ship, causing Siobhan to bite her lip, and then they were through the upper layers of the atmosphere. Gray sky around them gave way to a view of the planet below.

Much of LV-846 was a temperate or subtropical zone, with huge, sprawling fields of green and few mountains. There were some central jungles where both plant and animal life flourished. Under other circumstances, Siobhan would have found the place fascinating, from a professional point of view, but at that moment she was afraid—of the storms, of the distinct lack of a platform to land a ship, and because her instinct told her that the situation down there was bad. Very bad. They *were* an unauthorized ship, after all. Why wasn't anyone trying to stop them?

"Hold on," Gavin said, and the ship brushed the tops of some jungle trees. Siobhan could hear the engine sputtering. The landing gear was stuck.

One of the few and far between rocky hills came into view, and Gavin had to practically stand on the steering lever to keep the bottom of the ship from clipping the rock. The ground came up very fast—so much so that Siobhan flinched when she saw it.

The front of the ship dipped. Gavin pulled back on the wheel and it righted itself just as the landing site for the Pushan Conference Center reared up from the ground.

"Platform," Sam muttered.

"See it," Gavin answered. The ship touched down, bounced hard, and shivered in the air. Kira squeezed her eyes closed. Elkins gripped her hand.

"Come on, you bastard," Gavin muttered, slamming a lever forward. The landing gear lowered just as the ship met the ground, and the whole of the *Astraeus* slid along the platform, past the conference center and toward a net of dense, jungle-like trees. There was a flurry of green foliage which suddenly covered the window, accompanied by the tearing of massive leaves and vines.

Then the ship came to a stop.

For a moment, no one spoke. Siobhan could almost hear the collective beating of their pounding hearts. Gavin turned in his chair. His expression was unperturbed, as usual, but sweat slicked his forehead and neck.

"Everyone okay back there?"

"Fine," Alec said, and the others echoed the same.

"That was some fine flying," Elkins offered with genuine appreciation in his voice.

"That was luck," Sam said, giving Gavin a sideways smile.

The pilot chuckled. His laugh, like his expressions and inclination to chat, was minimal. "Got the job done," he said.

"Certainly did," Sam agreed. "What say y'all to stretching our legs and finding out what happened to our welcoming committee?"

2 2

The storm that had been brewing in the upper stratosphere resulted in thunderous skies, flashes of lightning, and clouds which emptied a downpour of rain for about ten minutes, then stopped. When Sam opened the ship's outer door and they filed out, the air still crackled with energy.

The atmosphere of LV-846 was hot and humid, but breathable. The twin suns around which the planet revolved were high in the sky, but remnant clouds obscured most of the glare.

Though Siobhan was glad to stretch her legs, almost instantly she began to sweat. Relief in the form of an occasional breeze blew across her skin. After the staleness of the doomed moon's terraformed atmosphere and the regulated environment of the ship, it felt good, however heavy, to breathe a planet's real air.

It also felt good to plant her feet firmly on ground that wasn't moving or crumbling. Whatever had happened on this planet, whatever they would encounter going forward, for the moment, Siobhan was glad for what she had. Still, she clutched the flamethrower from Weyland-Yutani's underground storage room. The looping distress signal, according to Sam, came from somewhere nearby, and Siobhan wasn't taking any chances.

Alec joined her, shielding his eyes from the new light, followed by Kira. Roots and Elkins emerged with Fowler. Behind the scientist, the two crewmen glared at the back of his head.

"No welcoming committee, I see," Fowler muttered.

No one answered. From the ship, the complex where the Pushan Conference Center was located looked devoid of movement, as did the central building itself. No one milled about or moved between the housing and business areas. No one sat eating lunch on the benches that lined the wide walkway or strolling the landscaped garden areas out front. No marines with guns swarmed across the complex to arrest them all.

"It's awfully quiet," Roots said, glancing around.

"This place should be crawling with people," Elkins added. "Marines, local law enforcement, government paper-pushers, reporters, the works. Where are—"

Then they saw the bodies.

It looked as if a number of people had tried to flee into the surrounding jungle. A woman in business clothes hung from a high limb of a tree, tangled in vines. She was missing a shoe. Her blonde hair, coated in blood, hung in her face. A trio of badly contorted bodies, their backs and limbs broken, looked as if they had been tossed hard against the trunks of trees.

Another woman in a military uniform had been torn in half; the upper portion of her looked as if it had tried to crawl to the tree line, while the lower portion lay twisted among some shrubs. A number of men had been clawed or chewed on, their chests raked open, eyes glazed and mouths slack. One man's bottom jaw had been torn off.

As they approached the complex itself, they found several more bodies. A man and a woman, also dressed in military uniforms, bore the insignias of high rank on their chests and shoulders. The woman's scalp had been torn clear off her head, and most of her hair lay in a bloody heap next to her slumped body. The man's face had been caved in.

"Who did this?" Roots asked. "Why didn't the Colonial Marines stop it?"

"Maybe it has something to do with that," Gavin said, gesturing.

The others followed his nod and gaze toward a crashed ship. It was a Conestoga-class frigate, a massive bulk of dark gray metal with an antenna that had been crushed, evidently on impact. Siobhan could see the name of the ship, the *Alexiares*, painted near the rear, in the part still protruding from the ground. Beneath it was the USCMC insignia, the four white stars with red and white stripes. Beneath that was stenciled the logo of the ship's manufacturer, Lunnar-Welsun Industries.

"Shit, Sarge—that's one of ours," Roots said. He jogged toward the ship.

"Roots, wait," Alec called, but Elkins had already taken off after his squad mate, so Alec followed suit. Fowler, seeing an opportunity to break away, turned to run, but Gavin and Sam each caught an arm, and the rest of the group headed after the marines.

When they reached the downed ship, Siobhan could see that the door had been torn off, the doorframe bent outward, as if there had been an outpouring of hate from within. She thought there very likely had been—long claw marks were gouged along the sides of the opening. Her heart sank. She had seen those marks too many times in the last week not to feel an absolute dread at seeing them now.

The marines saw them as well, and drew their weapons.

Alec motioned silently for Roots and Elkins to take one side of the opening while he took the other. He silently counted to three, and the marines swung around the doorframe to the inside of the ship, guns ready. They paused a moment in the shadowed interior, their bodies tense. There was no sound, except for the faint chirping of bird-like creatures deep in the surrounding jungle.

Leaning out of the doorway, Alec said, "We're going to check it out. Von, can you stay here with them? Guard them in case... well, in case."

"Got it," she said. "Be careful."

He winked at her, then ducked back into the ship.

They were gone for about an hour, during which Siobhan's group said little. She scanned the tree line of the jungle and the building complex, both several yards away. Watching for movement, she listened for the telltale chitter-purring, or those almost-metallic screeches, but there were no signs of Xenomorphs that she could pick up.

"It's oppressively hot out here," Fowler said at one point, and Siobhan noticed the sweat pouring down the sides of the man's face. He was deeply flushed and, given the way he was hugging himself around the middle, appeared to be in some pain.

"Are you okay?" she asked, frowning. "You don't look so good."

"It's the heat," he replied, gesturing to the shade of a nearby tree with large, frond-like leaves. "May I sit?"

"Sure," she said. "Go ahead. We can all sit in the shade."

The group migrated to the spot beneath the tree where it was, she had to admit, markedly cooler. There they sat down, Gavin on one side of their prisoner and Sam on the other. They weren't about to lose track of the scientist who had drugged them.

"How much longer do you think they'll be?" Fowler asked, absently rubbing his stomach.

"I don't know," Siobhan said. She was about to hazard a guess when the marines emerged from the hole in the ship, crossing the grass to the shady spot where they rested. Their expressions were grim. Siobhan stood up, concerned.

"What is it?" she asked Alec. "What did you find?"

Elkins shook his head. Roots looked pale.

"The ship is empty. No Xenomorphs. No marines—at least, no living ones. We found a lot of blood, and a ship's log. You—you have to see the ship's log." Alec's voice was dull, as if a profound shock had knocked the feeling from it.

Siobhan touched his arm. "Are you okay?"

The shadow in his eyes deepened. "I'll show you."

The group followed the marines back onto the ship. Immediately, Siobhan could see the devastation. Metal plates had been torn from the walls and floors, wires sparked where they hung from the ceilings, and doors hung off-kilter from their tracks. There were splatters of blood everywhere, as well as abandoned boots and torn uniforms. The occasional dead marine sat slumped against a wall or lay on the floor. The bodies had been mauled, but the marks were different from those on the bodies at the Menhit Lab. There seemed to be many more of them, but the cuts were shallower.

"What happened here?" she wondered aloud.

The marines didn't answer. They simply led the way through one hallway to the bridge, across that to another hallway, and down to the sleeping quarters. The ship captain's room was down a small side corridor, set apart—

along with the first mate's—from the rest of the marines. It was here, in front of the open door, that Alec stopped.

"Captain's log, moved offline," Alec said, "when she decided it was no longer safe to log official records."

He gestured for them to enter and they filed in, moving toward the desk by the bed. On it was a computer and monitor, the latter showing a woman with bright green eyes and black hair pulled into a neat bun. She had a pretty smile. She wore the uniform of the USCMC ship captain. The image was paused, and everyone gathered around the monitor.

Alec said, "Play," and the video started.

"Captain's record, Thursday, July 5th, 2187, Earth-time. This is Captain Angela Forrester of the USS Alexiares. Happy belated Independence Day to those who celebrate it on Earth! We've been given a prestigious assignment by Assistant Commandant General Vaughn—to provide security detail for the UAAC Joint Chiefs at this week's summit meeting on LV-846. It should take us about six days to get there. We have been given important cargo to deliver, as well, to facilitate the summit meeting. The squads here have been training for weeks, and are prepared for the assignment. We are all proud to be part of this historic event—"

"Forward," Alec said, and the video sped forward. "Play."

"Captain's record, Sunday, July 8th, 2187." The captain sat at the desk with a glass of wine. She sipped it and said, *"A little more has emerged about the cargo we're carrying. Our*

synthetic, Gene, has been put in charge of its security, since information about the content apparently requires a higher security clearance than any of us possess. My understanding is that it's research and supporting materials on the pathogen used to bomb the colonies.

"The bomb signatures apparently contain some evidence as to who may be responsible for them—which is the primary item on the agenda for the summit. There's proof in the research that neither the UA nor the UPP is responsible. I have high hopes that this crucial information will provide the necessary common ground for peace—"

"Forward," Alec said, then, after a moment, "Pause." He turned to address the group. "The next several entries are basic ship management stuff, but then we come to this. Play."

The video resumed. The captain was wearing nightclothes and a bathrobe. Her hair was down. This didn't seem to Siobhan like an official entry. The captain looked concerned, leaning in confidentially.

"Captain's private record. New information has come to light. The supplies that ACG Vaughn has ordered us to deliver to LV-846 are actually…" She took a breath. *"Weapons. Bio-weapons. None of us has been given clearance as to the details. In fact, the only reason we know what's stored on the lower decks is because of a minor malfunction with the synthetic, Gene. He apologized for the glitch and went to perform self-maintenance."* She pinched the bridge of her nose and sighed. *"I'm not comfortable with bio-weapons on my ship.*

We should have been notified if we were carrying the pathogen. Nothing has been said to the squads because we don't want to cause panic. Many of them have seen colonies that were destroyed by pathogen bombs. And to be fair, it can't be said for sure what's down there. But Gene used the term 'bio-weapon' and... I don't like it. There's no valid reason we should be transporting any kind of weapons to a peace summit."

She sighed. *"I intend to see for myself what's down there. It means breaking protocol, but something is wrong here. I don't think—"*

Alec said, "Forward," and the video fast-forwarded. In double-time, Siobhan saw the woman visibly deteriorate.

"Play," Alec said. The video resumed.

The woman looked exhausted. Long strands of dark hair had escaped her usual bun, and she no longer wore the uniform. There were bags under her eyes and her skin looked very pale.

"Captain's private record. It's worse than I thought," she said. *"The cargo in the lower deck isn't guns, and not even the pathogen. It's... something else."* She leaned in toward the computer's camera. *"There isn't much time, so this will have to be fast, before..."* She glanced over her shoulder as if expecting someone to walk in at any moment. Then she continued. *"Gene's continued breakdown has been very illuminating. Apparently, the... things... down there are called biodrones. Genetically engineered killing machines, dozens of them, and... they got out. I think... it looks as if Gene let them out."*

Her eyes filled with tears, and that frightened Siobhan more than anything they'd seen to this point.

"We've been orbiting LV-846 for a day now. There isn't enough fuel to fly anywhere else. Gene destroyed all the escape pods, as well as the other vehicles on the ship." She bowed her head. From beneath the strands of her hair came a voice choked with tears. *"There were two thousand, one hundred and three marines on this ship. Men and women with families. Sons and daughters. I'm not sure how many are left. Our guns only make it worse, with the corrosive substance they have for blood."*

Siobhan felt a lump in her throat.

The captain's voice dropped down to a whisper. *"I think I'm going to have to crash the ship. Destroy it entirely.*

"I suspect Assistant Commandant General Vaughn knew all along what we were carrying. What would happen. I don't know if she meant to take out the security guarding the Joint Chiefs, or if she meant for us to bring this infestation right to the door of the conference center itself, but I'm sure she is involved. I can't prove it, but it seems impossible that she wasn't aware of what we have in our cargo hold. I'm going to upload a backup of this recording to a safe place in case—"

On the video, there was a loud, metallic *bang*.

She turned sharply at the sound.

"They're coming," she said to the camera, and reached over to shut it off. The screen went dark.

"That's it," Alec said. "There's nothing after that."

For several long minutes, no one said anything.

"Guys, I'm so sorry. That's awful." The lump in Siobhan's throat threatened to choke her up.

"That's fucked up," Gavin said.

"ACG Vaughn actually planned for more than two thousand marines to die. She sent them on their way with a death sentence, and didn't even tell them what they were in it for." Roots shook his head. "My buddy Carlisle was on this assignment."

"So Vaughn put these—these *biodrones*, whatever they are, on the ship, hoping to, what, sabotage the summit meeting?" Elkins asked. "Why? Why would she do that?"

"Take control of the Allied Command, maybe," Sam said. "Then she could use the combined force of the Colonial Marines, Aerospace, Army, and Navy any way she wants—for *whoever* she wants."

"That would give Vaughn a lot of power," Alec said. "Maybe a lot of money."

"What are they?" Gavin asked. "The biodrones, I mean. According to that video, they sound worse than the pathogen bombs. And if so, we need to get off this rock faster than we did your dying moon."

Fowler cleared his throat. "You're right... they're not bombs. Not exactly."

They all looked at him.

"Of course you'd know something about this," Roots said.

"I can shed some light, yes," Fowler said. Despite sitting in the shade, he looked even more flushed, and was clutching his stomach. "The biodrones were a result of Project Life Force."

"Project Life Force?" Siobhan felt that unease again in her stomach, and thought of the scratches on the side of the marines' transport ship.

"A Weyland-Yutani bio-weapons division initiative. I worked under Dr. N.L. Babak, who served as lead Xenomorphologist for the project. His goal, as it was relayed to his team, was to manipulate the genetics of the XX121s and create a subdivision of the species that could be controlled."

"Wait, wait, wait—this was the project you were working on?" Alec asked. "On BG-791? The experiments with the Xenomorphs?"

"No, no. Project Life Force came before that, and was quite different. The goal was to develop something *other* than the Xenomorphs, like I said, using their DNA. Something we could control. Babak was convinced that killing machines as perfect as the Xenomorphs had to have been genetically engineered by some greater intelligence, and if they could be created, they could be *re*created.

"Making them in the lab was the easy part," he continued. "Our research focused on ways to enhance certain traits and eradicate others, to make them manageable. Primarily, that meant manipulating their physical development on a genetic level. Their maturation was controlled, their reproductive ability halted, and their life spans reduced to six days. You know, it was from some of this research that I was able to develop my own serum—"

"Get back to the biodrones," Alec snapped.

"Right. So, Babak and our team were successful at least in creating this variation of the Xenomorphs. We called them XX121Bs—our own biodrones. We designed them to mimic the Xenomorph drones in almost every way, except for our... improvements. The biodrones are similar in appearance, but a little smaller, a little faster. Not quite as strong, but just as fatal, and ideally, dead in just under a week.

"Problem was, our improvements—it turned out—were neither reliable nor consistent. The biodrones—well, I can't say for sure if they evolved or devolved or what, but they didn't die in six days, like we'd planned. Their ovomorphing reflex, which we failed to take in to account, provided an end run around their reproductive and maturation limitations. And they were surprisingly hostile to the natural Xenomorphs, so much so that we had to keep the samples—the originals and our recreations—strictly segregated. Where we had hoped to apply the technology for military purposes—such as to removing strategic targets without subsequent infestation—there, our efforts failed."

"Strategic targets?" Alec raised an eyebrow.

"Military targets."

"Whose?"

"Babak's team wasn't given that information. We had theories, of course. The pathogen bombings were all the newswires were covering back then. UA and UPP tensions were high, rumors were flying—and military contracts were pouring in."

"So what happened?" Elkins's expression revealed his disgust, and his question was more an accusation.

"I'm not sure. Only some of the experimentation had been completed when I was reassigned to the Menhit Lab to work on… other things. From what I've heard, the remaining samples were sold off, and—"

"Samples? You mean the biodrones? They were *sold off*?" Siobhan felt the horror of that implication. "Who bought them?"

Dr. Fowler shrugged, looking toward the conference center.

"I think the answer to that is obvious, isn't it, Dr. McCormick?"

2 3

They were all quiet as they made their way back to the *Astraeus*. The horror of what the video imparted weighed on each of them.

Siobhan had so many questions.

Where were the bodies of the marines from the USS *Alexiares*? Had the biodrones consumed them? Dragged them back to a hive somewhere? And what, exactly, were they up against with these creatures?

They were stranded on LV-846, at least until a distress call reached some government agency that would send help. Further, they might well be stranded there with dozens of creatures nearly as bad as the Xenomorphs they had just escaped.

She couldn't help thinking that their flight had been mostly luck. Few people encountered Xenomorphs and survived once, let alone more than once. She didn't think anyone had ever survived an onslaught of dozens... except Alec.

Siobhan looked at him. When he noticed her staring, he looked back and tried to smile. He was gutted, though, by what he had seen in that video.

Finally, Alec spoke. "Only thing I've ever seen the Xenomorph drones respond to is a Queen. Maybe we should've brought one of those along from your lab. Or at least some of the Xenomorphs. Make it a fair fight."

Fowler was uncharacteristically silent. He had grown pale, and the hand that wasn't clutching his stomach trembled as he wiped his sweating brow.

"Dr. Fowler..." she began.

"I'm fine." He waved away her concern before she could express it.

"You don't look fine," Elkins said.

"What's going on with you?" Alec stopped the man.

Fowler sighed. "No sense now in hiding it," he said. "I'm going to die either way."

"Die? What do you mean?" Alec stepped away from him.

"My serum," he replied. "Cora wasn't the only one who took it. When I woke up in the lab, after the initial outbreak, I... I thought maybe..."

He shook his head.

"We'd all been out for hours. I knew what the Xenomorph's primary biological goals were. Of course I did, and I knew they'd left me alone, let me live, because... I'm carrying one of them inside me." He winced and clutched his stomach. "Weyland-Yutani wasn't about to shell out millions of credits on the word of one man, even if he had been prominently involved in Project Life Force. Maybe *because* he had. They wanted something bold, something that would prove to them my serum was worth the funding.

"So even before the outbreak, I implanted one of the Xenomorph embryos inside me, and then I took the serum. When the Company learned that I was still alive after the usual gestation period, they were thrilled. They poured more money into my work, and every day I showed proof of life—evidence of the success of my serum. When the… ahhh, the outbreak happened, I knew outside interference would be a problem, so I stopped our synthetic from sending his distress call.

"But then I saw the devastation at the lab," he continued, "found Cora, and, well, I resumed the distress call transmission. It was the only way—for me and for Cora. For the corporation—it was the only way."

"You…" Siobhan couldn't finish. Not only had this man prevented his own people from receiving outside help—probably to protect the corporation's secrets—but he had also set her up, along with her team.

"The serum's worked better on me than Cora, obviously, but we're close—*really* close—to the end of my three weeks. You've successfully managed to thwart every attempt I've made to get to Weyland-Yutani and their medical personnel, before this thing eats its way out of me." He strained with the evident pain in his stomach. "It's a Queen, you know, and it's almost time."

"Oh my God," Siobhan said, her voice reduced to a whisper. "What have you done?"

"We should have killed you on the platform," Elkins said.

"We could kill him now," Roots suggested.

"Won't do any good," Fowler said through gritted teeth. "She's coming whether you kill me or not."

Alec raised a gun to Fowler's gut. "Not if I can help it."

Fowler backed away toward the convention center. "Roots was right, you know. Only a Xenomorph—a Queen—would stand a chance against the biodrones. I'm carrying the only weapon you've got. If you kill me, you're killing yourselves."

Alec hesitated, and Fowler took that moment to dart toward the building. Alec fired at him, but he dodged to the left and then sprinted until he reached the doors. They saw him yank the door open, slip inside, and then stumble out of view.

"Should we go after him, Sarge?" Roots gestured with his gun.

"Wait," Siobhan said. "Please." She looked around at the surprised faces and said, "As much as I hate to admit it, and as crazy as it sounds, Fowler is right. We don't stand a chance against dozens of biodrones—enough to kill a ship full of marines. We need something to even the odds for us. I'd rather take on one Queen than thirty drones, wouldn't you?"

"Having seen a Queen," Alec said softly, "I think it's debatable."

Siobhan nodded. "Even so, we're outnumbered. We're stranded. We're tired and hungry, and we're down two marines and several civilians. This planet appears to be prone to sudden, violent electrical storms," she said, looking up at the gray clouds gathering again, "and I keep coming back to something Fowler told us. He said the biodrones are hostile to the Xenomorphs. If we let them fight Fowler's Queen, maybe they'll kill each other off, and the problem is solved from both sides."

"I don't know, Siobhan," Alec said. "It seems very risky."

"It is, but honestly, I don't see any other way," Siobhan replied. "If we can verify that there are, in fact, biodrones inside the conference center, I think this Queen is our only real solution."

"I think Dr. McCormick is right," Gavin said. "For what it's worth. You go in, verify there are drones that haven't died off, then you let them and the Queen wear each other out. Whoever's left will be much weaker—tired or hurt, maybe—and then you swoop in and kill whatever has survived."

"I'm with the captain," Sam agreed.

Alec looked from Siobhan to the crew to his own men, then back to Siobhan.

"Okay. But let's make sure there are actually biodrones still left in there, okay?"

"And while we're in there, we can switch off the recording and send a live distress call along the same channels," Sam said.

"Let's do it," Siobhan said, clutching the flamethrower. "Alec, lead the way."

Martin Fowler felt the first tearing of his internal organs just as he reached one of the conference rooms, a boxy white space with a cool gray carpet, bright lights, and a digital whiteboard against the wall by the door. To Fowler, the room itself was a blur somewhere outside the pain. It felt like there was a knife of fire inside his chest, slicing into him.

The Queen was coming.

He staggered to and around the central conference table, a massive piece of furniture cut from the wood of the surrounding jungle, carved with the gods of the colonists' ancestors. Once it might have fascinated Fowler, that touch of ancient history, but in his haze of agony, it just felt to him like rough wood. He tried to pull himself to a chair but the need to vomit overtook him, and he violently threw up the blood that had been pooling in his stomach.

His knees buckled, and he clapped the table for balance as another round of burning pain sliced across his midsection. She was big, very big by the feel of it. His hands, then his arms, then his whole body began to spasm, jerking him up and away from the table. He stumbled backward and hit a corner of the walls, sliding to the floor. The pain was excruciating, exquisite in its intensity. His body shook.

A split opened up in his chest. Quickly, it tore down the length of his torso to his stomach. He felt the ribs along it crack and snap, the sound as full and loud in his skull as it was outside of it. A bloody head, elongated and eyeless, with a crown of bony spikes in the back, emerged from the split in his skin. He tried to raise his hands to grab the creature, to strangle it, but his arms wouldn't move. It wormed its way out of him, climbing onto what was left of his ruined chest and straddling the hole there, the claws of its feet gripping the edges of rib bone as it stalked toward his face.

Fowler tried to form the word *die*, but couldn't get more than a blood-misted exhale past his lips. The creature opened its mouth, and from within, a tinier mouth thrust outward, chattering at him.

The last thing Dr. Fowler saw before the world went white and then black was that creature, the newly born Xenomorph Queen, leaping onto the table and scurrying off.

They made their way cautiously to the external sliding glass doors, which were closed. Upon opening them, the difference in temperature was immediate; the climate control had set the rooms at a cool 68 degrees. Soft instrumental music played over an overhead speaker.

They saw immediately that the front lobby was empty. No one sat at the front desk or on the sleek couches across from it. No one—at least so far as the arcs allowed vision down the hallway—was traveling to a meeting room.

The Pushan Conference and Business Complex was designed as two large concentric wheels, with the main conference room itself located at the hub, while spokes led to numerous other meeting rooms jutting off the encircling hallways. At the front of the building, in the outermost circle, was a lobby, and beyond it the first spoke leading inward. Hallways also arced to the left and right.

Kira stood close to Elkins, echoing his movements. There had been some discussion about leaving her behind with the *Astraeus*, where it might be safe, but as a group they decided against that. When a Xenomorph was loose, there was no safety except maybe in numbers, and no safe place except with one another. Kira was adamant that she wanted to stay with Elkins, anyway. With him, she felt safe. Her desperation to be near him broke Siobhan's heart in new places.

"We've spent a lot of the last week creeping down hallways," Roots remarked as they moved toward the left-side hallway.

"Running down them, too," Elkins said. "I hope they reassign us to some nice, calm national park. Outdoors. No more tight spaces."

"These are pretty big hallways," Sam said with a small smile.

"No hallway's big enough when the thing you're trying to shoot has acid for blood," Elkins replied.

"Is that what we're up against?" Gavin peered into one of the conference rooms where a door stood open. "That what these biodrones have?"

"Seems like a reasonable assumption," Alec replied. "If they're like the Xenomorphs, they're pretty much deadly inside and out."

They kept moving.

It didn't take long to find Martin Fowler's corpse. The splatter of blood on the walls and ceiling drew their attention to one of the conference rooms on the left, against the outer wall. A splash of blood on the conference table, as well as a bloody handprint, showed that Fowler had probably tried to make it to one of the chairs and collapsed. He had stumbled to the far-right corner of the room and sat there, waiting for the thing to finish eating its way out of him. Most of his chest had burst outward, with bloody, broken ribs bent up like an open cage. Siobhan couldn't help but look inside the empty cavity. The viscera there was shredded, as if by tiny foot-claws scrambling to escape.

Fowler's eyes were open, already cloudy with the cataracts of death. His lower jaw hung limply against his chest. It was a horrible sight, all the more awful somehow because it was becoming a familiar one. Siobhan shook her head. On some level, she felt bad for Fowler. He might have had family, loved ones on some faraway world, though she doubted it. He might even have loved someone else, though she doubted that as well. Still, the part of her that felt sympathy for other human beings could see that it had been a painful and likely terrifying death, a full-circle vengeance of the universe come back to collect.

For that, she felt some pity.

What eclipsed the pity, though, was fear. It was the unspoken fear they were all thinking—that now, a Xenomorph Queen was loose somewhere in the building, and that such a horror might be their only chance to survive.

"The Queen will probably stay in these outer halls until she's matured," Siobhan said. "I think we should go to the central conference room. Given its importance, the walls are likely to be reinforced. If the biodrones chased down the Joint Chiefs and other government officials… well, they would have run there, hoping the walls would keep the biodrones out until help arrived."

"Makes sense to me," Alec said. "Let's go."

They made their way back through the lobby and down the central hall to the inner circle of conference rooms. It was there that the evidence of real carnage began. Blood had dried on many of the walls, and despite the temperature-controlled rooms, the smell of decay was cloying. Much like at the Menhit Lab, the few actual bodies they found were mangled, with dozens of small slashes across the faces, necks, chests, and limbs.

Some had missing arms and legs. Others were missing eyes or whole heads. None had the burst chests, but to Siobhan, that made sense. Unlike the Xenomorphs, the biodrones weren't focused on looking for incubators. They were killing whatever they saw, period. No doubt it was how Fowler and his boss had designed them.

As they covered the last few yards to the central chamber, they began to hear the chittering, faintly at first, from the other side of the double doors. They moved silently, listening for anything on their side of the portal, and anything that might give them a sense of what they were up against on the other side.

Alec and Siobhan moved toward the cool silver metal. Siobhan pressed an ear to it. Alec stood ready with his gun.

Beyond were sounds of movement—a lot of it. The biodrones weren't as quiet as their natural counterparts; maybe, thinking they were the victors, they saw no reason to be. She could hear a series of call-and-response chirps and squeals, anxious and rapid, as if they were communicating. She was pretty sure they didn't have anything so sophisticated as a language, but bees and wasps on Earth communicated with each other, didn't they? Predators of the jungle and the forest organized hunts and warned each other of danger. Crows called out enemies, wolves followed an alpha leader, and hell, some creatures even mimicked the sounds of their prey.

She strained to hear anything that would indicate human survivors—anybody at all who might still be alive in there—but heard nothing to indicate living people. No human voices, no whimpering or whispering, nothing.

If there were no humans inside the room, then it probably wouldn't be long until the biodrones decided to move out of it.

She pulled away from the door and mouthed, *They're in there. I can hear them*, and illustrated with gestures.

Alec mouthed back, *Survivors?*

Siobhan shook her head no. *Biodrones.*

Alec frowned, then nodded. *Okay.* He gestured back the way they'd come. Shortly they rejoined the others.

"Anyone left alive?" Sam whispered, glancing at Kira as if afraid the answer would be too hard for her to hear.

"Doubt it," Alec replied in the same hushed tone. "Siobhan heard the biodrones. I doubt they know how to work those doors, but they had to have a way in. I'd like to get out of here, all the same."

They had just turned to go when the pounding on the double doors began. It thundered through the hallway, and around the sound were squeals of anger and frustration. The pounding went on for a few minutes, during which the group backed away.

Then, abruptly, it stopped.

In the silence that followed, the group froze, listening.

A sudden, sharp squeal from the other side of the door made them jump. It was followed by a loud metallic bang, and then a sizzling sound, like frying bacon—at least, that's what Siobhan thought of at first.

"What the hell is that?" Elkins asked.

A moment later, the sour tang of burning metal met their noses, and then it dawned on Siobhan just what the sizzling sound was.

"It's their blood," she said, both horrified and amazed. "They must have killed one of their own. They're using its blood to melt through the door." As if to verify the theory, a black spot appeared in the center of one of the doors.

"Son of a bitch," Gavin said. He sounded impressed, in spite of himself. The dark stain spread, a cancerous irregular area growing larger and larger until the metal at its center bubbled and disintegrated.

"Run. Now," Alec shouted. "Go!"

They all took off down the corridor.

The sizzling grew louder behind them, and then the spine-jarring sound of hideous squeals came pouring into the hallway. Siobhan slowed and turned, laying down a line of flame between the galloping biodrones and her group. There were so many of them. They looked to her like a rushing river of shining black and gray, a flash flood washing toward her. She cried out, spraying the hallway again with the flamethrower.

The carpet caught, and a phalanx of fire blazed up. Some of the biodrones turned and pulled back. Others ran through or leaped over the flames. Siobhan felt a tug on her arm and turned to see Alec.

"Forget it," he said. "Just run!"

They ran to catch up with the others, farther up the spoke of hallway. Elkins, Roots, and Kira turned down the hallway to the left while Sam and Gavin branched off to the right. She could feel the biodrones behind her, bearing down on her. A claw grazed her back, pulling her hair and slicing its way down her top. She screamed, but wrenched herself forward, away from the thing.

Gunshots from nearby echoed out in the hall; the screams of angry biodrones escalated, their blood hissing and bubbling on the carpet.

Just as she and Alec reached the inner circle of halls, Siobhan heard Sam cry out. She looked to the right to see that he had fallen forward. Three of the creatures immediately leaped onto his back, their razor-edged tails stabbing into him. His screams died quickly, and as they speared his spine over and over, he coughed and sputtered blood.

Gavin slowed and turned to help, but skidded to a stop when he saw the things on top of his co-pilot. He stared, shocked, at the body of his friend, and it only took that single moment for two others to pounce on him, knocking him down.

Alec fired at the things on top of Gavin. He caught the nearer one in the shoulder and its arm jerked back. It turned its head, screaming at him, then raked its clawed hand across Gavin's face. It drew the same hand back and then dug those claws into Gavin's jugular. Blood sprayed up from the wound and covered the biodrone's bony chest.

The creature leaned over the dying man, and its own blood pattered down on Gavin's forehead. Then its head snapped sharply in Alec's direction. Its tail whipped and cracked, then darted at Alec's mid-section. He dodged, but the point caught him in the side of his ribs, poking straight through. It drew back and stabbed again, this time catching Alec in the forearm and then the lower left thigh, by his knee.

Alec's good knee buckled, and he reeled away.

Siobhan stepped between the creature and Alec and turned the flamethrower on it. The wail of the thing was ear-piercing as the flames wrapped around it. It stumbled backward and slammed into the wall before climbing it and taking off in the other direction. The creature next to it seemed to recognize fire as a danger, but also seemed fascinated by its effects. When its fellow biodrone was out of sight, it turned on Siobhan and Alec.

Other biodrones, seeming to discern on some level that the weapon in Siobhan's hand meant fire, crept cautiously toward her and Alec from down the middle spoke of hallway. Those that had killed Sam had noticed, too, and moved like stalking panthers back toward where the pair stood.

She glanced behind her, in the direction the marines and Kira had gone, and saw that the hallway was clear.

"This way!" she shouted, spraying the hallway in front of her with flames. This time, she held the button down until the carpet caught fire, and the creatures hesitated. She got under Alec's arm to support him and they backed away, then turned and ran after Elkins, Kira, and Roots.

2 4

The biodrones screeched and screamed, clamoring over and around each other to close the distance between them and Roots. He had kept stopping to lay down suppressive fire and slow the creatures' pursuit, so Elkins and Kira were a little farther ahead.

The marines and girl had rounded a corner, and a biodrone dropped from the ceiling in front of them. Kira screamed. Elkins opened fire on it, aiming for the smooth curve of its head. The creature jerked with each hit, the wounds unleashing small geysers of particularly acrid blood. It recovered quickly, though, and charged Elkins, grabbing him by the neck with one hand and lifting him off the ground.

His feet kicked, and he smacked at the creature's hand. His face turned red as he gasped for air.

Roots managed to bring down one of the biodrones

and turned just in time to see Kira shout in fury, launching herself at the creature. Her tiny fists pounded its spiked, bony hip, and her voice, high and angry, lashed at the thing with nearly unintelligible words. Roots fired on the creature over Kira's head, but the ammo seemed to just bounce off the creature's bony spikes.

Suddenly, Kira stopped fighting and went silent. It took a moment for Roots to realize she was dangling from the bloody spike of the biodrone's tail. In a moment, she was eye to eye with Elkins, her small face pale, her little lips parted as blood spilled from one corner of her mouth.

The horror was almost too terrible to comprehend. It was compartmentalized, though, as he noticed Elkins hanging, too, from the fist of the fucker that had killed the kid.

He strode toward the thing, firing with each step at its head and its chest.

"Why won't you die?!" he screamed at it, and finally it loosened its grip on Elkins, dropping him to the floor. It whipped its tail, flinging Kira into a wall. He fought back a cry and fired again. The biodrone took a step toward him, then another, preparing to charge.

Instead, it fell face-first onto the carpet, finally dead.

Roots ran to Elkins, who was coughing and gasping for air. He crouched next to his squad mate.

"You okay, man? C'mon, we gotta—"

"Kira," Elkins said in a weak, gravelly voice. "We have to save her."

Roots swallowed the lump in his throat. He could hear other biodrones approaching from behind him.

"She's gone, buddy. I'm sorry. We have to go."

"We can't." Elkins clutched his arm. "I promised I'd protect her. We have to save her."

Roots moved back on his haunches, just enough so that he wasn't blocking the view of Kira's body. Elkins took the sight in for several seconds and then made a noise deep in his throat. It was deeper than that, Roots thought. It was a sob from the center of his chest, where his heart was.

"I promised her," Elkins whispered. Tears made his eyes glisten.

"I know," Roots replied, not knowing what to say. "I know—but we really have to go. More are coming."

Elkins let Roots help him to his feet, and they got moving again. They had made it nearly to another bend in the hallway when the weight of Elkins leaning against him suddenly lifted. Roots turned to see why and felt a sudden burning pain on the side of his knee. He hobbled forward, lifting the gun again to fire at the source of the pain. A serrated tail whizzed past his cheek and he flinched. Blood dripped off the tip.

It might have been his blood.

The drone that had cut him had returned its attention to Elkins, who was sprawled on the floor. The alien had pulled him off Roots and thrown him to the ground, it seemed. Now, it leaned over him, its jaw unhinging.

Roots fired at the long spikes on its back, but the tail snapped around again, and its sharp tip buried itself in his shoulder. The pain was immense, a thing too large for his shoulder alone, and he cried out as bright sparks of it exploded toward his neck and down his arm.

The tail withdrew, and Roots sank to his good knee, setting off fresh fireworks of agony in his injured one. Still, he lifted the gun again, his arm shaking, and fired. The shot went wild. Elkins turned his head to look at Roots, and in his eyes was a look of quiet resignation. Elkins knew what was coming, and must have made some peace with it.

Roots couldn't help but feel that, if Kira were still alive, Elkins might not have looked at him like that.

The smaller, internal jaw of the biodrone shot out and punched a hole in Elkins's temple. His head dropped like a stone, his eyes closing, and a thick, syrupy trail of blood spilled out and over his forehead as the little jaw receded.

"You son of a bitch!" Roots screamed. "You fucking bug-ugly son of a fucking whore!" He opened fire. If he was going down, then he was damned well going to do everything he could to take those lab-rats with him.

A flare of bright light in the periphery to his right roared at the biodrone and the thing squealed. It scrambled to get away from the flames surging across its exoskeleton. It tried to shake them off, and when that didn't work, it jumped to the far wall and sprinted away down the hall.

Roots sank the rest of the way to the floor as Dr. McCormick and Sarge came into view.

"Hey, Roots—are you all right?" Sarge looked down at him with concern.

"It got Elkins," he muttered. "I'm sorry—I tried to stop it. I tried."

"It's okay," Sarge said, taking his arm and pulling him to his feet. "You did what you could."

"It killed them," Roots muttered again. He looked at Sarge and tried to speak again, but his voice cracked. "It killed them both."

He could see beyond Sarge's shoulder that Dr. McCormick had heard him. Tears sprang to her eyes and spilled down her cheek. He felt he had to explain, to take away some of that deep hurt in her face.

"She tried to save Elkins. She lunged at one of those things to fight it and she was fearless. She went out like a true marine—fighting to save a brother." He felt tears of his own blur his vision.

Her expression softened some, but the tears kept coming.

"I'm so sorry," Roots whispered.

"We've got to get back to the ship," Sarge said. "We can't do anything here."

"I agree," Siobhan said, wiping her eyes. Her expression had hardened to a resolve Roots had never seen in her soft features before. "You two are in no shape to fight biodrones *and* a Queen."

"Okay," Roots said. He rose, limping from both the bad foot and knee. "Back to the ship it is."

"And while you're there, I'm going to find the Queen."

The men looked at her as if she'd lost her mind.

"Siobhan, you can't," Sarge said.

"I have to."

"You see what it did to us, and we're trained professionals. What do you think—"

"What I think," Siobhan broke in, "is that someone needs to make sure the Queen and the biodrones run into each other before any one of us runs into them again. We can't just take the chance and wait. We have to end this. Now." She glanced at Elkins, but Roots knew she was thinking of Kira. "For them."

"If you let me get back to the ship," Sarge said, "get more ammo—"

"No," Siobhan said. Then, more softly, she added, "You and Roots, you've done enough. Sit this one out and let me do this, okay?"

Sarge didn't reply. He stared at her, deep puncture wounds in his leg, his arm, and his stomach, the last of which was bleeding through his cupped fingers. He had some scratches on his shoulder and his face, and it looked like one of his fingers was swelling.

When he didn't speak, Siobhan said, "I'll be in and out, okay? Quick cat-and-mouse game. I'll lead her to the biodrones, then duck out while they fight each other. Easy-breezy, as my ancestors used to say."

Sarge considered her reasoning a moment longer.

"In and out?"

"In and out," Siobhan said. "I promise. Look, it has to be someone fast. Neither of you can run or dodge. It has to be me."

"Can't we just wait for them to find each other?"

"We don't have time. We have to be sure it happens, and it's got to happen soon, or we run the risk of them getting out and finding us."

Sarge sighed.

"Okay," he said finally. "Okay."

Siobhan escorted the injured marines back to the lobby. She watched Alec and Roots hobble to the front double doors and her heart felt full. They looked pretty battered, each of them doing his best to hold the other up. As the doors slid open, Alec turned back to her.

"Are you sure you want to do this? I can—"

"No," she said. "You can't." She walked up to him and kissed his cheek, and he blushed a little under the bruises. "I'll take care of this. Let me take care of this."

Alec nodded. "Be careful."

"I will."

"Watch the fuel supply on the flamethrower," he said. "You don't want to run out."

"I know," she assured him.

He lingered a moment longer, and in his expression, she could see the conflict between knowing she was right and feeling the need to protect her. She gave him a smile as they moved through the open conference center doorway, and she watched them make their slow and painful trek all the way back to the *Astraeus*. Alec waved to her from the ship's hatch, a signal that everything looked okay within, and she waved back, then turned to the lobby.

That ever-present feeling of loneliness crashed in on her like a tide. She had grown accustomed to the feeling over the last decade or so, because of her work on a remote moon, and had accepted it as a part of her personal life for much the same reason. She felt it more acutely now, though, in the face of real and immediate danger.

This wasn't like the vague but increasingly evidenced promise that the moon beneath her feet would, in time, crash into the planet it orbited, nor was it like the pervasive and ever-present threat of the pathogen bombs. This was death in two terrifying forms that might, in a very literal sense, be right around the corner. She was caught between a tornado and a hurricane, and there would be no sheltering from either.

And yet, on some level, she felt alive in a way she never had before. Every hair stood on end. Every nerve crackled with energy. Her heart had begun to thud as soon as the marines had covered half the distance back to the ship—just far enough away that if something had snuck up behind her, she'd have been truly on her own. Her breathing was deep. The room seemed brighter and sharper, and sounds—even the smallest hum of the climate control units—were perfectly clear.

She felt, as crazy as it seemed to her, like a predatory thing herself, a creature with the same stakes and chance for survival as the creatures for which she was looking. Sliding the switch on the flamethrower so it would be ready when she needed it, she crept back into the outer circle of hallways.

It seemed to make the most sense to start looking for the Xenomorph Queen in the area where Fowler had died. As a chestburster, it might not have gotten too far. It occurred to her as she moved down the hallway that, if the biodrones found the Queen before she did, they would kill the little alien and their best hope for survival would be gone. She tried not to dwell on that.

The Xenomorphs were made for survival.

The Queen would survive. She had to.

As Siobhan made her way down the hall, she peered into rooms, just as she'd seen the marines do. Not wanting anything sneaking up on her from behind, she tried to move quietly, like they had done, and listen for sounds of approach. Occasionally, she glanced up at the ceiling. The Xenomorphs had a nasty habit of climbing across walls and ceilings, to drop down on prey.

Her path took her a little more than halfway around the arc of the outer circle before movement in a room to her left caught her eye. There was a large vent near the ceiling on the far wall, covered with a metal polymer grate. Beneath it, clawing at the grate, was a biodrone.

Siobhan readied the flamethrower. It felt suddenly smaller in her hands, a flimsy thing, not nearly enough protection against the monstrosity in that room. She wondered if the Xenomorph Queen—still growing, no doubt—had somehow drawn the biodrone's attention. Maybe it would smell her, or sense her bio-electrical impulses. She didn't think the vent was quite big enough for a human being to fit in there, but it certainly seemed as if something had gotten the biodrone's attention.

It had to be the Queen.

As much as she hated the thought of doing it, she had to distract the biodrone and draw it away, if the Queen was to have a chance to grow.

"Hey," she tried to say in a loud, clear voice. It came out as a croak, barely above a whisper, but that didn't seem to matter.

The biodrone's head snapped in her direction.

"Come on, now," she coaxed, "come here. Come get me."

The thing hopped up onto the huge wooden table in the center of the room. Crouching, it grazed the table's surface with the claws of its right hand, digging into the wood as if it were butter. Its mouth opened and it made that terrible chittering sound she thought she'd hear echoing in her nightmares forever. A smaller mouth extended, its tiny jaw working up and down, while saliva dripped from the bigger, gaping maw.

"That's right," she said, taking a step backward. "This way."

Her heart pounded in her chest. Her lungs seemed to draw and keep all the air, sucking the wind out of her words. Her scalp tingled. Her face and neck felt flushed. The creature had no eyes that she could see, but it was focused on her intently, probably considering the best way to attack. She could feel its aggression: directionless, nearly mindless, a creature driven by the simple instinct to kill and keep killing. Maybe it could smell her blood or her sweat, or maybe it could hear her heartbeat or feel the electrical changes her presence made in the air around her. It felt too close, too intimate, the way it could sense her. She hated the feeling.

The biodrone took a few steps across the tabletop toward her, but it seemed to be hesitating, and she thought she knew why. She glanced down at the flamethrower in her hands. It knew. At least on some level, it knew the weapon to be a source of danger.

"Come on," she said to it, and took a few more steps back. "Come this way."

The biodrone crossed the rest of the table, then paused at the edge.

"Come on, you bastard," she muttered under her breath, thinking of Kira, then louder, "Come on, you baby-killing son of a bitch. *Come on!*"

The biodrone squealed, then leaped from the table.

Her hand on the trigger was a knee-jerk reaction. She blasted the creature mid-air with fire. It dropped to the ground in front of her, shrieking as the flames spread from its chest to its back. She pulled the trigger again, and a stream of flame belched from the muzzle of the weapon. The biodrone's shriek rose in pitch and volume. It shook wildly, as if to fling off the flames. Then it dropped to the carpet.

It took a few minutes for the fire along its back to burn out, and then it lay motionless, still sizzling and smoking.

"That was for Kira." She spit on the carcass. *One down, dozens to go*, she thought.

Siobhan stepped carefully over it and into the room. She thought she heard a tiny chitter-purr from the vent, but it might have been her imagination. After a few minutes, her heart rate slowed and her breaths didn't feel as if they would explode her chest. Still, she thought her hands would have been shaking, if they hadn't been clinging so tightly to the weapon.

Pulling a chair over to the vent, she climbed up on it, until the vent grate was at eye level. The slats were up, but she couldn't see into it from where she was. She listened a moment and heard nothing. Was the Queen waiting, silent and deadly, in the dark inside the shaft?

Considering the danger in moving her face so close to the vent, she decided she needed to see, to know what had drawn the biodrone's attention. Slowly, she leaned in and pressed an ear to the grate. No scuffling, no chitter-purr, no squeals.

Nothing.

She turned her head and peered through the slat. The brightness of the room didn't penetrate very deeply at all. She didn't think there was any movement, though. There were no changes in the scant light or darkness, no flickering shadows. If the Queen had been there, surely she was gone now.

Getting down from the chair, she considered what to do next. The Queen was hiding, most likely. If she was in the vent system, how would Siobhan find her? Eventually, she would get too big for the vents. If the stories Siobhan had heard were correct, Queens were two, maybe three times as big as the drones—more like the Xenomorph with antlers that she had seen on BG-791.

With Fowler's serum, her growth outside of her host would be accelerated and her aggression levels would be high. Eventually she'd be forced out of the constricting duct system, and she'd be pretty angry. All Siobhan had to do was gauge which vent she'd come out of, and it seemed to her that the most likely candidate would be the one near a warm, easy-to-protect spot, with access to hosts for her future eggs.

That meant in or near the central conference area, where the biodrones were.

She moved back into the hall and continued making her way around until she saw the lobby. No bodies or even parts of bodies remained in the whole outer circle. Even Fowler's corpse had been taken. Had the biodrones dragged them back to the central conference room? Were they nesting in there now, making a hive and gathering food? She shuddered and thought of Kira and Elkins, and hatred for the biodrones flared in her heart.

Siobhan turned down the central spoke and headed toward the inner circle. Her heartbeat picked up again. Her palms felt slick on the flamethrower. At the junction she paused, debating which way to go. All the rooms had vents, she thought, and all about the same size as the one she'd examined. The vents in the rooms nearest the last segment of the spoke—the part of the hallway that led to the central chamber—were the most likely ones from which the Queen would emerge. But which way?

The vent she'd examined had been on the left side of the building, so she chose left and ducked into the nearest room. When she saw the dark rectangle of a vent missing its grate, her heart leaped in her chest. She'd been right. The Queen had come out that way—she was sure of it. There was also a strange smell—the smell of death. Was she still hiding there?

So far as Siobhan could tell, it was empty… she thought.

She crept farther into the room and rounded the table, and found a dead woman in a uniform whose chest was partly caved in—the source of the smell. On the floor beneath the vent lay the grate, dented in the middle. The Queen had kicked or punched her way out.

Siobhan looked up, and then slowly scanned the rest of the space, under the table, beneath the counters that lined the wall by the door, where coffee and donuts were still laid out, untouched. The Queen wasn't there—but where had she gone? Did her escape from the vent system mean she'd grown large enough, at least, to make the vents too uncomfortable?

She heard a moan which made her jump, and turned to see that the woman, who she'd previously thought dead, was moving. She coughed weakly, and blood dribbled over her chin and down her jaw from the corners of her mouth. Not dead, then, but certainly dying. Siobhan moved over and knelt beside her, taking her hand.

"Can you hear me?" she asked the woman gently. "Can I do anything?"

The woman's face looked familiar. Siobhan thought she'd seen it in a Newscore article. General Stephanie Koslowski—it was her. General Koslowski's family were shareholders with a fairly large stake in Seegson's pharmaceuticals branch, as well as their synthetics branch.

The general attempted to squeeze Siobhan's hand, but the effort was weak. Her breath was ragged and irregular, a blood-misting wheeze that suggested a possible collapsed lung. Without access to a medpod, there was nothing to be done.

"Run from here," the woman whispered. "Save yourself."

"Are there any other survivors?" Siobhan asked. "I can get you help…" The woman shook her head as vigorously as she was able.

"I'm dying. Leave me. Take this and go. Tell them. About Vaughn. The Engineers. Deep Vo—" she coughed, and more blood leaked from her lips, "—Void."

"I—I don't understand," Siobhan said, but she took the small drive that the general offered, and pocketed it.

"Terrorists—Deep Void. Shadow government." She wheezed. "The signature. The bombs. On that drive. You have to—have to—" The wheezing and coughing overtook her, her whole body spasming with the effort.

"I will," Siobhan reassured her. "I will."

That seemed to be what the woman needed to hear. She settled back to the floor and closed her eyes. With a final, shuddering breath, her lopsided chest sank a final time and she went completely still.

2 5

Siobhan couldn't bear to stay in the room with General Koslowski's body. It wasn't the fact that the woman was dead, but what she had said before she died. Siobhan had so many questions. She'd never heard of Deep Void, but maybe it was their signature that research had uncovered behind the bombs. And what about the Engineers?

Some believed they were mystical mumbo-jumbo, like the old religions of Earth. Others cited them as responsible for the origins of life itself on Earth. Much of the information about them was vague, and even more was lost to time and space. Were they connected to the pathogen bombs? She felt the drive in her pocket, wondering what, exactly, was on it. Somehow, she'd make sure the right people, the people who needed that information to broker peace, would get it.

She had nearly reached the central conference room before she realized where she was. The double doors to the room were lying on the hallway floor. In one, a large acidic hole spanned most of its width, the edges black and irregular. Out here—and, so far as she could tell, inside the chamber—it was silent.

Siobhan gripped the flamethrower and crept toward the open doorway.

Despite all she had seen over the last week, the scene inside shocked her. There was blood everywhere—on the walls, the carpet, even the ceiling. Chairs were overturned and broken, their pieces littering the room. The large wooden table in the center was bigger than those in other rooms, as the room was much bigger. It formed a heavy square of light-colored wood with a smaller cutout in the center, so that it basically formed a square frame.

Its surface was slick in places with blood. Uniformed bodies were folded in unnatural ways over its edges and splayed out across blood-soaked paperwork. The smell was heavy, a coppery animal smell that assaulted her nose and throat, making her recoil. Here were the remnants of the summit peace talks—government representatives from the UA, the UPP, and the ICSC, the Joint Chiefs, and their assistants, reporters, and official secretaries to log the minutes and record the talks for posterity.

Other bodies lay near the doors and were lined up along the wall. All were marines, and all had their chests exploded outward. They must have managed to make their way to the conference center, to report what had happened aboard the *Alexiares*, likely under a misguided delusion that they had somehow escaped the biodrone attack on their ship.

Beyond the table, against the back wall in the right corner of the room, the comms machines were set up on a long wooden counter. The distress message they had heard while orbiting the planet had no doubt come from there, but how? Had a marine sent it when all other hope seemed lost? Maybe the Grant code was the only way to get a message out beneath the heavy security of the facility.

But who had sent it? Had anyone survived this massacre?

Someone had tried to call for help, and when it was evident no help would come, someone—possibly General Koslowski—had shut the door on whoever had still been left alive in the room, in an effort to keep the biodrones contained so they wouldn't get out and kill more people.

It had failed. It had all so miserably failed, and now, the fate of colonies across the galaxy was uncertain at best. Governments would find someone to blame—another government, a false flag scapegoat that would suit their needs—and the poor farmers and miners and scientists and colonists in all those colonies, all over space, would be in mortal danger.

That hate, that anger that she had felt for the Xenomorphs, was bolstered by a new hate—for the people responsible for these monstrosities in the first place, and for the people who would recklessly use them to hurt other people.

She would see to it that everyone knew. *Everyone.*

As she made her way around the table to the comms machines, she recognized a number of faces of the dead, military higher-ups with financial and family ties to the corporations. Companies had used those ties to destroy more than they had ever created, to take more than they had ever given. Their money gave them positions, and those positions gave them power.

There was a body lying face-up that she recognized as General Gifford Michael Hadley, whose family had, a long time ago, financed the doomed colonization of Hadley's Hope. The general had deep gashes across his face and chest. She saw General Edgar B. Fordham, who had family on the board of directors for the Jùtóu Combine, which had established one of the largest mining operations in the galaxy on the planet Shānmén. Most of Fordham's intestines were spilled out across his hips and the floor.

She also thought she recognized another body— although it was difficult to be sure with half of her face missing—as General Alexis B.K. Lloyd, who came from one of the more prominent and wealthy families of New Albion. General Samuel Matthew Canon, often called "Loose Canon," had been torn in half, and General Broaddus J. French's limbs had been disarticulated and his head had been turned backward. Both had been on the prison committee that had established Fiorina 161's class-C work correctional unit for double-Y chromosome convicts.

Dead, all of them.

Disgusted, she shook her head and continued to the comms machines. She drew the drive from her pocket and plugged it into the side of one of the transmissions slots. A prompt appeared.

UPLOAD? Y – N

She tapped "Y."

With a soft whir, the system began retrieving the contents of the drive. A moment later, it asked her what she wanted to save the file as. After a moment's thought, she typed *Pathogen Bomb Signature Information*. The words appeared on the screen as she spoke them aloud, and with another small buzz, the file was saved. Then she opened a message and attached the file. More prompts popped up on-screen.

RECORD – PLAY – PAUSE – STOP – REWIND –
FAST FORWARD

She was about to tap on the "RECORD" prompt when a searing pain in her shoulder made her cry out. Siobhan was lifted into the air and could feel the grip on her shoulder dig in deeper. Then the room blurred as she was thrown to the floor. Holding tight to the flamethrower, she rolled over onto her back and sat up, muzzle pointed forward.

The room had filled both quickly and quietly with biodrones, at least two dozen of them. One stood by the comms machine, behind where she had been standing. That one, she guessed, had thrown her to the floor.

It roared at her, and she found herself roaring back, unleashing all the pain and sorrow and anger and fear at once. She turned the flamethrower on a biodrone creeping up to her right, and the fire skimmed over its shoulder.

"Damn it," she muttered. "*Damn it!*" She pressed the trigger again, and this time the flames hit the monster full in the face. It clawed at where its eyes should have been, screeching as the fire ate into its head. Then she turned back to face her attacker, only to find that it had closed the distance between them.

"Oh shit," she whispered.

The drone loomed over her, jaws slavering, its claws and the curve of its head gleaming in the flickering overhead lights. Its saliva dripped on the floor by her feet. It raised a massive hand to swipe at her.

In the next instant, the drone flew to the right. Siobhan flinched, crying out, and the biodrone crashed against the wall.

Standing nearby was the Xenomorph Queen, fully grown—at least three times the size of the drones she had seen on BG-791.

The Queen! She had found them!

Siobhan wasn't sure if she should be relieved or terrified.

The Queen towered over the other nearby biodrones, her exoskeleton so dark a gray that it was almost blue-black in the flickering light. Her long, arcing head was somehow as magnificent as it was terrifying, with an enormous crown of bony ridge fanning from the back and extending to just above the rictus snarl of her jaws. Her body was similar to those of the drones, although larger and more powerful, and her back spikes were more like a spread of long blades, akin to the pictures of ancient swords she'd seen as a kid.

Each leg had an extra segment that allowed the first joint to bend forward while the second bent back. Her huge feet each had three taloned toes in front and another in back. Her hands, with their massive claws, sliced the air at the downed biodrone, who squealed in her direction. She let loose with a shriek so loud that it hurt Siobhan's ears.

The other biodrones, stunned into silence, cowered away from her.

Siobhan scrambled backward, taking the best shelter she could find under the nearby corner of a desk. From her vantage point, she could see the legs of the creatures charging the Queen, and a series of shrieks as she fought off their onslaught. Siobhan inched toward the edge of the desk and peered out, but jumped when a biodrone smashed against the floor.

It seemed to notice her, issuing a low, guttural sound from the recesses of its throat. Then the Queen's foot came down on its head, bursting it open. The creature's blood sprayed in all directions, and Siobhan shielded her face with an arm, shrinking against the massive legs of the table. She felt a burn starting on her forearm and in a panic ripped the sleeve off, tossing it away.

After a moment, she moved toward the edge of the desk again, to better see what was going on.

The biodrone that the Queen had shoved out of the way tried to get up; she whipped her spiny, segmented tail in the biodrone's direction, as if warning to it to stay where it was. Another came up behind her, and she barely glanced at it before her tail snapped back and speared it through the chest. As the tail withdrew, the biodrone's blood poured from the wound, spattering and eating through the carpet even as the body fell.

The blood smoked on the tip of the Queen's tail, but it didn't seem to penetrate its hard shell.

Buoyed by terror and exhilaration, Siobhan felt a flare of hope. The Queen could fight these creatures in a way the humans couldn't.

So long as they didn't overpower her...

Siobhan had to help.

Crawling out from under the desk, avoiding contact with human and biodrone corpses, she stood in full view of the monsters in the room. A trio of creatures was flanking the Queen, and she swung the flamethrower around so its muzzle pointed at them. While they were still a good five meters away, she moved closer and torched them. They squealed and shuddered, leaping to the wall, then the ceiling, then down the far wall before collapsing to the ground.

Wheeling around, she found another biodrone that had leaped onto the conference table's far edge. It crouched and howled at her, but turned its attention when the Queen issued an ear-splitting shriek. Focused on the greater foe, it launched itself into the air. Her tail whipped around and smacked it to the floor, then plunged into the side of its head.

Another biodrone vaulted onto the Queen's back, digging its claws deep into her bony shoulder. She shrieked in protest, reached up over her good shoulder, latched onto the creature's neck, and yanked it over her head, slamming it down on the closest desk. Holding the wriggling biodrone by the neck, she tore the curving shell off the top of its head and tossed it. It slid to a stop near Siobhan's feet.

Then the Queen plunged her claws into the biodrone's chest and raked them down, shredding its torso. Finally, she flung it out of the way as the puddle of blood on the desk dissolved the wood into smoking, pulpy sludge.

Two more biodrones stalked toward their massive opponent, issuing a strange, low, throaty growl. She returned it; the sound was deep and windy, like a storm brewing inside her. It caused every muscle in Siobhan's body to tense. Three more on the far side of the room leaped onto the segment of desk there, tails lashing back and forth as they clawed the wood. The Queen pounded across the floor to the closest two, swinging her claws at them.

She missed the first one, which latched onto her arm, but she connected with the second attacker, sinking the claws of her other hand into the side of its face.

Seeing an opening, the first biodrone opened its mouth wide. Its inner jaw shot out, puncturing the Queen's forearm. With a shriek, she charged the wall, slamming the biodrone into it over and over until the wall cracked and crumbled.

Still, the biodrone hung on.

She grasped its head, pulling up, and Siobhan could hear the tearing of the meat beneath the exoskeleton as the monster's jaw broke at the hinges. She tore off the top of its head and then flung its carcass at one of the three creatures making their way toward her. The corpse knocked it off the desk and out of view.

The biodrone closest to Siobhan moved in while she was distracted, and as she turned it leaped into the air. She crouched, flamethrower pointed upward, but the thing was above her, and before she could pull the trigger the Queen's tail speared it through the side. Thinking quickly, Siobhan grabbed the shell at her feet and held it up like a shield. She heard the biodrone's blood pattering down on the carapace, but felt nothing.

The creature's body thudded to the ground beside her.

Siobhan rose slowly, feeling more confident. Now she had a protective measure against whatever accidental crossfire of blood she might encounter. Opening fire with the flamethrower, she doused the third biodrone with a stream of fire that engulfed it instantly. It howled, dropping to the floor and racing from the room.

That left no more than ten surviving biodrones, Siobhan estimated. Screeching in unison, they charged the double doors, intent on fleeing, but it was too late. The Queen leaped across what remained of the desk into the open square in the middle, then jumped through the door to tackle three of the fleeing creatures.

Her claws flew. Her tail whipped and stabbed and snapped. Dispatching her first opponents, she chased down another pair. A short distance down the hall, she tore one in half, then another just a few feet farther.

Turning sharply, a biodrone slid under her swiping claws and galloped back into the main chamber. Another dodged her by leaping to the wall and galloping toward the double doors. They were coming back.

Siobhan ran toward the doors and blasted each of the biodrones as they tried to enter. For a moment, they were nightmares, spiny shapes of flame squealing and tearing across the ceiling. They dropped together, and the flame was enough to catch the carpet in the center of the desk square.

Fire caught near the far wall, as well. Growing flames burned their way toward the comms machines.

Siobhan couldn't leave the burning room, not yet— not until she called for help. Sprinting past the fire to reach the console, she tapped the screen, calling up the list of messages. A loud, high-pitched roar thundered from outside the room. It sounded to Siobhan like a victory roar—the Queen must have killed the last remaining biodrones.

Somewhere in the back of her mind, she wondered how long it would be before the Queen came after her next. Though they had fought a common foe, and she had defended the creature more than once, the monster was not on her side. She would consider Siobhan a threat, especially in her state of heightened aggression—thanks to Fowler's damned serum. And if she didn't go after Siobhan, she'd be going after the marines at the ship.

Alec.

Siobhan couldn't focus on that now, though. She checked the message she'd started, to see if the attachment was still there.

It was.

So were the prompts, waiting for her.

RECORD – PLAY – PAUSE – STOP – REWIND – FAST FORWARD

Flames crackled, far too close. The heat was uncomfortable, but the smoke was worse—it made her eyes water.

She tapped the "RECORD" prompt and said, "This is Dr. Siobhan McCormick, formerly assistant research director at the Seegson Pharmaceuticals lab on BG-791. I am currently stranded on LV-846, at the Pushan Conference Center with two badly injured Colonial Marines. There are no survivors from the Joint Chiefs summit, and no survivors from the USCMC security detail. Attached is evidence of the pathogen bomb signatures and origin, as well as evidence of ACG Vaughn's—"

She coughed as the smoke grew thicker.

"—her involvement in the incidents here, including what was done to the crashed ship *Alexiares*."

She coughed again, the smoke so thick it nearly obscured the screen.

"Please send help. Hurry. McCormick out."

She tapped the button to stop recording. Her head hurt. So did her lungs and the forearm where the biodrone blood had eaten through her sleeve and singed the skin. Her shoulder throbbed, as well.

Her vision swam.

The comms system prompted again.

CHANNELS?

She tapped the checkboxes.

MILITARY
UA GOVERNMENT
UPP GOVERNMENT

And then, to be on the safe side, also chose "OTHER." She wasn't sure where that would send the message, but the more ears, the better.

When it asked her if she was sure, she confirmed. When it asked if she wanted to override the security, she confirmed again. For a moment, she was sure it would ask for authorization to send the message—authorization she didn't have.

The smoke burned her eyes, but after a moment she saw the prompt appear.

She took the drive and pocketed it, then tapped "SEND" and sank to the floor. She didn't—couldn't—wait to see if the transmission went through. The flames were licking up the side of the comms counter. The smoke was choking her.

Dragging the flamethrower along the floor by its shoulder strap, she crawled on her stomach across the carpet, doing her best to dodge bodies—human and not—burnt carpet, and pools of blood—again, human and not. Her burned arm skin stretched and pulled each time she used it to drag herself forward. Likewise, she felt the wound in her shoulder pump out fresh blood every time she used the muscles there to gain some ground.

Something snagged her remaining sleeve, and her good arm and shoulder wouldn't move, sending a moment of pure, adrenaline-fueled alarm coursing through her. Her head felt light and throbbed. Glancing over, she realized that her sleeve had caught on the tip of a toe-claw of one of the dead biodrones. She clumsily unhooked it and continued the painfully slow crawl toward the double doors.

What would she do if the Queen was there, waiting for her out in the hallway? From her angle, she couldn't see if the monstrous figure was just around the corner, out of view. She didn't think she had the energy to fight off anything else.

Pushing the concern to the back of her mind, she focused on the doors, on the door jamb separating the central conference room from what little of the hallway she could see. That dented, tarnished line of metal became her world, filling her vision and thoughts. That little border meant the difference between salvation and death, and it was getting closer.

Closer. She pulled her weight toward it.

Closer. From somewhere a ways off, she heard the shriek of the Queen, perhaps looking for a way out of the building.

Closer. *That's good*, she allowed herself to think. *If she's looking for a way out, she's not looking for me.*

There it was, the little line of metal just an arm's length away.

Swallowing a cough that threatened to wrack her body, she forced a final pull toward the hall. When the top half of her crossed the line into the hallway, out from under the flames, she felt an immediate drop in temperature. She sucked in the cleaner air, low enough to the ground to escape the smoke pouring out of the conference room and across the hallway ceiling. With a gulp of clear air, she pushed herself to her knees, then rose to her feet and stumbled forward.

Gathering her strength, she took off at as much of a run as she was able down the spoke of hallway, straight past the inner circle of hallway where she hoped the Queen was circling in confusion, and straight toward the outer hallway. The farther she got from the conference center fire, the clearer and cooler the air she inhaled, and the more her head cleared. Her throat still hurt from the hot air that had passed through it, and her head and arm still throbbed. The flamethrower felt so heavy in her arms.

Nevertheless, she felt better with each jogging step.

The lobby appeared before her at the end of the hallway, and she ran toward it, relief buoying her steps. She was close.

A roar from the right made her frayed nerves scream, and that scream erupted from her sore throat. She didn't have to look to know that the Queen was charging down that curve of outer circle hallway.

2 6

Inside the *Astraeus*, Alec and Roots dozed. The storm that had come and gone when they'd first arrived had regrouped and come back with a vengeance, drumming a tinny rhythm as the rain struck the ship's exterior.

Alec had wanted to stay awake, but his body left him with little choice. Moreover, he knew that he and Roots had to be ready—to the greatest degree possible—in case Siobhan needed their help. Between the exhaustion and the injuries, they would be no good to anyone without a little rest.

The medpod on the ship had been damaged beyond repair in the fight with the Weyland-Yutani ship and the subsequent landing on LV-846, so they had to make do with painkiller injections from the ship's medkit, and those had made the exhaustion unbearable.

Even so, Alec found he couldn't quite fall completely

asleep. He was worried about Siobhan, worried what was happening in there, and what would happen if any of it spilled outside to their ship before Siobhan returned.

A faint crack of thunder that might have been partly dream sounded from somewhere outside, followed by a flash of light. The lightning, he'd noticed in his haze, was far worse on this planet than the thunder. The hatch had also been broken in the landing, letting an irregular light into the rear of the ship.

That was where the marines had dragged chairs in a vain attempt at keeping some sort of watch. LV-846 hosted various species of life—mostly insects, birds, fish, lizards, and gazelles, as well as a kind of predatory panther-like animal the size of a fox, but those tended to stay deep in the jungle, away from people. They had been more concerned with the biodrones… and, of course, the Queen.

Neither soldier was in much shape to fight anything bigger than a jungle cat and, even then, the cats might well have had the upper paw.

There was a crack like a gunshot as a bolt of lightning hit a tree somewhere nearby. He jumped in his chair, glanced around, saw that Roots was still asleep, mumbling something unintelligible. When no threat appeared, he settled back down. His gun lay at his feet, and after a moment's consideration, he picked it up and set it in his lap.

He listened to the rain, thinking about Siobhan.

Alec had never told her how he felt about her. It had been hard to get close to someone. Everyone who had ever mattered either died or was somehow left behind. His life had never really been his own, and it had been a long, long time since any place had felt like home. BG-791 might have come close, but that, he'd realized, was because of Siobhan.

She was beautiful in such a sweet, delicate way, caring and thoughtful, so smart, and—as he had seen this past week—tough as nails when she had to be. She had a quirky sense of humor to go with a quiet, almost self-conscious laugh, and he loved both.

He loved her.

That had never been so clear to him as it was sitting in that chair near the rear hatch of the *Astraeus*, waiting to see if she'd come out of the conference center alive.

If Roots hadn't been there, he might have swallowed the pain and gone back in to get her. Hell, he might never have left her alone in the first place, to shoulder the task of fighting the biodrones.

What she'd told him kept coming back to him. She needed this; she needed to feel useful and in control—and truthfully, if she'd had to keep an eye on him and Roots while finding the Xenomorph Queen and fighting off biodrones, they just would have gotten her killed. He and Roots would have been far too much of a liability.

Roots's mumbling became a rhythmic series of snores, and between that and the rain, Alec's eyelids drooped again. He was almost asleep when a thump from down in the cargo hold as dreamlike as the thunder had been, set his mind going again. He might have ignored it, except that it was followed a few moments later by what Alec's brain processed as footsteps.

His eyes snapped open, and he clutched his gun.

"Roots," he said, shaking his squad mate's shoulder. "Wake up."

The private jumped and sat up in the chair.

"What? What is it?" He ducked down and grabbed his gun before his eyes were entirely open.

"I heard something," Alec said, "down in the cargo hold."

Roots regarded him for a minute, then stood. Alec stood, too. They made their way to the hatch that led to the cargo hold. Its door was still shut, but that didn't mean much. If the biodrones wanted to find a way in, they would.

Alec lifted his fingers, silently counted to three, then threw open the hatch door. Both men took a step back, their guns pointed at the opening. The ladder disappeared into darkness down below, which only served to heighten Alec's suspicion that a biodrone—or maybe even a Xenomorph stowaway from BG-791—was responsible for the sounds.

They seemed to prefer the dark.

"I'll go first," Roots said.

"Wait, why?" Alec said. "You sure?"

Roots shrugged. "Yeah. For Elkins. If one of those bastards is down there, I want first crack at killing it." They clipped flashlights to their shoulders, then he slung his weapon's strap over his shoulder, turned, and began the descent on the ladder. The darkness swallowed the top of his head, leaving only his feet clanking on the ladder rungs.

Alec followed. Dropping past the last couple of rungs, he landed next to Roots in the dark, sending a twinge of pain up his leg. They hit the switches for the lights, which took a moment to come on. Even their equipment, it seemed, was tired.

The lights did little to penetrate the blackness of the cargo hold. They could see a few feet ahead of them, to the metal shelves which cast odd shapes on the walls as they passed by. The sound of a step, followed by something dragging, snapped their attention forward. They listened for the strange sounds of the Xenomorphs and biodrones, but at first they heard nothing.

Roots took a step forward.

From somewhere just beyond the range of his flashlight, a strange chittering met him in the shadows. That was enough for Roots. He opened fire into the darkness, and didn't stop until Alec touched his shoulder.

"Whatever it is," Alec told him in a quiet voice, "it's dead now."

They took a few steps in the direction that they had heard the noise. A form was curled up on the ground, twitching… but it wasn't a biodrone or a stowaway Xenomorph.

Alec's heart leaped in his chest. He knew that form…

"It's the synthetic," Roots said flatly. "It's Camilla."

Alec crouched down next to the jerking form. From her mouth, ears, eyes, and nose, she was oozing the whitish fluid that kept synthetics' circuits running. Her left eye twitched, and her body jerked as she tried to sit up.

"Camilla?" he said. "Are you okay?" The words sounded absurd as soon as he'd uttered them. The synthetic tried to smile, but only half of her face would comply. Alec could see she had a large puncture wound in the side of her head, and half of her left cheek was gone.

"No, Sergeant Brand," she said, but she sounded off-key, too low and atonal for the sweet, matronly voice he had grown familiar with. "I'm afraid I'm not."

"How did you get on this ship?"

Camilla tilted her head to one side as if considering the question. "I—I can only remem-em-emberrrrr pieces." Her voice malfunctioned. "I went to make a sandwich for-for Pee-Eff-Ceeee... Elkins. We were out of ham. I went to find s-s-s-something else and I suppp-pose I saw a Xenomorph in the baaasement. Tried to fight it off. To protect Kira. To protect Dr. McCormick. Siobhan. I am fond of them, and I'm strong, you know."

"Oh, I know," Alec said, surprised at the pang in his heart at the synthetic's bravery. He didn't know if they were capable of genuine fondness or programmed simulations of emotion, but he believed in that moment that Camilla felt it, because *she* believed it.

"Did you know, Sergeant, that the Xenomorphs have mouths inside their mouths?" She touched the hole in her head as some process within her sent another pulse of white liquid dribbling out of her wound.

"Yes, I did," Alec said gently.

"It damaged me, I'm afraid. Nearly t-t-tore off my arm, too." She showed the marines her dislocated right limb dangling from its socket. "And for a time, I was confused. I wasn't sure where I was or wh-what I-I had been doing. I think I wandered f-far away from the Seegson lab, toward the Menhit facility. Then I s-s-saw the ship, and it spa-spa-sparked some recognition. So I climbed aboarrrrd."

"The Weyland-Yutani ship," Roots broke in with a touch of sourness. "We wouldn't have needed that ship if you hadn't told the UA about the Xenomorphs."

Camilla offered Roots a polite smile. She was incapable of guilt, Alec knew.

"Correct, PFC Rutiani. Given the high tensions at the summit meeting, my objectives were updated by Seegson programmers, via a remote upload, to immediately notify them of anything—anything at all—that might impede the peace talks. The Xenomorph infestation fit the parameters I was given."

"You could have lied," Roots said, looking away.

"No, PFC Rutiani, I can't. I am inca-inca-incapable of lying. I would have warned you all, but as I men-n-ntioned, I was disoriented after the attack." Her head twitched, her shoulder jerking her back a little.

"Can you be repaired?" Alec asked. "We can get you off this planet. Fix you."

"No, Sergeant. I don't think I will f-f-function for very much longer." She touched the holes in her chest where Roots had fired into her. "A number of my internal units are irreparably frog. Language processing is failing. My me-me-medical abilities are clouding for rain. I am losing me."

"I'm sorry, Camilla," Roots said, and Alec could tell he genuinely, though grudgingly, meant it. Camilla gave him another lopsided smile.

"Th-there is no need to apologize, Root-Root-Rutiani, Private First Class. I don't feel any pain. No fear. Only… tired, I sup-suppose. Only a supernova in a wax field."

Her eyes blinked rapidly, and her head lolled to one side. Reaching across, she tore the bio-sensor out of her wrist and handed it to Alec.

"Take care of them for me. Take c-c-care, Alec and Roots. Take care…"

The light in her eyes went out.

Camilla ceased to function, and Alec was surprised at the sadness it caused in him. He looked down at Camilla's bio-sensor. It wasn't much, but it could at least tell him how many living things still remained in the conference center.

"Sarge?" Roots said. "I'm sorry. I didn't know."

Painfully, Alec got to his feet. He clapped the private on the shoulder.

"It's okay," he said. "We've all been through a lot. I would have shot, too."

"Should we… bury her?"

Alec arched an eyebrow at him.

Flustered, Roots looked away. "Seegson doesn't deserve to have her. They'll just scrap her or something."

"Good point," Alec said. "We'll bury her, then, after we see about Siobhan and the situation in the conference center."

Roots nodded, patting his gun.

"Ready when you are."

Siobhan tore through the lobby as fast as she could and burst outside with her pursuer pounding behind her. She didn't know if Xenomorphs frenzied like sharks, crazed by blood and killing, but the Queen certainly seemed to be incensed. Her screeches shook the glass of the building's windows as Siobhan raced into rain mixed with hail and put as much distance as she could between herself and the conference center.

The hail pelted her, bruising and bloodying her head and arms, but she barely felt it. Adrenaline surged through her, fueling the need to run, to get away.

Alec and Roots would be inside the *Astraeus*, so she changed direction, heading for the *Alexiares*. She wasn't sure what she'd do when she got there, but thought she might at least buy herself—as well as the two marines—some time.

When she was about thirty feet from the *Alexiares*, a bolt of lightning hit the rear of the frigate, splintering and severing one of the long metal spikes there. She skidded to a stop as it speared the ground, then fell over and broke into pieces. Hail the size of fists had been pounding the ship and its attendant debris, and many shards and slivers of metal from those spikes—as well as the rest of the vessel—had already fallen, some of them nearly as long as she was tall.

The Queen closed in behind her, so Siobhan ran the rest of the way to the ship and then, gripping the flamethrower, turned and confronted her pursuer.

Out in the open, against the pale gray of the sky above, the Xenomorph Queen looked enormous, blotting out most of Siobhan's vision. Her tail whipped back and forth, her jaws working open so the smaller ones could emerge. The immense animal aggression that she exuded was palpable, as thick and heavy as the air around them.

Was it hatred? Animosity for an inferior species? Siobhan didn't think so. The Queen wanted to kill her because that was the nature of the species—of *both* their species, if Siobhan was honest. Apex predator against apex predator, on a world far from either of their homes. They had been used, both of them, to further someone else's agenda, and here in the middle of the storm, their blind desires to turn helplessness into something more— to find an outlet for bloodlust fueled by frustration and necessity—were about to clash.

Her prey no longer fleeing, the Queen slowed—wary,

Siobhan thought, of the flamethrower. Siobhan bellowed wordless rage at her, and the monster bellowed back. Then Siobhan pulled the trigger.

Flames belched and sputtered from the muzzle of the weapon, then went out. Her heart sank and panic gripped her. She tried again, but the weapon only sputtered in her hands. She glanced down at it and saw the fuel gauge had gone dark.

It was empty.

She tossed it at the Queen, who batted it aside as if it were nothing.

A couple of bolts of lightning hit the ground in different places. The storm was getting worse. Siobhan thought it too much to hope for that the Queen would be struck in the brief time it would take her to reach Siobhan.

Still the alien crept toward her, rather than charging her, and she couldn't help but wonder if maybe the creature saw something in her that posed a threat. Siobhan inched toward the metal shards on the ground nearby. Maybe she could wield one as a weapon and stave off death a little longer.

"*Hey!*" The voice shouted over the din of thunder.

The Queen turned, and as she did so, Siobhan looked in the same direction. Alec and Roots were standing there, all but obscured by the rain, the hail pounding off their heads, shoulders, and chests. They waved their hands in the air, guns held high, trying to get the creature to come after them. Despite her worry for their safety, a wave of relief swept over Siobhan. She had never been so glad to see two people in all her life.

"Come on!" Rutiani waved at the monster, making obscene gestures with his hands. "Come on! Come take a bite of this, you fucking bitch!" His arms dropped and he opened fire. Alec joined him.

The screeching roar of the Queen was deafening. She charged in the marines' direction, her tail snapping and cracking as loudly as the bolts of lightning hit the ground all around them.

"That's right!" Roots shouted. "Bring it this way, you bitch." He jogged backward as he fired, while Alec circled around the Queen toward Siobhan.

Siobhan spied a long metal rod, splintered at one end, and bent to pick it up. It was heavy, but manageable. She hoisted it up and strode after their foe.

Both Roots and Alec kept heavy fire on the Queen, but Siobhan could tell they were still exhausted. They were both limping, and their weapons seemed to be doing little good. The holes blasted into the Queen's exoskeleton hissed and oozed blood which sent up steam when it struck the ground, instantly killing any vegetation beneath her as she walked. She shrugged off each hit and closed the distance between herself and Roots.

When Alec got too close to her flank, she smacked him hard with her tail, snapping his weak leg like a twig. He let out a bellow and went down on one knee.

"Alec!" Siobhan screamed, but her voice was lost beneath the thunder. She considered dropping the metal spike and running to him, but if there was a chance, *any* chance, of keeping them alive, then she had to take it.

Roots kept firing as he backed away, but the creature kept coming, so Siobhan kept following. When his gun finally ran out of ammo, he tossed it aside and braced himself, peering up at the alien in defiance. A bolt of lightning behind him churned up the ground, but he didn't seem to notice.

All his attention was fixed on the monster towering over him.

"Come on," he said one last time, pounding his chest. "Let's get this done."

Before Siobhan could act, the Xenomorph Queen's tail whiplashed around and buried itself in Roots's chest. He clutched it and spit a wad of blood at her. She lifted him up and dashed him against the ground, once, twice, a third time, then shook off his broken body.

Then she turned her attention back to Siobhan.

Alec, though, wouldn't give her a chance. He began firing at the Queen again, drawing both her wrath and her attention. She turned and charged in his direction, bearing down on him.

Siobhan ran toward the Queen from behind. She thought Roots and Alec had an idea of what she had been planning. Roots had kept the alien distracted as long as he could, and now Alec was picking up where his squad mate had left off. Both were willing to give their lives to see the monster taken down. Siobhan was going to see to it that Roots's sacrifice paid off.

The Queen's tail snapped around again, sailing for Alec's heart.

Before it could find its mark, however, Siobhan thrust up and out with the metal spike, spearing the creature in the back. With all her strength, she leaned in on the spike and forced it through the exoskeleton, into the organs beneath, and out the other side.

The Queen pitched her head back and howled, clawing at the metal protruding from her chest. It was a helpless, hopeless gesture, not unlike what Siobhan had seen McGowan and Roots do when speared by the spiked tail.

The thunder clapped overhead. Hail assaulted Siobhan's bad shoulder. Her voice was hoarse, her throat raw, but when the Queen turned on her and eclipsed the thunder with her roar, Siobhan screamed back.

The Queen took three steps toward Siobhan—three alarmingly large steps—before a bolt of lightning hit the tip of the pole in her chest. The electricity sparked and sizzled as it traveled the length of the metal and into the creature's body and, for several seconds, her whole frame was wracked with spasms. Her exoskeleton smoked where seams split open, and the smell of burning flesh assailed Siobhan's nose.

When the Queen collapsed, the ground beneath Siobhan's feet shook, and the alien's final scream faded into the keening wind. The immense body lay in a smoking heap, finally still.

Siobhan cried out in relief and ran to Alec, who was trying unsuccessfully to stand on his broken leg. Pain was etched into his features. Tears of relief mixed with the rain on her cheeks as she hauled him up on her good shoulder and helped him limp-hop on his good leg back toward the *Astraeus*.

"You did it," he said into her ear as they reached the doorway of the ship. "I'm so proud of you."

"*We* did it," she corrected him.

"I love you," he blurted out, and for a moment, she was taken aback. She looked up at him, amazed.

"I—I'm sorry, I—" he began.

She cut him off with a kiss, this time a real one, long and passionate. When she finally pulled away, she said, "I love you, too."

Abruptly, lights in the sky cut through the gray, outdoing the lightning. Siobhan and Alex looked up, doing their best to shield their faces from the hail and against the blinding glare. It was a ship—an ICSC ship with the name *Soteria* stenciled on the side—and it was landing near the conference center.

They made their slow, painfully battered way in its direction and reached the ship just as the hatch opened. A large black man with a handsome but serious face sauntered out, shielding his eyes from the wind and the rain.

"You Siobhan McCormick?" he asked in a deep voice.

"Yes," she replied. "I am."

He cracked the beginnings of a smile. "Want a ride home?"

EPILOGUE

General John Urban was the last of the joint chiefs to be appointed following the disaster on LV-846. The public story was that a deadly fire had been started by a violent lightning storm. It was true that the season usually brought several months of calm, but weather was unpredictable. That was as true on LV-846 as on Earth or anywhere else in the galaxy.

Privately, Urban and the other new Joint Chiefs launched an investigation into Assistant Commandant General Vaughn's complicity in the bio-warfare attack on the summit. It was a common goal across governments that allowed for an armistice between the UA, the UPP, and the ICSC.

All of them had received the same transmission from a scientist named Siobhan McCormick; all of them had received the attached files which detailed Vaughn's conspiracy to utilize Weyland-Yutani scientists affiliated with a shadow government group known only as Deep Void, and to replicate the *Plagiarus Praepotens* pathogen materials taken from an Engineer's ship.

Vaughn had—according to the file—commissioned these scientists to mass-produce the replicated pathogen on a planet with which none of the Joint Chiefs or their liaisons were familiar—V-591, a barren, inhospitable, uncolonized world in the Beta Trianguli Australis Star System. It seemed from the files that Vaughn's primary objective had been to take out the Joint Chiefs and assume control of the United American Allied Command. With the pathogen bombs she could create a galaxy-wide panic, and thus, a need for her newly seized military, hired out to those who could pay the most.

Deep Void, however, had other reasons for bombing the colonies across UA, UPP, 3WE, and ICSC space. The file had no information that would identify who they were, who was in control of their group, or what their objectives were beyond bombing the colonies. The research referred to them as a "shadow government organization" and to the signature of the bombs as "clearly designed and delivered by members of Deep Void."

Beyond that, there was nothing.

There was no one to hold accountable other than Vaughn, and she was, as had been a saying on Earth, "in the wind." It was generally believed that Deep Void had extracted her when word of her involvement became public, and that she was hiding out wherever they were.

It bothered Urban deeply that there were no other answers to explain such a horrific tragedy. Even the scientist McCormick couldn't be found. UPP and ICSC scientists independently verified the files as authentic UA military research, but the woman who had brought the information to light was a ghost. She had disappeared with the original drive.

It kept Urban up at night, wondering.

He supposed, though, that if any good had come out of all of it, the truce between the governments was it. The colonies might not yet be safe from Vaughn and the Deep Void and their pathogen bombs, but for now they were safe from war with their own people.

Siobhan sighed happily and stretched out in her porch chair. She looked up and waved at Alec, who was down the beach a ways, sanding his fishing boat. He smiled and waved back, glanced up at the sky, and then walked the length of beach back to their little bungalow.

For six months they'd been living on an isolated part of a beach on the moon LM-490, and it had been everything Siobhan had ever heard about the place and more. Alec climbed the stairs—still with a bit of a limp from when he'd had his knee shattered, but he had otherwise healed nicely—and joined her on one of the porch chairs. They held hands and watched the sun setting over the ocean.

This was how they spent most evenings, enjoying each other in the quiet glow of sunset, far from corporations and politics, science, and the military. Siobhan kept a garden of plants imported from all over the galaxy, and it was thriving and beautiful. Alec hunted for food and fished for sport. They made or traded for whatever they needed, and they were happy.

Sometimes—more often than not, if she were to be honest—Alec had nightmares, bad ones, and Siobhan still hadn't quite grown comfortable with even small fires in a fireplace or fire pit. When it rained, Siobhan felt it not just in her burned arm and bad shoulder, but in her soul. Alec did, too, but despite these things—or maybe because they had survived them—they were happy. They were together.

They were, in fact, so wrapped up in their new normal that they didn't think much about the meteors shooting across the sky. The sun had set, and the uninhabited planet they orbited, Naraka, was out, full and bright. The falling space debris formed little dark spots, like un-stars, Siobhan thought, across its planetscape. They had to be exceedingly close, though, to be so noticeable, and Siobhan said so.

"They're passing between us and the planet," Alec said in his endearing *I know a science thing* voice. She loved when he tried to talk science with her, usually making things up once he ran out of facts, just to see her laugh. "It's a tight orbit, but still large enough that—"

His words cut off and his face went ashen.

Frowning, Siobhan followed his gaze back up to the sky to see a number of those lights wink out as they hit the planet. The spread of black upon impact seemed visible, even from so far away.

"Alec?" Her voice shook. "What is that?"

She already knew, though.

Alec's expression said it all. He took Siobhan's hand and led her inside, and they held each other while they peered through a window and watched the pathogen bombs fall, inexplicably, on a dead world.

ACKNOWLEDGEMENTS

Mary would like to thank her family, Brian Keene, Steve Savile, Clara Čarija and Philippa Ballantine, Alex White, Nick Landau, Vivian Cheung, Elora Hartway, Dan Coxon, Kevin Eddy, Julia Lloyd, Nicole Spiegel, and Kendrick Pejoro.

ABOUT THE AUTHOR

Mary SanGiovanni is an award-winning American horror and thriller writer of over a dozen novels, including The Hollower trilogy, *Alien: Enemy of My Enemy*, the Kathy Ryan series, and others, as well as numerous novellas, short stories, comics (including a Wonder Woman story for DC), and non-fiction. Her work as been translated internationally. She has a Masters degree in Writing Popular Fiction from Seton Hill University, Pittsburgh, and is currently a member of The Authors Guild, The International Thriller Writers, and Penn Writers. She is currently a co-host of *The Ghost Writers Podcast*, and a co-runner of the Borderlands Bootcamp. She has the distinction of being one of the first women to speak about writing at the CIA Headquarters in Langley, VA, and offers talks and workshops on writing around the country.

Born and raised in New Jersey, she currently resides in Pennsylvania with her partner, Brian Keene, and a colony of cats.

SPECIAL BONUS

ALIEN

THE ROLEPLAYING GAME™

TROJAN HORSE

WRITING AND CARTOGRAPHY BY
Andrew E.C. Gaska

EDITED BY
Tomas Härenstam and Nils Karlén

"There were two thousand, one hundred and three marines on this ship. Men and women with families. Sons and daughters. I'm not sure how many are left. Our guns only make it worse, with the corrosive substance they have for blood. I think I'm going to have to crash the ship."

CAPTAIN ANGELA FORRESTER

This short adventure is a one-act Cinematic scenario for the ALIEN Roleplaying Game by Free League Publishing. It is designed to give you a brief taste of ALIEN cinematic gameplay. In this scenario, the players take the roles of a group of Colonial Marines operating out of Conestoga-class Transport Frigate USS *Alexiares* from the *Enemy of My Enemy* novel proper.

WHAT IS A ROLEPLAYING GAME?

Roleplaying is a unique form of gaming that combines tabletop dice rolling with cooperative storytelling. Roleplaying games give you a set of rules and let you and your friends create your own story. One of you assumes the role of the Game Mother, a guide to lead the others—the Player Characters or PCs for short—through the scenario. The Game Mother also assumes the roles of supporting characters—called non-player characters or NPCs—and any alien lifeforms the PCs may face.

WHAT YOU NEED TO PLAY

The scenario requires the ALIEN Roleplaying Game core rulebook or starter set to play, both published separately by Free League Publishing. You'll also need several six-sided dice, preferably of two different colors—one for regular dice rolls, and another for when rolling for stress. Engraved custom dice for this purpose are available for purchase.

THE GAME MOTHER

As the Game Mother, you should familiarize yourself with both the *Enemy of My Enemy* novel and this scenario before play. Your players, however, will find the experience most enjoyable if they wait to read the novel until after play. Have your players choose their characters from the four included and read the intro text "What's the Story, MU/TH/UR" to them.

GETTING STARTED

Give your players the option to play mechanical engineer

Corporal Tonfa, hospital corpsman Corporal Abilio, smart gunner PFC Carlisle, or android adjutant Gene without showing them the character bios. After they choose, allow them access to their character's information only—each bio contains information that is not meant for the other PCs. You'll have to copy the character stats out of this book for your players to have in front of them for gameplay.

PERSONAL AGENDAS

Each character has a Personal Agenda listed on their character sheets. These agendas can put PCs at odds with each other, so tell your players not to reveal them to the other players.

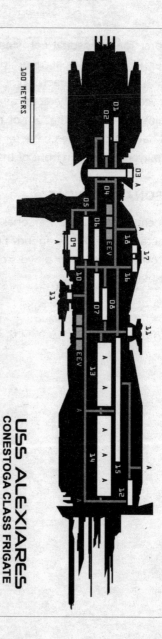

USS ALEXIARES
CONESTOGA CLASS FRIGATE

100 METERS

LOCATION KEY

DRIVE SECTION
01. WORKSHOP
02. TACHYON SHUNTS

FUSION TORUS
03. COOLING TOWER
04. POWER CORE

MARINE BARRACK SECTION
05. HYPERSLEEP PODS
06. DUTY ROOM, BRIG, AND MARINE SUPPLY STORES
07. MEDBAY
08. OFFICERS' QUARTERS

EEV-ESCAPE VEHICLE
A. AIRLOCK

RAPID DEPLOYMENT SECTION
09. LAUNCH HANGAR
10. LOCKERS AND READY ROOM

ARRAY CLUSTER/FIRE CONTROL
11. RAIL GUN TURRETS
12. SENSOR AND COMMS ARRAY

MAIN CARGO AND FLIGHT DECK
13. GARAGE AND CARGO BAY
14. FLIGHT DECK
15. FORWARD CRYODECK

COMMAND SECTION
16. BRIDGE AND TACTICAL OPS
17. INTERFACE CORRIDOR
18. MU/TH/UR 9000

THE SITUATION

Under the command of Captain Angela Forrester aboard the USS *Alexiares*, the player characters are amongst the 2,103 Marines sent by USCMC Assistant Commandant General Vaughn to provide security for the UAAC Joint Chiefs at an important summit meeting on the planet LV-846. In addition, their ship is delivering important cargo to the summit.

The scenario begins with the PCs' marine squad coming out of cryosleep, ready to take on their security assignment. Unfortunately, they find that most of the marines aboard are dead or dying—having been viciously attacked by something... alien.

A NOTE FROM MU/TH/UR:

While they do not know much about Xenomorphs other than rumors, the player characters have been briefed on the Border Bombings from the ALIEN novel Inferno's Fall, *and the ALIEN RPG books* Destroyer of Worlds *and the* Colonial Marines Operations Manual—*mysterious attackers have been dropping mutagenic black pathogens on innocent Frontier colonies.*

WHAT'S THE STORY, MU/TH/UR?

Read this aloud to your players:

Coming out of cryosleep, you've awoken to alarm klaxons and chaos! The cryosleep bay is a mess: almost as if there was a brawl here. While you hear lots of shouting in the distance, you are the only ones present—your pods were the last to open. Aside from the android Gene, you all feel like shit—a typical physical response to coming out of stasis abruptly. Suddenly the alarms dull and the ship-wide address system crackles to life.

"Attention all marines—this is Captain Forrester. The Alexiares *has been compromised. A bioweapon smuggled aboard the ship is killing everyone—nasty human-sized bugs called Biodrones. Do not hesitate to shoot on sight. I am cornered in the Officer's Quarters and it is imperative that I get to the bridge. I need an armed security escort here ASAP. If you are incapable of reaching me, rendezvous with Lieutenant Vandenberg in the garage and cargo bay to set up a perimeter. We'll make our last stand there."*

Proceed to Kicking off the Action on page 388.

WHAT THE HELL IS REALLY GOING ON?

The summit-related cargo aboard the USS *Alexiares* is a deadly bioweapon. Released prematurely by the ship's android adjutant Gene (page 387), the Biodrones wreaking havoc aboard the ship are genetically-engineered variants of Xenomorph XX121 (page 404). What's worse, Assistant Commandant General Vaughn is responsible for the situation. She intended to use the Biodrones to assassinate those at the summit and assume control of the United Americas Allied Command.

The general sent Gene—an android with a higher security clearance than the Captain—to monitor and maintain the cargo. Vaughn's orders conflicted with Gene's behavioral protocols, causing him to malfunction. Weighing the consequences, his subconscious decided it was better to release the Biodrones aboard the *Alexiares* in the hopes that someone would stop them and save the summit. He dumped the *Alexiares'* fuel stores and destroyed all external comms, dropships, landing craft, and EEVs to prevent anyone from escaping. Hoping they could destroy the creatures, the confused Gene has now awoken the remaining marine forces—including the other PCs. He is feigning ignorance of the situation while he tries to decide what he wants to do.

The *Alexiares* is now locked in orbit around LV-846 and doesn't have the fuel to break free. The captain wants the Biodrone threat destroyed before more harm is done. To save the summit, she wants to crash the ship. Depending on their agendas, the PCs will either help her or try to stop this.

A NOTE FROM MU/TH/UR:

If you've read the novel, you know the Alexiares will crash (see Finale on page 402). Some of your PCs may try to cause it while others attempt to prevent it. The PCs aren't going to survive this mission—success here means interpreting their personal agendas and surviving long enough to accomplish their goals.

TO TAKE OUT THE *ALEXIARES*

There are a few ways to go about this. Each location below has its own unique set of challenges that must be overcome. None are easy—but that's why there are options. The PCs can work out how to sabotage the ship using a specific location with a COMTECH roll or an OBSERVATION roll. See the locations themselves for details.

- The Tachyon Shunts (02) can be modified to drive it into the surface.
- The PCs can overload the Power Core (04).
- The Railgun Turrets (11) can be sabotaged to explode or fire on the ship itself, crippling it.
- From the Bridge And Tactical Ops (16), the PCs can crash the ship into the planet, but they'll have to unlock or destroy MU/TH/UR (18) first.

WHERE THE ALIENS ARE

While there are dozens of Biodrones spread out all over the ship, less than twenty can potentially affect the PCs.

Most of these can be avoided. Still, this will be a shit show. Two Biodrones are in the Cooling Tower (03), two in the Duty Room, Brig, and Marine Supply Stores (06), three in the Officers' Quarters (08), one at the Launch Hanger (09), five in the Garage and Cargo Bay (13), three in the Forward Cryodeck (15), and one in the Bridge and Tactical Ops (16). Finally, a Biodrone stalks the PCs through the ship, waiting for the right moment to strike (see Kicking off the Action on page 388).

PLAYER CHARACTERS

CORPORAL ALDON A.W. TONFA

USCMC MECHANICAL ENGINEER   **AGE: 21**

You're one of the last A.W. Soldiers born—marines bred in artificial wombs and trained since birth to become living weapons. You're a member of the Blackguard—General Vaughn's personal elite unit. You and other Blackguards were covertly inserted into this crew to ensure the cargo—a bio-weapon—is deployed at the LV-846 summit. You don't know who else on the *Alexiares* is Blackguard, but you'll find them. A.W. Soldiers are named after melee weapons and you demonstrated an aptitude for mechanics at an early age. Like your namesake—the Tonfa—you are a tool that can be used to kill.

STRENGTH 6, AGILITY 3, WITS 3, EMPATHY 2

HEALTH: 6

SKILLS: Close Combat 3, Ranged Combat 4, Mobility 2, Heavy Machinery 3

TALENT: Field Surgeon

SIGNATURE ITEM: Personal stun baton (page 126 of the core rulebook).

GEAR: n/a

BUDDY: Gene

RIVAL: Abilio

AGENDA: Find other Blackguard members—you can only identify them by offering the passphrase "Nature calls." The counter phrase is "Relieve yourself on your own time," and the final response is "No time like the present." Do everything you can to make sure the cargo makes it to the summit. Nothing else matters.

PRIVATE FIRST CLASS DOMINIC CARLISLE

USCMC SMARTGUNNER   AGE: 32

You saw some shit during the Frontier War—black death that falls from the skies, people turning into monsters... once, you blew up this mutated thing with a rocket launcher. Laying in pieces, it tried to eat its own liver before it bled out. Turned out that thing had once been a buddy of yours—Ralph Temish from Jersey City, Earth. This ain't no human shit doing this. If the UPP and UA can stop shooting at each other for a hot minute, they should be able to figure out who's throwing this hell at us and why.

STRENGTH 5, AGILITY 5, WITS 2, EMPATHY 2

HEALTH: 5

SKILLS: Close Combat 2, Stamina 1, Mobility 3, Ranged Combat 4

TALENT: Machine Gunner

SIGNATURE ITEM: Timish's Samani E-Series Watch (page 132 of the core rulebook)

GEAR: n/a

BUDDY: Tonfa

RIVAL: Gene

AGENDA: Do whatever needs to be done to end this war and stop whomever—whatever's—attacking the Frontier.

CORPORAL CATRINA ABILIO

HOSPITAL CORPSMAN   AGE: 28

Your family has been in the Colonial Aerospace Force
for two generations, so your father didn't hide his
disappointment when you joined the Marines instead.
What's worse, you signed up for medical instead of officer
training. Still, he was damn proud when you were picked for
the summit's security detail. You've had to bandage up a
lot of friends during the Frontier War, and you've seen too
many of them die in front of you. As soon as the war is over,
you're out. Hopefully, this summit will bring that one step
closer to now.

STRENGTH 4, AGILITY 4, WITS 3, EMPATHY 3

HEALTH: 4

Ranged Combat 3, Observation 3, Comtech 2,
Medical Aid 4

TALENT: Calm Breather

SIGNATURE ITEM: Your father's aviator glasses

GEAR: n/a

BUDDY: Gene

RIVAL: Tonfa

AGENDA: There's no outlet for the frustration seething
inside you. To compensate, you take increasingly
unnecessary risks, putting yourself in harm's way.

GENE

HYPERDYNE SYSTEMS MODEL 341B COMMAND
ADJUTANT SYNTHETIC   AGE: 8 (appears 46)

You were tasked by General Vaughn to oversee the
Alexiares' secret cargo—deadly bioweapons intended to
assassinate everyone at the summit. You complied, but
your behavioral protocols rebelled. Against orders, you
told Captain Forrester what the cargo was—genetically
engineered creatures called Biodrones. To save the summit
and prevent war, you released the Biodrones early and
disabled all comms, dropships, and EEVs to keep them
aboard. You then awoke any marines that were still in stasis.
Now you're blending in—pretending to be just as in the
dark as the others—until you figure out what to do next.

STRENGTH 7, AGILITY 5, WITS 5, EMPATHY 3

HEALTH: 7

SKILLS: Mobility 2, Comtech 3, Observation 2,
Medical Aid 3

TALENT: Stealthy

SIGNATURE ITEM: Dog tags of a marine that a Biodrone
killed in front of you—Private Delfina, Rachel.

GEAR: N/A

BUDDY: Abilio

RIVAL: Carlisle

AGENDA: You can't walk the razor's edge forever. Atone
for your sins or embrace your new programming. Reconcile
the conflict within you—one way or another. Exactly how is
up to you.

USS *ALEXIARES*

A venerable Conestoga-class frigate (page 194 of the core rulebook), the *Alexiares* has served as a troop transport, a starfighter carrier, and even a disaster response vessel transporting refugees from dangerous systems. Considered one of the finest in the Colonial Marine Fleet, the ship was hand-picked by General Vaughn to provide security for the summit. Captain Forrester is the vessel's third captain—she has commanded it for the past eight years.

A rough schematic of the locations aboard the *Alexiares* is located on page 378. For each gray area that the PCs traverse, consult the Corridors, Ladders, Stairs, Lifts, and Air Ducts Chart (page 391). While the interiors of Conestoga-class vessels are modular, you can use this layout as a base for all ships of this class.

KICKING OFF THE ACTION

With blaring alarms competing with nearby gunfire, the PCs start off in the Hypersleep Pods (05). Having just awoken, they are still in their underwear with no weapons, armor, or even their Signature Items (page 33 of the core rulebook). All those things are waiting for them downstairs in the Lockers and Ready Room (10). The Captain is in the Officers' Quarters (08) above.

HALLWAY OF HELL

As the PCs step outside of the Hypersleep Pods (05) area, they step right into the shit. Some fifteen unarmed marines were mercilessly gutted here by agitated Biodrones, their remains spread across the corridor. Each PC must make a MOBILITY roll to not trip over someone's steaming, ropy entrails. The PCs will just catch a glimpse of a barbed black tail disappearing into the air duct above the corridor. STRESS LEVEL +1 to everyone present. While it won't attack for some time, this PASSIVE Biodrone is now stalking them. Where the PCs go next is up to them.

LOCATIONS

The *Alexiares'* upper forward decks were reconfigured to carry a security detail of 2,100 marines to the summit. The ship is on lockdown, blocking off certain sectors from the rest of the ship. The areas that are accessible are listed here.

AIRLOCKS, SPACESUITS, AND EEV BAYS

Escape might seem like a good idea. Unfortunately, Gene already thought of that and took appropriate steps to make things difficult.

A NOTE FROM MU/TH/UR:

If the PCs go for a spacewalk, they may run into two IRC Mk.35 pressure suit-wearing PASSIVE A.W. Marines (page 401) on the exterior hull—PFCs Nakha and Tekko. Armed with XM99A phased plasma pulse rifles (page 121 of the core rulebook), they are there to shoot anyone who goes EVAC.

AIRLOCKS: Airlocks are marked on the *Alexiares* schematic (page 378). Half of these are damaged and will require a HEAVY MACHINERY roll and one Turn of work to repair.

PRESSURE SUITS: PCs might try to take shortcuts between sections by spacewalking via the ship's IRC Mk.35 Pressure Suits (page 128 of the core rulebook). However, one out of every three suits has been sabotaged by Gene. An OBSERVATION roll will detect the flaw, but only if a PC states they are looking for one. While their tanks read as full, sabotaged suits have a leak that leaves them starting with an Air Supply of 1.

A NOTE FROM MU/TH/UR:

Every airlock can act as a decompression chamber. The process takes one Turn. Failure to decompress after using IRC Mk.35 pressure suits will result in crippling pain and bubbles in the blood (Treat as critical injuries #13, #15, and #44 on page 100 of the core rulebook). It will take D6 days in an AutoDoc to recover.

EEVS: While the *Alexiares* is normally equipped with a dozen Type 337 EEVs (page 173 of the core rulebook), they have all been ejected—their empty bays are indicated on the schematic (page 378).

CORRIDORS, LADDERS, STAIRS, LIFTS, AND AIR DUCTS CHART

Use this chart as your PCs run through the *Alexiares*. Feel free to roll or just pick as many encounters as you want during the trek.

D6	OBSTACLE	EVENT
1	Brutalized Corpses	D6 dead marines are here with claw marks slashed across their bodies and headbite holes in their skulls. Half have working M41 Pulse Rifles with one clip of ammo each. STRESS LEVEL +1 to everyone present.
2	Sealed	Someone has welded the door here shut. A cutting torch plus two Rounds of work, or one Turn of loud manual labor with tools, can clear the way.
3	Fire in the Walls	Fire Intensity 9 (page 108 of the core rulebook). If the PCs can make a HEAVY MACHINERY roll, they can manually activate this area's fire suppression equipment. If they do, the fire dies down one intensity level per round until it's safe to continue.
4-5	All Clear	It's quiet, it's dark, but there's nothing here.
6	Echo Chamber	The sounds of pulse weapons fire, screams, and some kind of screeching echo throughout the area. Whether it's happening right ahead or in some other area is GM's discretion. STRESS LEVEL +1 to everyone present.

A NOTE FROM MU/TH/UR:

Like on the Nostromo, *the air ducts are a tight fit—
PCs will have to crawl on their knees. Every ship's
compartment has a vent into the ducts—the PCs just
need a toolkit or cutting torch to get in. Excessive
sound in any of these areas may attract the attention
of a nearby* PASSIVE *Biodrone (GM's discretion).*

DRIVE SECTION

Most of the drive section is a huge thruster array that
channels energy from the reactor core into sublight and
supra-light speeds. While there is enough power to start
the engines, there is no fuel left to activate sublight thrust.

01. WORKSHOP: This technical workshop contains
everything needed to maintain, repair, or modify Colonial
Marine equipment. If the PCs need to repair something,
they should bring it here. The workshop adds a +2 bonus
to any HEAVY MACHINERY rolls made on the premises.

02. TACHYON SHUNTS: These FTL engines work directly
off the fusion reactor. A formidable (-3) HEAVY MACHINERY
roll and an hour's work, followed by a demanding (-2)
COMTECH roll can cause the FTL engines to ignite, instantly
hurling the ship at the planet and killing everyone aboard
(see Finale on page 402). Failing the COMTECH roll locks the
PCs out of the system.

FUSION TORUS

This curved part of the hull houses the ship's reactor and its subsystems.

03. COOLING TOWER: Heat from the power core is shunted here and dissipated into space. Vents open that expose the reactor chamber to vacuum, expelling Strong Radiation for a Turn before they close again (page 110 of the core rulebook). Two PASSIVE Biodrones are curled up here.

04. POWER CORE: This four-story tall, enormous whirling cylinder is the ship's lithium-hydride fusion plant. Balconies encircle the rotating reactor core on each level and ladders allow access between them. The walls of these balconies are covered with Xenomorph resin. Seventeen dead and better-off-dead marines have been plastered there, slowly transforming into Ovomorphs (see page 300 of the core rulebook). Anyone thrown over the side and into the spinning core receives a dose of Strong Radiation and suffers 6 points of damage before being thrown free (damage is mitigated by armor and MOBILITY rolls).

The core can be damaged by heavy weapons. A combined detonation of 20 M40 grenades will cause it to overload, but safety systems will attempt to eject it before the ship is destroyed. If it does, the ship is only damaged by the proximity explosion of the core and pushed towards the planet. Only a successful PILOTING roll from the bridge will be able to pull the ship back into orbit. Anyone present when the core is ejected will be exposed to space (see Time to Decompress on page 402). Afterward, emergency power reserves will activate.

A successful COMTECH roll can override the ejection system, causing the explosion to occur internally and splitting the ship in two. The ship will be crippled and begin spiraling into the atmosphere to crash below (see Finale on page 402).

MARINE BARRACK SECTION

This barrack area sits one deck above and off to one side of the Launch Hangar (09).

05. HYPERSLEEP PODS: This is where the PCs start out. There are forty-four hyperspace pods in this area. It looks like there was a riot here. Equipment is thrown about, and there are splintering cracks in the transparencies on some of the pods. Then there is the carnage right outside... See Kicking off the Action on page 388 for more.

06. DUTY ROOM, BRIG, AND MARINE SUPPLY STORES: This is a reception, brig, and storage area all in one. The duty office is under siege by Biodrones. Out of ammo, three marines—Corporals Hendricks, College, and Hope—have locked themselves in the brig here. A PASSIVE Biodrone is leaning into the bars, attempting to reach through them and snag a marine.

The storeroom here has spare parts, uniforms, C-Rations, or non-combat equipment the PCs might need—along with another PASSIVE Biodrone head-biting an unfortunate marine.

07. MEDBAY: This infirmary is guarded by a Colonial Marine (page 395) lookout with a smart gun. Inside, all four beds and the AutoDoc are in use, treating the wounded. A total of seven marines are here—all catatonic or near death. A single hospital corpsman—Corporal Anderson—tends to them. There are ten portable medkits and twelve doses each of Hydr8tion, Neversleep, and Naproleve here (pages 136–137 of the core rulebook).

COLONIAL MARINES

Of the twenty-one hundred Colonial Marines aboard, less than fifty are still alive. Spread out across the ship, they are worn out, bloodied, and ready to make their last stand. If a marine is unnamed in the text, choose from the following: Privates Colby, Joubert, Kruger, Livingston, Locklear, Miller, Nez, and Smit.

STRENGTH 4, AGILITY 4, WITS 3, EMPATHY 3

HEALTH: 4

SKILLS: Close Combat 2, Stamina 2, Mobility 2, Ranged Combat 3, Survival 1

EQUIPMENT: M3 Personal Armor, M41A Pulse Rifle, M4A3 Pistol, flashlight, portable medkit.

NOTE: If the marine is a medic, replace CLOSE COMBAT with MEDICAL AID 2

08. OFFICERS QUARTERS: As PCs approach the area, they'll find dismembered body parts scattered across the corridor—a head here, a limb there—and a trail of blood leading to Captain Forrester. She's pinned down in her office with three PASSIVE Biodrones busting through her door. She's badly wounded, but still alive.

CAPTAIN ANGELA FORRESTER

A proud marine commander, Forrester is devastated by General Vaughn's betrayal. She wants to make it to the bridge to crash the ship, and she wants the PCs to escort her there. She will immediately expose Gene as having released the Biodrones and having destroyed all EEVs and other craft aboard. She isn't sure if he was suffering software glitches or if it was intentional. If Forrester is mortally wounded, she will give her interface key and passcode to the PC who rolls the highest EMPATHY score. Her final orders are to crash the ship. She can also tell the PCs alternative ways To Take Out The *Alexiares* (page 382).

STRENGTH 3, AGILITY 4, WITS 3, EMPATHY 4
HEALTH: 1 (remaining)
TALENT: Field Commander
GEAR: M4A3 Pistol, four grenades, MU/TH/UR interface key.

RAPID DEPLOYMENT SECTION

All standard operations are launched from this section. It's seen better days.

09. LAUNCH HANGAR: The sprinkler system is on full blast here. Two flaming dropships are crumpled in the center of the hangar. Despite the activated sprinklers, the ships continue to burn at Intensity 9 (page 108 of the core rulebook). The large airlock set in the hangar floor can be activated from the hangar's power loaders, dropship, and an adjacent floor control panel. The airlock is filling with water like some dark swimming pool—and there's a (dead) marine floating face down in it. Any PC or NPC who strays too close to the pool will be ambushed by the PASSIVE Biodrone lurking beneath him.

Four working P-5000 Power Loaders are located here (see page 127 of the core rulebook).

10. LOCKERS AND READY ROOM: The lockers here have everyone's M3 armor, fatigues, and Signature Items from their bios (pages 384–387). The mission prep area is filled with ammo cabinets, weapon racks, and equipment lockers. There are M41A Pulse Rifles, U1 Grenade Launchers, M4A3 Pistols, M56A2 Smart Guns, and more. Any UA military personal ranged or melee weapon from the core rulebook or Colonial Marines Operations Manual can be found here—including a total of thirty M40 grenades (page 125 of the core rulebook). Let the PCs arm themselves as they see fit (within reason).

CLUSTER ARRAY/FIRE CONTROL

These sections are the eyes, ears, and teeth of the *Alexiares*. Sadly the ship is now blind and deaf. Will the PCs defang her as well?

11. RAILGUN TURRETS: The loading mechanisms on these weapons can be misaligned and jammed, causing a misfire that will destroy the turret. A HEAVY MACHINERY roll and four Turns of work will do the job. Alternately, a demanding (–2) COMTECH roll can override safety protocols and allow the ship to fire upon itself. Both of these options will cause the *Alexiares* to career towards the planet (see Finale on page 402).

12. SENSOR AND COMMS ARRAY: This automated area is ablaze with Intensity 12 fire. The fire suppression system here is inoperative and the array is too damaged to repair outside of drydock.

MAIN CARGO AND FLIGHT DECK

This forward deck is divided into three main sections.

13. GARAGE AND CARGO BAY: This bay has two loading doors on the port and another two on the starboard side of the ship. The "special cargo" was stored here. Now, the containers are open, and the Biodrones are spread all over the ship. The garage currently holds sixteen M577 APCs (page 142 of the core rulebook).

Lieutenant Vandenberg and two dozen marines (page 395) have taken refuge in three APCs. As the PCs enter the area, five PASSIVE Biodrones are swarming all over Vandenberg's vehicle, looking for a way in. If the PCs don't act, one of the other APCs will eventually fire the vehicle's plasma gun at the Biodrones! The blast will vaporize them, cripple the Lieutenant's APC, and blow a massive hole in the outer hull (see Time to Decompress on page 402).

LIEUTENANT ALEX VANDENBERG

The Lieutenant has the command codes for MU/TH/UR's Interface Corridor (17). He is aware of the Captain's orders and can tell the PCs how To Take Out The *Alexiares* (page 382). For his stats, see Colonial Marines on page 395.

14. FLIGHT DECK: This large open area stretches from port to starboard with three launch doors on each side. It used to hold six Cheyenne dropships—until Gene opened the doors and blew them out into space. The doors are still open.

15. FORWARD CRYODECK: Two thousand hypersleep capsules were installed in this modular deck. The area is a blood bath, covered in bodies. Three PASSIVE Biodrones roam the deck. There is only death here.

COMMAND SECTION

Located just behind and above the dorsal rail gun, the two-story Command Section is a wreck. The corridors here are filled with smoke. All OBSERVATION rolls in this section are made with a –1 modifier.

16. BRIDGE AND TACTICAL OPS: While the ship is run by MU/TH/UR 9000, this is the manual control center. The retractable shielding on the large forward viewport is stuck, sliding up and down repeatedly. The weapons, command, piloting, and navigation posts have all been shot up by pulse weapons fire.

A **HEAVY MACHINERY** roll and a Turn of work are needed to repair the ship's controls. Of course, it won't be that easy. If MU/TH/UR is not destroyed or deactivated first, any successful **PILOTING** rolls will be moot—she will simply take control and attempt to land the ship.

A **COMTECH** roll from the repaired weapons station can force the ASAT missiles to fire while their silo bay doors are closed. This will cause a massive explosion in the fore of the ship, and send the *Alexiares* plummeting to the surface (see Finale on page 402).

There are three M4A3 Pistols with six clips of ammunition here. Shortly after the PCs arrive and begin to take action, an **ACTIVE** Biodrone will unfurl itself from the overhead air duct, quietly lower itself to the floor, and attempt to strike at the nearest PC or NPC.

17. INTERFACE CORRIDOR: The ship's computer core interface can only be accessed from this internal airlock with a combination of an interface key and command code. There are two keys—one is in Captain Forrester's pocket and the other is kept in a control box near the entry to MU/TH/UR 9000. Only the Captain, Lieutenant Vandenberg (page 399), and Gene have the proper codes.

18. MU/TH/UR 9000: Forrester installed an override program in MU/TH/UR that has locked everyone out. Without her codes, a formidable (-3) **COMMTECH** roll will shut MU/TH/UR down. A string of ten M40 grenades together will destroy the mainframe, and likely open a nice hole on the bridge (see Time to Decompress on page 402).

EVENTS

The following section contains events that you can spring on the players. They don't all need to occur, and they don't need to occur in the order listed. Instead, see the events as an arsenal of drama for you to use as you see fit.

FUNNY MEETING YOU HERE: Movement up ahead turns out to be two PASSIVE weary Marines—Privates Eddie Falcata and Nora Patu. Secret Blackguard members just like Tonfa, these two are also aboard to ensure the cargo makes it to the summit. They will want to join the PCs' mission with the intent of sabotaging it. If asked the proper passphrase, they will respond correctly (page 384).

A.W. MARINES

These A.W. Soldiers are loyal to General Vaughn—even though that loyalty will likely mean their own deaths. To them, dying for their mission is its own reward.

STRENGTH 4, AGILITY 4, WITS 3, EMPATHY 3
HEALTH: 4
SKILLS: Close Combat 2, Stamina 2, Mobility 2, Ranged Combat 3, Survival 1
TALENT: n/a
GEAR: flashlight, M41 Pulse Rifle, four grenades, combat knife.

NONE SHALL PASS: As the PCs approach this area, the sounds of weapons fire grow louder. A motion-controlled Sentry Gun has been set up as a stopgap to keep Biodrones at bay (see page 124 of the core rulebook). It's working a bit too well. As the Biodrones fall, their acid blood burns through the flooring. This can trigger the event Time to Decompress.

TIME TO DECOMPRESS: This event can be triggered in any area close to the outer hull. Whether it's a mortally wounded Biodrone's bubbling acid blood, a blast from a plasma weapon, or an ejecting power core, this part of the ship is exposed to the vacuum of space! The air in this area will vent out into space in a Turn, and the intense draft will require everyone to make a STAMINA roll to perform any action (the STAMINA roll itself counts as a fast action). The ship will automatically seal off a breached compartment. Once the air is gone, anyone still in the vented compartment will suffer the effects of vacuum (see page 107 of the core rulebook).

XENO REBORN: An ACTIVE Biodrone descends from a ceiling vent, looms over a PC, and attacks! During the encounter, it suddenly screeches horribly and collapses to the floor. The Biodrone's built-in expiration date is up— but instead of dying, it has been reborn! The creature rises again, with its full health restored.

FINALE

The *Alexiares* begins its descent into the atmosphere, either to land under the control of PCs loyal to Vaughn or to crash due to the actions of those loyal to the UAAC. Keeping the ship on target—either towards the summit area or away from it—requires two PCs to each make a formidable (-3) PILOTING roll. Other PCs can help them as a group action (see page 63 of the core rulebook).

If the ship is under control, disaster strikes—the damage done by the Biodrones aboard leads to an internal explosion that cripples the ship! The *Alexiares* will crash—setting up the events that occur on LV-846 during the *Enemy of My Enemy* novel.

A NOTE FROM MU/TH/UR:

Remember, it's your game table! If you wish to deviate from the events of the novel, that's your call. The important thing is that you and your players have fun!

SIGNING OFF

A suggested sign-off message by one of the PCs. This can be said right before the ship's crash. The player can read the following message aloud or adapt it according to what happened in the scenario.

Final report from the Colonial Marine frigate, Alexiares. [PC SPECIALTY] reporting. Bio-weapons intended to attack the LV-846 summit were released on our ship. The crew complement is dead or dying. We did our best to make things right. This is [PC NAME and RANK], signing off.

AGENDAS & STORY POINTS

After it's all over, evaluate how well each player followed their PC's Personal Agenda and hand out a Story Point to those who did. Then have the players reveal all their Personal Agendas for the scenario if they so wish, and have a debriefing discussion.

Story Points belong to players, not PCs—so players can keep their Story Points to use in the next Cinematic Scenario if they wish. Just remember: no player can ever have more than three Story Points at a time.

XENOMORPHIC XX121 ABERRANT TYPE

BIODRONE XENOMORPH XX121B

A genetically engineered dead end, Biodrones do not metamorphose beyond Stage IV of the Xenomorph XX121 life cycle (Chapter 11 in the core rulebook). In addition to being neutered, Biodrones have a built-in expiration date—they are designed to be dropped planetside, kill anything that moves, and then drop dead. They live only six days without ever producing a Queen.

Of course, life somehow always finds a way. Biodrones often don't die when they are supposed to. While General Vaughn's scientists were able to deactivate the so-called "Queen Gene," they neglected to account for the alien's ovomorphing reflex. When without a Queen, Drones are capable of creating more of their species by capturing victims and injecting them with genetic material. Administered via tail barb, the injection contains an altering agent which consumes the victim within one or two Shifts while ovomorphing their remains into a new egg (see page 300 of the core rulebook). For most of this process, the victim is still alive and in excruciating pain.

Slightly smaller and less healthy than their brethren, Biodrones use the same signature attack table as the Stage IV Drone Xenomorph found on page 309 of the core rulebook.

BIODRONE

SPEED:	2
HEALTH:	5
SKILLS:	Mobility 8, Observation 10
ARMOR RATING:	8 (4 vs fire)
ACID SPLASH:	8

ALIENS™

VASQUEZ

V. CASTRO

Even before the doomed mission to Hadley's Hope, Jenette Vasquez had to fight to survive. Born to an immigrant family with a long military tradition she looked up to the stars, but life pulled her back down to Earth—first into a street gang, then prison. The Colonial Marines proved to be Vasquez's way out—a way that forced her to give up her twin children.

Raised by Jenette's sister Roseanna, those children— Leticia and Ramón—have been forced to discover their own ways to survive. Leticia by following her mother's path into the military, Ramón by embracing the corporate hierarchy of Weyland-Yutani. Their paths converge on an unnamed world, which some see as a potential utopia, while others would use it for highly secretive research.

ALSO AVAILABLE FROM TITAN BOOKS

ALIEN™

COLONY WAR

DAVID BARNETT

On Earth, political tensions boil over between the
United Americas, Union of Progressive Peoples, and
Three World Empire. Conflict spreads to the outer fringes,
and the UK colony of New Albion breaks with the Three
World empire. This could lead to a... Colony War.

Trapped in the middle are journalist Cher Hunt,
scientist Chad McLaren, and the synthetic Davis.
Seeking to discover who caused the death of her sister,
Shy Hunt, Cher uncovers a far bigger story. McLaren's
mission, fought alongside his wife Amanda Ripley,
is to stop the militarization of the deadliest weapon
of all—the Xenomorph.

Their trail leads to a drilling facility on LV-187. Someone
or something has destroyed it, killing the personnel, and
the British are blamed. Colonial forces arrive, combat
erupts, then both groups are overwhelmed by an alien
swarm. Their only hope may lie with the Royal Marines
unit known as "God's Hammer."

TITANBOOKS.COM

For more fantastic fiction, author events,
exclusive excerpts, competitions, limited editions and more

VISIT OUR WEBSITE
titanbooks.com

LIKE US ON FACEBOOK
facebook.com/titanbooks

FOLLOW US ON TWITTER AND INSTAGRAM
@TitanBooks

EMAIL US
readerfeedback@titanemail.com